Sul

# Night Fire

## Books by Edward Kimbrough

FROM HELL TO BREAKFAST

NIGHT FIRE

# Night Fire

by Edward Kimbrough

Rinehart & Company, Inc.
New York Toronto

COPYRIGHT, 1946, BY EDWARD KIMBROUGH
PRINTED IN THE UNITED STATES OF AMERICA
AMERICAN BOOK–STRATFORD PRESS, INC., NEW YORK
*All Rights Reserved*

This book is for

*Thérèse and Hudson Strode*

# Night Fire

# Chapter I

It all began with one of those incidents which any man would be more likely to laugh at than to ponder over.

Ashby Pelham had been hunting. He left the sedge field along the river when darkness came.

He whistled the dog back from his circling and sent him, with a grinning oath, ahead of him, home to food. Then, with the sedge whirring to the thrash of his booted foot, he followed, gun a-shoulder.

From along the river to his back there came the last echoes of the evening church bells, borne up from town three miles away. To his left, a far way, he heard hounds baying, and in the same direction, but closer, he heard the Negroes singing, until suddenly their oil-rich voices ceased, so that it seemed that they too were listening for something beyond them. The lights in their cabins around the commissary flickered palely, but there was no sound, only the waiting stillness.

Vaguely, he wondered at this, but only vaguely. He did not think of himself as a mystic man, and he was not one to see in stilled voices a foreboding.

There was upon him, anyhow, that tiredness akin to a surfeit of drink or of love. His right knee ached and there was a soreness in the tendons of his legs, and along the ridge of his shoulders the muscles were fiery with fatigue. Yet there was in his very exhaustion a pleasant and dreamful unawareness. He could have lain there in the sedge with the thistles and beggar-lice and cockle-burrs pricking and itching his legs through the wool socks, with the clay cold and wet to his back, without pillow or fire or food he could have lain there and slept. It was a good way to feel, to feel that you could sleep anywhere without caring. And a man only felt so, he thought, when he had had enough of drink, or else enough of love, or else enough of exercise. At least those were the only times he knew when a man could sleep in a field and not care. It was a thing to think about, though, and to wonder what else there might be to make a man sleep easy.

But he was too comfortable to wonder about it long. He went up a knoll and through an oak grove and then scrambled down an embankment to where the barbed wire fence marked the road. He put his gun over the fence, leaning it against the lower wire, and then put a hand on the pine post and vaulted over. His feet hit the ditch bank with a thud. He wiped the pine splinters from his burned palm. Then he picked up his gun, shouldered it, and started up the road, in a direction away from the Negro cabins a hundred yards behind him. There was only a little gravel on the road. His feet plodded wetly on rain-packed clay.

A full moon, young and yellow in the night, breasted the trees along the ridge a far way from him. Its light goldened the road and the fields. He sang. *Oh, I'm a blasted rebel . . .*

It was a song he had heard all his life. It was a song his father sang to show that he was feeling good. Then, when Ashby had been in college, it had been the kind of song favored at drunken stag parties in the fraternity house, because it took no poet to add to it innumerable bawdy verses. So he had heard it casually sung for a long time, but the feeling he had for it was not casual. He called it, to himself, "the song about fighting." Cousin Evelina said that when he was no more than three, he would yell for the song about fighting. It was not, he knew, that it was a ballad about the Civil War; it could have been about any war, about any fight anywhere. He was a peaceful man, but a tune about battle made a strange yearning in him.

So he sang:

> Oh, I'm a blasted re-bel,
> And I'm right proud I am.
> I fought the dirty Yankees,
> And I don't give a damn.

He could not carry a tune. Evelina always said, "Ashby, you sound like a rooster with croup."

"I can hear it so plain in my head," he said, "that to me I sound like Caruso." Laughing at her and singing.

He broke his song to grin, thinking about that; and the song no longer in his ears, he heard, all at once, the sound of hounds again. They had come closer without his knowing it, so that he realized it was not the ordinary moon-baying of farmers' dogs in a yard somewhere. These hounds were moving, and, when he stopped to listen, he knew that they were not foxhounds either. He stood in the road and listened. They made a sound not melodious and excited like foxhounds on a trail, but harsh with a note of persistent cruelty in it. So that he knew they must be bloodhounds. That was why the Negroes had hushed their singing and waited. He could imagine the terror of their waiting, and he was suddenly angry that they should be frightened in the midst of song.

He narrowed his eyes as if to see a long way. The road had curved and he could not see the cabins at the commissary. But his ears said that the dogs had hit the road at almost the spot he himself had hit it.

Then he saw the lights coming, like a coterie of fireflies, growing larger and more distinct as they approached him. The sound of bloodhounds stirred and frothed his blood. He put the butt of his gun on the ground and leaned a little against the barrel, waiting.

They were very close. He heard the shouts of the breathless running men. Then he saw the dogs, leaping at their leashes; in the glow of moon and flashlight, they were red, their coats, their tongues, the gums atop their white bared teeth. Then they were on him; he stood facing them like a quarry backed to its extremest thicket and now proud and unafraid before his tormentors. They never got to touch him. The men dug their heels into the clay, pulled, cursing, at the leashes to hold them away from Ashby. The flashlights wavered, jostled in the shuffle. Then finally through the jumping dogs and cursing men, one man came, a man in a ten gallon black hat, with a flashlight in one hand and a pistol held rather nervously in the other. He came stumbling and kicking through the dogs toward Ashby.

He was the sheriff; Ashby recognized him in spite of the blinding flashlights. He had small eyes, and, when he took his hat off to shield them from the glare so as to see Ashby, his head was bald and waxy. "What you aimin' to grow up there?" the voters always asked him. "Votes," he would say, massaging the smooth pink expanse of his head. "A crop of votes, now I got it cleared for cultivation." People laughed at him, though he was really a serious man, and a man with a quick and violent anger in him. He had, on his neck, a peculiar growth of wild, purple flesh; it hung scrawnily there, and moved when he swallowed. For this he was called "Turkey." "Turkey" Littlepage, the sheriff.

Now he came up to Ashby, cautiously, once he was past the dogs. Though Ashby's gun was still serving him as a post to lean on, Turkey was not a daresome man. He lifted his flashlight in a wavering hand, and when he saw Ashby he became all at once tongueless with anger, as if a fire moved redly under his skin.

"I'll kill 'em," he said. He lowered the flashlight and his voice rose. "So help me God, I'll cut 'em up and feed 'em to the vultures." He was talking about the dogs. His flashlight pointed to them. He stomped on the ground in his anger. The dog wail rose; the hounds strained, and the men called to Turkey, "Who is it? Who . . . ?"

"Now, Turkey," Ashby said. Whatever anger had been in

him was gone now; glee was warm like alcohol in him. Behind Turkey in the confused light he saw the smiling mouths of the deputies, who now recognized him. "What you want me for, Turkey? That killing out on Watermelon Road? Or that store I robbed in Good Hope?"

Turkey never looked at him. He put his gun in his holster, and said, "I'll tie 'em alive and let buzzards eat their hearts." He still stomped, and then suddenly he kicked out aimlessly and struck a near dog in the chest; the dog's wail changed to quick yappings of pain. "Bastard," Turkey said.

Then he stood there looking foolishly at Ashby and then at the dogs.

"You say you want me, Turkey?"

"No," Turkey said. "No. I never wanted you and you know it."

"Yes, you did . . ." It was one of the deputies. He was an old man with a sandy mustache and a black hat like the sheriff's. "His pa sent word by you when we passed the house . . ."

Turkey looked malignantly at the old deputy. "What color hair has he got?" Turkey said, waving a finger in Ashby's direction.

"He towheaded," the old deputy said. "Blond like his Papa was . . ."

"Father?" Ashby said, to Turkey. "What did Father want?"

But Turkey paid him no mind. The finger still waved and Turkey still glared at the old deputy. "And what color eyes has he got?"

The old deputy squinted at Ashby and said, "Look blue to me."

"Do?" Turkey said, sarcastically. "And I don't reckon you would say that that sun tan he's got is exactly brown would you . . ."

"No," the old deputy said, his face straight. "I don't reckon I would."

"Then goddamit," Turkey said, "What are you doin' trackin'

him down when we was after a nigger? Or did he look like a nigger to you?"

"Why, Turkey," the old deputy said. "I couldn't see him no better'n you could. Nor no better'n these here hounds you got could smell . . ." It sounded as if the old deputy were laughing to himself.

Turkey's teeth clicked twice before he spoke. "Then don't go interruptin' me," he said. "Jest hush up. Ain't I got enough troubles without you . . ."

"But what did Father want?" Ashby said.

The sheriff turned to him. "Listen," he said. "Tell me something. Where did you hit this here road?" He pointed with the flashlight to the clay underfoot.

"Why, I reckon about a hundred yards this side of the commissary," Ashby said. "There by Big Sand Spring. Why?"

"I knowed it," the sheriff said. "Six hundred acres for you to walk over and you had to go and cross the trail in the only place . . ." He beat the flashlight against his thigh, accenting the words. Then he turned to the deputies. "Take 'em away. For Jesus' sake, take 'em away. Go back yonder to where we turned into this miserable road. Go back and take it up again from there."

"All right," the old deputy said. "But I can tell you now it won't do no good. If you was to start out looking for a man with these hounds, you'd end up on the trail of a possum." Ashby laughed. Turkey grabbed his hat off his head and threw it down in the road.

"Goldarnit," he said. "Who's sheriff around here? Will you git the hell . . ."

They went, then. The dogs, confused at being turned aside, howled louder than ever. But after a deal of pulling and cursing, the men got them off down the road.

Then Turkey found himself a big rock by the ditch and sat down on it. He put his flashlight on the ground beside him. With slow anger he rolled himself a cigarette. Ashby picked up his hat and handed it to him.

"Throw it away," Turkey said. He licked the paper. "Throw it to hell and back. I might as well catch pneumonia anyhow."

Ashby let the hat fall to the ground by Turkey's feet. Then he placed his gun carefully on the ground and squatted. "What did Father want?"

"I'm a ruined man, anyhow," Turkey said, not listening. "Them hounds are my ruination. It ain't been a week since they chased Senator Roberts. It looks like they got the devil in them for sho. They are gonna ruin me politically."

Ashby made as if to consider this gravely; he had a time keeping his lips straight. "I reckon you're right, Turkey. Seem to me I heard something about your chasing Brother Harkness clean up the steps of the Methodist Church last week. They tell me the Methodists are mighty put out about that . . ."

"Don't remind me," the sheriff said. His head was shaking as he struck the match. The purple flesh on his neck moved up and down. "It's humiliatin'. I ain't had a peaceful minute since I bought 'em. I curse the day I let ole Hell-fire Smith sell 'em to me."

"It just might be," Ashby said, "that you're not workin' 'em right. It seems to me like you're s'posed to let 'em loose. The way you keep 'em on a leash, the trail grows cold time they hit it good, and . . ."

The cigarette turned agitatedly between Turkey's lips. "What? You expect me to let them hounds loose? And have 'em git lost?"

"Bloodhounds? Get lost?" Ashby said. "Anyhow, I thought you didn't care anything about 'em. If they're ruinin' you . . ."

The smoke wreathed around Turkey's head, so that, red as he was anyway, it looked as if he were on fire. "They're ruining me politically. There ain't no use to let 'em ruin me financially, too. I aim to sell 'em. I'm gonna sell 'em to somebody that's as big a fool as I was. And I hope I don't never see one of 'em ag'in." He listened, for a second, to the far-off sound of the trailing dogs. He moaned.

"Well," Ashby said. "Who was it you were really chasing?"

"When?" the sheriff said. "I done chased might' nigh half the county by now . . ."

There was no humor in Turkey's voice. He could say a thing like that about himself and, where most men would laugh at themselves, Turkey would only be angry, first at himself and then at the person who saw his anger.

So it was that when Ashby said, "Tonight. Now." Turkey answered in that same measured, sarcastic voice, the sound with which he whipped his own rage.

"Well," he said, "Of course I ain't never sure. But I believe I was chasin' a nigger named Temptation Pelham. Ain't he one of your niggers?" He sounded gleeful, somehow, saying "your niggers."

"Temp?" Ashby said. He leaned toward the red point of the sheriff's cigarette. "Temp? What you chasin' Temp for?"

"To catch him," the sheriff said, almost biting his lip with the quick click of his teeth. "I'm gonna catch him if it sends me to my grave. Because when I left town, all the church crowd was out watchin' me, and if I go back without Temp, I ain' gonna have a vote from a single one of 'em." Then his voice changed, his eyes looked a far way. "You should 'a' seen 'em, Ashby. Cheerin' me on . . ."

"You look like a poet," Ashby said. "Or else like you got a stomach ache." He pulled a cigarette from the pocket of his canvas coat, struck a match on his heel—almost losing his balance as he did it—and drew the smoke into his throat and out his nostrils. "Well," he said. "That's what you bought 'em for. For the voters to cheer you . . ."

"God knows," Turkey said. "God knows I never thought . . ." He shook his head.

"But Temp . . ." Ashby said. "What'd he do?"

"He molested a high-yaller gal on Front Street," the sheriff said. "Or at least they said it was him, and I've done told all the church crowd it was him, when they asked me who was I goin' after, and so now it has got to be him, if I ain' gonna be even more humiliated."

"Molested a gal?" Ashby said. "You crazy? You know how old Temp is? Sixty-six."

The sheriff looked at him. "Hell," he said. "I'm sixty-one and I reckon I could molest a high-yaller if I wanted to. Don't you go tryin' to mess me up, Ashby. Them hounds are enough, without you tryin' to create doubt and confusion in my mind." He spat. "Sixty-six. You act like that's . . . Hell, last night . . ."

"I know," Ashby said. "I was at Miranda's last night." He chuckled. "Louise told me about you. You were about six sheets in the wind, too . . ."

"Ashby!" Turkey looked furtively around, his mouth twisted. "You always so open-mouthed, Ashby . . ."

"You mean about Miranda's?" Ashby said. "Why, the devil, Turkey, I'm the one oughta be lookin' to see if anybody heard me. The way Father and Evelina won't let Miranda's name be said, I . . ."

"I ain't talkin' 'bout that," Turkey said, squirming. "Though it has give me many a laugh, thinkin' 'bout one of you high an' mighty Pelhams . . ." He rubbed a hand over his waxy head. His eyes still looked about him, as if he expected someone to appear from out a thicket somewhere. "You jest don't seem to have any respect for anything, Ashby. 'Six sheets in the wind.' I'm the sheriff here and charged to uphold the dry law, and you go talkin' like that . . ."

"Why, hell," Ashby said. "There's nothing but bushes to hear."

"You always go making a man feel guilty about his little pleasure," the sheriff said. "Always look so mocksome, Ashby. Why, you as sinful as I am, Ashby . . ."

"Never denied it," Ashby said. "Couldn't look holy if I tried. But I just got to laugh when I see somebody like you looking like Saint Purity in a white robe . . ."

The sheriff shook his head; his mouth was curling angrily again. He dropped his cigarette on the ground and said, "I swear, Ashby, I been meanin' to talk to you a long time. Ashby, are you *sound?*"

"*Sound?*" Ashby said. "*Sound?* How you mean, *sound.*" He touched his knee with the flat of the hand holding the cigarette. "I have got a trick knee, but outside of that . . ."

"You know what I mean," the sheriff said. "I mean are you the kind of fellow somebody could trust, or have you got ideas?"

"Listen," Ashby said. Fatigued, he sat down on the road, the clay cold to his buttocks. "I want to talk about Temp. When did all this happen? This about the high-yaller? Because I saw Temp about three o'clock and I gave him five dollars. Over yonder in the west field next the river. I had just shot a single, and old Dan was retrievin' it, when Temp came up out o' breath and said he needed some money bad, and so I . . ."

The sheriff moaned. "You mean you give him money? Like that?" He looked up, starward; his hand rubbed back and forth, back and forth over his bare dome. "I swear to God, it look like ever'thing an' ever'body's ag'inst me. I reckon if a star fell from up yonder and plonked me on the head, I wouldn't even notice it. I'm a plumb humiliated man . . ."

"When did it happen?" Ashby said. Turkey stood up.

"It happened jest 'fore church," Turkey said. "This mornin' jest 'fore church. I tole you that. I tole you I tole the church crowd I'd catch him. And now they gonna be laughin' at me, a-joshin' and a-jokin' behind my back . . ." He plucked at his nose. Then he pointed his finger at Ashby. "It's you. A Pelham. Even think you don't have to observe the game laws. Huntin' in March. Dependin' on your name to keep you out of court . . ."

Ashby flushed. "Maybe so, Turkey. I never thought about season being over. You want to arrest me?" He rose.

"Naw, I don't want to arrest you. Anyhow, you could say the quails was pesterin' you and they wouldn't fine you." Turkey pointed his finger at Ashby again. "But it's jest like I said. You got ideas."

"Ideas? What kind of ideas? Hasn't been an idea loose around here since '65."

"Who ever heard of jest givin' a nigger . . . Why, hell, he'll use that money to go down on Ruttin' Row . . ."

"At sixty-six?"

"And he'll be doin' no tellin' what, gittin' me out all hours of night with them far-fetched hounds, to be laughed at . . ." The sheriff breathed like a winded horse. When he paused, his face was near to lavender in the moonlight.

"He said he needed it bad," Ashby said. "And I think enough of Temp . . ." He flipped his cigarette into the ditch.

"Well, he could 'a' got it off you had he been a cut-throatin' criminal," the sheriff said. "You a Pelham, ain't you? Sp'ilin' ever' nigger in the county. Runnin' Pelham Place like a fourteen carat, gold-plated nigger heaven, so that niggers that ain't on your place is dissatisfied where they are. It ain' good for business and a decent profit, Ashby, and you know it. Why, the fellow puttin' in the new factory says he never would 'a' come here if he'd thought he was gonna hafta mess around with a bunch of biggety niggers."

The sheriff's voice was unctuous now, pleading a little. Ashby said, "Well, I'd just as soon he hadn't come cluttering up our air with his smokestacks, if he came here just to gyp the Negroes. . . ." He was enjoying himself and his voice betrayed the fact. The sheriff took heart.

"I swear," he said, "Sometimes if I didn't know yo' grandpa was a hero in the War, I'd think you was a carpetbagger, Ashby. . . ."

Ashby laughed. "And I reckon that factory man is a son of the Old South in your eyes, eh, Turkey? Why, you know well as I do that this place . . ." He moved his head from side to side of the road. "This place is being run just like it was run before the War. Been run like this since 1840. Father wouldn't change it, and I'm too lazy to change it. So if I'm a carpetbagger, I reckon the man that made this plantation in the first place was one, but you all have got his statue up down yonder in front of the courthouse . . ."

Turkey looked at the ground and kicked at a clod with his

bootheel. "I was jest sayin' what folks all say about you all," he said. "Hell, the War's over, and . . ."

"Did you tell Father that when you went by the house?" Ashby said. "He'd be right pleased to know it. That is, if Lee won . . ."

Turkey looked more comfortable. "Always joshing," he said.

"You the one," Ashby said. "One minute callin' me a carpet-bagger an' next minute tellin' me I don't know the War's over. The thing is, I reckon, that we around here haven't changed, Turkey, and it's sorta confusin' to folks to see us doing like we did a hundred years ago. I don't know whether it's a right way to do or not, but it's our way, and . . ." He shrugged. "But I can tell you this," he said. "I'd give Temp that five dollars again, and if you aim to put him in jail on any kind of crazy charge like that . . ." He narrowed his eyes, watching Turkey. "Who ever heard of getting out bloodhounds because a Negro did what you claim Temp did? Acting like it's a terrible crime and running all over the country with those hounds . . ."

Turkey's eyes were small and glistening on him. "How do I know that's all he's guilty of? How do I know he wasn't the one that killed poor old Miss Lucy Weatherbee? I'm tellin' you, the voters is gettin' tired of things like what happened to Miss Lucy, and I aim to . . ."

Ashby put one hand on his hip. "By God, if I thought you'd . . . Are you standing there aiming to tell me you intend to blame all the crimes in Christendom on a poor old Negro like Temp, just because you . . ." He felt his anger in his teeth.

"I ain't the only one," Turkey said. "That's the first thing some of them in the church crowd thunk of. They said, 'Maybe he's the one killed poor Miss Lucy.' And another'n said, 'I bet he's the one robbed the Good Hope store.' "

"Good God," Ashby said. "You stand up there and try to tell me Temp's conducted a one-man crime wave, when he's been with me day in and out, and most of the nights, too, and couldn't possibly . . ."

"I never thought you'd do anything but take up for him,"

Turkey said. "He's a nigger, and you act mighty lovin' toward 'em sometime . . ." His voice was drawling, his lips curled a little with his sarcasm.

"And you hate 'em," Ashby said. "You'd do anything . . ."

"You damn right I hate 'em," Turkey said. "And if you think I am going to let this one get away, after being humiliated with them hounds, the way they run down Brother Harkness last week. . . . I've done told the voters I was gonna git a dangerous nigger with 'em, and I'm gonna do it."

Ashby put the butt of the gun down on the ground and leaned on the barrel. He said, quietly, "And you're gonna have Father and me to fight if you do. If you aim to blame all the crimes you can't solve on Temp, and then hold one of your little hanging parties just to clear yourself and those hounds with the voters—and exercise your anger at black skin . . . Well, you're gonna have a fight on your hands . . ." Ashby straightened then, and said, casually. "What did Father want?"

Turkey's eyes never moved. He answered the question—"Wanted to tell you something. Said to hurry,"—but his mind was not on what he was saying. His eyes were focused hard on Ashby.

"What ails you?" Ashby said.

"I'm thinkin' about yo' helpin' that nigger. . . ." Turkey clamped his mouth shut and doubled his fists.

"Why," Ashby said, "I helped out a man that said he needed help. I gave him five dollars, and if he had told me why he needed it, Turkey, I reckon I would have given him more. I haven't got a whole lot of patience with the way you spend yo' time runnin' 'round in a rage at some poor old Negro, and let all the white folks get away with more real devilment than a Negro could think up in a hundred years. . . . And I don't aim for you to make Temp a sacrificial lamb on your political altar." He half-turned.

"Oh. So you ain't got patience," Turkey said. "Well, Ashby, if I hear yo' helpin' any nigger to escape from justice, I'm gon' put you in jail, Pelham or no Pelham. . . ."

Ashby turned and looked him in the eyes. "Why," he said, grinning, "I'd tell you now, Turkey. I reckon knowing how you are, he's already in Memphis now, whether he's innocent or guilty. And if he isn't, I'd take him there myself before I'd let him fall into your hands. . . ."

Then he turned and left the sheriff standing there in the road. It seemed to him that he had won a kind of victory. He went toward home.

## Chapter II

He had gone only a little way when he saw Num. The river mist was coiling now all about him, but he knew it was Num even at a distance, even through the moonlighted night.

It seemed that he saw the cane first, the glint of gold on its head. Num carried it lightly in one black hand; old as he was, he never put it heavily on the ground to lean upon it, but swung it lightly, with a nimble, dandified gesture.

Then Ashby saw the slow splayed feet and the body bent from the hips so that the tails of the "preaching coat" he wore stuck out far from his calves and flapped in the air. The coat was an old one of Ashby's Father's. Num had seized on it one day twenty years ago, had grabbed it from a parcel being fixed for the Salvation Army.

"Where you going to wear it?" Father had said, his mouth spreading as if to josh.

"Preachin'," Num had said. A single finger had rubbed wonderingly along the coat.

"You're not any preacher," Father had said.

"I am now," Num had said. "Now I got me a preachin' coat."

He had been then, for a while. He didn't appear any more in the colored gallery of the Presbyterian Church. He had been the last Negro who ever came there anyway, and sat there all alone in a cane-bottomed chair. When the white folks would look up at him, he bowed with a grave gesture, holding one thin hand parallel with his face, as it moved downward, as if he would have tipped a hat had he been brash enough to wear one in the Lord's House. Then, for almost a year, when he had got the coat, he had not been there.

They had known what he was doing; he was preaching, word for word, the sermons he had heard over all the years in that very church.

"He could have made a fortune on the stage," Father had said. "He can remember anything and mock anybody." They had thought about how he could mimic Dr. McAllister, the pastor: the every gesture there, down to the slow batting of the left eye and the peculiar sideward and upward motion of his head at emotional moments.

One Sunday while he was gone from the church, Father had looked at the empty balcony and wondered. "What I wonder," he had said, "is how the Negroes are taking to Presbyterianism. And I reckon Num is no doubt throwing in a little Shakespeare, too. I'm afraid he is confusing souls . . ."

"It's heathenish," Evelina had said. "A mockery. It is." Ashby had stirred restlessly on the slick oak pew at her tone; but then she had laughed. She reached for the blue hymn book with a plump gloved hand; on her revealed wrist, a little circle of a watch ticked conscientiously as always.

Father had winked at Ashby. When he winked it was like a blanket passed over firesmoke; the thing done, the smoke of his eyes was bluer than you remembered it before.

"You just miss him up there in the balcony on Sunday like we do," Father had whispered, uncrossing his legs to rise for the song. "You wouldn't mind how much he said his sermons, if he were . . ."

"Sh-h- . . ." she had said, and opened her little mouth to sing.

It had not been long after that that Num came back to the balcony. He came without telling them he was coming, did not even drive into town with them as he had been used to do right after breakfast. He came alone, a little late, and they were singing the Doxology when Ashby saw him and tapped Father's hand. Even then, when Ashby was only fourteen, Father was fifty-four. And, seeing Num there, where he had been for so long and had been gone for what seemed an even longer time, he sighed even as he smiled; he liked things as they had been.

They had met Num that morning after church. He waited for them beside the car, wearing his preaching coat, his eyes already yellowed a little with age, but his flesh still at that time smooth and polished as slick dark wood, so that it seemed a finger rubbed across it would squeak a little with its hardness. "Well," Father had said. Ashby knew Father was happy because of the way he wet his cigar: with a slow and conscious moving of his tongue.

"Yassuh," Num had said. "It ain' no use tryin' to make nothin' but a Baptist out o' a nigger. They claim sprinklin' can't wash away all they sin. You got to scare 'em by a nigh-drownin' in Jordan to make 'em believe they saved. Yassuh."

But he had preserved his preaching coat. He had worn it every Sunday since then, in the balcony, where he sat now more proudly than ever, since he sat by special dispensation of the Elders themselves. The way that had come about was that the town grew, and new people came into it and some of these demanded that he be kept out of the balcony so that white folks could sit there. Father had been angry. He had gone to the session meeting, and Ashby knew he was full of a great anger because of the way he walked, the legs taut, and the chest thrust out so that the wingbones of his lean back showed through the dark wool of his coat. When he had come home, it had been agreed that Num could sit there unto death. "Unto death," Father had said, pleased with the sound of it.

Num was a proud man, too, at the sound of it; he knew how it was to want a way of being preserved unto death. Unto death? After death. Forever, and ever, Ashby thought, when now he saw him there on the road, the unchangeable pride in his slow walk, the moon glint on the lightly-held cane, the head of white nap held straight in spite of the bent body.

And Ashby did not want to speak to him. He was peaceful now; his anger at the sheriff had been quick and clean and done with, unless the sheriff or chance should bring it back again. But the feeling Num always gave him was never that kind of swift lightning, soon gone; rather it was like an endless storm, grumbling and restless. He was a relaxed man, returning tired from a hunt; he had seven quail in his pockets, and the drunken peace in his mind. That peace was such that he did not actually want to go home. But, if he had to go home, he did not want to talk to Num. For a second he thought of slipping through the barbed wire and cutting off across the winter-dead cotton field and coming on the house from another way.

But then Num turned, his white head cocked, as if by twisting his neck he could aid his eyesight. He looked older than Ashby ever remembered him. In the night light, going toward him, Ashby saw with a start the blurred eyes and the no-longer-taut skin, the skin now dried, wrinkled like a piece of dark paper crushed once and unsmooth forever. Then when he sensed that it was Ashby, he croaked. Hell, Ashby thought, hell, now he will say . . .

"Huh . . ." Num said. "You went a far piece. Huntin' on the Lawd's Day, unmannersome as ever . . ." He spat on the road. "Jest like *him*. *He* was a moon-burned man. . . ."

Ashby's hand was hard on the gun butt. Goddamit, he thought, if I did a hula dance in the moonlight, he would say, just like *he* did. . . . But he said nothing. He did not ask Num who *he* was. He knew, and knew that if he were to avoid the stories, he must be quiet. He made a grave bow to Num, without opening his mouth.

But Num said, "He . . ." and his voice came hard through his timeworn throat. Num told the tale.

I have heard it seventeen hundred and seventy-six times, Ashby thought. It was the Shiloh story. Number one, Ashby thought. The Number One story about the Number One man. The man was Ashby Pelham, too—Colonel Ashby Pelham, C.S.A. And the tale, now coming relentlessly from the old dry lips, was the story of how the Colonel Ashby Pelham had been shot at Shiloh when Num was seventeen.

"I was seventeen," Num said.

"So I've heard somewhere before," Ashby said.

But Num paid him no mind. "Miss Lucy was 'bout twenty-five. And yo' Papa not born yet. Three months 'fore he was born, it was . . ."

When Granny was twenty-five, Ashby thought. They went to Shiloh that night because she knew he had been shot. How? Intuition. "A feelin'," Num said. "It was a feelin' she had." The Scotch have visions, Ashby thought. So she and Num went and found him and everything that has happened to them since has happened only as it has been reflected from that night. They drove twenty miles there and found him with the hole in his neck. He was, tales said, the man who had shot a yellow ribbon from his fiancee's hair at a hundred paces; the shot had been witnessed by her father, who had promptly had a heart attack, and, with the imperiousness of the ill, had ordered her to marry a less daring man of his own choice. She (who was now Granny) had done so, but that other Ashby had followed her on the river boat which she and the less daring man had boarded for their honeymoon. The boat had caught fire the first night, while she and her groom danced in the saloon. Ashby had saved her, and then later married her, a widow who had never been a wife—nor ever wanted to be a wife except to

Ashby. It was that Ashby, also, who had carried messages through the enemy lines, concealing them in tobacco padded in his jaw. It was he, too, who could quote Shakespeare and the Bible and write an appropriate Latin phrase at the top of an essay on government. He could, they said, write a lyric to make a lady smile as easily as he could deliver a political speech to make a man cheer. The tales grew with the telling, but they all said he was a man who could face the devil with a grin and had a quick hand to a pistol. That was the man they found with the hole in his neck on the field at Shiloh. And they, Num and Granny, brought him back in the carriage, and he waited, it seemed, waited to die until he was there in his own house on the blue-tapestried couch where the stain of his blood was yet, a brown splotch on the fabric.

Sometimes it seemed to Ashby they had all been stained by that dying. If he had died as a man, it might not have been so. But he had died as a legend and a hero, and, dying, had left his mark on them all, and on Ashby more than any, because he bore the name.

His hand was gripped to whiteness on the butt of the gun.

Then Num said, "All right. I ain' gonna say no more 'bout him." He raised his eyes. "You hit me once. Only time you ever hit me, when I was tellin' you 'bout him. . . . You wasn't old. Nine or ten, I reckon." His throat was aged and raw: his words rasped like gravel in his throat.

"I don't recollect," Ashby said, but he did. The feel of that past moment was on him now, the taste of lemon, sour in the glands of his jaw and the aching ring in his ears, when Num said, "They named you wrong. You ain't no Ashby Pelham. No wonder yo' Granny don't love you like she love him. Behavin' the way you do. You couldn't be no Ashby Pelham if you tried."

He remembered hitting Num. He remembered his fist swung without aim, he remembered the gristle and bone toughness of Num's ribs. He remembered saying, "I could. I could be Ashby Pelham. I could, I could . . ." His fists beating into gristle, into bone. Num had never moved, had never tried to stop him.

So that he had turned and fled, crying, the tears dropping off his chin and splashing in the dusty road that led to the pasture.

One moment he was like that other one, another moment he was not and could never be. Once, a time later, Num had again said that to him: "You never could be like him." But then he had only said, "What of it! I'm not him. I'm me. I'm this Ashby Pelham. I wouldn't be that other if I could. I wouldn't want to."

But Num would always counter that with the question: "Is it enough?"

"Enough?" he would say. "What you mean enough?"

"Enough not bein' him. How is not bein' somebody enough? If you ain't somebody, then you got to be somebody else. You can't be nothin'. . . ."

The look was on Num's face there in the road, then. The question was there, unspoken.

And he knew the answer. It was not enough. It's not within a hog bristle of being enough, either, he thought. It's as far from enough as I know, but what enough is, I don't know.

He put the gun down on the ground, the butt between his boots, the barrel resting against his abdomen. He knew it was not enough, because, with Num having said nothing, with Num standing silent watching him, the question had been asked and it had been answered. He felt that familiar souring in his jowls and that tautness in the windpipe.

Usually when the question ached in his throat and was like an itch on his mind, there were things he did. He got his gun and Don and went hunting. Or he fought his Tatori fighting cocks in the Hamilton barn, with slow cursing concentration and swift exchange of wagered greenbacks.

Sometimes he drank, not too often; corn liquor, aged in charred kegs in the wine cellar under the kitchen. He drank it from a silver flask a girl had given him in college. She had been called Honeybreeches, even by her own family who did not, presumably, know the origin of the name. It was a sort of state-wide joke, the old folks calling her that, not knowing she had been a kind of carnal communist. With a sort of innocent pleasure, she had taken the gifts her men brought her, but never had she favored the men in turn with anything save herself. So that it was a matter of surprise and then for bawdy cracks on the campus when she had given Ashby the flask. On it was engraved "For Ashby from Honeybreeches. December, 1929."

It was this flask he reached for now, when the question asked itself there on the road with Num. It was cold to his hands; moonlight glinted upon it. He always felt a shock on first seeing it, and then he looked at it wryly, remembering.

Now it was Num who put the remembering in words. Always, Ashby thought. Always.

Num said, "Ain't that the flask . . .? That the one Miss Carol broke her 'gagement 'bout?"

Ashby half-closed his eyes. "You got any salt on you?" he said. "If you have, I might be able to find a cut somewhere on me and you could rub the salt in, and I reckon get a heap of pleasure out of it. . . ." He let his breath out with a snorting sound.

"What?" Num said. "What?" He put a hand to his ear. "I jest rememberin' Miss Carol."

"You got might' nigh a monopoly on remembering, to hear you tell it," Ashby said. "But I reckon I can compete a little with you in remembering Miss Carol." He pulled his lower lip over his top one, nervously. She had been a breathless kind of girl. She had had all of Cousin Evelina's specifications: she was a Southerner, a Democrat, a Presbyterian, and a blue-eyed blonde—the last being important to Evelina, who had notions about race purity. But what had been important to him was that breathlessness, the enthusiasm and wonder that was in her. "Like she just arrived on a train," he had said, describing her once, "Like she just got here and can't wait to see and say and do everything."

It was this very quality about her that he had not properly realized. He had treated Carol as if she were a fragile miracle, fragile because she was a lady and Ashby Pelham had been taught to treat ladies so, and a miracle because he was in love with her, and he had never been in love before and did not know quite how to do. What she could not bear, when she found out, was that he had treated Honeybreeches as a woman, while he was treating her as a fragile miracle. He knew now he had wanted Carol as a woman, but he had not known it then, not consciously, because they had reared him to think that there were women and there were ladies and a man kept them separate in two parts of his mind.

Well, that was one part of the legend he would never believe again, he thought. Honeybreeches' flask had taught him that, anyhow. So he always lifted the flask to her, to Honeybreeches.

He did it now, watching Num out of the corner of his eye. And Num said, "Why come you gonna drink? Ever' time I see you, you got the restless foot. Got to shoot. Got to gamble. Got to drink. Got to . . ."

Ashby held the flask still. "Got to sit on my tail on a fence post and broil in the sun hollerin' at hands in the field," he said. "Got to scrape my belly oiling the gin, come baling time. Got to run for the doctor when babies are coming in the quarter. Got to rub my nose in the ledgers to keep Bluson Larkin from gypping the hands at the commissary. You act like all I do is . . ."

He shrugged. Then he slowly, deliberately, unscrewed the top of the flask.

"Yes," Num said. "He was one to drink. He . . ." Then he slowed his moving hand and gazed down at the road. He touched a piece of clay with the gold-topped cane. He hit the clod with the cane as if it were a golf ball.

Ashby, the rim of the flask cold on his lips, lowered it. Then, silently, with slow deliberate anger, he screwed the top on. With one hand he took up his gun while with the other he slipped the flask back into his hip pocket.

"All right," he said, roughly. "Let's go." He turned abruptly and stepped away. Num came after him. "What does Father want anyhow, besides somebody to talk to?" He slowed.

Num took up his slow pace. "It's that Temp," he said. His voice was quavery, with contempt or pain, Ashby did not know which. "Gittin' hisself in law trouble. He ain't none o' mine. He was got without me bein' there. He a child o' midnight sin, an' I said so. . . ."

"Where is he?" Ashby said. "I gave him money. Did he get off?"

"No," Num said. "He come to the house, aimin' to walk th'ough, and throw that sheriff off the trail, but yo' Father found him, an' make him stay there, an' sent word to you. . . ."

Ashby stopped and turned his head down to Num. "You mean he was there when the sheriff went by with the hounds, and Father sent word to me by the sheriff . . .?"

Num nodded. "Yassuh . . ."

"I be damned," Ashby said. "If Father's not . . ." He shook his head, grinning. "That sheriff would have apoplexy if he knew."

They walked on. "Temp never had no business doin' it," Num said. "He never did nothin' ag'in the law, but he never had no business doin' nothin' that could look like it was ag'in the law."

"Well, what did he do anyhow?" Ashby said.

Num, shuffling to keep up with him, moved the cane with an agitated hand. "He didn' do nothin' but try to stop that daughter o' his'n. . . That gal he got on that high-yaller from Memphis, that he married in Oxford that time. . . . She was misbehavin' unladylike down on Front Street, an' he . . . She hollered when he tried to stop her. She say he wasn't none o' her papa, when he is. She called for the law, an' Temp slap her to hush her up, an' she holler louder, an' when he hit her ag'in, he got sceared and run. He ought not to run. If he'd thunk how that sheriff likes to use them hounds, an' will believe any tale to git a chance to use his hounds, he might not. But he did . . ."

Ashby laughed. "I thought," he said, nodding. The whole situation pleased him, the way, unwittingly, they had outwitted the sheriff. "I thought, when that sheriff said Temp had molested a gal . . ."

"Nawsir," Num said. "Temp couldn't molest no gal. Temp ain't had no nature left in him fer a long time now. Used it all up a time ago. He couldn't molest no gal any more'n I could. But he never had no business bringing this trouble on me, old as I am. . . ." His voice had a wet sound in it.

Ashby said, "Now here. He's innocent, and that's all there is to it, and so what is all the ruckus about? You all can make more racket over nothing . . ." He shifted his gun to the other shoulder.

"It's my name," Num said. "I don't want my name bandied about by the law. I named Pelham like you, an' it ain't a name I hold light, like you seem . . ." He coughed, a rasping sound. "For one of my name to go to jail. It don't look like I could stand that."

He was shaking. When Ashby looked at him, he could see the trembling, the hand palsied on the cane.

Ashby stopped. "All right," he said. His voice was soft. "You don't worry. We'll tend to it." He put his hand on Num's shoulder. "You just forget it, you hear. Hear?"

"I jest can't stand for one of my name to go to jail," Num said. "And he got to get away from here, till the Senator . . ." His breath was short. He said again, his chest heaving, "The Senator . . ." He called Father that most of the time; he liked the sound of it, Ashby thought, it was a comfort to him to say the word. They all wanted titles, like royalty. Father had been senator for six months thirty years ago. Another man had had to die and Father had had to have a friend in the governor's chair to appoint him. But now he was called Senator. "The Senator," Num said again, "He say we got to hide him till that sheriff git over his madness. He gits a mad spell on him, and there ain't no sense in him. He white trash, and they all like that. So we got to hide Temp. . . ."

"Well," Ashby said, "I'll help. Wherever you all want him hid."

They walked on. Num said, "We can't hide him here. That sheriff likely to come a-snoopin' back up yonder tonight, and there wouldn't be no talkin' sense to him."

Ashby could feel, without looking, Num's eyes watching him. "You want me to take him off?" he said.

"If you would," Num said. "I'd sho' be thankful. . . ."

"All right," Ashby said. "I'll take him off tonight." Their feet made sucking sounds on the wet clay. They were not a far way from the house; he could see the lights from it first, and then he saw the house itself, blue-white in the encircling trees. "It looks like a tomb," he said. "I'll be glad to get away from it for a while. I'm glad of the excuse. . . . Maybe I'll go see Uncle Ephe."

"Our house? You talkin' 'bout our house?" Num said. The road rose gradually. "That the finest house in all this county. That glass in the stair-window come from over the ocean. Bohemia. And they brung them pines along the drive clean from California by oxcart . . ."

"As if we didn't have enough pines here already," Ashby said. He was glad to hear himself saying it. At least, he thought, I am back to where I can mock them. I reckon it is because I am going somewhere. I reckon that is it.

"But them pines is different," Num said.

"Uglier," Ashby said. "And more expensive . . ."

But Num had his eyes fastened on the house now. "An' them mantles was carved in Italy . . ."

"What you doin'?" Ashby said. "Practicin' yo' garden club speech on me? You better save it up, Num. For the spring, when the old women come nosing. I get enough of living in a museum, anyhow . . ."

But thinking about leaving, knowing he had a thing to do, he was gleeful. "Or I tell you what," he said. "If I manage to make myself come back by spring . . ."

"By spring . . .?" Num said. "What you talkin' 'bout?"

"You never know where a man will end up," Ashby said.

"You ain' got no feelin', have you?" Num said. "No feelin' that somethin' goin' to happen . . .?"

"No,' Ashby said. "I leave that to you an' Miss Evelina. No, what I started to say is that, come spring, you could dress me up in a gray uniform and put me in a glass case and tell everybody I'm Colonel Ashby Pelham dug up. And you could charge the garden club ladies a quarter to see me, and we could make us enough money to pitch a good drunk. . . ." His hand was on the cold iron of the gate latch.

"Mocksome," Num said. "Mocksome like always."

# Chapter III

He hurried toward the kitchen wing, because his feet were muddy, and if he went the front way, Evelina would say, "You ought to have come 'round back. Just look at all that dirt you've left all over our clean front steps." So he wiped his boots on the back steps, balancing himself on one leg while he ran his foot down the edge of the step so that the mud came off in gobs. Num waited patiently behind him.

Through the glass door, he could see her, Evelina, sitting beside the kitchen fireplace, next to the stove on which she had placed a tablecloth and a bowl of narcissus in token that no work was done in that house on the Lord's Day. Evelina was a one for tokens, for symbols. It was not what a thing was, he thought, but how it looked. Or how it sounded, when said. There was a place on the river called "Polecat Point" because of the sulfurous odors there where the sewers from the town drained into the river. Though the name was by now so well-established that no one else even thought of the meaning when saying the words, Evelina would never say them at all. She always referred to the place as "that spot where the lovely willows are." Father laughed at her about it.

Whenever they joshed her, she could laugh at herself as much as they could laugh at her; but none of the joshing changed her. It was as if she said to them, "It does sound ridiculous the way you put it, but just the same, I know what I'm about, and I'm right. . . ."

So that, since she never changed, Ashby knew exactly what she would say when he opened the door and stood there in the warm kitchen facing her. And she did. He said, "Howdy," sniffing the odor of wax and narcissus and mellowed apples, and put his gun against the wall and held the screen open for Num to come through.

And Evelina said, "You ought not . . ."

"Ought not, ought, ought not, ought . . ." he chanted and went over to her and scratched a finger under her full-fleshed chin. Her nose was in a perpetual quiver; sometimes she would close one eye and wrinkle one nostril up, as if the little nose itched and she was too much a lady to scratch it. When she did that, strange gentlemen had sometimes thought she was winking at them. She had had her bottom pinched more than once because of it. She always exhibited the proper mixture of outrage and pleasure about such encounters.

"Ought not what?" he said. He put a hand in her hair, trying to muss it, but it was thick and held securely in place with numerous large horn hairpins, so that it could not separate but could only rock as a single mass under his touch. She had once been what she called "a titian," but her hair was now whitening; he had nicknamed her because of it.

"Pinky," he said. "Ought not what, Pinky?"

"Hunt on Sunday," she said. "You ought not to." She shook her head. But she said it so without emotion, so as if it were a thing of habit now unfelt, that he only grinned and backed to the spitting fire. He felt his boots and his pants steaming and the heat crawling pleasurably up his legs and thighs and buttocks. Then, lifting her blue eyes to him, she said, "Sacrilegious."

Again the word did not seem to have any real emotional meaning to her. They talk, he thought, in words that don't mean anything, not even to them; or don't mean anything now if they ever did. They say *honor* and *duty* and *loyalty* and *love* but there's nothing in the words when they're said. Yet they live by them. You can depend on them being honorable and dutiful and loyal and loving; you can depend on Father and Evelina being that way, because they don't know any other way to be. But when they say the words, they don't mean anything.

He was aware of Num standing impatiently by the door, but he only winked at him and then turned back to her.

"Why," he said, "what do you mean 'sacrilegious?' " He frowned. "I don't reckon you could get much closer to God than I got out yonder. . . ."

She sniffed, the little nose twitching.

"I bet," he said, "I bet you don't even know what the sermon was about this morning. . . ." He thought about her in church. The temperature was never right: she would have sworn she went for the good of her soul, but it was her body she worried about once there. Church was always too cold or too hot, drafts and steam plaguing her in alternate waves. She would beckon imperiously to an usher and hiss loudly, "Would you mind closing that window?" And five minutes later, fuming, as if the Lord and the usher had plotted together against her, she would lift the finger again. "Too hot. It's too hot now. . . ." The usher closest to their pew was old Joe Scanlon, and he was not up to all the exercise Evelina put him through. "By the good Harry," Father would say, "She's gonna kill him. And neither she nor Joe has heard a word of a sermon since her old age settled in her ankles."

"Sermon?" she said now, straightening herself in her chair. "Of course I know what it was about . . ." Her teeth scraped her lower lip for a second.

"Well?" he said. He grinned at Num but Num only fumbled with his cane, waiting.

"It was . . . it was . . ." she said. "Well, I thought it mighty funny if you ask me. A funny thing to preach about . . ." She moved her head in pretended outrage, her lips pressed together.

"Well?" Ashby said. "What was it?"

He could see the doubt on her face and the faint pouting turn of her lips. "A mighty funny thing. He preached about 'beer.' "

" 'Beer?' " Ashby said, and then covered with his hand the laughter exploding from his mouth. He shook his head at her, mock serious. "Pinky, you're going to hell for sure. 'Beer'!"

"Why," she said, "That's what he preached on. What are you laughing at?"

"Because it wasn't about beer," he said.

"And how do you know?" she said, stiff-backed now, prideful.

"Why," he said. "I stopped in and had dinner with the Trents. And they happened to mention it. . . ." He closed one eye slowly at her. He took a step away from the fire; he could smell the leather of his boots burning.

"You mean you went to Sunday dinner at the Trents in huntin' clothes?"

"Ah-ah," he said. "Don't go changing the subject. Besides since you won't feed me anything here . . ." He looked at the stove. "But the sermon was about . . ." He licked his lips. "Not beer . . ."

She shrugged and made out not to listen.

"But 'Fear'!" he said. "And you listened to it for forty minutes, thinking he was talking about . . ."

He leaned against the mantel, laughing at her. Her mouth was set in a straight line and she moved her little head angrily from side to side. "Well," she said, "Like I say, if that ole Joe Scanlon would quit rattlin' those windows . . ."

"Why," he said. "You made him do it. You the one set him to fussin' with 'em . . ." Then she laughed, a tentative, half-embarrassed laugh.

"I reckon I did," she said. "I reckon I did."

He leaned and patted her shoulder. "That's all right," he said. "You just keep on goin' to church even if you never hear the sermon, and I reckon you'll make heaven."

"Well, you ain't . . ." Num said, suddenly. "You gonna be late at the judgment, you are, if this the way . . ." He had not moved from the center of the room. Now he looked over his shoulder, with a gesture like the tic of a man who feels himself followed.

"Okay," Ashby said. He slid his hand into his coat pocket. "Catch," he said, and tossed a cold bird across to Num.

"Lawd . . ." Num said. His cane clattered to the floor, but he caught the quail, by one foot. "Hah!" he said, gloating. "Th'ow 'em here. I show you how I catch 'em."

Ashby threw them, one by one, counting. ". . . two, three . . ." Num grunted, swooped, and cradled the bodies in the crook of his arm. ". . . seven . . ." Ashby said. He took a handkerchief out and wiped a clot of blood and two feathers from his thumb.

"Well, Pinky," he said. "I'm off . . ."

"You ought not to sound so cheerful about it," she said. "When I think of poor Temptation . . ."

"Why," he said, "I can't get in a Scotch gloom about a trip. And Temp's gonna be all right, after all. . . ." He looked at the watch on his wrist. "Lord," he said, "Eight-fifteen. I got to rush."

"That sheriff gon' be doublin' back this way soon," Num said. "I wish you'd hurry, 'stead o' talking."

"All right," he said. He held a hand up to Evelina. "See you, Pinky . . ."

"Was Carol home?" she said. "At the Trents?" He didn't answer.

"Oh, yes. It's tonight she's coming," Evelina said. He only looked at her.

"And I'm going," he said, and turned abruptly, a kind of sickness in him. He went through the pantry, heavy with the winey odor of fruitcakes and an open jar of brandied peaches on a tray. In the dining room, in the half-light from the hall he heard his Father's voice, the full-throated monotone. That voice was the only thing about him that seemed alive and his own; all else seemed dead, a way of acting and thinking that belonged to another time and another person. Only his voice was alive, a strong and vibrant quality.

Ashby listened, still for a second. He could always, wherever he was, recall that voice to his mind; to recall what it said was harder and sometimes to recall what his Father looked like was almost impossible. It was as if he were half-hidden in a mist, as if the blue of his eyes was seen behind a smokiness. Ashby could say to himself that Father was a lean man with a thin face and wiry white hair; that he wore white shirts and old-fashioned string ties and dark blue suits. But having said that, he had still not seen his Father in his mind. And whenever the word *father* came quickly to his mind, he saw not Father but the image of Colonel Ashby Pelham as they had described him to him. Just as all his life it had been Granny who had meant *mother* to him. For nobody had ever said to him, "What would your Father think?" but "What would Colonel Ashby think?" Just as, since his Mother had died when he was born, they had said, "Your Granny won't love you unless you be like Colonel Ashby."

Ashby heard Father say, "Since she fought back, you have perhaps a chance of correcting her behavior. If a woman fights you, then she is half-won to your way of doing. It is when a woman pretends to submit that you are lost, because then her very helplessness will induce in a man a pity and softness which will allow her to dominate him completely. She has . . . uh . . . no ethics about her. If feigned submission is a way to achieve dominance, then she will live a life. . . ."

There was a silence for a second. Then Temp said, "Uh . . . Yassuh." He did not sound, Ashby thought with a grin, he did not sound exactly enlightened. Yet he and Num would sit spellbound by Father's talk and never understand any of it, although Num could reproduce it the next day, almost word for word.

"Yes," Father said, "It is an interesting subject, the relationship . . ."

And Ashby, going toward his voice, thought, He could sit and talk quietly about one of his interesting subjects with this house crumbling down about him, and never notice a piece of plaster falling at his feet or a joist giving away under him. Not that that house could fall down: it was as scrupulously preserved as the legend they lived with.

He went into the library. Father was sitting in the tall, blue leather chair beside the fireplace, a book in his lap with one finger holding a place in it. His white hair was mussed a little and the contrary cowlick in the front stood straight up. He looked reflectively down at Temp who sat on a stool at his feet. Temp had an expression of slightly confused contemplation on his brown face; his wide lips were slightly parted, and the gold-rimmed glasses he wore because he liked the dignity of them had slipped down on his nose, and he peered over them so that he could really see Father. Neither of them heard Ashby until he said, "Howdy . . ."

Then Father rose and said, "See? I told you he'd get here soon." Then to Ashby, "You took a heap of time. I told that sheriff . . ."

Ashby laughed at him. "You're a one," he said. "Sending the sheriff after me to get me home to spirit away the fellow the sheriff was after all along. . . . I bet Turkey would have apoplexy if he knew."

Father smiled and then said, "I don't like that man. It gives me a certain pleasure to outwit him."

"Me, too," Ashby said. They all three stood before the fire.

Temp plucked at Ashby's coat. "Does you hear 'em?" he said. He leaned toward the river windows.

"Can't say I do . . ." Ashby said. "But I'll get dressed and we'll be gone . . ." He looked at his Father. "I got seven quail."

"Good," Father said. "Why don't you take them to Granny? You could just as easily go by Ephe's, and she would like them. I told her she ought to stay with us till bird season was over, the way she likes them . . ." He put his arm around Ashby's shoulder. He smelled the plain white soap, cigar smoke and brandy. "I'm glad you don't mind doing it," he said, as they went together toward the hall.

"I don't mind," Ashby said, "I'm sort o' glad to get away. Like Num says, I got an itch in me . . ."

He looked up to see Num in the hall. "You ain't got enough itch now," Num said, his eyes pleading. "I sho wish you'd hurry." He peered over their shoulders at Temp. "That boy is in a fix," he said.

"You go on in and keep him company," Father said, "Mr. Ashby is gonna hurry."

"Yassuh," Num said. He went past them, and they walked on to the foot of the stairs.

"It's Num," Father said. "I believe he'd die if they took Temp to jail, and the way that sheriff is, he'd take him to jail tonight, while he's mad, even if he knew he was gonna have to let him out tomorrow because he was innocent." Father jerked his head toward the library, where they could hear Num. "You know how he's always been about Negroes who get themselves in jail. . . . 'Trash . . .' he says. And 'I a Pelham, and a Pelham ain't never been in jail.' Well . . ."

Ashby nodded, smiling. "Lord," he said, "I can hear what that sheriff would say. He wouldn't believe me if I told him I took a trip in the middle of the night to save a nigger's pride in his name. . . ."

Father stiffened. "Ashby!" Then his hand, still firm if white and dry, clung hardly to Ashby's arm. "You sound like white trash. Don't say a thing like that. . . ."

Ashby felt his face grow hot. "I didn't mean it the way it sounded," he said. "I just meant that's the way it would look to other folks. I know Num's got as much right to be proud . . . I started to say as I have, but I don't take any pride in a name, I think a man . . ."

But Father cut him short with a hand like a meat cleaver, chopping.

"You say that," Father said. "But you can't help acting like your blood and raising taught you. What you're doing tonight . . ."

"I'm doing because I want to," Ashby said, seeing the redness of his face in the gilt-framed mirror opposite him. "I want to help Num out." He felt a beginning of anger between them. He put one foot on the stair-carpet.

His Father's face was taut and there was a flush around his eyes.

"My Father . . ." Father said. "When he was district attorney, heard one night that a mob of white trash had taken a freed Negro from the jail and were about to lynch him. Already, even then, before the War, the hate was starting here. . . ." Father shook his head. "Anyhow, he heard about it. There was a bitter rain, but he rode through it. He swam the river in it. The mud on the road was up to the horse's knees. They had the Negro standing on a barrel under that oak that's still yonder in the Trent's pasture. They stood there with torches, those that the rain hadn't put out. There must have been a hundred of 'em. And the Negro on the barrel and the rope already around his neck when Father got there. They were ready to kick the barrel out from under him. He got there just then and rode his horse through the crowd, hearing them say his name, 'Ashby Pelham, it's Lawyer Pelham . . .' They scattered and dropped their torches. They saw him do it only by a clap of lightning. They say the lightning clapped at that very minute when he reached out with a knife. He went through the whole crowd, a lone man with nothing but a knife, and reached out and cut that rope. Then he took the Negro up on his own horse and rode back through the crowd and not a man dared touch him."

On Father's face there was a look of pride and glory. But Ashby's hand kneaded the stair-rail. He closed his eyes, and let his breath out. Then he opened his eyes.

"Why did you have to tell me that old story again?" he said. "Good God, why couldn't you let me do this because *I* wanted to, not because *he* did a thing like it ninety years ago?"

"But, Ashby, I . . ." Father said.

But Ashby's feet were already thudding on the stair-carpet, stepping two at a time, and his hand reaching for the flask.

# Chapter IV

He got drunk and he stopped off at Miranda's.

It was revenge of the kind which Evelina would have described as "cutting off your nose to spite your face." It was a gesture akin to his deliberately failing the West Point examinations when they had got him the appointment, saying, "*He* was a soldier. Now we will have another Colonel Ashby Pelham in this family." Or like the fact that, half-yielding to them, he had got the law degree which, now framed, hung on the wall of his bedroom; but had never practiced law, and deliberately called himself a "farmer" when he could at least have assuaged their feelings by styling himself "planter." Or like his having joined in college a fraternity which was not the fraternity Colonel Ashby and his Father and Ephe had belonged to.

To go to Miranda's was a gesture of the same kind, even if they never knew he went there. Because, in the first place, Miranda was the final mockery of them all, of Father and Granny and Evelina and Ephraim. Miranda was a caricature of the Pelham mind, and there he could laugh at that mind, temporarily freed of it, for the moment only a sardonic observer.

Then, too, it was a part of his living which no one could compare, favorably or unfavorably, with Colonel Ashby Pelham's life. If they knew what Colonel Ashby had done when, unmarried, being man, he had needed woman, they left their knowing unspoken. They never acknowledged the flesh if they could help it, anyway. "You would think," Ashby had said once, "that all Pelhams were got without carnality. Immaculate conceptions, the whole damn tribe." Ashby himself had often suspected that some of the lighter Negroes on the place had more claim to the name Pelham than merely their self-seized right at emancipation to name their families after their white folks. But though the Pelhams might hint, delicately, that *some* respectable white men had of yore had a yearning for a dark and velvet skin, they never even admitted that a Pelham male had any carnal needs, black or white.

So that to go to Miranda's was one thing for which there was no pattern; it was a doing which was his own.

When he left the house he had not voiced in his mind any intention of going there. He was merely angry and a little drunk, and when he had established Temp on the floor in the back, seeing him settled on pillows and covered with a sleeping bag, he had let the top of the car down and had driven, with the wind biting his face, seventy miles an hour into town.

His very leaving had been like the blind striking out of a

man enraged to sightlessness. And his stopping at Miranda's was so. He found himself on the familiar street, before the familiar place, and he made the tires squeal with stopping. Then, sitting in the car, dappled with moonlight through the live oaks above him, he was pleased, and laughed at the very aimlessness of his stopping there.

He fumbled on the seat beside him and found the flask and turned the top with quick fingers. He lifted it to his lips. His Adam's apple moved to the gurgles. The whiskey was sugar and flame in his throat, an aching fume in his nose.

Temp's head appeared above the back of the seat.

"You took the hide off my bottom stopping that way," he said. "Where we?"

Ashby closed the flask and slid it beneath his coat into his back pants pocket.

"Miss Miranda's," he said. "Miss Miranda's Boarding Home for young Ladies." He pointed to the sign above, suspended from the live oak.

He turned in his seat and followed Temp's eyes to the house. It looked like the home of a maiden lady, perhaps the last survivor of her family, who now lived in genteel semi-poverty compared to the day fifty years ago when the house itself must have been built: who took in boarders and required that they be mannersome and quiet and not cook in their rooms, and that, above all, they sit and listen to her tales of former affluence and her gentle hints that she had had a lover killed in some never-identified war. It looked like all the houses around it. It stood behind an iron fence, beyond the length of a yard cluttered with shrubs, a lily pool, a great yellow pottery frog and two green copper statues of Venus and Cupid flanking its walk—the last articles being a mark of its age and respectability and having nothing whatever to do with art or bohemianism. Protected by all this, the house itself was tall, with a peaked roof and a great octagonal tower on one end. Atop the tower, a gargoyle weathervane of tin, patterned by the moon behind it, stood still with rust. From the tower, across the front of the house, a porch stretched, its joists and posts decorated with wooden lacework; along the porch, in the dim light, there was a row of green rockers, turned back-side before and leaned against the wall, awaiting summer evenings. The clapboard walls were painted gray: it was a dull and respectable looking house. He laughed at that; looking at it, he found the humor bubbling out of him.

But it was a sort of angry humor, and Temp said, "You laugh devilish. How come we stop here? You ain' gon' git out an' leave me here? How come we don' go on to Mr. Ephe's?"

He had not thought of a reason before, but, pressed, he thought of it then. "Because we'd get there about three in the morning and wake 'em all up. And so we might as well dawdle and get there at a decent hour . . ."

"Yassuh," Temp said. He must have been on his knees; still only his head showed. "But I jest as soon not dawdle this close to that sheriff . . ."

"Whatever happens, you just stay in this car," Ashby said. "Nobody will find you here. . . ." He slid toward the door nearest the curb.

"That ain't our Miss Miranda, is it?" Temp said, from behind him. Ashby said nothing; he made as if to be watching for some movement behind the shaded windows of the house.

"A town nigger tole me t'other day it was. I say how long she been here, and he say a long time, maybe ten year, and I say couldn't nobody tell me our Miss Miranda would've come back to our town and not come home in no ten year. Not even after . . ." Temp rumbled in his throat. "And I say if she been back so long, how come I ain't seed her? And he say she never go out o' that house. Jest stay inside all the time so nobody ever see her. Is you seen her?"

"Yes," he said, not turning, one hand on the cold metal of the door handle.

"There," Temp said. "There. I said she wasn't our'n. I said didn't none of our folks keep no boa'ding house. Some sho-nuff white folks does, I said, but my white folks is sho-nuff *and rich.*"

Ashby opened the door and stepped out onto the curb.

"Somehow," Temp said. "Somehow I sorta wish it was our Miss Miranda. It ain't right. Miss Evelina and Mr. Ephe ain't seed their own sister in over twenty years. It ain't . . ." He wet his lips, his head still just showing over the side of the car. "Well, she run off with that trash, Mr. Jason said. He—the trash—he sold snuff. Mama Rose Snuff was what he sold. It was right good snuff, but he was trash. I 'members though he had a gold tooth and it was the prettiest tooth I ever saw. . . ."

Ashby tried to imagine Miranda young and fleshly enough to run off with a man, and could not; he tried to imagine her marrying a snuff salesman with a gold tooth, and that was even harder. Nothing can really happen to them, he thought. What they really are can't be changed. Even now she and Evelina are sisters, though Miranda has been through a deal of living and Evelina through almost none: because nothing has ever really happened to either of them. For they are like deep rivers pelted with rocks: their surface ripples a moment and then goes on as before; and all the things that had happened to them had been no more than this, than rocks peppered into a river.

Temp was still talking. "Here!" Ashby said. "You hush up. And get down there on your pallet. And stay scrooched up, because if somebody saw you, you'd be jailed before you know it. . . ."

"Yassuh," Temp said. Then he looked at Ashby, a frown between his eyebrows. "How come you goin' in there? I might git awful cold out here, and . . ."

Ashby reached into his pocket. "All right, damn you," he said. He grinned. "Take it." He handed the flask to Temp. "But don't you get drunk and do something foolish. You do, I'll let that sheriff use that new travelin' electric chair on you. . . ."

"Yassuh. Thank you, suh," Temp said. He shook the flask beside his ear, grinning at the wash and gurgle.

"Hush!" Ashby said. "Here comes somebody." Temp's head dropped. Ashby turned, and waited to be sure that the man passed on.

The man walked with a slow and powerful tread on the brick walk. Then, very near Ashby, he stopped.

"Howdy," he said, softly, and then stood there on the walk looking up with grave eyes at the sign on the board. There was a kind of deliberate slowness about him that was somehow tense. He was a big man, as tall as Ashby, and massive in addition, so large that he seemed to bulge in his clothes; and not only physically did he seem confined, but there was something like the quieted fury of a relaxed tomcat pent within him and likely to break forth. But Ashby felt this only for a second and then wondered why when the man turned gentle dark eyes on him and then shook his bare head confusedly and took a slow step away.

"You looking for something?" Ashby said, wondering at the man's bewilderment.

"Yes," the man said, stopping. "I reckon I am." He had a slow deep voice: it made a sound like a rich whisper. "I reckon. But I don't reckon this is it. A fellow told me . . ." He looked at Miranda's house and then craned his neck to look back at the sign. "He didn't say it was a boarding house. He said . . ."

"You looking for a woman?" Ashby said. The man looked down at his feet and said nothing. "Hell," Ashby said. "I'm not a pimp for the place, but if you're looking for a place named Miranda's where there are girls, then so am I, and this is it."

"But it says . . ." the man said, his thick eyebrows raised questioningly at the sign.

"That's just a sign," Ashby said. "You don't believe everything you read, do you?" He was enjoying himself; he was just drunk enough to find a grin in everything.

The man lifted his face; his large mouth worked strangely.

"It sounds crazy . . ." he said. "But I . . . I never been to one. I . . ."

"Well," Ashby said, one eyebrow lifted, the other eye half closed, "You're lucky. Practically bragging . . ."

"No," the man said. "Not that. I mean . . ."

"You're not fixing to tell me you're a virgin, are you?" Ashby said.

The man scuffed one shoe on the other, like an abashed boy. "No . . . I . . ." he said. "Well, when I was a kid . . . Girls then. But since . . . since . . ." He let his eyes look on Ashby. "I'm a lonesome man," he said, the words hurried and embarrassed. Then he turned abruptly. "Well, I reckon I'll be goin'. . . ."

The word was in Ashby's mind, ringing. "Lonesome?" he said. "Yes. Lonesome . . ." There was a lone feeling in him at the sound of the words, and he did not want the man to leave, feeling that way, lonely. "Here . . ." he said. "It's not a heap better in there, but you forget about it for a while."

The man turned again and for a second the explosive quality was in his eyes; then they softened. "They say only gentlemen go in this place. I'm afraid . . ." He spoke very slowly; he looked down at the blue plaid suit he wore and then looked Ashby up and down, noting the dark blue of Ashby's suit, the white shirt, the dark tie, his eyes taking Ashby in with careful appraisal. "I reckon I'm not . . ."

"Are you worryin' about what you got on?" Ashby said. "Because if you are, you ought to know a gentleman's not clothes, any more than that sign tells what this house is. And if it's how to act, then I can tell you all you got to do is be quiet and never say around Miranda that you know what kind of house it is." He was at the gate, his hand on the latch.

"Not let on?" the man said, "Not say what kind of house . . .?" He was beside Ashby at the gate.

"Yes," Ashby said. "She believes that." He jerked his head toward the sign. "She thinks she means this is a boarding house. To see her in action you would think she was running a boarding school for ten year old virgins. Why, she never even admits to the girls in there what goes on. She just charges them 'room and board.' Of course, the room and board is about three times what any other house on the street charges, and none of the girls in the place does any visible work, but Miranda goes through all the motions of keeping a regular, but sort o' high-falutin', boarding house. Miranda's a gal, I tell you . . ." He laughed, looking toward the door; then he opened the gate. "After you . . ." he said.

The man looked up at the house for a second and then back at Ashby. "Go on," Ashby said.

Then, hesitantly, the man walked through.

When Ashby knocked, a Negro maid opened the door. The hall behind her was dim, a white and blue room.

"Howdy do, Mr. Ashby," she said.

Ashby fumbled and handed her a calling card. "Miss Miranda?" he said. The maid opened the door wider and they stepped inside. Behind him, the man whispered, "You got to have a ticket? I haven't got . . ."

"Hush," Ashby said, the sound hissing in his teeth. "It's a calling card . . ."

"Miss Miranda is in. I'll tell her you're here," the maid said. She rapped on the parlor door to Ashby's left.

Beside him, the man said, "Calling card? I haven't got any calling card. Why, you mean you got to . . ."

"Sh-h-h," Ashby said. The maid went through the door, though they had heard no answer. Then Ashby turned to the man. In the heat of the hall, the whiskey ran swiftly in his veins, and he saw the man only as a sort of blur, but he could see the astonished mouth, half open, and he grinned at that. "It's part of the illusion. Like the sign."

"Illusion?" the man said. His eyes were big with a childish wonder.

"The game," Ashby said. "You got to make out you're a gentleman calling on a lady. The printers in this town got all the work they can do, printing calling cards for folks that never had any use for 'em before, but now got to have 'em to come to Miranda's. . . ."

The man cut his eyes at Ashby and then turned and shook his head. "It ain't no use," he said. "I wasn't born a gentleman, and I don't know how to do. I reckon I jest better . . ."

"Here . . ." Ashby said. He caught the man's sleeve, because there in the parlor door was Miranda. Seeing the little nose and the blue eyes, like Evelina's, he could imagine her rising from her maidenly place by the fire to come greet them. She looked as if she might be preparing to give a text to a Sunday School class. She was not uncomely, merely unfleshly, more unfleshly than even Evelina, because she was taller and more spare. She had what is known as "good bones," and her skin always looked as if it had just had a good scrubbing with health soap after which it had been taken for a good walk around the block in the wholesome air of outdoors. Her gray hair, the only thing about her that seemed old, was put up in the most unworldly fashion possible, drawn into a tight knot on the nape of her neck; her eyes had a look of far pride in them. She lifted her hand and Ashby stepped forward and took it lightly in his own.

"How do you do, Ashby," she said, in a measured voice. "It's good to see you." As if, he thought, she had not seen him last night. As if he had come calling after a long absence.

"Thank you, Cousin Mi . . ." He gulped and a little frown crossed her face. Mentally, he damned Temp for reminding him; it was a relationship he never put into words, because he knew she did not like it. They never acknowledged it in any way; they behaved as old friends. "Miss Miranda . . ." he said, and she smiled.

"And this is a friend of yours?" she said, looking at the man.

"Yes," Ashby said. He saw the man open his mouth, presumably to say his name, and he spoke quickly. That would have been another thing she would not have liked, for Ashby not to know the name. She did not approve of gentlemen introducing casual street acquaintances to a lady in her home. So he made a name up, quickly. "This is Carter Thomas, Miss Miranda . . ."

"So good to see you," Miranda said. She inclined her head slightly toward the man, smiling.

"But . . ." the man said. Ashby narrowed his eyes and the man, befuddled, sighed. "Yes'm," he said. "Thank you, ma'am."

"Ashby always has such mannersome friends," Miranda said.

By now the man's face was flag red.

"Let's go into the parlor," Miranda said. "Perhaps you would like a sip of wine?"

She went through the door, into the room where the lamps were muted, and the fire was a flameless heap of live red coals. The man tugged at Ashby's sleeve.

"Wine? I don't care much for wine. It gives me headaches. . . ."

"Not this wine . . ." Ashby said. He laughed shortly, and then, standing in the center of the parlor, the laughs still came in spite of him, and they bubbled through his lips with little popping sounds.

The maid, who was now spreading coal on the fire with a shovel, turned to Miss Miranda. "Wine?" she said.

"If you please, Mattie." She watched the maid through the door, and then seated herself on the carved loveseat by the fire. "Sit down there across from me," she said. "It's so good of you to come see an old lady like me. . . ." She touched a wedding band on her finger. In the lamplight, she smiled. The last duchess, Ashby thought. The last one on the whole earth.

Beside Ashby on the sofa across from Miranda, the man stirred agitatedly. "Yes'm . . ." he said, his mouth open as if he intended to say more. If I don't watch him, Ashby thought, he's likely to be asking her where the beds are; he's in such a stew now, I reckon he'd do it without thinking. He touched the man's knee, quickly.

"Carter is a lawyer," he said.

The man's mouth remained open and his soft dark eyes looked accusingly at Ashby.

"How nice," Miranda said. "So many lawyers in my family. Are you a statesman, Mr. Thomas?"

"Uh-h-h . . ." the man grumbled.

"Politician," Ashby said. "Miss Miranda wants to know if you're a politician. . . ."

She stiffened. "I said 'statesman,' Ashby," she said. "I did not say 'politician.' There is a great difference." Then she smiled at the man. "I'm sure Mr. Thomas could never demean himself to the level of politics. . . ."

Never, never, never, Ashby thought, the drink chasing glee through his veins. Oh never to the level of politics. Statesman or nothing.

"Yes," he said.

"Ah . . . our wine . . ." Miranda said.

Mattie put the tray down on the coffee table between them. There were three tumblers with ice in them, an ice bucket; and an opened bottle of soda resting beside a tall bottle full of a rich brown liquid labeled *Sherry*.

"Soda, sir?" Miss Miranda said to the man. The door closed softly behind the maid.

"With wine?" the man said. "I . . ."

Again Ashby touched his knee. "Carter likes soda with his wine."

She filled the tumblers half full of the dark liquid and then added the soda. Ashby rose and handed the man his drink and then sat down with his own.

Miss Miranda lifted her glass. "To our good fortune," she said, and in her thin throat a pulse beat prettily.

She drank. Ashby closed his eyes and drank deep, the drink tasting mild to his throat. When he opened his eyes, Miranda had gone toward a sound at the door, and there the man beside him was, sputtering, a thin trickle of the drink dripping off his chin.

"Wine? Wine?" the man whispered, hoarsely.

"Hush," Ashby said. From a vineyard full of corn—wine, he thought. "This is Miss Miranda's wine."

"Why," the man said. "I'd swear it was whiskey. . . ."

Ashby looked at him and grinned. "And I'd swear those females upstairs aren't what she calls 'em either. But I don't reckon it makes any difference what you name 'em. . . ."

The man rubbed his forehead and watched Ashby. "I jest ain't a gentleman," he said. "I reckon I better get outa here. I would feel more to home in a asylum."

"Hush . . ." Ashby said. Miranda came toward them from the door.

"I wonder if you'd be so good as to excuse me for a moment. I have some business in the library. . . . But, Ashby, I've sent Mattie after Miss Louise, and she'll be down to talk to you until my business is done. . . ." She extended her hand to the man. "So good to have seen you," she said. "If I should be detained too long to see you again, do come again. . . ." She patted Ashby on the sleeve and then went from the room, pausing only a second at the door to smile on them, and then closing the door softly behind her.

"Whew!" Ashby said. He sat down: "Is this place hot to you?" He took a long drink.

"I been cooler," the man said, "on a July day in a feather bed." He was standing there with his feet spread apart and the drink in his hand and a look on his face like that of an innocent in hell.

"I have some lovely young ladies residing with me," Ashby said, mimicking Miranda. "They cool off gentlemen so delightfully. But understand, they never demean themselves to the level of whoredom. Oh, no, my friends, they are ladies." His lips curled and he put his face in one hand and shook his head, laughing silently. Then he sobered. "I must be drunk," he said, "to mock her that way. Out loud. But . . ."

The man was drinking with slow desperation, steady sips.

"She's kinfolks," Ashby said. "Or to me she is. In my house they never say her name. I reckon because she's beaten them. They disowned her and she ended up madame of a whorehouse, but she's beaten them like they never got beat before. She came back when the man left her. They thought they were rid of her. They figured she had gone without any trouble, without even blotching the escutcheon. And now she's back and throwing ink on the family coat of arms every day, and nothing they can do. She's a living mockery of them all, because she has done everything they would condemn and yet she hasn't changed a bit, she is just like always, just like them. It's them that've been hurt, because they look on their healthy state as the reward of virtue, and yet she . . ."

He shook his head, and looked through an alcoholic haze at the man; but the man's face was passive and blank, and he was applying himself with a kind of quiet frenzy to the drinking of the whiskey.

"Or maybe, you know," Ashby said, "Maybe she's revenging herself on marriage. On the whole damn institution. After what happened to her . . ."

The man never moved. He stood with that same quietness, his legs still planted wide, the drink still to his lips and down, to his lips and down.

"Or maybe," Ashby said, "She never did it for any of that a-tall. There wasn't anything else she could do, I reckon. She was brought up to be a lady, helpless. And a lady proud, too, so that when the man went back on her, she couldn't come back to our house, and she had to do something, helpless as she was. You never know about any of them. Maybe she doesn't know what she's doing." He lifted his empty glass and looked through it. "They can delude themselves into believing anything. Maybe she did all of it, coming back and running this house, without ever thinking to revenge herself on anybody or anything. Or maybe she chuckles to herself at night—oh, a most lady-like chuckle—to think about Father and Evelina and . . ." He leaned back and closed his eyes; his head seemed to bob on dark waves. "I am a bit drunk . . . And how are you. . . ."

He had started talking to the man with laughter in him, but now the laughter was gone, and the memory sharp as ice of Father and Evelina and Num was back on him.

"Why, honey . . ." the woman's voice said. He did not open his eyes. "You're drunk, honey . . ."

"Hush up," he said. "You hush." He still did not look at her; he knew the smell of her, violet soap, mixed with the kind of clean-odored talc they put on babies. She was close to him, but he did not move.

"Is you mad?" she said, cooing. "Did somebody make him mad, Ashby-Washby?"

"Goddamit," he said, "I never said anything about being mad. And you better hush that indecent talk before Miranda hears you. You're supposed to be a 'lovely young lady.' " He got up, looking away from her and went over and stared into the fire.

"What you need," she said, "is a drink. Here, honey, I'll fix you one. . . ." Her hand came around him and up toward the glass which he held loosely in a hand resting on the mantel.

"Go away and hush!" he said. He turned and she stood there, backing off a little from him. Her eyes were wide and black; she was all black and white, white skin and white teeth and black hair and eyes and dress. She pushed a lace handkerchief in and out of the pocket of the black dress. "I don't need a drink," he said. "I don't need a drink or anything else. Except a whole new . . ." He did not say it; he did not know what he started to say. Maybe it was "life."

The man looked confusedly from one to the other. "Now . . ." he said, placatingly, "Now . . ."

Louise came over to Ashby and touched his shoulder. "I didn't know you had the grumps really," she said. "I wouldn't have said nothing, Ashby. . . ."

He shrugged her hand off and stared at her feet.

"My," she said. "You're handsome when you're mad, Ashby. I never saw you that mad before." She laughed, a sound like icecubes in water. "Today must be a crazy day. A day like when everything changes. What's happened to you, Ashby?"

He didn't look at her. "What's all the talking about?" he said. "Have you got a gal for Carter here?" He jerked his head at the man.

"Why, Ashby, honey, you haven't even introduced me," she

said, her big eyes slanted toward the man as if she had just seen him. "Why, Miss Miranda . . ."

". . . wouldn't approve," Ashby said. "Say 'hell.' "

" 'Hell,' " she said. "Why?"

"Say 'damn.' "

" 'Damn,' " she said. "Why?"

"Nothing," he said. "I just wanted to make sure you were still corruptible. I always said that someday Miranda was gonna go too far in this thing and wake up some morning and find her stock in trade marked 'Guaranteed Genuine Ladies, One Hundred Per Cent Pure.' " He was grinning again; he stood there by the fireplace grinning at both of them, her and the man.

"Oh, Ashby," she said. She came and leaned against him and nuzzled her nose into his shoulder, just in the spot where the collarbone reached the ridge of the shoulder.

He jerked. "Quit that. Miranda's gonna come in here and catch you leading me astray in public. And if you do that one more time . . ." He rubbed his shoulder. "I'll be sho-nuff astray . . ." He really laughed then.

"Oh, you!" she said and she smiled, pleased, at him. "Y'all come on," she said, "I got to see Miss Miranda a minute about something and then . . ."

She took Ashby's hand and they went into the hall, the man following. "You boys wait on the steps," she said. "I won't be but a second."

She knocked on the door there by the stairs, directly across from the door to the front parlor. It was Miranda's voice which said, "Come in. . . ."

Ashby and the man sat down side by side on the steps in the quiet and empty hall.

"Well," Ashby said, "You still sane?" He reached for his cigarettes.

"I don't understand anything," the man said. He sat very still and brooded, his eyes focused on something a far way away.

"What kind of girl you want?" Ashby said. He extended the crumpled package of cigarettes toward the man. "Have one?"

"No thank you," the man said. Ashby lighted his own cigarette while the man brooded again. "I reckon," the man said, "I reckon I want a medium-sized one. . . ."

Ashby opened his mouth, intending to be humorous, but he heard the sound before he said anything. He turned and there was a girl coming down the stairs, a stranger to him. "How about this one?" he whispered, and the man turned and looked up, too.

They stood up, jostling each other, and turned to watch her come down. She came slowly, smiling slightly at them, one hand on the bannister. Ashby noticed her neat little feet and the perfect turn of her ankle. Her hair was dark blond with sunburned streaks of gold in it. She had freckles which she made no effort to hide, and her cheeks were naturally pink, as if she had just run a long way. She was not beautiful; she was almost plain, but there was this about her, she seemed filled with a great energy and simplicity.

The man's hand touched Ashby. "Yes," he said. "Yes." With one hand he fussed with his dark untidy hair. In the split second before the girl was upon them, Ashby was suddenly irritated that the man should have seized so quickly and avidly on this one. Then the girl was there, on the next to last step, and out of the side of his eyes he saw the tongueless eagerness of the man and so he shrugged the feeling away.

"Howdy do, ma'am," Ashby said.

He heard her catch her breath, as if she were both surprised and pleased that he had spoken to her. "Why, hello," she said, and the catch of breath seemed there again. He thought he must be remembering again, because it was a lovely sound to him that he had heard a long time in his mind, and was likely to hear in strange places. I must be drunk, he thought, really drunk.

"My name is Ashby Pelham," he said, his eyes on the man because he somehow did not want to look at her, or rather wanted to, but was somehow afraid to. "And this is a friend of mine. . . ."

But the girl was saying in that voice that was breathless, that was really breathless, that he was not just imagining, "Ashby Pelham? Are you kin to Mr. Ephraim Pelham?"

"Why . . . yes . . ." he said, thinking fast, wondering if Ephe had habituated houses like this, and then what she, the girl, was doing in this place, and. . . He shook the thoughts away with an impatient gesture of his head. "You know Uncle Ephe? He's my cousin, but I call him . . ." Then he patted the man on the shoulder. "This is Carter Thomas. This is Carter Thomas, Miss . . ."

"Landers," she said, lifting her chin. "Laurel Landers." Then she turned her head a little and in that voice of hers said, "I'm so glad to see you, Mr. Thomas."

The man couldn't say anything. And I myself, Ashby thought, feel just as much a damn fool. A girl in a house like this walks down the stairs, a girl not even particularly beautiful, just a plain girl, and she opens her mouth and two grown men stand cockeyed before her, drunkened by her.

And, feeling foolish, and having to do something to cover the man's silence, he bowed to her. "How are you, Miss Landers?"

She laughed, a little, caught-breath laugh. "I'm fine," she said. "I just came today. I got in on the train tonight. . . ."

*Like she just arrived on a train,* he thought, *like she just got here and can't wait to see and say and do everything.* It looks like I got an echo in my life, he said to himself. Or else the record's stuck. It keeps repeating.

"Oh," he said, "Just today . . ." He wanted to take her and without a word lead her out the front door, but he called himself a fool. A drunken fool. She's twenty-one, he thought. So he said casually, as if she didn't matter, "I came to see Louise . . ." He wondered if he saw a little blink of disappointment in the gold eyes. "But my friend," he said, hurriedly. "Are you engaged tonight, Miss Landers?"

"Why, no . . ." she said. She had a way of tilting her chin up when she was pleased; or at least it made her look pleased. "You see, I'm so new. I haven't even unpacked."

"Then would you be so kind . . ." He waved a hand at the man, who just stood there, staring at her.

"Why . . ." she said. "I don't know. . . You see, I haven't even met my landlady yet, and I don't know . . ." There was nothing coy about her. Her eyes were wide and frank, and she spoke as if she were really wondering whether it was the right thing for her to do. But though there was no coquetry about her, there was that tone in the words that was somehow intimate, a sound of hurried confidence. It seemed to Ashby that she was whispering to him alone.

"Oh, that's all right," he said. "I'll tell Miranda I introduced you two. Miranda and I are old friends. . . ." He wanted to get her out of his sight before he did a fool thing, before he leaned and kissed her there before the man or took her hand and led her without a word out the door to the car and away from there. He put a hand on the man's shoulder and one on the girl's, and, achingly conscious of the hand that touched her, he propelled them toward the second door across the hall. "This is a private parlor," he said. He opened the door and they went in ahead of him. She seated herself before the fire and smiled up at him; she had a minute gap between her front teeth, and it made her smile peculiarly innocent and young. The man stood helplessly watching her.

"Aren't you going to join us?" the girl said, her head lifted up to Ashby.

"Later maybe," Ashby said. "I've got to go out to my car a minute. . . ." Not having thought until then about Temp, and not even then thinking there was any need to see how Temp was, but speaking only to avoid saying, "Join you? Not if I can help it. Not after . . ." Then he half-bowed and said, "Be seein' you." He went out of the room, drawing the door shut behind him.

He heard her say to the man, "And what do you do, Mr.

Thomas?" with the eagerness there in her voice, like a child just discovering all the knowledge there is to ask questions about.

He sat down on the steps again, cursing himself. He knew he had imagined her. He had looked and listened to her through the rose mist of alcohol. If he were to see her tomorrow, she would be unrecognizable. Yet even telling himself this, he was glad for what happened then.

Mattie came out of the room where Miranda and Louise were. She carried a scuttle-full of ashes, heavy enough to take both her hands.

"You mind closing that door for me, Mr. Ashby?" she said.

"Sho, Mattie . . ." He stood and dropped into the scuttle the cigarette he must have lighted unconsciously a few minutes before. Then he reached for the door as Mattie, moving down the hall, said, "Thank ya, sir."

But he did not close the door immediately. Because he heard Louise say the name. "Landers. Her name's Landers . . ."

"Why, that's a good name," Miss Miranda said. "A good name."

"That's what I'm telling you," Louise said. "She don't know . . ."

". . . doesn't . . ." Miss Miranda said. "Do watch your grammar, Louise."

"Yes," Ashby whispered. "For God's sake, Louise, your grammar."

"All right," Louise sighed. "She doesn't know where. . . She thinks . . ."

There was a hiss behind Ashby. He closed the door softly and turned. The man was there, his face befuddled. Ashby went over to him.

"She won't let me kiss her," he said. "I don't know what to do. . . ."

By God I won't do it, Ashby thought. I'm damned if I will tell him. . . But he said, "Why, hell. Just kiss her. You're big enough."

"But . . ." the man said. "She don't act like she expected me to kiss her. . . ."

"The devil," Ashby said. "She's just been told about how Miranda does. . . Just a case of over-tutoring, I reckon. Go on and make out she's a lady that you got to seduce. . . ." He felt guilty and unhappy, and the man had a grieved expression on his face.

"I don't know how," the man said.

"Everybody knows how," Ashby said.

"But how will I know what to say?"

"Biology," Ashby said. "Biology will put a tongue in a man who never had a tongue before. . . ." Except me, he thought. Because if it had put a tongue in me, I would tell him now to get the hell out of my way, and I would go in there where she is and find out if I really saw her straight when she came down those stairs.

"It's mighty peculiar, the way she is. . . ." the man said and his face disappeared behind the door.

Then Ashby, hearing the echo of the man's words, "It's mighty peculiar . . ." suddenly saw it all. He tiptoed quickly back to the other door and put his ear close to it. "Eavesdroppers will be hell's burners," Num always said. But he intended to hear about Laurel Landers, already knowing what he would hear, already laughing a little with relief at the knowing.

Louise was talking. "But I tell you she thinks this is a boarding house. . . ."

Miranda's voice was cold as doom. "And what is it if it isn't a boarding house?"

But Ashby barely heard her. The laughing relief went all through him, and he trembled all over, like a kid who had escaped a punishment he thought certain to come. She didn't even know where she was, he said to himself, didn't even know where she was. He rested his head against the door jamb. Within the room, Louise was saying his very words, stubbornly.

"She's a nice kid and she don't know where she is."

"I hope all my girls are nice girls," Miss Miranda said.

"But . . ." Louise moaned. "But, Miss Miranda, I'm telling you she came in and we thought she was the new girl coming from New Orleans, and so we gave her the front room, and now we know she's not the one . . ."

"I shall attend to it, Louise," Miss Miranda said.

"Well," Louise said. "You better 'tend to it now, because there's no telling what might happen, with her not knowin' . . ."

"Louise!" Miss Miranda's voice was almost loud.

Ashby did not listen any more. He went over to the room where the man and girl were and knocked on the door.

"Carter!" he said. He heard their voices cease and then the man was at the door.

"You want me?" he said.

"Come out and close the door," Ashby whispered.

The man pulled the door to but kept his hand on the knob.

"How you coming?" Ashby said.

"I can't . . ." the man said. "I . . ." He looked as if he had been ruffling his hair, or as if someone had just awakened him from a nap: he was mussed and mystified.

Ashby grinned. "I reckon you can't," he said. "She's nice. She's here by mistake, and she doesn't know . . ." He put his hand on the man's elbow. "I tell you what," he said. "You let me introduce you to Louise, and I'll go in there and just talk to Laurel."

"No," the man said. "I reckon I'd like to talk to her myself. I reckon I'm right glad she's not . . ."

"Now," Ashby said, disappointed. "You didn't come down here for talk. You'll like Louise. Louise is . . ." He made motions in the air with his hands.

"You trying to palm me off?"

He turned and Louise was there. She didn't seem either angry or glad, merely questioning.

But he said, "Why, no, Louise, but . . ."

Then, before he said anything more, the man said, "Well, I'll be seein' y'all. . . ." and went through the door back to Laurel.

Ashby looked angrily after him. Louise came up beside him and her hip touched his and she put an arm around his waist. But he kept his eye on the door for a long while. Then he said, "Well, at least she'll be safe. She couldn't be any safer with . . ."

"Who?" Louise said, uncuriously.

But he never answered. He was trying to think straight, and all that came out of the thinking was that he did not want to leave her there. He wanted to go in and get her away from there. Yet he couldn't just go in and pick her up and carry her out the door. He would have to tell her why, and that would be one time he would be tongue-tied. The cat would certainly have his tongue if he had to tell her she was in a—he grinned wrily—a cat house. But even if he could manage to tell her, how would it make her feel toward him? She was bound to feel a little foolish, if not downright outraged, and it might be that she couldn't help but connect him with those feelings, so that he could see it all ending in her disliking him, the way a person will connect bad tidings with their bearer, no matter how innocent the bearer might be. On the other hand, if he waited and let Miranda think up a logical and ladylike reason for Laurel having to move out, then Laurel might never know about what kind of place she had been in at all; and that would have the extra advantage of her not connecting him with a place like that. So that, when he found her, wherever she might go, they could start to know each other without having Miranda's house like a fateful joke between them.

No, he would be a fool to do anything about it now; yet knowing that did not make him any happier. He was an unhappy man, standing there staring at the closed door and thinking about Laurel.

He was so unhappy, so drunk on whiskey and his own misery, that when Louise nuzzled her chin again into his collarbone, he grabbed her and kissed her till his lips hurt. He kept thinking, though, about how it would be to kiss Laurel, and when they went up the stairs together, their bodies touching awkwardly, he wondered how it would be to walk that close to Laurel, to feel the touch of Laurel.

He was a miserable man, but a man couldn't just sit and be miserable, a man had to do something. And there was Louise and Louise's room.

But none of it did any good. Even afterward, when Louise was asleep in his arms, he was the same way, only more so. He could laugh at himself for being pricked by adolescent emotions, a conscience at having come upstairs with Louise, at having been unfaithful to Laurel fifteen minutes after he could not have imagined being so. He could even laugh at that, at the few seconds he had seen her. Not long enough, he told himself, to know what color her eyes were. But he knew. They were gold. He knew all about her. Whatever she had felt, he had committed himself to her five minutes after he laid eyes on her. And that was probably as adolescent as the unhappy guilt in him now, but nevertheless it was there. He felt like the devil. The very devil.

He reached a hand and loosed Louise's arms from around his neck and slipped from her. A man had to move. A man couldn't just stay still and think. In the darkness he found a towel and dried the perspiration from his body, rubbing his flesh angrily as if to mortify it, as if to cleanse it with hurt.

He paid no attention when he heard the first shout from downstairs, so busy was he with the towel. He was pulling on his undershorts when he heard the sound of rough laughter and a door slamming downstairs. They were strange sounds in Miranda's house, but this he never reflected on beyond the initial surprise at hearing them; for he immediately was concerned about her—Laurel. He fumbled, found his undershirt, stuck his arms and head through it.

Now he heard loud cursing only barely muffled through the door. He lost his balance in his haste to get his pants on. His shirt was half-buttoned, his tie only caught under the collar, his coat over his arm when he hurried from the room. He blinked in the hall light. He looked down over the bannister. Miranda stood at the door of the parlor where the man and Laurel were. She rapped with spare knuckles sharply.

"Mr. Littlepage . . ." she said. "Mr. Littlepage . . ."

Ashby thought, Littlepage? Did I tell her his name was Littlepage? And if it was the man she was talking to, where was Laurel and what was happening in that room?

He was going down the steps, his feet drumming. "What is it?" he said. "What is it, Miss Miranda?" He breathed hard.

"Ashby . . ." she said, sucking in her breath. "Ashby, see if you can get this door open. . . ." Then she rapped again, saying, "I won't have it. I won't have it."

He heard a sound like fighting behind the door; some glass fell and cracked on the floor. He put his shoulder against the door and lunged. "Who is it?" he said, backing off. He tossed his coat to Miranda.

"The sheriff," she said. "And one of his deputies." She made a steamy sound through her teeth, as if she were cold, but she could only have been cold with anger if she were. "That poor dear girl . . ."

He lunged at the door just as she said it; the door made a cracking sound, trembled, but did not open. "What?" he said. "Laurel. What's happened "

"Nothing," she said. "Only the sheriff . . ." She spoke clearly and precisely then. "He is behaving in a manner unbecoming a gentleman," she said. Her lips were tight and bloodless.

"I wanted to hit him once before this evening," Ashby said. "Now he's gonna wish he never . . ." He thrust his shoulder again at the door; but it was opened without his ever having touched it, and he fell against Laurel. Her arms caught him and for a second they embraced each other. Her hair was in his mouth; in the moment he noticed the soap-and-water freshness of her.

She made a soft sound in her throat and then stepped loose from him. A little deputy with bandy legs, still wearing his black hat ducked past Ashby and caught her by the arm. In the middle of the room the man had a strangle hold on Turkey Littlepage and Turkey's face was all over the color of the flesh on his neck. The man was full of a great electric anger and he kept shaking the sheriff as if the sheriff were a sack he was trying to empty of something; he just shook Turkey with that wordless anger.

But Ashby no more than glanced at the man and Turkey. He heard Miranda say to the little deputy, "Take your hands off her. . . ."

And he turned to where the little deputy had Laurel pinned against the staircase. The little deputy was saying, "I got to do what the boss says. He told me this was the one, the new one you got from New Orleans. I don't see why we got to have all this fuss, when you know the new ones have always been his first, always have been . . ."

Miranda said, "I don't know what you're talking about."

But Ashby didn't say anything, because he had turned and grabbed the little deputy by the collar. He jerked him back so hard the collar ripped; he swung him around and, scarcely looking at his red-veined face, he let his fist swing. The little deputy ducked, so that Ashby's fist knocked his hat off and skimmed along his greasy black hair. Then, head lowered, the little deputy rushed goatlike. Ashby stepped aside, grabbed the deputy's coat and swung again. He hit cleanly on the right jaw, a good solid crack. The little deputy howled, put a hand up, then shut his eyes, swayed and fell limply on the blue carpet. He kicked and groaned a second and then lay still. . . .

When Ashby could look for her, Laurel was gone. "Where is she?" he said.

Miranda didn't answer. "Get them out. Please, Ashby, get them out."

"You 'tend to Laurel," he said. "Miranda, you 'tend . . ." He was shouting; he suddenly heard himself shouting.

He was aware then of the man in the hall, with Turkey Littlepage slung over his shoulder as if he were now an empty sack. And Turkey, his windpipe freed, was yelling, "Goddamit. Goddamit. I'm the sheriff here. Whether you know it or not . . ."

"Hit him," Ashby said to the man. "Let him down from there, and hit him. . . ." He kept wondering about Laurel.

He heard a squeal from somewhere and, looking up, saw two of the girls leaning over the bannister. A man wandered at that moment drunkenly up to them, dressed only in his underwear. The girls pushed him away. One of them pushed him through the open door to a room and shut it behind him.

Miranda was stiff-backed. "Get back to your rooms," she said, in a measured voice. "Is that any way for young ladies to act?" And when she caught Ashby grinning at her, she pursed her lips and looked at the sheriff over the man's shoulder. "Well, are you going to hit him or not?" she said, grimly. "The gentlemen in my family have always been good at fisticuffs, but perhaps you . . ."

"Oh," he said, "*how* I'm going to hit him!"

The sheriff was pounding the man on the back. "Goddamit," he yelled, "I'm the sheriff. . . ."

Ashby's voice was louder than Turkey's. "Put him down," he said to the man. "Put him down where I can hit him."

But the man was going toward the door. "I'm gonna throw him out the door and let his head crack," he said. "I'm powerful mad at him. . . ."

"No," Ashby said. "I got a thing to settle with him myself. . . ." He was at the door, but the man had already jerked it open.

There were three deputies there. You could say that about Turkey, he always traveled in a crowd, Ashby thought, even as he tried to close the door. But the man blocked it open, and before he, Ashby, could get it closed, the deputies pushed through. Ashby heard himself say, "Watch out . . ." and he hit out at the nearest deputy, hit blindly.

Then he felt himself being tackled and falling, his knees pinioned, his head striking the carpet with a thud. Somebody had hold of one of his arms and when he reached out with the other one, the deputy rolled him half over and sat on him. He smelled the rank odor of the man and heard his breathful muttering. He struggled. "Damn you, damn you . . ." His mouth was touching the carpet; he could feel the grit on his lips. Then he heard the metal click against his wrist. All the time there was the noise of struggling around him. They must be on the man, too, he thought. But he couldn't see, for struggling, himself.

"You be still or I'm gonna knock the p-winding hell outa you," the deputy on him muttered. Then the deputy reached under him and grabbed his other arm and pulled it to the other handcuff, in spite of his struggling.

Then he and the man were both lying there, handcuffed, and the sheriff and the deputies stood there looking down at them. When the sheriff saw Ashby he closed his eyes and opened them again and then again closed them. "I be gawd-dammed," he said. "This is one time you done done too much, Ashby. This is one time you done humiliated me. . . . I'm the sheriff and I'm owing some respect, and if it hadn't been for you. . . I could 'a' handled this fellow. . . ." He had a gun.

"I saw about how you and that little deputy put together were handling him," Ashby said. "I saw it."

Turkey said, "Twice in one night. Twice I got to . . ."

Ashby made as if to get up. "Git down there," Turkey said. "Ain't I had enough . . ."

Then Miranda was there beside the sheriff. "Mr. Littlepage . . ."

"Yes, ma'm," he said. He looked at her. Then he held up his hand. "Now don't you come telling me. . . ." he said.

"I think you owe me an apology for your behavior," Miranda said. Apology, Ashby thought, apology. They would ask for manners in hell. They would.

"It ain't my fault. It ain't none of my fault, Miranda, and you know it. . . ."

Turkey was almost wordless with anger, anyway, but even so he never got to finish what he was saying then. Because there was a sound of feet coming down the stairs and Ashby heard Louise's voice saying his name. "Ashby, Ashby . . ." There was a kind of wildness in the sound, as if she had seen a nightmare. Then she was on her knees beside him and she was just saying, "Oh . . . oh . . . oh . . ." over and over.

Miranda said, "Louise . . ."

Ashby said, "What's the matter with you?" Her face was close to his and she didn't say anything, just looked at him out of her black eyes. Then she said, "How come you had to get in it?" He didn't say anything. "It was that girl, wasn't it? That girl? When they told me upstairs she was the one in the room, and how you had done. . . . It was her . . ."

"I just wanted a fight," he said. "I been spoiling for a fight all day. And this was a beaut." He grinned at her, feeling like an idiot lying there on the floor. Then he had to ask. "Where is she? Where is Laurel?"

"She's gone." Louise said. "She left a while ago, the back way. . . ."

"Gone?" the man said, half rising.

"You git down 'fore I blow your top off," Turkey said, handling his gun carelessly. Then, "Gone? You mean she's gone?" He looked at the deputies around him. "Two o' y'all go find her. You find that gal. Ashby Pelham made me lose that nigger, but he ain't gonna make me lose two things I want in one day. . . ." The deputies went out the door.

Miranda said, "Louise, go to your room. Louise!"

Louise stood up over him. "Oh . . . Ashby . . ." she said, and then she turned and ran down the hall, and he could hear her feet going up the stairs. But he thought about Laurel. Gone. Where?

"Now, Mr. Littlepage," Miranda said, sounding steel-nerved, braced. "You will please apologize to me and to these gentlemen. And you will remove those handcuffs and then you will leave my house. . . ."

Turkey looked at her with his mouth open. His eyes bugged

with astonishment, then with anger. "Don't you come telling me what to do, Miranda. I ought to close you up. . . ."

She never blinked. "Close me up? And how would you do that? I run a perfectly respectable boarding home for young ladies," she said, her voice not quavering, so that the sheriff looked at her as if he thought he must be hearing wrong, that she should say the thing so easily. "And I might remind you that this house has never seen such ungentlemanly conduct as yours tonight. In fact, I wouldn't mind telling the court that, if you . . ."

He held up his free hand. "Now Miranda," he said. "Don't do nothing far fetched. I never aimed to provoke no trouble, but this here big fellow tried to keep that girl away from me, and I've had a mighty hard day of it, what with my hounds never finding that nigger I went after because Ashby, here, had to go and mess the trail up, and so I was mighty mean-hearted and discouraged when I come in here, and was looking forward to . . ." He was having a labor of breathing. "When I think about Ashby. . . ." He closed his eyes.

"Well," Ashby said, "You better be thinking about lettin' me and my buddy loose. You better be thinking about it hard. . . ."

Turkey made his lips mean and glanced at the deputy beside him to see how the deputy was taking such back talk to the sheriff and then looked at Miranda and down at Ashby.

Then he said, "No sir. I'm taking you two along. Making me lose that gal . . ."

"Just get your hounds," Ashby said. "The way they can find things, you ought to have her. . . ."

"You hush up, Ashby," the sheriff said. "And git up. I'm gonna put you in jail. I couldn't live 'round myself if I let you loose after what you done done to me today."

Miranda said, "I'm going to ask you just once more. . . ."

"And I'm gonna say no," Turkey said. He kicked Ashby's foot. "Git up. I'm a plumb mad man. And . . ." He looked at Miranda. "And all yo' lady ways ain't gonna change me."

Ashby got up and the man with him. The man said nothing. He only breathed with slow heavy sounds and stared straight ahead of him.

"Never mind, Miranda," Ashby said. "I *was* gonna tell him where he could find Temp . . but . . ." He shrugged.

"No sir," Turkey said. "You don't fool me that-a way—I ain't a fool. Come on now. . . ."

The deputy pushed the big man. "Get on through." The big man went through the door and Ashby after him. At the last minute, Miranda caught his hand.

"Don't worry," she said, leaning through the door toward him. "I'll 'tend to this. . . ."

With his handcuffed hands he patted her wrist and grinned. "I didn't have anything special to do until tomorrow any-how," he said. But only to make her feel better. Going down the walk with the sheriff dragging the little deputy he had knocked out and with the other deputy ahead of him, he wasn't worried about jail. He was worried about her, Laurel, and only a little less about Temp. But he knew that he would just have to wait the cooling of Turkey's anger, unless he called Father, and he did not intend to do that unless Turkey stayed angry too long.

The other two deputies met them at the gate. "She got away," they said.

"Goddamit," Turkey said, "Goddamit. I would like to hang you, Ashby. I would take a pure pleasure in it."

Ashby grinned back at him. They were going past his car and he saw Turkey glance at it. "And you were gonna tell me where that nigger. . . . I reckon you'd ride me right to him, wouldn't you? If I was fool enough to let you loose to drive. . . ."

For one second Ashby saw Temp's gleaming eyes watching them. Then he said, "Why, yes. Although I reckon you could be within ten feet of him and not find him, Turkey. . . . Like you got mighty close to that girl and . . ."

"That's all right," Turkey said. "I ain' a easy man to fool. Not easy a-tall, as you'll find, Ashby. . . ."

Ashby had to laugh at him, because Temp was safe there a few feet away, and Laurel was no telling where, but safe, too. So that even going to jail with a headache, he had to laugh still.

"What you laughing at?" Turkey said.

Ashby didn't say anything.

# Chapter V

But there was not even the relief of laughter in jail. There was a sickness in him. He thought of Temp, lying there terrified in the cold, cramped in the car, waiting for him. He thought about Temp being hungry because he would be afraid to move from the car to seek food. He was ill with guilt.

He thought about Laurel, too, and wondered where she had fled in the middle of the night, and whether or not she was safe wherever she was, and how she would look on him if ever he saw her again.

The thinking was a sickness beyond flesh and blood, and all he had with which to meet it was, as usual, the self-mockery that never failed him. Nobody else, he thought sardonically, would get himself chased by bloodhounds and then go on from there to spirit a Negro away from an angry sheriff, and on the way stop at a refined cat house and fall in love with a girl and go to bed with another one, and get in a fight with the sheriff over the girl he's in love with and wind the evening up in jail. He had, he thought, a special capacity for aimlessness, a talent for allowing fate to push him around, just as some people had the ability to rub their stomachs and pat their heads at the same time.

And so now he was in jail. He was lying in the bunk, naked, with only the sheet covering him, because the sheriff had taken their clothes when he locked them in. "I ain' gonna have no escapin' from my jail," Turkey had said. "I don't reckon even a crazy a pair as you would go wanderin' out o' here jaybird bare. . . ."

So the both of them were locked in the cell with no clothes on. They lay across from each other and stared into the pale light of the single bulb in the corridor and heard the intermittent hissing of the radiator. The man had not spoken, except for a brief argument with the sheriff about his name. When the sheriff called him a liar, the man merely shut up, on his face and in his hound-soft eyes the injured innocence of a child unjustly accused.

Suddenly now, on his bunk, the man moved under the sheet.

"I got to talk some," he said.

Ashby didn't say anything. He thought: All right, talk. But just don't go over what happened tonight. Just don't try to make sense out of it. And don't nag at the future, at tomorrow. Fate pushed me in here, now I'm going to let it push me out.

The man was sitting up now, his bare feet on the floor, his sheet draped like a toga around him. "I aim to thank you for helping me in that fight."

"I just wish I'd got a crack at Turkey," Ashby said.

The man didn't say anything for a second. He just looked down at his feet, and in the shadow, draped in the white sheet, he was still as a statue.

Then he said, "I never got to tell her . . . I never got to tell Laurel about me. . . . I never got to tell . . ."

Ashby leaned up and propped his head on his hand: My, God, Ashby thought, the man was in love with her. He almost thought: In love with her, too. In love with her like I am. But he couldn't be sure. He might have imagined her. It might have been nothing but drunken imagining. But the man didn't think he had imagined her.

Ashby said, "What did you aim to tell her?"

"I knew she wasn't any . . . she wasn't one of those kind of . . . I knew she wasn't . . ." the man said. "Before ever you told me. And I didn't know how to talk to her, and I wanted to tell her about me, and why I didn't know how to talk to her. But I never got started. . . ."

"What were you gonna tell her?" Ashby said. If the man wanted to talk, he was going to let him. It would be one decent thing he had done that day. He would look a little better in his own sight if he could act decent to this man. And, anyhow, he liked him. He was a strange man. Gentle and bewildered there outside of Miranda's house. Then, an hour later, with the sheriff, he was fierce and purposeful.

The man's head was lowered. The light through the bars touched his shaggy hair, so that it was a bluish color. Then he looked over at Ashby, his eyes illumined, a sort of damp light in them, a glistening.

"I wanted to say to her," the man said, and it was as if he were not talking to Ashby, but to the girl. "I wanted to say, 'I was born in a shanty. A mill shanty. It was three feet from other shanties on each side. Sometimes in summer you had a time breathing in it. The way it was on the mud flats . . . Then the first frost, we stuck rags and cardboard in the cracks. A flat is the hottest place in summer and the coldest in winter, I reckon, and in a shanty like that . . .' " The man shook his head. From the corridor, from another cell, there came snoring.

"She wouldn't have minded that," Ashby said. "If she was a right kind, she wouldn't have minded where you were born. I don't guess it matters, anyhow. We're all kin. . . ."

But the man scarcely listened. "I wanted to tell her I slept twenty-two years in a shanty like that, when there was one for us to sleep in a-tall. Me and Papa. Mama was dead. I mind when she died. There was a heap o' dyin' in those days. There was privies back of the shanties, along the creek. . . . Us kids used to play in the creek. There wasn't any place else. An' we never knowed it was—well, it was thick and dirty water, but about germs . . . Anyhow, there was always, seem-like, the typhoid fever gettin' folks down and they dyin' off. They died and was buried. When one died, it always seemed like there was another fellow in from the country to take his place in the mill. The shanties was always full, even with all the dyin'—dyin' was sort of casual-like, you might say. And Mama's dyin' might 'a' been, too, except for Papa. . . ."

There was no self-pity in the man. If he took himself seriously, as Ashby had thought, it was only himself as a part of something else, a part of a way of living that he had thought a lot about. So that hearing the man tell about these things which had happened to him, hearing him speak of these things in that curious monotone, Ashby had the feeling that the man was trying to understand something important. There was a purpose in this man, and, sensing it, Ashby knew again a sort of self-sickness. He did not say anything; he only waited for the man to go on. The man put his tongue to his lips.

"Papa was a man with a fire stoked up inside him. He was bigger'n any man I ever saw. And he was a talker. Talked like the Bible, he did; it was all he read. It was that talking—well, I never got much chance to talk around him. I had to listen. I been a listenin' one most ever since. . . ."

Again it seemed that the man was explaining not to Ashby but to the girl, Laurel.

"Maybe it's been better. Because his talking—well, he was the best worker the mill ever had. And they aimed, two or three times, to make him foreman. Ever' time he talked. He said he'd change things a heap was he foreman, and if they didn't aim to have things changed, then they needn't make him foreman. 'I don't aim to be a cattle-herder,' he told ole man Ammett, that owned the mill one time 'If you aim for me to prick your cattle on for you, then I say no. I'll work with human beings, as an equal, but I'm not gonna set myself up as Lord God Almighty and my neighbors down below me as the beasts of the field.' " The man coughed. "So he wasn't foreman. . . ."

Ashby nodded. There wasn't any bitterness or any heroics in the man's words. He liked that. It made him believe the man, and believe in the father he was talking about. He wondered if he, himself, might have believed easier in Colonel Ashby Pelham and the stories about him if they hadn't been so hell bent on making the Colonel a hero. If they had just made him a man, maybe, he, Ashby, could have believed in him the way the man believed in his father. And that could have been all the difference if they had asked Ashby to be a man and not a hero. But they hadn't.

The man was talking, his voice still toneless, his eyes not yet seeing Ashby, but someone else. "When Mama died," he said, "Papa just stood there a time looking at her. I couldn't 'a' been more'n six, but I mind how she was layin' there, little and still on the ragged comforter, and the hot sun seepin' in through the thousandfoot-a-night vines on the porch, the sun a-touchin' his face, and it strong and brown enough to 'a' been carved out o' sandstone. I reckon I had a cryin' inside me, but I couldn't let him see it. I just stood watching him, first the moanful way his eyes were, and then the hardness comin', the madness. If ever I think of God, I think of him lookin' like he did then—full of sorrowing and angriness both. I mind I said to him, 'What is it?' and he looked at me and knowed . . . knew . . . what I was talkin' about. He said, 'It's that I'm full of the righteous anger of the Lord, my God. And that I will never forget who and what did this to her. Yea, if I must go hungry and ragged all my days, I will root out and destroy it, root, branch, bud and seed I will destroy it. . . .' " The voice was quiet as ever, and the very unemotional quality of it was more powerful than any histrionics could have been. Ashby wondered how it was to have a righteous anger; he knew anger, but a righteous anger was something he didn't know. Where did you find a righteous anger? And was that the thing a man needed?

He didn't look at the man. The man knew something he didn't know, and perhaps would never know. He wanted to hear the man talk on, but he didn't look at him.

"A long time later I heard about it," the man said. "That day I only knew that he had left me to sit beside her. But he told me later that he went to the mill to ole man Ammett's office. And they say his talkin' stopped ever'thing and all the shuttles were still. I don't know what he said. I only know that all the folks marched out of the mill that day. I saw them coming home, and him at their head, taller than anybody, and a kind of glory on his face. And everybody around him looked up. I was six, but I remember it, because I hadn't ever seen folks looking up like that. The folks I had known all looked down. But that day . . ." The man's face was lifted, his mouth parted, and he was sitting straight so that the light striped by the bars touched his mussed black hair. "Those faces, looking up . . ." he said, remembering.

It was a thing Ashby had never thought about, where a man's face looked, down or up, and why. He had always looked any man in the eye, he had always looked straight ahead, and he had never wondered at it. But he knew he hadn't done anything to deserve the right to look straight ahead. Anything, that is, outside of being born to the name Pelham. So he stirred under his sheet at what the man had said. He had his palms lapped together under his head and he stared at the gray ceiling of the cell.

"But the way it was . . ." the man said. "They moved us out of the shanties. The sheriff and his deputies came and moved us out and lined up before the houses to protect the niggers they were moving in. They moved our broken-down beds and our quilts and the apple boxes we kept things in. . . . And then, with all of us standing there in the middle of the street, lookin' at the sheriff's men and behind them at the scared niggers tryin' to slip along like they wasn't there at all . . . With us standin' there not knowin' where to go, and the niggers movin' in our houses . . . That day Papa stood up on one of the apple crates. There was somebody amongst us who cussed; more than one, I guess. Ole man Ammett's sheriff and ole man Ammett's deputies were there to protect the niggers, but our folks cussed 'em, the niggers, standin' in the road, dusty. . . ."

"Did you cuss 'em?" Ashby said. "What about you?"

"No," the man said, "I never . . ."

"How come?" Ashby said. "If they were moving in your houses, taking your jobs . . ."

"Why," the man said, "I tole you I wasn't but six. But I don't reckon I would have cussed 'em anyway. I didn't hate 'em. Do you hate niggers?"

"No," Ashby said. "Why should I?" But he thought, they never took my job and my house. It takes a big man not to hate somebody for doing that.

The man went on. "Papa got on his apple box," he said. "And he looked down at his folks. And he said, 'Curse not your brethren!' 'Them? Niggers? Our brethren?' the folks said. Mad at him now. Had put up with his doing this long, because they were busy hatin' the niggers and ole man Ammett for puttin' them in our places. But now they saw that it was Papa who had brought it all on. And he said to 'em, 'We are all of us the disinherited. Us and them. If you must curse, curse those who make us hate one another. Curse them who grow rich out of our hatred, black for white and white for black. What have we, any of us, here . . .' And he swept his long arm over them all, niggers and white folks alike—'What have we, black or white, except backs strong and willing to work? Nothing except labor to sell, and that at a whore's price. And why? Because if we don't, the blacks will!' "

"Yes," Ashby said, "I can see what he meant. I never thought about it, but . . ." But what he really wondered at still was the man's being able to see it that way, without hating. He could understand his own lack of hatred, his Father's attitude toward Num and Temp, could understand Colonel Ashby Pelham's knife flashing out to cut the rope that night in the Trent pasture. He could understand his Father persuading the session to let Num sit in the balcony of the Presbyterian Church. But the thing that this man's father had said, passed understanding. He had stood and watched Negroes move into the only houses his folks had, taking the only jobs his folks could get. And he said . . . "You mean he . . .?" he said, again.

The man nodded. "Does it make you mad?" he said. "If it makes you mad, I . . ."

"No," Ashby said. "It doesn't make me mad. Why should it?"

"It does most folks," the man said. "That sheriff now . . ." He shook his head. "It made our own folks mad there that day. They looked at him and they were mad. One fellow hollered, 'Nigger-lover!' And others of 'em kept saying it over. And then he roared at 'em. . . . He said, 'Don't be fools. Don't you see? We aimed at living like a man ought to live, and ole man Ammett said, *Get out. If you got to be human beings 'stead o' slaves, I'll get somebody who ain't so uppity. I'll get niggers.* And so he got 'em. And now if they should ever ask him the same thing we did, he'll say to them, *Get out. I'll get white trash.* And that will go on to time's end, if you are fool enough to curse one another.' 'What you want us to do?' they said. 'Why,' he said, 'Stand beside your brethren, no matter his color. Speak with one voice. And then where can Ammett turn? How will his mill run then?' And they said, 'Stand with niggers?' "

"I never thought of it," Ashby said, quietly. "It's a thing I never thought about before. I reckon I must have known it was that way, but . . ." He found his cigarettes under the pillow and lighted one and sat puffing. "I just never . . ." he said. The man sat in that great stillness of his for a second. Then he spoke again.

"I sat in the road in the cinders, by the white pine apple box, where he was standing. And I watched 'em walk off, cursing him and cursing the niggers. And they went back that very day to ole man Ammett and told him they would do whatever he said. Ole man Ammett knew they'd be back, I reckon. And he knew that they'd give in, that they'd forget everything. They did. They told him they'd do whatever he said, if only he would give them their houses back and move the niggers out. I didn't know that that day. He told me a long time later, Papa did. All I knew that day was that he strapped our iron bed on his back and made up a bundle of clothes and we went together up the street and on out of town. . . ." Now there was just the faintest drawn look on the man's face, and the slightest look of an old sorrow around his mouth and in the crowfeet around his dark eyes.

Ashby did not know anything to say; all his life he had been a man to talk lightly, and whatever he might have felt he still could not say a serious thing. He was, he guessed, a jokester. Or somehow, beside this man, he seemed to be, and his life seemed a kind of comic existence, unreal even to him.

"He used to call that 'The day of the vision.' Maybe he was crazy, the way some folks said. Only a thinking came to him there that day in the cinder road that had never come to him before. And I reckon it was something he had to tell, because we went a long hard way together for him to tell it. We went a long journey, mill working. And always, when he went to tell his vision, we had to take to the road again. There weren't any ears to listen. The po' white folks hated it because they'd been taught to hate the niggers more than they could ever hate the men that owned the mills. The niggers hated it because they'd been taught to hate 'white trash' more than they could hate the mill owners. And you know the mill owners would hate it. There is a heap of hate loose in the world, but it look like to me sometimes there is more of it here where we are than anywhere. Because there are some here that get rich out of it, and they mean to see the hate stay here, and grow. . . ."

"Go on," Ashby said, in the silence. "Go on. I want to know what happened to you." He had a notion that, happy or not, this man at least had something which he lacked. He couldn't name what it was, but he knew that the man was not aimless. Whatever he was, he was not that. That was one thing he could feel about him.

"So then," the man said, "One day when we were working a way away from here, he heard about the strike in Milltown. I was grown then. I was twenty-two. And we came home. He came home to tell the vision all over again, where he had started telling it. But when we got here, it was different from the last time. Ole man Ammett had done like always. He had fired all them that struck and sent for niggers to come. But the niggers never got there. The white folks had guns to use against 'em. And the niggers was too scared. Papa told the white folks how it would be. 'All right,' he said, 'Go on with it the way you are. But you won't gain anything. Ole man Ammett can hold out a long time, longer than your stomachs can. And even if you do hold out he can just close the mill. He can do that. He'll eat still.' But they laughed at him. 'No,' they said. 'This time we got him *and* the niggers beat. This time . . .' Then, finally, one night when he was talking to 'em before the church, the righteous wrath got into him. 'Oh, brethren,' he said, pleadin-like, 'They have treated you as less than men. And so you act like animals. Like cornered rats your turn snarling on your own kind, instead of on the ones who've cornered you. . . .' "

The man cut his words short and straightened a little.

Ashby knew what he was about to tell. He said, "He ought to have known . . ." But then he thought, "What if he did know. It was a thing a man had to say. He had to tell the truth, whatever . . ."

The man said, "The bullet went through the kerosene lamp hung up before him. He had one hand up in the air, and he went down with his long finger still pointing up. . . ."

Ashby said, "I'm sorry." He was thinking, Does every man have somewhere in him a tale about a hero? And if he has, what does it do to him? For me, I have had to mock it, but this man does not mock it. And perhaps I wouldn't either, in his place. Maybe in his place I would believe it, too, since I had seen it with my own eyes, since in a way I had shared it.

In the quiet there was only the steamy sound of the radiator and the low breathing from the other cells.

The man shook himself. "Well," he said, "It came about the way he said. The mill was just closed down. In fact, ole man Ammett was so stubborn about it, he let the mill go bankrupt before he'd open it. And he died of it, a little after. And there we were, all of us together, in Milltown, worse off than ever. I stayed on, because it would have seemed like leaving him. . . ."

"You didn't find the one . . ." Ashby said, "the one that shot . . . ?"

The man shook his head. "I never knew who it was. I never tried to find out, and Lord knows the law wasn't interested. The law was pretty glad to have him gone, I reckon. Anyhow, they all of them killed him, or maybe none of them; hate done it. And then when he was proved right, the men began to drop into the shanty where I was, and ask what to do. Not that I knew, any more'n they did. But it was like they was shamefaced, and like they thought I was him come back. . . ."

Ashby stirred and blew smoke toward the ceiling. That was a thing he knew, too: being looked on as the reincarnation of someone else, being not you but another man returned from death.

"And one day," the man said, "they said there wasn't anything they knew how to do except work in a mill. And there stood that mill not being used. And that it wasn't right. And they asked if I would go see about renting it. And I said even if we had it where could we get the cotton? And they said to make a borrow from the bank. And I said how, with what to put up? They said try. Try for us. And I said if I tried, it would have to be his—Papa's—way that the mill was run. And they said all right."

The man nodded to himself, as if to say, "That's how it was."

"Well, the bank that owned the mill was just paying taxes and gettin' nothin' back. So they said we could rent it and pay 'em at the end of the year. They didn't have nothin' to lose, anyhow. But there wasn't any money to start it runnin'. Not a pound of cotton . . . And nobody to lend us money to buy it with. Then one night when I was sittin' figurin', ten of the men came up on the shanty porch. 'We got a bale o' cotton,' they said. 'Where you get it?' I said. 'Fellow give it to us.' I knew they was tellin' a story. I knew that that was a stole bale o' cotton. But they wouldn't tell it any other way, than that some fellow had give it to them. They was hungry and their wives and their chillun. I don't reckon that made it right, but I went ahead and used it. I took that bale o' cotton and we made it into unbleached domestic. Unbleached because we didn't have any bleachers, nor nothin' else much. And we sold it and made enough to buy more cotton and make more. And little by little we growed—grew—so that the time came when the mill was ours and runnin' steady. . . ."

He didn't seem to have any self-pride about any of it. He was proud of a thing done and not of his doing it when he said, "You ought to see the way it is now. Niggers there workin' too the way he knew it ought to be, and no hatin'. I can show you, don't you believe it. Because it's my mill now, or at least in my name, it and three others. But it's really theirs, all them that work there, because without them there wouldn't be any mill, but without me, there would still be their sweat to run it."

Ashby put his cigarette on the concrete floor and watched it smoke a second. "So you really are Bevo Banes, like you told the sheriff," he said. "And he wouldn't believe you. . . ."

"Yes," the man said. "Which is what I'm aimin' to say. The thing that is on my mind, that I wanted to tell her, Laurel . . . Here I am, belonging to this town, and the sheriff don't know me a-tall. It's like I live in a place where the world is walled out, and it's not a way I like, but nothin' I can do about it. . . . I'm a lone man, because I been so busy I never had time to be nothin' else. And now that I got time, I don't know how . . ."

Ashby sat and looked at him for a long minute. Then he said, "You listen here. I don't know what you want, but I want to tell you you got an important thing. That vision you talk about—that's a thing that counts."

The man looked uncertain. "You never had a vision?" he said.

Ashby laughed. "Never a vision," he said, "except a sort of second-hand one that never seemed to belong to me . . ."

"I don't reckon you can know," the man said. "Until a test comes. A vision is something you got to put to a test, and then it's your vision, no matter who had it first-hand."

"I never had a vision," Ashby said. "Nor any righteous anger, either. Maybe it's what I need." He leaned toward the man who sat brooding at the floor. "What do you want, more than that?"

The man turned his soft eyes on him. "I want a woman and I want to be a gentleman. A vision is all right. But a empty bed and aloneness in a man . . ."

Ashby lay back on the bunk, shutting out the man's face. Lying down quickly like that, he felt a little drunkedness still in him. And he thought, he thinks it is Laurel he needs, to have Laurel and to be a gentleman. And I reckon I think I need Laurel and a vision. But what we have both got in our mind is the story of our fathers. The father that in his case happens to be his own, in mine, I reckon, is Colonel Ashby Pelham. I don't reckon we needed even to be connected by blood for that matter. Because a father is a state of mind, a father is a sort of hero that a man makes up in his mind, that a man wants to be like. But what a man has to know is *how*? A man knows what winds his father stood against and what rivers he dammed. But what he has to know is what winds rise up in his day, and what rivers flood?

He half-sat to tell the man what he had thought, but he never said a word, out loud. To himself he said, I must be awful drunk. And slept.

# Chapter VI

Ashby awoke to jail smell and jail sound, the smell of ammonia, sweat, and antiseptic, the sound of Negroes at the far end of the corridor singing. In him, he had a sense of failure, sickening as the familiar over-sweet taste of a hangover in his mouth. And against the failure as against the hangover, there was no remedy but a jeer. A jeer was the only protection he could always count on.

So he lay on the bunk, listening to the distant singing, and saying to himself, Yah, now you're in jail. Let Papa tell you about the time he was in jail. Papa is the only Pelham in history to be incarcerated in a common jail. Uncle Vance was in a Yankee prison in Indiana—but a prisoner of war is a hero not a criminal. But Papa Ashby, he was just a pure-D thug, locked up for drunkedness and assault and battery and probably for other assorted crimes like attempted rape in a cat house. He set out to play cops and robbers and outwit a sheriff who did not, God knows, need much outwitting, and he ended up behind bars with a bad taste in his mouth and a terrific thirst. That was back in the thirties, son, when they gave you the Medal of Honor for a hangover and the key to the city for a night in jail. Papa was a great man in his day. . . .

He turned over and blinked at the thin sunlight. Down the corridor the Negroes sang, *I'm a pilgrim and a stranger, travelin' through a foreign land. . . .* Then there was a high jeering voice, calling down the length of the corridor, reverberating in the honeycomb of cells, "Boy, don't you wish you was traveling." Ashby rose and went to the watertap and drank straight from the tap, gulping the water thirstily, thinking, Hell, yes. I wish I was traveling. I wish I had gone on last night with Temp. It does look like at thirty-four a man could stop being a fool. Only I don't know what else I'd be, and I reckon, not knowing, I had as well be a fool as anything.

When he had drunk all the water he could, he stood beside the corner bucket. The sound was like birdshot on a tin roof, louder than the undiscouraged but softened singing down the way.

He returned to his bunk after one curious and impatient glance into the corridor. They have likely got drunk with my money, he thought. But no, a sheriff gets his whiskey free. Listen, son, you run for sheriff when you grow up. That's the job for a bright boy.

He stretched out again on the bunk and lay there grinning sardonically at the dark water-stained ceiling. He turned on his side and looked across the cell at Bevo. In the first sun, Bevo lay there, his huge muscled arm writhing as he scratched at his head.

"Bedbugs?" Ashby said.

Bevo took his hand away and looked at him.

"Dandruff," he said, with that gentle dead seriousness on his face. He sat up on the bunk and still keeping his nakedness covered by the sheet put his feet out on the floor, wiggling his toes in the patch of sunshine.

"Athlete's foot?" Ashby said, watching the toes.

"No," Bevo said. He looked bewildered again.

"Too bad," Ashby said.

"How come?" Bevo said.

"So much fun to scratch," Ashby said. He stuck one foot

out of the cover and, doubling himself up, began to scratch his toes between thumb and forefinger. "Ah-h-h- . . ." He groaned, pleasurably. He held his mouth half open.

Bevo regarded him gravely. He's taking it hard, Ashby thought. It's come to him that he's in jail. He was so busy talking last night, it didn't worry him. But now he looks hang-dog.

Bevo opened his mouth. "I . . ." he said. Then, "I ought to 'scuse myself for the way I talked last night. About myself, I mean. You never talked none about yourself, and I . . ."

"Hell," Ashby said. "No use apologizing for that. I mean, if a fellow wants to talk, and needs to, I'm glad to listen. I might want to talk myself, sometime, and need somebody to listen."

"It was just . . . It was Laurel." Bevo leaned a little, his hand dropping the sheet, so that only his abdomen was covered and his big chest moved with breathing. "You remember how Laurel was?"

"Yes," Ashby said, "I remember." He wished he hadn't. He wished he had never seen her, but if he had to see her, he wished he could have forgot. He wished he could think now that she was something he made up in his drunkedness. He wished he could think that, looking at her, he had really seen Carol, and had felt a sentimental shock which a man might mistake for something else. But he had felt something else, and he still felt it, an emotional reaction he had never felt in the presence of Carol or Honeybreeches or Louise. He did not know why and now he wished he hadn't. "I am in favor," he announced suddenly, "Of no complications. Or complex situations. I am going to be a Presbyterian and let predestination . . ." His voice trailed off. He did not even know what he was going to let predestination do.

"I got to find her," Bevo said. "I got to."

"Well, if you want me to help you . . ." Ashby said. Then he wondered why he said it, since he had the immediate problem of getting out of jail and taking Temp away, and, in any case, would not know where to look for her even if he had the opportunity. And what, for that matter, if he found her? He could imagine himself finding her and then sending word to Bevo, "Come quick. Found Laurel behind the barn." Then he could imagine the three of them standing, staring, and wondering what in devil's name to do next. And yet, when he thought of it, he reckoned he might do just that. Bevo was not the kind of man a man could deal from under the deck with. He had a quality of honesty in him that would make any other man play according to the rules with him. So that perhaps he, Ashby, would do just that. Perhaps he would wire, "Found Laurel behind the barn." Then maybe they would run a footrace to see who got her. Or toss an Indianhead penny. Only Ashby did not think they would have much chance to do either. Not any time soon, anyhow. Not soon.

"I got to get out o' here," Bevo said. "I got . . ."

"So have I," he said. He began to laugh to himself, thinking. Bevo looked at him, curious. "You know why?" he said, "You know why I got to get out o' here?" Bevo shook his head. Ashby closed his mouth to cut off the laughter and then ran his tongue along his curling lips. "I got to get out o' here to spirit away the nigger the sheriff talked about being after last night. You remember?"

Bevo nodded. Down the corridor the Negroes still sang, voices pulsing.

"Well," Ashby said, his voice low. "He—the nigger—was right there in my car when the sheriff and all those deputies went by. In fact, he stuck his head up to watch us. And that sheriff never saw him. After he'd spent all Sunday chasin' him with those far fetched hounds of his, and there he was, in ten feet of him. . . ."

Bevo smiled. "Well," he said. "And he never knew it . . . And now you gonna git out and slip him away. . . ." He laughed, shortly. It was the first time Ashby had ever seen him laugh.

It was then they heard the sound of footsteps in the corridor. Bevo stood up, letting the sheet fall from him; he stood there naked and unconscious of being so, watching and waiting.

"Looking for somebody? A confederate with a handsaw?" Ashby said. Bevo turned his grave face round to Ashby. Ashby grinned.

"Well," Ashby said, "Whoever it is, I must say you're in fine fettle to entertain 'em. Especially if it's female . . ."

Bevo looked quickly at himself, his nakedness. He reddened and stepped hurriedly, lumberingly to the bunk and covered himself with the sheet. He sat there impatiently with the sheet held up around his neck.

"You look," Ashby said, "like a statue about to be unveiled."

The Negro voices thrummed into silence; the footsteps came on.

The woman spoke before Ashby saw her clearly; the sun had not yet touched the corridor.

She had a strong, hoarse voice.

"Brothers, are you saved?"

Ashby saw her mouth first, thin lipped and small, and then he saw the peculiar scarlet sunbonnet she wore. He merely stared at her and said nothing. He was conscious of Bevo stirring uncomfortably.

Then Bevo said, "Yessum . . ."

"Are you sure, brother?" the woman said, her eyes now directed toward Bevo. Ashby could see behind her a man, a little rabbity man peering over her shoulder.

"Are you sure you saved, brother?" the little man said. He sounded apologetic, as if he had just stolen the idea from the woman. But he probably apologized all the time for merely existing, Ashby thought; because, though the woman's mouth was small, everything else about her was bold as sunlight.

"Yessir," Bevo said to the little man. "Three times."

Ashby grunted, audibly; but it had no effect on anybody.

"How long ago, brother?" the woman said. She had a long

tip-tilted nose that Ashby imagined must get in her way when she was peeping through keyholes.

"Now," Bevo said. He frowned, remembering. He held the sheet tight around his throat. "I reckon it was twenty-seven years ago. Yessum. It was when I was twelve."

"All three times?" the little man said, making another tip-toe appearance over the woman's shoulder.

"Yessir," Bevo said. "A preacher's daughter got me to do it."

"Eve started it because Adam needed a bath," Ashby said.

The woman turned to him, her mouth like two halves of a biscuit pressed together. She opened her mouth to say something and then she leaned her head closer to the bars and looked again. They were both looking at him now. She turned her head slightly toward the little man.

"Ashby Pelham," she said.

"Yes, ma'm," Ashby said. "Have I had the pleasure?"

The woman looked as if she were going to whistle, or perhaps to crow, but at any rate not as if she were going to be able to talk at that moment. She made her mouth into a tiny circle and then opened it wide and exhaled his name triumphantly, "Ashby Pelham." She shook her head, holding her mouth with tight pride, as if to say, "I tell you about the sinfulness in the homes of the mighty."

Then she turned to the little man. "You see?" she said. "I told you the Presbyterians was jest as worldly as the 'Piscopals. Now you see." Then she looked back at Ashby, who lay grinning at her, and she applied her tongue to her palate several times in long slow clucks of pure joy. When this was done, she turned abruptly to the little man.

"Horatius," she said, "Let us sing." Ashby heard her foot pat three times and then the song came. It came in one single high nasal whine, so that the two voices, the man's and the woman's, were almost indistinguishable; or perhaps the little man was not really allowed to make any sound at all, and just opened his mouth for the looks of the thing. Ashby could see Bevo squirming and looking at the floor.

They sang:

Come to Jesus, thine the glory,
Come to Jesus, a-men.
Come to Jesus, thine the glory,
Revive us again . . .

"As if being in jail wasn't bad enough," Ashby said, not looking at anybody.

But the voices went on, like a noon whistle stuck till one o'clock. The corridor was quiet; no voice joined them.

"After those Negroes," Ashby said, "This sounds like a patent medicine advertisement."

Come to Jesus, thine the glory,
Come to Jesus, a-men . . .

"Try salvation," Ashby said. "Guaranteed to work in ninety days, or your money back. In hell."

He was having a fine time. He was full of mockery and he had thought of a way to get the sheriff up there. He lay there grinning. He remembered an Irishman he had roomed with in college who used to describe him in this state as "grinning like a skunk eatin' briars." He had never known why a skunk should either eat briars or grin about it, but it was a good expression.

The singing stopped abruptly and he waited for the woman to say what he knew she would say.

"Let us pray," she said. "Let us pray, sinners."

She looked through the bars at them. She looked as he had known she would, as if she expected them to do something.

"Let us pray, sinners," she repeated, in a loud voice.

"Yes ma'm," Bevo said. But he didn't move.

She stared at Ashby. "Mr. Pelham, let us pray."

"You pray," he said. "I'm plumb wore out from all that singing."

She fixed her eyes coldly on him for a moment; then she turned to Bevo.

"Let us pray, brother," she said.

"Yes, ma'm," he said. "I'm ready."

Ashby waited. Then, "Is that the way you're going to face your Lawd?" she said. "Halfway in bed, like that?"

Bevo looked at her helplessly. "I . . . I . . ." he stuttered.

"Don't you know the proper way to pray, brother?" she said.

Unhappily, his eyes met hers. Ashby watched. "Yes, ma'm," Bevo said.

"Then let us kneel," the woman said.

"Yes, brother," the little man said, as if he had just thought of it. "Let us kneel."

Ashby chuckled, and then the laughter came out in steamy sounds from his nose. The two waited at the door. Bevo sat helplessly, not moving.

"Brother . . ." the woman said.

"I'm not dressed," Bevo blurted out. "I'm . . ."

Ashby sat up on his bunk. He looked out of the corner of his eyes at Bevo. "He's a nudist," Ashby said. "He was run in for being a nudist. He runs around naked, absorbing God's sunshine."

Bevo said, "I don't. I never . . ." but the woman had already drawn back a step, her eyes foolishly wide and the clucking noise coming again from her mouth. "Oh, brother . . ." she said.

The little man threw his hands toward the ceiling. "Brother!" he said.

"But it ain't so," Bevo said. "I swear . . ." He sat up.

Ashby waved an arm. "He converted me last night. We ran all over this county naked last night." He began to rise slowly on his bunk, looking straight at the woman, who stared fascinated. He shook a finger at her.

"Sister," he said, "Do you know the beauty of the human form?" He lowered his sheet an inch. "Sister, have you seen what a beautiful handiwork of God is man without clothes?" He was shouting at her now, and her mouth was in an unsteady oval, as if she could neither close nor open it. "Sister," he yelled, "are you hiding your light under a bushel petticoat?" He was standing erect now, on the bunk; the sheet was at his midriff. "Sister, prepare to feast your eyes on God's creation. Sister, look closely now. Look, sister . . ." He had dropped the sheet. But the woman was no longer there.

He could hear her and the little man going down the corridor, with quick feet and hurried outraged voices.

He lay back on the bunk, laughter pulsing through him. Bevo sat and looked at him and did not say anything. Finally Ashby was quiet. He turned his eyes to Bevo.

"You ever see anything like it?" he said, "You ever?"

"What did you go and do that for?" Bevo said.

"Because I got a kick out of it in the first place," Ashby said. "But mainly, I reckon, because it was a good way to get the sheriff up here. He'll be trottin' along that hall any minute now."

"Well," Bevo said, "I don't see why, but I hope he does. But you never had to make her think I wasn't a gentleman. . . ."

Ashby looked at him. "I been a gentleman for thirty years," he said. "It hasn't got me anywhere."

Bevo watched him. "Where did you aim for it to get you?"

"I don't know," Ashby said, his gaze in space immobile.

"Look like to me that's not the question," Bevo said. "Look like to me that being a gentleman is enough in itself. It's just a way of being that a fellow wants to be. . . ." He had his heavy-bearded face thrust forward now, across the space toward Ashby.

Ashby grunted and turned on his back. "That's what got us in this jail," he said. "Acting like gentlemen . . ."

"You sorry?" Bevo said.

"No," Ashby said. "I never had been in jail before." He chuckled. " 'You're not a man till you have.' " He rubbed a hand across the stubble on his jaw. "But I never thought I'd get in jail for acting a gentleman in a cat house."

"Look," Bevo said, unsmiling, almost grim. "Look. Where are you going if we get out of here?"

Ashby turned again on his side. "Why, to take Temp . . ."

"I know," Bevo said. "But where?"

"To my uncle's. He's my cousin, but more like an uncle. Uncle Ephe. Ex-governor. Ex-dandy. Ex-brother by his own choice to Miranda. Which is a secret he keeps . . ."

"That's what I want," Bevo said.

"What?" Ashby said.

"To go with you. To see how he acts. How a gentleman acts. I got to learn some manners for myself, so I know how to associate with folks. The way I am now . . . Well, at the mill, no matter if I did start out same as ever'body else there, I'm the boss now, an' it ain't like it used to be between me and the others, no trouble but just not free and easy like. And it's a lonesome way to be, but if I knew how to act . . ." His eyes met Ashby's. "Will you take me? I could help if there was any trouble . . ."

Ashby raised his eyebrows. "It's all right with me," he said. "Though I'm thinking you're likely to find that the manners of a gentleman can cover the morals of a tomcat. But if you want to go . . . Hell, I'd like company. Not that there's gonna be any trouble." He lay silent and unmoving while Bevo thanked him. "The devil," he said, finally. "Don't thank me. I only wish there could be a little trouble in it for us. When I think how I enjoyed that fight last night . . . If I could just have hit that sheriff, I . . ."

"I heard you. I heard what you said. . . ." Turkey was there in the door, his red nose stuck through the bar, the sun now far enough into the corridor to shine on his baldness.

"Well," Ashby said, knowing he had heard nothing about Temp, "if you'd quit wearing sneakers, you might get rid of your inferiority complex. But as it is, you know what folks think of you, slipping up on 'em like that. . . ."

"Now, Ashby," Turkey said, so that Ashby knew at that moment that Turkey was in his hands, since Turkey was wheezing, a sound which with him passed for joviality. He will be apologizing for the next ten years for putting me in jail last night, Ashby thought. The change of heart has come. "Now boys," Turkey said. When he leaned close to the bars, Ashby saw a swollen purple puff under one eye. "What's this I hear 'bout y'all running God's messengers out of here with that big tale about being nudists? You boys are gonna lose me the church vote, doing things like that."

"Why, I thought you'd already lost it," Ashby said. "But then, if we helped you lose it, I reckon you're grateful. Now you can go into Miranda's in broad open daylight drunk as a skunk and just not care what the church vote thinks. I reckon you came up to thank us." He spoke slowly, with mock soberness.

"Now, Ashby," the sheriff said. He wiped his forehead with a bandana. "You wouldn't want to cause me no trouble. . . ."

"No more than I can," Ashby said. "After what you've done . . ."

"Now, Ashby," the sheriff said. His under lip was stuck out pleadingly. "I've always boasted that I run a Christian jail. There ain't a more Christian jail in this state than this one."

"Have you told the Chamber of Commerce?" Ashby said. Out of the corner of his eye he saw Bevo's discomfiture. The hand still held the sheet doggedly against his chest.

"And for three years," the sheriff said, "I have had the pleasant little custom of having my friends in jail woke up by some beautiful church music and morning prayers. And now you have done spoiled it all. And all the blame will lay on me."

Ashby sat up. "Well, Turkey," he said, "I reckon the only thing you can do is let us out of here quick. Before we destroy the whole moral tone of the place."

The sheriff rubbed at his head with the bandana. "Now Ashby, I'm aimin' to let you out as soon as I can. At least I'm aimin' to let you out, Ashby, but this here fellow." He pointed to Bevo. "He started it all, an' then on top o' that he lied to me, tole me that big tale. . . . It was mighty ungentlemanly the way he done. . . ."

"Ungentlemanly," Ashby mocked. "Tryin' to save the virtue of a pure little innocent girl, and you call him ungentlemanly. . . ."

Pain lined the sheriff's face. "Now, Ashby, I've done repented my hasty acts, and if you was a Christian, you'd forgive me. I got tempted and I fell. . . ."

"Not as low as you wanted to, though," Ashby said. He closed one eye and inspected the sheriff out of the other. He could see Bevo peering from one to the other of them. "It just looks like to me," Ashby said, "it looks like it's my Christian duty to tell a few folks how you were acting last night. So you can make your repentance public."

"Now, Ashby . . ." Turkey said, and the purple growth on his neck writhed. "Now there ain't no need of sayin' a thing like that. . . ." Then he laughed, with what was meant to be a comfortable sound. "You a great prankster, Ashby. . . ."

"There's one thing I have a hard time doing," Ashby said, his eyes unwavering on the sheriff, "and that is keeping my mouth shut. I'm the talkingest man in six counties and I just got to tell what I know. When I think about you and those hounds, and you drunk at Miranda's, and the good stories I could tell everybody . . ." He got up and went over to the door, the concrete floor cool to his bare feet. "Unless I got a good reason to keep my mouth shut. Like somebody doin' me a big favor. . . ."

The sheriff was busy with the bandana again. "Ashby, would you like your breakfast now. I could have a good breakfast . . ."

"No," Ashby said. "What I would like is my clothes and an open door."

"All right," Turkey said. "Jest as soon . . ."

"Now," Ashby said. "We got to get out of here now."

"I can't now, Ashby," the sheriff said. They stared at each other. Bevo sat and watched them. "I can't. In a little while . . ."

"It's gonna be a pity about that church vote," Ashby said.

He kept thinking that he ought to have thought about the church vote last night; but he was having a fine time using it now.

The sheriff held on to one bar of the door. "Why did I ever mention it?" he said. "I don't see why I had to come up here blabbing. . . ." He was not looking at Ashby. "I'm the dangdest fool," he said, angry at himself now, without humor. He turned his eyes to Ashby again. "You ain't got no business being so unchristian, Ashby. Your father . . ." He stopped. His mouth opened, closed, and then he grinned slowly. "What," he said, "What if Senator Pelham was to hear about this? What if, instead of lettin' you out with no charge, I was to tell . . . What if the Senator was to know you'd been in jail?" Turkey was pleased with himself.

"Wouldn't surprise him," Ashby said. "He wouldn't be finding out anything about me he didn't know, because I'm not a good hypocrite like you, Turkey. But now that church vote would really be finding out, if I . . ." The sheriff held up his hand, but Ashby went on. "Are you gonna lose the church vote by bein' stubborn, Turkey?"

Misery weighted the corners of the sheriff's mouth. "It ain't stubbornness, Ashby . . ."

"Then what is it?"

"It's . . ." The sheriff made a knot in the bandana. "The damndest things," he whispered to himself, "the damndest things ever can happen to me. It's humiliating." Then he passed his eyes sort of skittishly over Ashby. "It's this way. I had your and his suit down there in my office . . ."

"Oh, Lord," Ashby said.

The sheriff nodded. "And some of the boys was admirin' em. The deputies. And before I knew it . . ."

"They've gone off with our clothes. . . ." Ashby said. "It wasn't enough to put us in jail, but . . ." He stepped close to the door.

The sheriff held up a hand. "Now Ashby," he said, "they jest put 'em on to wear 'round the pool hall. First they bet whether they would fit 'em, and then when they did, they decided to wear 'em 'round the pool hall to show 'em off before I knew it . . ."

"It does look like with all the graft they collect from bootleggers and whores that they could afford to buy whatever kind of suits they want," Ashby said.

Turkey held up the hand again, a sign like a benediction.

But Ashby said, "Well, what are you gonna do?"

Bevo spoke then. "Go get 'em."

Turkey turned on him. "Don't you talk to me. You ain't no gentleman."

Bevo reddened, but stared hard at the sheriff.

"Go get 'em," Ashby said.

"Now, Ashby, I've sent a nigger after 'em, and as soon as they get enough of showin' 'em off . . . See, Ashby?" Turkey was hoarse.

Ashby sat down on the bunk. He looked at Bevo and then at the sheriff. "I have had some crazy things happen to me. But I never got put in jail for defending a lady in a cat house from a drunken sheriff and got put in a cell with a millionaire mill owner and had my clothes stolen by the deputy sheriffs to show off at a pool hall. I never had that happen to me before."

The sheriff seemed relieved. He leaned close to the bars and pointed a finger through them at Bevo. "He been tellin' you them lies, too?"

"I never said I was a millionaire," Bevo said.

But Ashby was watching the sheriff, his arms folded and his mouth grim. "Don't you go adding slander to your sins, Turkey," he said. "You leave him alone. You walk easy."

The sheriff laughed as if he had not heard. "He told me he was Bevo Banes. Bevo Banes. Yessir. Fellow like him claiming to be Bevo Banes." He gazed at Bevo. He shook his bald head. Bevo dropped his eyes in helpless, quiet anger.

Ashby smiled. "You know Bevo Banes?"

"I know he ain't him," the sheriff said.

"You ever see Bevo Banes?" Ashby said.

"Why, no," the sheriff said. "I've seen that Hampton fellow that works for him. I've seen Hampton at the Chamber of Commerce. But Bevo Banes . . . Ain't much of nobody seen Bevo Banes. He sends Hampton out to 'tend to business outside the mill. Timid sort of fellow, he is, they say. He jest lives out there with his millworkers. . . ."

"That's me," Bevo said, nodding. "That's me, I reckon."

Ashby did not say anything. He merely nodded and gestured with his hand toward Bevo.

The sheriff did not want to believe it. "He ain't old enough."

"I'm thirty-nine," Bevo said.

"He ain't got no millionaire look about him," the sheriff said.

"Sheriff," Ashby said, "meet Bevo Banes. You've put a millionaire in jail. I reckon next time you run for office, your opponent will get a big campaign fund from Bevo Banes. . . ."

Belief pushed painfully into the sheriff's mind. He looked at Bevo. "I wouldn't want no hard feelings. . . ."

"That's all right," Bevo said.

"It's not all right," Ashby said. "Nothing is all right unless you get us out of here. . . ." He rose. "And quick."

The sheriff backed away. "I'm mighty sorry. I done repented ever'thing I done, Ashby. If you boys will jest be patient . . ."

"What about our clothes?" Ashby said.

"I swear to God," the sheriff said, "if I have to walk down and undress that pair in front of the preacher on Main Street, I'll have them suits here in a hour. I'm put out with the way they been actin'. I try to treat my friends right in jail, and I ain' gonna have no such carryings-on. . . ." He smiled, sickly. "You boys jest wait a little while. I'll be back. . . ." He went waddling off, and they heard him muttering along the corridor.

Ashby sat rocking and grinning to himself on the bunk. "I wouldn't take a crop of dollar cotton for that look on his face."

"Even him," Bevo said, standing now impatiently by the barred door. "Even him. I don't look like a gentleman to anybody."

# Chapter VII

They had washed and shaved and fed themselves. They had tended to the needs of Temp, and now, in the car, had left the town safely behind. Temp slept, his body loose and sprawled on the back seat, the gold-rimmed glasses he wore resting precariously near the tip of his blunt nose. "You need glasses, Temp?" Father had said, when Temp had told him how much they would cost. "Yassir," Temp had said. "I needs 'em." "For seeing?" Father had said. "Yassir," Temp had said, "For seeing." "Whose seeing?" Father had said. "Yours or those field hand darkies?" Temp had grinned and Father had given him the money. They both knew—glasses would mark him, better than a white shirt, as no field hand darky, the sign of his pleasant snobbery.

Ashby suspected that they hurt his eyes. He looked over the top of the rims most of the time. But when he went to town on Saturday, he stood on Front Street, looking through the lenses, and sometimes ostentatiously reading a newspaper, his head bent and brow furrowed in a gesture so identical with Father's attitude in his library, that Ashby wondered if he had copied Father consciously or had just absorbed by intuitive osmosis the white man's manner. The other Negroes on Front

Street watched him respectfully, awesomely: he had gold-rimmed glasses through which he actually read, and he had more gold teeth than any Negro in that county, teeth for which he had sacrificed perfectly good bicuspids. The red-ginghamed black girls smiled archly at him. He watched them gravely, remembering perhaps; but he left them to the rutting bucks. His fires were ash, and decorum was now his passion.

Which was why Ashby resented for him the indignity he had suffered from the sheriff. When, out of jail, he and Bevo had returned to the car at Miranda's, Temp had uncoiled himself from the cramped floor of the car, where he had slept the frightened night, and had looked at Ashby thankfully, but with pride sapped—no longer marked, apart, aloof, but one with those others of his color who knew how it was to flee into burrows. The mark of distinction—the teeth, the glasses—meant nothing. Like a field hand he had been chased and like a field hand he had run. He hung his head.

He hung his head, Ashby thought, exactly as he might have hung it if somebody had yanked his glasses off and ground them underfoot and then jerked from his mouth the golden teeth. A man needed the symbol of the man he would be.

*All I can say for Grant,* Granny always said, *is that he would not take General's Lee's sword at the surrender. For a whiskey-swilling hog of a man he had that strange moment of rare insight. A soldier beaten is a soldier still, and if he cannot be a soldier in his mind, I don't know what he can be. He'd be nothing, nothing. In his mind a man makes the man he'd be, and if you destroy the man in his mind, there's nothing left. Nothing. Maybe Grant knew that at Appomattox that day. Anyhow, there was more of God than rum inside him then. He could have disinherited Lee, and he didn't.*

*Disinherited.* He made the word soundlessly with his lips and looked covertly at Bevo beside him to see if he had noticed. He could remember the way the word had sounded in her mouth. It had sounded like a small quiet yawp of doom. And she had meant it to sound so: to divest a man not alone of his legacy but of the badge of his legacy was unutterable shame to her. Let him keep his badge, for God's sake. Leave him his little ribbons, his medal struck in bronze; let him hang his sword where he may look upon it.

Yet a man could keep a badge and it have no meaning: Temp still slept there with his glasses, his golden teeth. And it might perhaps be even worse that a man should have had no badge, ever, no sword at all, nothing to be deprived of. Like, Ashby thought, like me and Bevo. He glanced again at the man beside him. Bevo sat edgily on the seat, his great bulk unmoving but taut. He wants to be a gentleman, Ashby thought, or he thinks he wants to be. He wants to find whatever it is that marks a gentleman: a way of tying a tie, perhaps, or a way of speaking. But of course what he really wants is to belong to some identifiable species of humanity. Because he lives now in some uninhabited middle ground. He has done his father's work and now finds no more to do. When he was fighting his father's battle, he belonged in a certain place. But now he belongs nowhere. He is not worker or rebel or gentleman of leisure. He is unsworded.

And so am I, he thought, and have been always. He let his eyes go far down the road ahead. It was warming as they went southward, and the land, near to the March burgeoning, had the haunted look of late afternoon at winter end when the purple earth smells of charred pine and rank swamp-muck. The sun labored against the mist of the hills, and its light curdled yellowly in the milky wood smoke. Many years he had seen the land like this, yet today it seemed new. On Traveler, Lee without a sword might have found the Arlington hills strange ground and the sea-spermy odor of the Potomac a foreign smell. Unsworded, a man belonged nowhere.

"What you thinking about?" Bevo said, suddenly. "You look like you talking to yourself."

"Am," Ashby said, and grinned, musingly. "Like a damn neurotic." He let the car coast down a hill. "Too much Byron and Shelley. Too damned much heart clutching. Country's full of it." Bevo nodded, abstractedly, and, wandering in some mind-country of his own, said nothing.

Still, Ashby thought, the land had a strange look on it. Oh, if somebody should ask me what land is this, I could answer, talking easily and familiarly, and not necessarily like a travel brochure.

I could say there are hillsides in it rutted and gapped, barren now, so that the empty shacks perched upon them rot and tumble about their tenantry of field rats and spiders. And there are other hills not yet sterile, but upon them the cotton grows weakly and the stunted corn withers untasselled, and these are the province of humped men who curse alike the unproductive earth and the ironic fecundity of their own loins which get, from the racked fertile bodies of their wives, numberless plague-ridden children the land cannot nourish nor the sky succor. And yet there is also the Delta, flat reaches of rich loam where cotton pushes waist-high on a tall man, and the tall men—and their firm silken women—attend only to the god river and his son soil, and paganly gamble every day on the whim of their capricious lords. Yet outside of river and soil they have no masters, unless it be their own private ghosts, which they have had the leisure and the wealth to nurse, until now their every mansion is ghost-ridden. *The Delta?* Granny always said. *I approve of it. It's the only place I know where God works for us against the Yankees. Everywhere else the Yankees steal what we have and take it North. But there God steals the Yankees' topsoil and brings it South. Although someday, no doubt, they'll try to reverse the Mississippi River and take the Delta's black dirt back to Illinois and Iowa.*

"What you laughing at?" Bevo said.

"Thinking what Granny said about the Delta," Ashby said.

"I worked once in a lumber mill in the Delta," Bevo said. "Saw a fellow get his arm cut off. He held a handful of sawdust to the stump to stanch the blood."

Ashby grunted. Yes, and there are the sawdust piles burning day and night in the lumber towns, the treeless, sun-stricken towns of houses huddled together in the center of circling acres of raw stumps.

"He was from Oxford," Bevo said. "Stood there holding the sawdust to his bleeding stump and turned to me—I hadn't moved since it happened—and said, 'I got to go home. I reckon I'll jest git myself on to Oxford.' That's what he said, and Oxford fifty miles away. He took two steps north, though, before he fell."

And yes, Oxford. There are towns with courthouse squares where the Lost Cause is commemorated with an iron cannon and a marble soldier with a marble musket. The square is stained with amber spittle, the grass of it worn by heel-rocking politicians, and the air of it laden with the flat malarial voices of countrymen. But radiating out from it there are oak-roofed streets, lined with Victorian gingerbread houses set behind wrought iron fences. People sit on their galleries and rock and peer sharp-eyed at young couples in the summer-evening air. They lick their lips like lechers, following the pairs with their eyes.

"I think," Bevo said, "I think he was a nigger, but I'm not sure. Nobody troubled to ask him. He was that near to white, and labor was short, so that even the boss never bothered. He lived with the white workers."

There, Ashby thought, but not at home. At home he lived in an unpainted shack in niggertown. A creek full of sewage overflows it regularly in spring, overturns the outhouses and licks at the precarious brick pillars on which the warped timbers of the houses rest. In the jazz joint with its windows encrusted with dust and dead flies, he drinks moonshine from a tin can and dances with the yellowest girl in the room and sings with a gramophone in a loud hoarse voice that drowns out the sound of the spiritual from the African Baptist church next door. A pair of dice rattle in his pocket.

"I never knew anything about him except that he said he'd worked once at a . . . house in Memphis."

"Cat house?" Ashby said. He let the wheel straighten after a curve.

"Uh."

Ashby grinned. "In college, we used to go to Memphis. If somebody asked us what for, we'd say for an Arkansas ride. Every whore in Memphis was born on a farm in Arkansas."

"They say New Orleans is the place," Bevo said.

He nodded. "Was," he said, thinking, Maybe I should count the ruins, too. If you're going to tell about a land, you can't leave out the ruins. There are the shells of houses standing gaunt on land the wild grape has reclaimed. A corner of tumbled brick, a lone column yet upright, a marble statue of some naked Grecian maiden with a drop of rainwater in her navel, a burial ground with moss greening the Latin inscriptions, one great fire-blackened chimney towering above the oaks—there are these to mark what has gone.

"Was?" Bevo said. "Ain't it still?"

"What?" Ashby said.

"New Orleans?"

So much is gone, he thought. Even since I have lived. "No," he said. "Not like before. Basin Street is gone. The girls don't sit any more in red kimonos on the stoops of their cribs and part their garments to show off their sagging wares." He laughed shortly. "Oh, you can still walk through that New Orleans smell of wet rope and caulking tar and chicory and women, but no gray shutter'll open and a female voice call, so that, looking up, you'll see her nakedness in the dark window. There used to be a house where you handed the Negro butler ten dollars in your hat, and named your pleasure for the night. They had octoroons, with high cheekbones and smooth gold skin and the blackest hair and bloodiest red lips you ever saw." He shook his head. "All gone now. The cribs cleaned out, and they're gonna put a housing project there. And all over the Quarter, the historical associations of clubwomen are busy 'restoring' the place. Without the girls of course. They only want to paint the husk, and the life that was in the husk—well they forget that. So the Quarter's gone—what in hell do walls, painted or unpainted, mean by themselves anyhow. It's what they hold. And that's gone."

"You mean the girls?"

"No," Ashby said. "A whole way of living."

"Does it matter to you?"

"No." That was what was wrong: there was nothing in all the land that mattered. Even could he have brought back that Vieux Carré of fifteen years ago, even could he have restored the mansions the wild grapes had taken, there would have been no meaning in it for him.

What was he anyhow to that land or that land to him? He farmed it, somebody might point out. But the fact was that a hoe or a cultivator had no special meaning for him. He neither liked nor disliked them. They were not Lee's sword. A man without a sword, without a pair of gold-rimmed glasses: he is a stranger in his own land.

"Do you believe that the earth belongs to the living?" he said, all at once, to Bevo.

" 'The earth belongs to the living?' " Bevo said.

Ashby nodded. "I think Jefferson said it. It's something Granny's always saying. I don't know that I believe it." It was darkening; he gazed intently ahead and then reached and switched on the lights. "I think maybe we're all born disinherited. I think we've got to make the earth ours. We've got to buy it all over again."

"With what?" Bevo watched him curiously.

"With . . . our sweat, I reckon. With—hell, I don't know what with. But I don't feel like an old citizen here. I don't really feel there's any place I belong. Because I haven't paid for any place." He laughed. "I'm talking like a Presbyterian. Presbyterians are forever in debt—to God. Maybe we all are."

"I don't belong anywhere, either," Bevo said. "But I'd think you would."

Ashby shook his head. "Listen," he said. "When I look out yonder . . ." He nodded his head at the rolling land, deep purple with sundown. "It all looks strange. I don't belong to any of it." He touched his lips with his tongue. "I thought once this morning that if it'd been possible for us to take Temp's case into court—if I could have fought that sheriff in court—I would have earned a place in this land. Then it would have looked different to me."

"It might yet," Bevo said. "You might yet have to fight them over Temp. If a fight is what you need . . ."

Ashby nodded. "A fight." He stopped again, and wet his lips with his tongue. He did not find it particularly easy and natural to talk about himself. But he went on anyhow. "When I was four, I learned how to write. I took a book out of the library and I copied the word off the title. I learned it all by myself. Wrote it on a tablet that had thick gray paper with blue lines. The word I wrote was *war*. I remember I made it three lines high. And when I showed it to Father and he smiled and said, 'Why, yes, you've made a word. Now you can make a lot more.' 'How many?' I said. 'Why, as many words as there are in the world, and more, I reckon, if you care to make new ones up.' I remember laughing like in a delirium. I was a word-maker. I could take a pencil and make words and everybody would know what the words I made meant. Somehow that one word sort of joined me up with mankind. And for a while I didn't feel like a newcomer on earth." He grunted. "I didn't even feel little underneath those goddamned Corinthian columns. You know?"

Bevo sat, his face half-turned, listening. "I reckon," he said.

"Well . . ." Ashby said, baffled for words. "Hell, you remember the first girl you ever had?"

"You mean . . . ?" Bevo said.

Ashby nodded. The car took the curve, sweetly, at sixty.

"You thought it would be like in books. Or I did, because—well, because of the way they brought me up, so that I had a hard time separating what the real world was like compared to the book world they taught me. And I thought having a girl would be—you know—sweet words and the flesh satisfied without the flesh ever really being there at all. You know how writers do it. It's like the ocean, like a wave lifting you up, up . . ." He grunted again. "Or like flying. Like flying higher and higher and then dropping. Always that way in books. Never flesh and friction. No arms or thighs, no damned anatomy involved; or none that you really feel. And hell, I believed it. Until I was nineteen . . ." He pulled the car to one side to let a truck pass; it was dark enough for the light to dazzle his eyes. "It was in the summer. I was going to summer school at the University, and a bunch of us had rooms in the upstairs of an old house. The woman that owned the house had died, and there wasn't anything downstairs at all, no furniture I mean. Some of the fellows pulled the mattresses off the empty beds, and lined 'em up in the vacant dining room. For strictly amorous purposes." He could see in his mind the long dark paneled room, the thin line of street light seeping through the heavy dusty draperies. He could smell the musty mattresses, and hear the orgiastic sounds, liquid, smothered. "Well, that was where I learned what the books never tell. Her name was Freddie, and she was a blond country gal, who had taken up her profession because she just plain liked it, and not because of any mean stepfather or of any dirty cad's deserting her at the wrong moment, the way the books explain it. She just plain liked it, and she didn't make anything poetic out of it either. And when she got through with me—well, I don't know, that was another moment I felt bigger than those damned columns. I felt big enough to raise up some columns of my own kind, and not just go on living in the shadow of some blasted columns made by somebody a hundred years ago who had copied 'em from somebody who lived a couple of thousand years ago. I belonged to the living." He shook his head. "But it didn't last. The feeling."

He pulled a cigarette from the package in his coat pocket and pushed in the lighter on the dash; he brought it glowing to the cigarette and the smoke snaked around him.

"There's something more than the word and the woman,"

he said. Then he shrugged, and said, jeeringly, "Papa wants a sword. Papa wants to be a hero. Papa even likes to pretend that maybe that sheriff is chasing him now, instead of telling his fat wife good-bye and setting out to seek him a virgin."

"Maybe he is," Bevo said.

"Is what? Chasing us?" Ashby said. "Hell, unless somebody saw us and phoned him, I don't reckon he's even given Temp a thought. And even if he did . . ." He grunted. "I'm a man that's been overfed on romantic pap. I need me some corn whiskey to take the taste out of my mouth."

"Now?" Bevo said.

"Why not?" Ashby said.

"No reason, I reckon."

Ashby reached and opened the compartment on the dash and pulled out the flask with Honeybreeches' name on it. With one hand on the steering wheel, he shook it. No sound.

"Damn," he said. "I forgot. Temp." He dropped the empty flask on the seat.

"It don't matter to me," Bevo said. "I wouldn't want to add any whiskey to those onions I ate. Between them and that stuff that deputy sprinkled on my suit, I reckon I smell loud enough anyhow, without adding any whiskey."

Ashby laughed. "That deputy's toilet water does sort of smell like essence of polecat, doesn't it? Well, when we get to Ephe's you can go in town and buy yourself another suit."

Now that he had thought of it, he wanted that drink. He wanted to feel the sharp burning sweetness of alcohol on his tongue and he did not mind the idea of drunkenness. There was no reason for getting drunk, but neither was there any reason for not getting drunk. There was no reason in the world why he shouldn't get drunk. "I know what we'll do." He stepped on the accelerator and watched the dash needle touch seventy-five. Through the crack in the window beside him, the wind whistled thinly. The purple land went swiftly past; the hills dropped and settled into flatlands. Temp slept silently.

"You're goin' mighty fast," Bevo said.

"I'm a fast man," he said, grinning. "I figure on plunging us into adventure, as the books say."

"Jest so you don't plunge us into no ditch," Bevo said.

The swamp was thick on either side of the road now. It was quite dark. On the back seat, Temp began to snore, softly. The side road appeared before Ashby expected it. In the darkness, only a white post marked it. He stopped the car so quickly that it slid several feet, tires squealing, before it jerked to stillness. Then he turned in the seat and backed carefully to where the post was, and then drove from the highway and over a clattering wooden bridge which crossed the ditch and into the tree-canopied darkness of the swamp road. He stopped the car and sat a moment puffing his cigarette. Then he reached again into the open compartment and found his flashlight.

"What you aim to do?" Bevo said. His voice was hushed, the way a man's voice often is by darkness.

"Come on with me," Ashby said.

"Where?" Bevo said, still whispering.

"See a friend of mine," Ashby said.

Bevo nodded. "Temp comin' too?"

"He's asleep," Ashby said, glancing toward the back seat. "No, he'll be all right." He turned off the lights and stepped from the car onto the mucky road. Bevo followed and stood beside him. Ashby closed the car door quietly, so as not to awaken Temp.

"A swamp is a whispery place," Bevo said.

"Come on," Ashby said, whispering back to him. He bounded into the woods, through the tangled vines and bushes that switched his face, walked a way through the wet undergrowth until he came to the place he knew. He put out an arm to stop Bevo. He heard their breathing in the dark, quick steamy panting. Then he reached in his pocket and found his wallet and pulled a bill out. Only then did he turn on the flashlight. He found the stump, marked with a cross in white paint. He put the bill under the rock and then, very deliberately, standing exactly over the stump and rock and bill, he flashed the light three times; off and on and then off again, he made the signal, then waited, and repeated himself. He did this perhaps a dozen times before anything happened. Bevo stood close beside him, quiet except for his heavy breathing; he was a man who could wait and wonder in silence. Then at last the answer came: three lights from a distance, so far they seemed no more than firefly size.

"Look," Bevo said.

"Yeah. Come on. Back to the car."

Bevo followed him. "But he answered you. Why don't we wait here? What is it anyhow? You flashin' that light, and then that other light . . . 'Minds me of a picture show."

"When we see that light flash again . . ." Ashby said, ducking under a branch and onto the road, "we'll go back and there'll be a gallon of the best rye a man ever tasted, sittin' right side that stump."

"Why don't you jest go git it," Bevo said. "Why you got to go through all that light flashing?"

"So if Jake up yonder should ever get caught, I couldn't say he'd ever sold me any whiskey. So nobody could ever catch us, me payin' him and him givin' me the whiskey straight. The way this is, it's like he just finds a ten dollar bill and I find a gallon jug in the swamp. Just accident, you might say. . . ." He laughed in the darkness and leaned against the car.

Bevo stood in the middle of the road, and regarded him a moment in silence. "But you know. You know it's Jake and Jake knows—well, he knows it's somebody wants whiskey. So even if you never see one another, you still know it's Jake you're buying whiskey from."

"Why, now," Ashby said. "How do I know it's Jake? It might be any of a hundred folks. I couldn't swear in court it was Jake. I don't see him in yonder. . . ." He pointed into the thick trees.

Bevo let out a loud breath. "It looks like to me you got to have a mind all twisted up like a pile o' thread. . . ."

"For what?" Ashby said.

"To be a gentleman," Bevo said. "You say what you don't mean, and don't say what you do mean. You do one thing and call it another. Miss Miranda serves straight whiskey and calls it wine. You buy whiskey from a bootlegger and talk about losing a ten dollar bill and just 'finding' a gallon jug o' whiskey. I ain't nothin' but a plain man, that says what he aims to say, and calls what he does by its right name, and I reckon I never will learn . . ." Bevo stopped, suddenly, and his whole huge figure leaned forward a bit, ear cocked toward the highway.

They both heard the sound almost as soon as they saw the parked car on the shoulder of the highway. The sound was a voice, and a familiar one. Ashby, hearing it, felt the blood freeze in him, and then as quickly pump forcefully through his veins; the taste of sudden excitement was sharp on his tongue.

Before he could speak, he heard the smothered fear in Temp's voice. From the back of the car Temp muttered, "Lawd God. Lawd God . . ." His head peered from the back window.

The first voice, on the highway, was loud now. "Dadgumit, I'm gonna git me some deputies that ain't always about to wet thei' pants. I never heard o' nothing like it in all my days. . . ."

There was no doubt now. It was Turkey.

"Lawd God," Temp said. "It's him. Mr. Ashby . . ."

"Hush," Ashby said. "Be still . . ." He heard the men in the bushes, just off the highway, the lash of branches and the rustle of leaves as they moved into the underbrush of the swamp. He put his hand out toward the car, not turning his eyes from the direction of the sounds. He thought of the pistol in the compartment; he calculated how swift he could grasp it. His mind worked fiercely, thinking of what he would do if they continued to come, if they advanced nearer.

Then he heard the plaintive rasp from Turkey's throat. "You gonna stop in purgatory to piss on the way to heaven," he said.

Ashby, tense with waiting, felt the laughter grip the muscles in his stomach. But Bevo, who had walked a few paces up the road, still stood immobile in the darkness, his eyes straining toward the highway and the lights of the deputies in the swamp to their right. And Temp moaned softly in his throat—an unearthly, fearful sound.

"Hush," Ashby said. "They're only taking a leak, but if you don't hush, they'll be . . ." Now the sound of what the deputies were doing came to them, and above the steady jet, the wailing anger of the sheriff.

"Nobody never told me a sheriff had to be wetnurse to his deputies. As if I ain't got enough with them hounds and with the Christian vote gonna leave me on account of how Ashby Pelham done this mornin' in jail, and with . . . As if I ain't plagued enough, I got to stop a manhunt on account of yo' dadblasted bladders. . . ."

Bevo was back, beside him again. "You hear him?" he whispered. "He said 'manhunt.'"

Ashby, head thrust forward to listen, was full of both laughter and sudden worry. He nodded. "We're not the only men he could be . . ."

"Hell, Turkey," a deputy said, "If you would feed us better whiskey, we might could hold the dew in the lily a little longer . . ."

Ashby chuckled, but the sheriff's voice cut through the sound he made. "Oh, my God," the sheriff said. "Will you please hurry up. That there Ashby Pelham will be clean to the Miss'ippi River by now, the way you all . . ."

"Well," one of the deputies said, "We ain't got no business crossin' the county line after him anyhow. I never heard o' nothing crazy as this."

"You hear?" Temp said. "Lawd, Mr. Ashby . . ."

"Hush . . ." Ashby said. There was no laughing in him now.

"Oh, you never," the sheriff said to the deputy. "Crazy, is it? Well, I want to tell you you oughta consider yourself lucky to be in on this. You needn't quote no law about county lines to me. I know it. But I know too that I'm gonna find that Ashby and then I'm gonna git the sheriff of whatever county

I find him in and have that sheriff arrest him and then turn him over to me. Him and the nigger. And I got reasons for doin' this myself instead of jest leavin' it to some no 'count sheriff in some backwater county. I got reasons bigger than a deputy can understand, and so I ain' tellin'. But somethin' mighty important is liable to happen to ever' blest one of us, and what are you doin'?"

"What's he talkin' about?" Bevo said. "How does he know we got Temp? And why's he so hell bent . . . ?"

"Sh . . . h . . . h." With his mind, Ashby urged the sheriff away, waiting tensely and crossing his fingers against Jake shining the flashlight too soon.

"Hurry up . . ." Turkey said. "Or have you thunk up some other job you got to do?"

They heard the deputies leaving the woods now. Then the car door slammed, and there was the sound of another door opening. It was then that Bevo whispered, "There's that fellow's flashlight. . . ."

Ashby said, "We can't answer it. Not yet . . ."

"Fer God's sake," Temp whispered from the car. "Fer God's sake, Mr. Ashby, let's us go . . ."

Ashby said nothing. He gripped the barrel of the light in his hand, waiting. Then he heard Turkey.

"Did I see a light in that there swamp?"

"Lightning bugs," a voice said. "Do you aim to go, or you want us to git them bloodhounds and let 'em lose you in the swamp?"

"You a fine one to ask me do I aim to go," Turkey said. "You bladder, you!" Then Ashby heard him climb muttering into the car and shut the door. The motor started and he saw the red taillight of the car disappear.

"Thank God," Temp said. "Thank God. But he after us." His voice was that of a terrified child awakened from a nightmare. Ashby touched his hand where it lay on the window ledge of the car. Temp's face, the gold-rimmed glasses reflecting the least bit of starlight, looked up at him. Ashby patted the hand.

"Get up off your knees," he said, "and sit back on the seat and relax. He'll never get you."

"That fellow's flashin' ag'in," Bevo said.

Ashby handed him the light. "Flash right back," Ashby said. "And I'll run in and get it."

"The Lawd led us off that highway," Temp said.

"I needed a drink," Ashby said. "It was the devil that saved us."

"Don't talk that-a-way," Temp said. He held tightly to Ashby's hand. "This ain't no time to make the Lawd mad."

"You goin' get that whiskey?" Bevo said.

"I don't aim to leave it," Ashby said. He turned toward the swamp.

"Well," Bevo said quietly. "Maybe you will need that sword."

Ashby leaped the ditch, laughing. "A cap pistol," he said. There was nothing to do but outrun the sheriff and get to Ephe's ahead of him. "I reckon a cap pistol will do for this."

"Maybe," Bevo said.

# Chapter VIII

They came to Ephraim's after a long journey by the devious back country roads. As they rode along beside the swamplands that stretched down to the river and were here marked with black and white signs bearing the name Ephraim Pelham and the legend POSTED, KEEP OUT. Bevo joked with Ashby. "For a man that thought escaping that sheriff was a cap pistol job," he said, "you have sho taken us a ride. Through every hog-rut in the state. Or don't you think you'll have as easy a time shaking the sheriff as you said?"

"I don't know," Ashby said.

Bevo stirred uncomfortably on the seat. "Well," he said, "we have sho played the dad-gumdest game of cops and robbers anybody ever played."

"Yes, maybe so," Ashby said. "You're likely right. I reckon I inherit a tendency to cops and robbers, anyhow. You might, to be exact, call it an old Southern tendency. Or does everybody have it, everywhere wars are remembered? Well, anyhow—we didn't call it cops and robbers. I came up before movies." He mused. "We played what we called 'dueling.' And we played 'War Between the States' and always had our biggest fight over who was going to be the Yankee." He could remember the dust in the stable yard sifting through his toes. They had peashooters which Num made of bamboo cut at the river bank. Their ammunition was hard green chinaberries from the trees next the stable. And now Dale Tarnin, who had nearly always had to be the Yankee because he was smaller and because his mother had come from Cambridge, Massachusetts, and so was what Num called a 'bluebelly' (Ashby had been long learning the term was figurative, and had yearned for one sight of her strangely-hued abdomen)—now Dale Tarnin, who had so unreasonably insisted that if he had to be the Yankee then he must be acknowledged winner of the battle, was dead of typhoid induced by raw oysters bought in Tampa, Florida from a Negro huckster who had unwittingly dredged them from a part of the bay too close to the sewerage pipes. Dale was dead and Bill Fitzpatrick, who had always found himself a cock feather for his straw hat and by virtue of it had become General Jeb Stewart and proceeded to pull his rank on Ashby who was always only Colonel Ashby Pelham, was now a retired Naval flier, ten years out of Annapolis, less than that out of Pensacola, and less than that out of the plane in which he had crashed in a field in South Alabama, whence he had been taken with only one leg and an even more painful wound somewhere inside him which Ashby saw only on those occasions when, in the midst of a chess game on the veranda, Bill would look up at a sound, and watch with a veteran's regret the slow and beautiful wheeling of a blue and silver plane. "General Stuart," Ashby would say. "Your move." "Yes, Colonel." Bill would smile. And when Ashby won, he would say, "Why, you bastard, you! Colonel Pelham, hell! You're Tecumseh Sherman in disguise. Picking on women, chillun and wounded soldiers . . ." The memory of dead battles, fought and now meaningless, was sharp in them. "A drink, General Sherman?" He would look a moment at Bill, standing cane in hand on the fine aluminum leg. "Sho, General Stuart. Anything you say, sir." The memory was sharp.

It was sharp in him in the night when over the silken shuttle of the motor, Bevo said, "Cops and robbers." Perhaps it was childish to look for a battle, as childish as the night dreams of adolescence when in the close miasmic night he had lain awake and dreamed of saving fair women from the cold stone towers of some Gothic bluebeard. He thought of that dream that morning when, having passed the long miles of swampland which bordered Ephraim's acres, he caught sight of Ephraim's house with the great cupola and realized that it had always been that cupola—though it was made of wood and he dreamed it stone—in which his fair lady had been imprisoned. And Uncle Ephe the bluebeard? He did not remember.

They came on the place by a back road that bisected the land and ran along the side of the house into the highway. Ashby stopped the car by a springhouse on the pasture rim. It was here that, without thought, he reached into the dash compartment for the pistol and put it into his coat pocket. When he stepped from the car, he made some overly casual remark about how the land there deep in the south was greening already and how the breeze that touched him was spring-laden.

When he made a movement as if to go on to the house, Temp complained briefly. He had not forgot the last time he had been left for "a little while." "Can't us go with you? You ain' got to leave us . . . ?"

"I got to make sure," Ashby said, and arrested his hand just short of patting the gun which bulged in his pocket. He looked at Bevo, as if he waited for Bevo to say, "Still playing cops and robbers?" But Bevo only nodded, quietly, and Ashby turned and walked swiftly along the gravel road through the wet fog of morning, his eyes on the house ahead. It stood on a rise of land, white in the sunlight, its wooden turrets and gables, its elaborately-paned windows, its five chimneys, its towers and bays giving it a look of harlotry in that land, like a bold woman trying to appear what she was not. It was no Gothic castle, but plainly only a wooden imitation, and Ashby wondered that anyone could have built so ugly a structure and one so foreign to the soil it stood upon. Granny had given Ephe the money to build the house when he was married, since the home place had been left, naturally, to Father and then in turn was to go to Ashby. But when Granny had taken Ephe and Evelina and Miranda as her own children when Great Uncle Dave and Great Aunt Martha had died swiftly in a yellow fever epidemic, Granny had always looked on them as heirs to whatever the Pelhams had. So Ephe had got this house, and, though Evelina had never left the home place nor ever asked more than to live there, Ashby suspected that Granny had given Miranda the money which eventually bought the house she came home to when she left the snuff salesman.

Looking on the naked ugliness of the house ahead, Ashby remembered Granny, a long time ago, saying, "I hate Ephe's house. But then Ephe never belonged in the home place, and I reckon he belongs in that place he lives in, though it's not a house that belongs to . . ." And, in the way she had, she had waved her hand around the garden, taking in the clematis and smilax and magnolia and oak, and said no more.

He had not thought about that in a long time, but now he remembered wondering what she had meant that day: she and Father both had a way of talking in strange half-hints about Ephraim. Even when Ephraim had been governor of the state, Granny had never shown any pride in him; when folks spoke of the fortune Ephe had made from his cotton mills, Granny's nose wrinkled in an imperceptible sniff; and she went reluctantly each year for her winter visit to his house: but of these things Ashby could never remember hearing the reason. He himself did not know Ephraim, but he took it as natural that a man did not ever know or really understand his own folks. He had hunted and played poker and drunk and swapped stories with Uncle Ephe, and they had remained to each other no more than pleasant strangers. They met perhaps twice a year, briefly.

Now he was at the gate to the back drive, and he opened it and went through, along the brick pavement and the rock-bordered flower beds massed with pale and sickly chrysanthemums.

Everything about the yard was swept neatly. No leaves were allowed to enrich the soil there, and here in the back, screened from the front yard by the precisely-cut privet which flanked the house on two sides, no grass grew under the trees and the ground was red and sterile in its swept cleanliness. Ahead of Ashby, to one side of the back yard, was the long garage and stable, and attached to it the brick cottage, which, of all the buildings there, seemed the only structure to have sprung from the land beneath it, and so seemed beautiful. He had always looked on it with a strange fascination; around it the Cherokee roses, with trunks of a size he had never seen in their wild cousins, twisted their thorny branches through a welter of ivy, and though their vines were now bare with frost, he could remember them in June, their great white blossoms luminous in the night. In that barren and geometric yard, the cottage alone was wild and rich; the leaves filled its sagging gutters and piled up around the rose and ivy roots. He had never understood that, either; it was now the house that Tilda, the cook, lived in, but why it should be spared the rake and broom and pruning shears and the tape measure which had been imposed on the rest of that ground, he could not understand. Once he had tried to ask Aunt Semantha, but the mention of the place had set her to staring into some time he knew nothing about and then to crying those soundless tears which she tried to pretend did not even exist, and he had never said anything about it again. He was aware always that in this place there were unanswered questions and legions of old remembrances.

He felt this in looking wonderingly for a moment at the cottage. Then he turned abruptly from it and from his own thought, went to the back door and knocked. Tilda came, her red sandals flapping rythmically at her thin heels: he watched her through the glass of the door. She turned the knob and put only her head out. Her hair was elaborately coiffured. It was straight and shining black but she had curled it under at the back of her neck and had made this same kind of undercurl straight across her forehead. She smelled faintly of rum.

She blinked a second at him. "Well," she said. "Mr. Ashby . . ." Below the fiercely black hair, her skin was the color of a flooding river, a light creamy tan. She was perhaps thirty-five, he guessed, for certainly she had been in that kitchen some twenty years. And though she did not at first glance seem that old, when he looked closer he could see that there was about her a kind of distraught virginity, a certain miserliness in the way she seemed to shrink her body, which a man would know instantly she had never used at all, but had hoarded in a cask her mind had made.

He grinned at her. "Howdy, Tilda." How many times had he turned from the dream of a fair woman rescued from the silo-like towers of that house and bestowing on him, her hero, a square of lace-edged linen scented with lilac and a chaste kiss and so sending him off celibate to even greater chivalries, to a dream of Tilda, who had been his boyish vision of earth, his shameful fantasy of hot bronze skin and what he could remember Great Uncle Vance calling "breastworks worth a campaign, gentlemen, worth a frontal assault and God knows promising delight to a flank attack." And now she stood there before him, having swept the door open, and she was so unearthly, so lost to flesh that the red shoes below the hem of her white uniform were somehow outrageous, like the painted whore-face some maiden ladies will adopt desperately at fifty, as if color could hide the wastage of their lives.

"Why you come to the back door?" she said.

He did not answer her. He went past her into the kitchen, hot and filled with the odors of a breakfast he saw they had already eaten: the plates yellow with egg were piled on the sink and the coffee smelled cold and creamy. He felt his tiredness and his hunger.

"Where's everybody?" he said. He hesitated, one hand on the door to the butler's pantry which led to the dining room.

"Your Granny out taking the sun and gettin' 'dew in her joints,' as she say," Tilda said. "And Mr. Ephe . . . He in his office, talking to the governor on the long distance, last time I listen. . . ."

He grinned again at her. She was always listening; she was a great polisher of doorknobs, and keyholes attracted her like a drug. Snooping, Uncle Vance used to say, is a disease of virgins.

"And Miss Semantha," she said, her soft eyes unfocused, so that she did not notice his grin, "she in the parlor havin' her tea."

"Tea?" he said. "Granny got her in the tea-habit?"

Tilda licked her lips. In one hand, a dish towel hung limply. "We got to have our tea," she said. "Me and Miss Semantha. We got the high blood pressure." When she leaned toward him, her uniform parted from her and he could see the silken skin of one virginal breast, and he could smell the rum stronger now.

"Yessir," she said, pleased about something, a mysterious smile parting her lips. "Yessir. Got the high blood pressure."

"And you take tea," he said, musingly, pushing his flat palm against the swinging door.

"Yessir. Miss Semantha can fix up tea mighty good. I never tasted any tea like it."

"Uh-h-h," he said, absent-mindedly, wondering why she tried to hold him there with words he had no interest in. "Well, I'll go on and see 'em. I . . ."

"Mr. Ashby. Wait." She held one smooth dark hand out toward him. A strange light burned yellowly in her eyes. On the hand held out to him there was a blueness beneath the nails. The whitest octoroon sometimes has it, he thought. "If she ask you where it is, tell her you don't know. Tell her if there's chopping to do, I can do it for her. I tried to make her let Wesley do it, but she wouldn't. Said it was a thing she had to do. It's 'cause it's my birthday she's brooding about it. But I got a right to chop 'em, too, I reckon, and I could . . . But don't you say nothing to Mr. Ephe. He won't hear of 'em being chopped. Make out like he aim to protect her. But it's not that."

He took his eyes away from the blue nails. "What?" he said. "What are you talking about, Tilda?"

But she did not hear him. Her lips were parted and moving, but no sound came. She was holding some intense communion with herself. He reached out a tentative hand to touch her; then shrugged and turned and pushed the swinging door open and went through the inevitable fruitcake and brandy odor of the butler's pantry and into the dark dining room, a beamed room with a huge green tile fireplace surmounted by a mahogany mantel generously carved. The place had two towering glass-enclosed cabinets chocked with assorted beflowered china and crystal, some of it marked, he knew with the dates and names of long-past expositions. The room had the damp mustiness of all sunless spaces, and even the odor of the recent breakfast could not abolish that smell always there.

The great sliding doors to the parlor were open. He went

through them and came on Ephraim's wife, his Aunt Semantha, where she sat before the fireplace. He stopped just inside the room and looked at her from behind. She was a thin, fragile woman, full of a strange nervous intensity, unable somehow to relax or to let anyone else feel at ease about her. She had fierce black eyes, and though her hair had once been black by grace of God, it was now so by grace of her beauty parlor. Her flesh was pallid and taut on her bones. She had once, Ashby was always told, been very beautiful. And even now, though she moved with the jerky motion of a puppet, and her thin mouth twitched constantly and her voice was often strident there was a certain beauty of frame about her, and a certain quality which made a man think, "I bet once she was a fine woman . . ."

Ashby cleared his throat. But she did not move. She sat staring into the fire, and when he stepped slightly toward her, to one side, he could see the wide black eyes fixed on the flames. He saw also the teapot before her, the cup and the bottle of rum. Then he saw her reach for these, pour the tea and add the rum to it: half and half, he judged, but perhaps not. *No wonder Tilda . . .* he thought.

"Aunt Semantha?" he said, softly.

The cup rattled in her hand. She turned her head with that ungraceful trembling and jerking which was now her way, and looked at him with eyes that saw no more than her eyes had seen in the flames.

He went toward her. "It's Ashby," he said.

"Ashby . . ." she said, and her voice was low and wondering, and less intense than he had expected. But her eyes were duller than he had ever seen them. They seemed unfocused, wavering.

"How are you?" he said and leaned and kissed her lightly on the forehead: the skin was parched. She nodded and held the cup clutched in both hands.

"Tea," she said. "Have some tea. Good for blood pressure."

"Is?" he said. He sat in the chair beside the carved mahogany and leather loveseat where she perched uneasily.

"Good," she said, nodding to herself. Then she leaned toward him, the dullness suddenly going out of her eyes. They fixed on him. "You see the ax, Ashby? When you came in, did you see the ax anywhere?"

"Ax?" he said. He looked at her uneasily, remembering Tilda's talk of "chopping." He had known a long time that Semantha drank, surreptitiously, but this was the first time he had ever seen her so disorganized and unaware. To the family she had been for years "Poor Semantha." But he had never seen her as she was now. "Ax?" he said, again. For a second he thought to ask her what it was she wanted; but he wanted to see Ephe and get Temp settled and face the problem of what he was going to do once Temp was safe. So, restlessly, he pretended he had misunderstood. "Where's Uncle Ephe?" he said.

Her mouth twitched. "You mean 'the governor?' The governor's in yonder. . . ." She jerked her head toward the hall and Ephraim's office. "Foreclosing mortgages and countin' his money." She made a short bitter laugh in her throat. She drank hungrily of the cup, the liquid gurgling down.

Ashby stood. "I reckon I'll step in to see him."

She didn't say anything; her eyes were back on the flames.

He stood indecisively a moment, watching her, a nagging doubt about leaving her in his mind. Then he went into the hall and was about to rap, one hand lifted, when his eyes went toward the leaded glass windows on either side of the front door. His hand dropped.

For there, through the glass, he saw the sheriff's car and beside it the sheriff, his hat revolving in his hand and his purplish throat moving convulsively as he talked to Granny. Granny stood at the gate, very straight and dignified, her white head still, in the way she held it since the cataracts had so dimmed her sight that she must concentrate intently on any person she faced.

The sheriff seemed in a state of controlled wrath. He started toward the gate once, but Granny never moved and Turkey stepped back helplessly.

Watching, Ashby found himself half crouching, as if to hide. He stood like that a second without decision. Then he rapped quickly on the door to Ephraim's office.

"Come . . ." The voice was bass, half-bored, half-annoyed. Ashby opened the door.

Ephraim sat at his desk, facing the door, a telephone in his fleshy hand, and on the hand a lodge ring, glowing redly. He lifted black unbrushed eyebrows at Ashby, made an attempt at a smile with his large mouth, and went on talking.

His voice rasped. "Listen," he said into the phone, "I been running cotton mills for twenty-five years without having the state legislature . . . All right, then. Well, the governor said he'd veto any damn workmen's compensation bill that came his way. So if you boys in the legislature just got to toady to a bunch o' radical labor leaders, why . . ." He paused, breathing hard, the veins reddening in his choleric face; with his free hand, he scratched annoyedly at his thick white hair. "Now, listen, Lem . . ." he said. "You know well as I do that the labor vote in this state don't count enough to bother, and never will long as we got a poll tax. . . . That's right. I know it's right. All right, Lem. And we'll get together about that other business. . . ."

Ashby watched Ephraim impatiently for a moment, then switched his eyes to the window, watching the sheriff. Any minute, he thought, Turkey will get past Granny and come in here and I won't have a chance to get out or explain to Uncle Ephe to keep quiet and keep Aunt Semantha and Tilda quiet about my being here. And then I reckon I'll have to chase over half the state, running from that damn sheriff.

With half his mind he was tense against the immediate danger; and yet with the other half, he almost wished the sheriff would get past Granny so that he could face him, and they could fight it out. He gripped his hands in his confusion. He looked at Ephraim over his shoulder. "Yeah. Yeah. That's right . . ." Ephraim said.

Turkey had not yet by-passed Granny. He was arguing

with her desperately now, his hands moving in the air, and behind him the deputies leaned out of the car watching him. Ashby found a half-chuckle escaping his tightened lips, to think of Turkey's frustration. Then he saw Granny hold up her hand and put a finger to her forehead as if thinking. Then she leaned a bit toward Turkey and said something to him. Turkey cocked his head on one side, disbelieving. Granny spoke again. Turkey nodded reluctantly. He asked Granny something, and Granny answered. Then the sheriff bowed to Granny and turned and got in his car. The exhaust gas spouted whitely in the cold air. Granny stood very still watching the car move off.

"Well . . ." Ephraim said. "Well, boy."

"Howdy, sir," Ashby said, not turning for a second so that he could see the car safely out of sight down the highway. "Yessir," he said, then, and turned to Ephe. He put out his hand and Ephe's hand met it, damp and hot and heavy. Ephraim's eyes, gray with strange yellow flecks in them, looked at him with searching pleasantry. "How are you all?" Ashby said.

Ephe grunted. "All right, I reckon. Glad you've come. Your Aunt Semantha's not . . ." He spread his hands and did not finish. "Well, you'll brighten up the place. Mama's pretty bad . . ."

"Granny? She looked fine to me." He started to tell Ephe about her and the sheriff, but Ephe was talking.

"Oh, nothing really wrong with her physically. Or mentally either, I reckon. She can still outthink anybody old or young. . . . But you know how she is. Take up any habit anybody else has got. She got more habits than a dog's got fleas, and she don't get rid of 'em any easier, either. She's got to have her cup of coffee at six o'clock. And at seven-thirty, at breakfast, she got to have tea. And a Coca-Cola at eight-thirty. And goes on all through the day, hollering once an hour for Tilda to bring her this that and the other." He shook his head, his mouth spread as if to grin. "And makes everybody go to bed at eight-thirty, because that's her habit and she doesn't want anybody up talking about something she might miss hearing." He sat down at his desk again, took up a cold but half-smoked cigar and motioned Ashby to the chair across from him.

"I thought you meant she was sick," Ashby said, sitting down. Around the walls, behind glass doors, legal books and old red and gold bound volumes filled the shelves. Ephe's law degree hung framed behind his head, beneath a picture of Robert E. Lee. There were photographs around the room of Ephe making speeches, of his inauguration as governor, of him with an arrow pointed at his head sitting in the crowded banquet room at the Democratic National Convention of 1920.

Ephe spoke and Ashby's eyes returned to him. "No," he said, "Not sick. But just afraid of getting sick, which is just as bad, I reckon. She's heard Tilda and Semantha talk so much about sickness, she's taken up the medicine habit, now. I have to hide all the medicine in the house. She'll snoop around and find a half-empty bottle of some prescription some of us have taken five or six years ago, and she'll decide it ought not go to waste . . ." Ephe was grinning. "She's Scotch. And first thing you know, she's taking the stuff. Whether she's got what it cures or not. Why, she's treated herself for everything from hemorrhoids to hallucinations since she's been here. Can't resist a patent medicine advertisement . . ."

Ashby laughed. Ephe winked with sly pleasure.

"Oh, well," Ashby said. "I reckon when you're old as she is. But it doesn't sound like Granny. Her mind was always . . ."

"Still is, like I said. I never meant to say her mind was failing. It's not. She's got as good a memory as I have, which isn't the best in the world, but for a woman over ninety. . . ." Ephe shook his head, his chin jutted. "No, I tell you," he said. "I believe she got some kind of an obsession about dying. I think she's hell bent on living, Ashby, and all this medicine-taking is just like—well, just precaution. To keep her from getting sick and dying." Ephe spread his hands again. "Well, she's older now than I'll ever be. . . ." He looked regretful. "And maybe she's got a reason. But she sho wants to be Mrs. Methuselah . . ."

"That's just what I do want to be. . . ." Her voice had a smothered laughing in it, but she stood there looking at them with an exterior of haughty anger, as if she dared them to smile.

"Mama . . ." Ephe said. He rose, and Ashby stood quickly.

"Howdy, Granny," Ashby said, and went toward her. He bent and kissed her forehead, and she patted his back, straining her eyes through the pink-tinted glasses to see him.

She was neither tall nor short, and her flesh was amazingly unwasted for her age, so that, though she was slender, she had none of the flabby skin and bone appearance of women grown too old. Her face was thin, with a small nose, her cheeks patterned with uncountable wrinkles. Her white hair was piled heavily over her forehead.

"I knew you must be either here or on your way," she said. "All the time I was lying for you out there." She had a low, beautiful voice, and when she had looked at him a second more, she directed it toward Ephraim, while seeming not to see him at all. "They all talk about you," she said. "When you get old, they all . . ." She was making her way to a chair by the desk. Since her eyes had become bad, she always walked with heavy feet, as if to convince herself that the floor beneath her still held firm. He wondered how she had got so quietly to the door of the office.

"Now, Mama . . ." Ephe said. He was still standing behind the desk and in his hand the cigar revolved between two hairy fingers.

"Of course I want to be Mrs. Methuselah," she said. Ashby sat down in the leather chair facing her and Ephraim. "It looks like I've got to be, if I'm to see . . ." She sighed and looked intently, but without seeing, toward Ashby, the skin crinkling around her dim eyes. It was a sign that she wanted to talk; it was the way she looked when she wanted to start on a long monologue: she seemed to forget where she was, and her words seemed to come from far way in time, to be spoken in a voice other than her own. "Ashby . . ." she said, and the way she spoke the name, caressingly, let them know that it was not the Ashby in that room, but the other one, her husband.

"Granny . . ." Ashby said, thinking to make her tell him about the sheriff before she should lose herself in the legend she lived in.

But she paid him no mind. "Ashby . . ." she said, still talking of that other one. "Ashby had a wish all his life. They always say that women want the race to go on, that they are the ones who . . ." She paused and put one white hand on Ephraim's desk, beside her chair, and Ashby thought for a moment she had forgot what she started to say. Then she said, "It's men. A man wants immortality. A real man does. A real man can't stand the idea of not leaving his mark on the earth. A man wants to mark the land he lives in, and the men he lives with, and he wants to mark his children. He wants children to mark, more than any woman ever thought to want them—more than . . ." She shook her head, impatient for words. "And he wants them to be him all over again, he wants his image to be immortal. . . ." The words came slowly, with pauses for breath and thought. She had her hands folded in her lap; they were small, but strangely square and strong, white on the black of her dress. "Ashby wanted it. And never saw his son. Nor his grandson." She leaned her head toward Ashby. "Nor ever knew others of his own blood." She nodded her head toward Ephraim, behind her. "Just as well," she said, abruptly. "None of you, none of you, his image. No immortality for him in you. None of you will leave the stain of your blood . . ." She broke off, then turned her head in Ephe's direction. "I'm waiting. He couldn't see for himself, and I'm waiting to see another Ashby Pelham for him. . . ."

Ashby stirred uncomfortably in his chair; always it was like this. The name was forever being spoken, and, spoken by her, it gave him a quick feeling of guilt. He looked at Ephe, wondering if in Ephe's face he would see the discomfort he felt in his own. But Ephe sat unmoved, lighting his cigar. He raised his eyebrows only when Granny chuckled.

"Maybe I won't have to wait so long," she said. "Maybe this Ashby . . ." She leaned a little toward him, where he sat suddenly warmed and comforted by her voice and look. He had the ridiculous feeling that he wanted her to hold him, as she had used to hold him when he was a boy. "Running from that sheriff. Slipping Temptation off," she said. "Ah, you act like a Pelham for once, boy. Like he did that time when . . ."

He felt himself flushing, and would not have interrupted her, would not have cut short the pleasing words except that he was afraid she would tell the whole story of the lynching. So he said, quickly, "What did you tell that sheriff, Granny? I saw you . . ."

"What are you two talking about?" Ephraim said, a little angry at not knowing. "What sheriff?"

"Why, I'm a fugitive from justice," Ashby said grinning. Granny smiled at him, and he told Ephe about the flight with Temp, leaving out only the excursion to Miranda's and the jail; he would not have been surprised had Granny known about that, but if she did, she would never admit it to him and he would certainly not be expected to confess it to her; it was the kind of thing they ignored. "And so," he said, finishing the story, "Temp's out yonder in the car down by the springhouse, along with a friend of mine who came along . . ."

He saw Ephe's face grow strangely sullen and the corners of his rubbery mouth turn down, but Granny was talking. "Yes. Yes," she said. "He had been hunting for you all night. Then he thought that maybe you might have come here. He lost you somewhere down the road. . . . And I told him . . ."

"But how did you know I was here? How did you know to send him off?"

She stiffened a little. "I have always known to be cautious when strangers come inquiring about my kin. I learned that when Ephraim's father, Dave, was hiding out at our place after Appomattox. Anyhow, I knew what to do. And I haven't any use for policemen and sheriffs. I never knew one who wasn't a little old no 'count man who never could be anything else, and once he gets a badge on, always turns into a bully and a liar . . ." She spread her hands. "Odious creatures," she said. "Awful. I never would tell a sheriff anything until I was sure I knew what he wanted to know. So I found out he was after you, and then I told him you'd called on the telephone and said you were going up in the Delta to see a girl. I even told him her name, so he would believe me. That little girl you went with that had the funny name—Honeybreeches Hunnicutt. I told him you'd gone to see her."

Ashby grinned at her, until his eyes met Ephe's. Then he saw that Ephe was standing now, glowering.

"I believe you have both lost your minds," he said. He looked at Ashby, and on his face there was not only anger, but a fear which Ashby saw but could not then understand. "You've got to take that nigger back right now and turn him over to Turkey."

Ashby stood a second in silent astonishment. Then he said, "Why . . . Why, Uncle Ephe . . ." Ephe's hands were trembling.

"Take him back?" Granny said. "He will not. Just because you've got a scalawag mind . . ."

"I'm not goin' to act as any underground railway for any nigger criminal," Ephe said, his teeth clicking shut.

Ashby was angry then, but only for a second. "Okay," he said, shrugging. "But for your information, he's not a criminal. He's innocent and I got him out of there before that po'-buckra sheriff jailed him without giving him a chance. You know how Turkey is, the way he hates Negroes. . . ."

Ephe came around the desk. "I'm not concerned with Temptation. I'm concerned with a bigger problem than Temptation. I'm worried about the whole black problem. Even if you don't, I know it's dangerous, and here you come heaping fuel on it. When the niggers all around us hear about it, they will think they can do anything and get away with it, and first thing you know, we'll be having riots. . . ." He sliced the sunlit air with his hand. "You're breeding disrespect for the law."

"Ashby always said," Granny said, sitting very still and not looking at Ephraim, "Ashby always said that when law and justice were not identical, a man had to choose between them and fight for one or the other."

Ashby was standing now. "Well," he said. "I reckon I better get cracking." He grinned, not only because he did not want to give Ephe the satisfaction of anger, but also because he was pleased at the idea that if the danger from the sheriff were real, he would save Temp from it by himself. He was hungry and tired, but the promised danger of a serious chase held at the moment a lure stronger to him than food or bed. For Temp's sake he wished they might have stopped at Ephe's, but for his own it did not matter where they stopped or whether there was any stopping anywhere. He was sick of nothing but inaction.

"Where are you going?" Ephe said, scowling.

"Somewhere," he said, with a quick movement of his shoulders. "This is likely nothing but a tempest in a teapot. But I don't aim to bet on it being no more than that. You see, I talked to Turkey last night, and I heard him hinting around about how Temp was likely guilty of pretty near every unsolved crime in the county. Turkey was humiliated and when he gets humiliated the only thing he knows to do is to go after some Negro. Well, I don't intend for Temp to bear the brunt of Turkey's craziness. So, until Father can attend to Turkey, can make him see reason, I intend to keep Temp out of his hands. Because if it served Turkey's purposes he's not above letting justice be done with a rope, and you know it. After all, election year is coming up, and he gets elected for maintaining what he calls 'white supremacy,' and . . ."

"You needn't jeer at it," Ephe said, shortly.

"Why not?" Ashby said. "A man's best friend is a jeer."

"If it weren't for white supremacy," Ephe said, stuffily, as if quoting holy writ, "we would all be mongrels."

Granny laughed, suddenly, a laugh not quite bitter, but satiric. She turned her head to Ephraim and laughed in his face. "You have done your part there, too," she said.

"Mama!" he said, the word abrupt and shocked. His whole bulky physique was tense and explosive now. He rolled the cigar agitatedly between two thick fingers.

Ashby looked bewildered from one to the other, wondering if he had understood the implication of what Granny had said, wondering even more at the sudden bitterness he felt between the old woman and Ephraim.

"Well," he said, "I never aimed to rattle any skeletons. I reckon I better take Temp on somewhere else."

"Ashby . . ." Ephe said. He looked a little guilty now, as if Granny had shocked him out of his anger. "Ashby . . ." he said, almost pleadingly. "Ashby, there's a special reason why I can't take Temptation in here now. It . . . It could ruin me if it got out. If it was known I was sheltering a nigger fugitive."

"A family Negro," Granny said. "Temp was born on our land and has lived there all his life."

"But Mama, you don't . . ." Ephe shook his head at her, helplessly.

"Oh, I understand," she said. She turned and started from the room. Then she stopped and looked at Ephraim. "Ephe, I'm sorry we had this disagreement. While I am under this roof, I don't intend to be a nagging old woman: here or anywhere else for that matter. But you have done a thing to me today . . ." Then she shook her head and there were tears in her eyes. She fumbled for a handkerchief and, finding none, blinked them back.

Ashby said, "It doesn't matter. We'll just take us a little longer automobile ride." He wanted to leave now. They were making the case of Temp into a more important thing than he now wanted to make it. The tension in the room embarrassed him, and left him almost fearful, as if, staying there, he might somehow fail in a fight which Granny already seemed to foresee. "Heck," he said, "I need a vacation anyhow. We'll go on over to New Orleans. . . ."

Granny looked at him. "You will go and get that man and Temptation and have breakfast here first. Then I will tell you where to take him. After all, not all Pelhams are scalawags. . . ."

"Yes," Ephe said, not noticing Granny's expression. His guilt faded and his face grew expansive, warm. "Yes, bring them up and I'll have Tilda cook you up a good breakfast."

"Thank you, sir," Ashby said. "But I reckon we best be going."

"No, no," Ephe said.

"You come back here and eat," Granny said.

Ephe came over to Ashby and put his heavy arm across Ashby's shoulder. "You know I'd take you in, if it didn't put me in such a spot. Someday I'll tell you, Ashby."

"That's all right," he said. He freed himself, more abruptly than he intended, of the heavy arm, and followed Granny to the door.

She put her hand out and held his wrist. "I wish I was young enough to really help you, go with you. If I were, that sheriff would never get Temptation. . . ." He tried to protest, lightly. "I'm proud of you . . ."

"Shoot, Granny . . ." he said, inarticulately.

She gave him a little push. "Go on. Hurry and get them. By the time you've finished breakfast . . . I'm going to take my morning nap, and when I wake from it in half an hour, I'll have thought of something. You go get them."

He nodded, letting her hold his hand tightly for a moment. Then, while she went slowly up the stairs, he half-bowed to Ephe and closed the door on the confused face. He started across the hall, but turned at the sound of Granny speaking to someone. Granny was half up the stairs, and when his eyes rose with the railing, he saw her—the girl. She was coming down the stairs, and as Granny passed her and went out of sight, Ashby knew he had seen that girl come down stairs before. Then he saw that it was Laurel Landers.

# Chapter IX

On each side of the stairs which curved down into the center of the hall with wax-gleaming mahogany rails and thick maroon carpets, there stood two lissome bronze Minervas holding aloft torches of orange bulbs shaped to resemble flame. It was in this light that he saw her. He put out a hand to where he thought to find one of the sliding doors into Semantha's parlor and touched instead the insubstantial velvet portieres and for a moment struggled with unbalance. When he looked again, he saw that the girl had moved to the other side of the stairs to let Granny pass, and he saw also in the faint flicker of her eyelids shutting briefly over the amber eyes that she had recognized him, but she said nothing as Granny, unaware of Ashby's still being there, went agedly up the stairs and out of sight.

I didn't dream her, he thought. I didn't dream her and I wasn't too drunk to know what I was seeing.

He could feel the blood race mercurially in his veins. As if I were fourteen and had just found out what a woman is made for, he taunted himself. He touched his tongue to his lips. As if I were fourteen. She moved down toward him, and he could see that she was not beautiful, or at least not beautiful in the sense he had always accepted, the sense everyone he knew accepted. Without having been aware of it, he realized he had been taught that beauty was largely artifice, the skin delicately colored, the lips deftly shaped with the aid of boxes and tubes and pots of chemical remedies for God's mistakes.

Now, gazing frankly at her, he saw that she was unlike any of the women he had thought of as beautiful. She was too openly flesh and blood. Her skin was scrubbed, suntanned and untouched by any chemical except lipstick. Yet she did not look unfeminine. In fact, he thought he had never seen anyone so completely feminine. She moved almost soundlessly, with an easy grace.

Then she said, "Why, Mr. Pelham, it's you." She came toward him. She wore a plain wool dress of a dull green color. "Why imagine . . ." she said. Then she laughed, opening her amber eyes wide and shaking her head so that the short brown-blond hair fluttered as if in a breeze. In any other woman, he thought, the gesture would have been coy. "When I think of night before last . . ." He wondered if he imagined that she was whispering to him, like a conspirator. With her voice, she was able to isolate them, to cut them off from everyone else; yet the voice was not intentionally alluring or purring with wile, like the voices of the women he knew, but only spontaneous, quick and natural as a child's.

"We're always meeting at the foot of stairs," he said. He saw her hand held tentatively toward him, and he held his own back for a second, and then touched hers quickly, finding it warm and firm, just as he had imagined it would be. Then, perhaps too quickly, he let it drop.

"But this time, at least, you don't think . . ." she said.

She leaned toward him. In the hollow of her throat there were three light freckles. As if it had been carved from some fine but flecked marble, he thought. He jerked his head up, took his eyes away from her throat and smiled at her.

She smelled like hay. There was no scent about her that was like anything but hay, fresh-cut and sun-warm. "You really didn't think I was that kind of a girl?" she said, eager about it, pretending a concern which the amusement in her eyes belied.

"Well . . ." he said. "A man can hope." He felt like an adolescent; there was something in her old with female knowing.

"Oh . . ." she said. "You're awful . . ." He wondered how she could say it so without coquetry, since she obviously did not believe what she said. "Awful . . ." she said, and her laugh caught in her throat.

A regular rake-hell, he thought. But scared to touch you.

"You should have seen me getting out the back way at Miss Miranda's that night. Running like outraged virtue and laughing to myself every step of the way. Oh, it was a wonderful thing to have happen to me, to go to a boarding house and find it was . . ." She was quite out of breath now, and so just stood there, shaking her head in merriment, the head perched forward a bit to see his eyes better.

He could only grin at her, his hands stuck in his pockets, his head turned down to her.

"It was wonderful, wasn't it?" she said. "Wasn't it the wonderfullest thing?" She had a gusto, a frank relishing of experience he had never seen in a woman before, and she communicated it to a man, so that he felt like hurling hammers about the heavens for her own special amusement. Ashby felt like a boy on the verge of flexing his arms to show off his muscle.

"Wonderful . . ." he said.

"I'm so glad you've come," she said. "So I can talk about it. I couldn't tell Mr. Ephe, and certainly not your Granny or Miss Semantha." She was really whispering now and he was drunkened with the sibilant intimacy of her voice.

He said, urgently, "I've got to go to my car." And did not move.

"Why yes," she said, and as if she knew he had asked her to come without any words, "I'll go with you. Will I need a coat?"

"No, I don't think so. It feels like spring here," he said.

"Yes," she said. "I thought I felt spring when I woke up." She sniffed, "Let's go out where we can really smell it. Is that your car I saw down by the pasture?"

"Yes," he said.

"Oh, it will be good to get out," she said. "I was coming for a walk when I saw you. Or maybe a run. I wanted to run and run . . ."

She put her arm through his. "Ready, Mr. Pelham?"

"If you run," he said, "I'll be chasing you." He grinned as if he were joking, but he saw in his mind's eye the picture of the satyr chasing the nymph, in one of Father's Greek books. He knew that, running, she would look like the nymph in the picture: he saw her barefooted with a loose girt robe, he saw her supple legs flashing in pasture sunlight, and he saw the wind in her hair which was shorter than the picture nymph's but which would flutter feather-like when she ran into the breeze. While he thought of her running, they moved past the stairwell into the back hall and to the door. He reached and opened the door and they went through greenhouse-sunparlor where the goldfish fountain tinkled into a marble pool. They went through the glass door into the clean-swept yard. He turned to look down at her, and as he did, he saw the black of Semantha's dress and hair just as it disappeared into the cellar door under the kitchen. He stopped suddenly, wondering with vague unease. Laurel stopped with him. She looked up at him curiously.

"What . . . ?"

"Nothing," he said, and led the way on. "I thought I saw Aunt Semantha."

"Oh, did you?" She looked over her shoulder. "I don't see her. I feel so sorry for her. She must be dreadfully ill."

"I don't know," he said.

"Sometimes at night I hear her crying. I never heard such crying. It tears your heart out to hear it. It never lasts long, though, because Tilda gets up—she sleeps there at the foot of Miss Semantha's bed most of the time now—and she gets up and gives her a sleeping tablet. I wonder really if I should be here. Mr. Ephe had invited me to come, or I never would have, but when I saw how sick she was, I thought maybe . . ."

"Yes," Ashby said, the breath going out of him painfully

all at once, as if he had been struck in the groin. What, after all was she doing here? What was she to Ephe? *Mr. Ephe had invited me.* And that night at Miranda's she had asked about Ephe. He had a sudden nauseous thought of the two of them, Laurel and Ephe, together. He felt a quick anger at Ephe, at the thought of Ephe stealing, with the sly leering of an aged dandy, into her room in the night and there . . . He found himself wanting to loose her arm from his, hating her, and yet half-laughing at himself for thinking that she would waste herself on Ephe, that she would let him touch her.

She stopped and closed her hand around his arm. "What's the matter? What do you look like that for?" They were at the gate, standing on the gritty brick driveway, and she held his elbow and shook it. In the wrought-iron of the gate an oak leaf was caught; in the breeze, it vibrated, but it was too well caught to come loose. His throat vibrated like the leaf and yet the tightness in it would not loosen for him to speak.

He shook his head and tried to say, "Nothing," but the word would not come.

"What," she said, shaking his elbow.

With one hand he gripped the gate latch. He felt himself pull the other loose from her hand and he felt his face contort. "What . . ." he mumbled through the ache in his throat. "What are you doing here? What are you to Ephe?" He heard his voice swell with anger.

"Oh . . ." she said. "Oh . . ." She put the back of her hand to her mouth, in an amazement which widened her eyes, and which he did not for one second doubt. Then she laughed, still holding that white firm hand to her red mouth, laughing through the parted fingers, and then speaking through them. "Oh . . . you thought . . ."

Roughly, he pushed the gate open, so that it swung and clanged against the brick pillar. "I never thought anything," he said, ashamed now that he believed her, and, worse, confused because he had showed her that what she was to Ephe mattered to him. He walked with rigid back toward the road.

He heard her behind him, the quick tap of her heels on the brick bridge over the road ditch. "Aren't you going to close the gate?"

"No," he said. "I got to drive the car through."

He turned onto the gravel road. "Oh," she said, half-running to keep up with him. She touched his elbow again. "What are you mad for? Because you thought . . ."

"I'm not mad," he said. "I never thought. I just asked you a question and instead of answering it, you laughed, and so . . ." He shrugged and did not look at her, but he slowed his pace.

"You never should have asked it," she said. "Not the way you did. Because you should have known. Even if you did meet me in a bad house, I . . ."

He stopped and looked at her. Her head still shook a little, protesting, but when he turned, she smiled and he could see the tiny space between the two front teeth and the way in her agitation she bit at the pink tip of her tongue, like a child trying to drive a nail and holding his tongue between his teeth in fierce concentration. He looked out over her head at the pasture beyond the hedgerow of whitening plum bushes.

"All right," he said, mockingly. "The Southern lady is insulted. If your father or brother or sweetheart will send his seconds to me, I will be glad to meet him. Maybe it'd be a good thing to revive the duel anyhow. Like my Great Uncle Vance used to say, 'Boy, if we hadn't been a country of duelers, we might never have held out two years against the Yankees. Oh,' he'd say, 'I'm not talking about any practice in marksmanship. I'm speaking instead of the legend we used to duel over, the legend of the pure and virtuous female, which we actually believed, in spite of the fact that any man with eyes could see the country was populated with she-wolves gettin' a deal of vicarious pleasure out of the spilling of male blood over their non-existent honor. But nevertheless, believing it, and believing it was something a Yankee would never respect, believing that our women would be ruined by the Yankee soldier and the free nigger, we had the powerfullest motivation to win a war any country ever had. Why, dadgummit, boy, do you wonder we fought our damn hearts out, saving our pure women?' " He could feel his lips twist a little, as Uncle Vance's had twisted when he had talked to him, there in the front gallery at Pelham Place, in the shadow of the Corinthian columns.

"You hadn't insulted me at all," she said, quietly. "And I didn't think you meant to, until . . . until just then. That was a nice subtle Southern orator's way of insulting me, Mr. Pelham. If you were bent on doing it, I thank you for doing it so nicely." Then she turned, the sun glinting on the sheen of her hair. He watched her walk back toward the gate, pride stiffening her.

For a moment, his own pride held him still. Then he found himself running after her. He caught up with her.

"I'm sorry," he said.

She stopped and turned and looked at him with eyes in which there was no fire at all now. "Your apology is accepted, Mr. Pelham." She put out her hand to him. He seized it almost roughly. "I'm going in now."

He laughed at her. "That's a subtle little Southern lady's way of saying go to hell," he said, laughing. "The score's even now."

For a second her face remained grave. Then she laughed, throwing back her head so that he could see her throat quivering to her laughter. They laughed together standing there on the gravel road with the morning sunlight yellow on them. When the laughter was gone from them, she said, hoarse from the strain of the laughing in her throat, "One thing I kept thinking was how Slim would look if Aunt Martha informed him he had to fight a duel over my honor. Because Aunt Martha would do it, in spite of the fact that she's supposed to be an emancipated woman, and is more emancipated than anybody ever thought she could be when she had to become a stenographer at forty-five. I've lived with her nearly all my life, and she always astonishes me, bustling in at dinner time and telling me the latest joke from the courthouse—she works for a lawyer—and then the next minute saying grace with as fine a pious-lady air as you ever saw."

"Slim?" he said. "Who's Slim?"

"My stepfather," she said. "That's what I was trying to tell you before. Slim and Mr. Ephe are good friends—they are sort of business associates, and Mr. Ephe . . ." She shook her head, her hair goldened by the bright sunlight. "You'll never believe it if I tell you . . ." she said.

"Go on," he said, grinning at her. "What?"

"Mr. Ephe sent me to college," she said. "He sent me to college because he lost a poker game with my father. Slim, I mean. Slim didn't want me to go to college. Aunt Martha couldn't afford to send me, and Slim could, but he wouldn't, because he and Mother—well, they didn't get along very well. One of those . . ." She made a quick gesture with her hand. "Well, one of those marriages people like Aunt Martha always discuss by saying, 'I don't see how Sara could have married him and I never will. And your father such a fine man, and for Sara to re-marry the way she did, to a man like Slim Lorrimer . . .'" Laurel smiled. "You know?" Ashby nodded. "Well, Slim always blamed his and Mother's trouble on education. 'Book-learnin' put too damned many ideas in her head,' he'd say. 'Nigh drove me crazy tryin' to improve my grammar.' I guess he really hated her. I think when he was courting her, after Father died, she gave him self-confidence, the way she'd give any man self-confidence, because she'd been reared to say just the things to make a man feel important. And I think she felt he needed her. He was younger then, and not bad looking, in an awkward sort of way. Anyhow, she married him, and it was terrible from the first, and she died a little while after, which was a mercy, I guess. Aunt Martha took me and from time to time, Slim would come to see me. . . ." She seemed to shiver the least bit, even in the warm sun. He looked at her curiously, but she did not explain. "Anyhow," she said, "When I wanted to go to college, he got mad. 'Not on my money,' he said. 'I'm not making any la-de-da ladies with my money.' 'Oh, is that your money you have?' Aunt Martha said. Biting off a thread and dropping it in her workbasket. 'I thought it was money you'd stolen over a poker table.' It made him awful mad. He was fascinated by Aunt Martha, the way he'd been by Mother. They both infuriated him, and yet he kept coming back, like a man who goes out and sins and then comes back to church, regularly. I used to think sometime that they were like his conscience. He tried to ignore them but he couldn't. He could only yell and sputter at them. He did that that night. 'Any time I can steal enough to make a college education, I'll give it to her, by God,' he said. 'I wish you wouldn't take the Lord's name in vain,' Aunt Martha said, quietly. 'Are you playing poker tonight? 'Yes?' he said, surprised, making a question out of the word. 'Why?' 'I dare you to make the stakes a college education for Laurel,' Aunt Martha said. 'You dare me,' he said, sneering. 'Oh. The fine lady dares me, does she?' 'Yes,' Aunt Martha said, 'Are you man enough to take it?' 'I'll take your dare,' he said. 'Can I trust you?' she said. 'Who're you playing with?' 'Mr. Ephe Pelham,' he said. 'If you can't trust me, I reckon you can trust him.' 'Yes,' Aunt Martha said. 'I'll check with him tomorrow.' Well, Slim scowled at her a minute and then went out, slamming the door. But at midnight that night he came in, drunk, and dropped four thousand dollars in my lap. He stood there with his hands on his hips, swaying and glowering triumphantly at Aunt Martha. 'Can I trust you?' he said, mimicking her. So . . . I went to college. And that's how I got to know Mr. Ephe. I had the registrar at college send him my reports, because I felt since he was paying for it. . . ."

Ashby looked down at the gravel underfoot. "Oh," he said. "Well . . ." He smiled at her. "Well . . ." he said again, lamely.

"And if you want to know why I was at Miss Miranda's that night, it was because Mr. Ephe had got me a job over there. My job didn't begin for two weeks, and he had asked me to come here, but I decided to go there and get settled." She still spoke intensely, as if she were afraid he would not believe her. "Then, when I ran out of Miss Miranda's that night . . . well, I just decided between laughing to come on here, anyhow, and have my vacation. I didn't fancy spending it at Miranda's." She laughed again.

"Oh," he said. Then he smiled again. "Well, I'm glad you did."

"I'm glad you got out of jail," she said, her eyes full of laughter.

He nodded. It was her hair he smelled. It was her hair that was like hay; in the breeze, a wisp of it touched his nose, she was so close to him. He closed his eyes and smelled her. He backed off a little and stared at her; their eyes met and held for a second. Then she said, suddenly, "Come on . . ." and ran ahead of him down the road. He watched her run without moving. He watched the ripple of her body under the soft wool dress and he wondered who it was had said a woman naked was an unbeautiful object, because he knew how she would be without clothes, he could see her in his mind, and he knew she would be molded like the arcs a man makes in the air with his hand when he is describing a woman he has conceived beauteous and perfect in his brain. Only Laurel was here, and real. Yet what held him there rooted, watching her run, was that she was also the woman a man creates in arcs in the air and never thinks to find.

He had not moved, and finally, a long way down the road, she stopped and looked back for him. Behind her, he could see Bevo get out of the car and look uncertainly in her direction.

She called back to Ashby, "Come on . . ." Then she turned her head toward the car, and peered intently a moment at Bevo, now approaching her up the road, and then made a quick movement toward Ashby and said, "Why you've got Mr. Thomas with you."

"Yes," Ashby said, and started to walk toward her, watching with a dread in him the approach of Bevo, thinking, "Now what do I do? Say, 'Nice to have met you, Miss Landers. I'll turn you over now to your Mr. Thomas.' "

He started to trot, and she called, "Run, run . . ."

But he didn't run. He didn't run because over and above her voice, he heard the other voice, coming from behind him, coming from the back yard of the house. It was a thin shriek, like the sweep of a cold feather over his body, and he stopped quickly, half-turned.

"What is it?" Laurel hurried toward him. The shriek came again, and then he heard Ephe's name being called in Tilda's frantic voice, "Mr. Ephe, Mr. Ephe . . ."

He was aware enough to motion Bevo to get the car and bring it on up to the house, and to notice in the split second before he turned his back on him the look of patient wonderment on his face as he gazed gap-jawed at Laurel and then turned unhappily back toward the car. Then with Laurel beside him, Ashby ran toward the house, while Tilda's voice sank into a convulsive and fear-driven gibberish.

The gravel seemed slippery beneath his feet. He heard the small "Oh" sounds Laurel made in her throat as they went through the open gate and into the yard, the brick drive making a sound of sliding grit under their feet. Then in the middle of the yard he halted.

There, before the brick cottage where the Cherokee roses grew, lay Semantha on the ground, and bending over her was Ephraim, and moving her hands frantically in the skirt of her white uniform was Tilda, weeping. By the time he reached them, he had seen the raw split trunks of the gnarled roses, obviously hacked at with something sharp; and then he had seen the ax —a new ax evidently—glittering in the sun, its edge encrusted with mud and something darker than mud and more gelatinous. And when he got to Semantha where she lay, he saw the gash through half the thin leg and the blood dark as night pulsing onto the sterile swept clay of the yard.

# Chapter X

There was a moment in which no one moved and no one spoke, as if the spilling blood had entranced them. When finally Ashby dropped to his knees beside Semantha, and leaned close to the fine white face now torn by the rose thorns, he could hear her almost imperceptible breathing. One hand, mapped with thin tributaries of blood, was all about her that moved; with it, she dug into the earth. In the dark hollows beneath her eyes, two patches of glistening tears had formed.

Laurel knelt beside him. "Oh . . . h . . . h." He heard the sound she made but did not look at her.

"Get me a towel," he said. "Quick." He rose and went to the woodpile beside the garage, and picked out a new piece of split oak.

"Tilda . . . a towel." Ephe's voice sounded as if it had come from behind a hand pressed to his mouth. Then as Ashby turned from the woodpile, it became loud, for Tilda remained there in stolid horror, unmoving. "Goddamit, Tilda, a towel . . ."

Tilda turned to him with painful slowness and for a second stood rigid and regarded Ephe with hard dark eyes. Then the rigidity left her body, her flesh seemed to sag on her bones, and she wept. She went toward the cottage door, her throat full and strangled with weeping, and the sound in the yard was unearthly and chilling as her shrieking had been a moment before.

She seemed to Ashby to move with exasperating slowness, so that he went after her. He leaned over her in the darkened room of the cottage while she stooped beside a cedar chest and fumbled in the moth-balled odored interior for a towel. She found it, and he snatched it from her and hurried back to where Semantha was. But he remembered Tilda's eyes, like fire in that gloom, and her voice that sounded like drops of water steaming angrily across the hot iron of a stove-top when she said, as he jerked the towel from her hand, "I would like to strangle him with it. . . ." He could see in his mind the way the loose graceful hands had suddenly tightened and twisted in that split second and then how she had dropped them disconsolately by her side. Leaning over Semantha, trying to stop the spurt of blood grown brighter now and less thick, it seemed to him that those hands waited in the dark of that room still.

Ephe sat on the ground, looking at Semantha, with the intent stare of a man who actually sees nothing in front of him but envisions in his mind some secret long-past scene. Laurel knelt beside Semantha, holding the frail shoulders and saying, "Miss Semantha, Miss Semantha," as if with words she could undo what had happened, as if only by calling the name she could close the thorn-scratches and heal the ax's gash.

Ashby pulled up Semantha's dark silk skirt, feeling the act somehow obscene, as if he were violating not a living but a dead thing in fixing the tourniquet on the wasted white thigh. He twisted with straining muscles the towel around the leg, his hands tight on the oaken stick. The leg twitched, and Semantha moaned, softly. He held the tourniquet tightly, but turned his eyes decently away from the passionless white of her flesh. He felt suddenly and unreasonably angry at himself for wondering what he was aiming to save: life for a woman who had not known what it was and had not been able to reproduce it. It was a thing he had known about her before, he supposed, but the knowledge came with redoubled imagery at that moment.

He was angry at himself and he spoke angrily to Ephe and

Laurel, who crouched beside him, staring, both of them so obviously living in every bone and tissue, and crouching there, staring with the horrified fascination of the living at death finding the flesh.

"Well," Ashby said. "One of you might go get a doctor, or do you aim for me to hold this here all day. . . ." The blood from the gash had almost stopped; there was now only a faint gelatinous trickle into the clot on the red clay.

"I'll . . ." Ephe said. He swayed on his feet, his eyes lowered. "I hid that ax. Tilda took the other one away and threw it in a slough in the swamp, because Semantha was so bent on. . . But we had to have an ax, and so I bought a new one and hid it. I don't know how she found it, I put it behind the coal bin under some boards. I . . ." His voice had the puffy quality of a winter wind, now blustering loudly, now whistling thinly. His words rose over the sound of the car motor as Bevo and Temp drove into the yard.

"No use talking about it now," Ashby said. "I reckon you'd better call the doctor. And here's Temp to take her upstairs." Ephe nodded, and then straightened himself, the reddened beard-roughened fat of his undercheek moving to his dry swallow. Then he turned and went, almost running, his broad body looking purposeful once more as he rushed up the back steps to the hall door beyond the greenhouse.

Ashby looked toward the car. The sun on the foreshortened chromium radiator dazzled his eyes. Bevo and Temp got out on opposite sides of the car. Bevo half ran toward them, not because he saw Semantha, of whom he seemed unaware, but because he had seen Laurel. His eyes were fast on her.

Laurel stood and said to Ashby, "We better get her up in a hurry. We can get Mr. Thomas . . ." Then she turned to Bevo. "How are you?" she said, her face grave. Bevo nodded slowly at her, and swallowed so that his Adam's apple moved convulsively in his throat. He stared at her with bewitched eyes until Ashby said, gruffly, "Here. Are you going to help me get her up? And you, Temp. . . I got to hold this tight." He raised his face to Laurel's. "You get Tilda. I don't know what's happened to her."

"Yes," she said. "Yes." She turned away toward the cottage. Bevo's eyes followed her.

"What's she doin' here?" he said. "Did you know she was gonna be here?"

"No," Ashby said. "It was a surprise to me. I knew she knew Ephe, but. . . Lean here and help me."

"Oh," Bevo said, and then he looked down, still speaking. "I'm mighty sorry, Ashby. But that was Laurel. That was . . ." Then he saw the gash, the torn stocking and the towel-bound thigh. He looked on Semantha for the first time, and the words stopped in his throat. "What . . . what?" he said, his voice dry.

Across from Ashby, Temp leaned, saying her name. "It's Miss Semantha. Miss Semantha. And I can 'member when her and Mr. Ephe was married, and . . ."

"Quit talking like she's dead," Ashby said, sharply. "Get her legs, Bevo. And you, Temp, her shoulder." Bevo leaned and seized the thin ankles gingerly, his face turned away, either from the blood or from Semantha's nakedness. Temp, his spectacles resting dangerously near the tip of his nose, held her shoulders and began to back toward the house.

He kept saying her name. "Miss Semantha . . ."

"Quit saying that," Ashby said. "And watch it. Slow. Slow. You want her to bleed to death?" He walked, bent awkwardly, beside them, keeping his grip tight on the tourniquet.

They went slowly toward the house with the fragile body swaying limply between them.

At the greenhouse, Ashby said, "Reach behind you and open the door, Temp."

"I'll open it." Laurel was there, opening the door for them.

"You get Tilda?" Ashby said.

"She's coming in a minute," Laurel said.

"Keep an eye on her," Ashby said. "Be sure she comes. . . ."

"Yes," Laurel said. "As soon as I open the hall door for you."

They waited a moment in the greenhouse where the water tinkled in the goldfish pond and the house ivy swayed to the draft from the door. Then Laurel had the door opened for them, and they moved away from the one thick drop of red blood on the white marble floor.

They took a long time getting her up the stairs, past the lighted Minervas. Behind them, in his library, Ephraim was speaking brusquely over the telephone to the doctor. At the landing the stairs turned both left and right.

"Right," Ashby said, and Temp, facing him, went to his own right instead of Ashby's right.

"Other way, Temp."

"Yassir."

They made the final stairs and went through the second open door in the upstairs hall and laid her gently on the bed in her cold white room. Bevo back to the door, mumbling between lips that sounded frozen, "Reckon I best wait out here."

But Temp stood there by the bed on which Ashby sat still holding the tourniquet and watching the slow seeping blood gradually spread on the white organdy bedspread. Temp stood with his old black eyes staring over the rims of his glasses.

"I 'member the day she was married. Miss Evelina taken me to Blakeville to help out, and Gen'l Blake, her papa, kep' a-feedin' me muskydine wine to make me sing a song he liked that I can't remember now, but I can remember him, one-armed the way he was from the war. I 'member they had a confusion at the altar because she had to come in with him holding on to the arm he had and that put her on the wrong side of the altar, or something. I 'member there was talk about it before, but nothin' to do because he didn't have no arm on the side that he oughta had a arm on to give her away proper, and so. . . Anyhow, it was a fine wedding, the church all full of the whitest, sweetest-smellin' magnolias I ever seed, and the white ladies a-settin' there cryin' and Mr. Ephe fine and strong-lookin' in his frock coat. Her sister, Miss Adele, come back from Paris for the weddin', and stood there with that red hair of hers. She had a maid that talked French, and Papa—Num—was scared of her till he found it was French because he thought maybe it was Unknown Tongues, and wasn't sure the devil wasn't speakin' through her. When the weddin' was over, I drove 'em home in the carriage, and after the party, I drove 'em to the depot. I can see Miss Semantha now, in the depot, standing on the steps of the New Orleans train, one step below Mr. Ephe, and lookin' out at the crowd that had come to tell 'em good-bye, her face white as it is now, but holdin' her head proud and smilin' until Miss Adele ran through the crowd and stretched up and made Miss Semantha lean down to hear somethin' she had to say. I can see Miss Semantha's bent head now, the bunch of purple flowers on the top of her hat. And I can see the way she jerked her head up, sudden, and had a redness on her face and her lips quivering like she was gonna cry, and all at once she looked over her shoulder at Mr. Ephe, and she shut her eyes a second and then she pulled up her skirts and brushed past him—he tried to stop her, but she jerked loose—and ran out of sight into the train car. I 'member the general grabbing Miss Adele and putting her in the carriage I was driving when the train had left. He was mad about something. 'What did you tell Semantha there?' he said. I couldn't see them without turning, but I could tell he was mad. 'I told her not to be a bloody Southern ninny,' Miss Adele said." Temp looked at Ashby. "You know what she meant?"

Ashby nodded, but said nothing. With his fingers he felt for her pulse. "I didn't," Temp said. "And don't now." Ashby said nothing.

"The Gen'l got turrible mad. 'I never heard such talk,' he said. 'It comes,' Miss Adele said, 'from having read the classics.' I can hear her laughin' now. 'If I had been meek, like Semantha, and not read all your books, I would probably be as ignorant as she is.' I 'member her sayin' it 'cause it seemed funny to me thinking Miss Semantha was ignorant. The Gen'l said, 'And I don't know but what you'd be better off ignorant. If all you know is the kind of thing a lady . . .' Miss Adele laughed at him. 'Really, Father,' she said. 'Your mother . . .' the Gen'l said. 'You married her the way you would buy a statue for your garden. For ornament,' Miss Adele said. 'The way Mr. Ephe . . ." (she called him Ephie) 'the way Ephie married sister. No wonder you men keep yard-wives of flesh and blood. . . .' The Gen'l clapped his hand over her mouth. 'I forbid you,' he said. I heard her yawning behind me. 'Will you get my tickets for the twentieth?' she said, like she didn't even know he was mad. 'I want to be in England by July first.' 'Don't you light that cigarette in this carriage,' the Gen'l said. It was the first I knowed she smoked, but Celia the cook told me afterward she had got the habit mongst them foreigners and her room was a litter of butts. Celia said, 'She ain' like Miss Semantha. She got gen'l's blood. Miss Semantha meek-blooded, like her Mama. A lady.' "

"Yes," Ashby said. "A lady." He put his finger under her fine chiseled nose to be sure she breathed. A lady, he thought. But what madness had sent her out to chop those rosebushes, what failure in the perfectly-molded, well-manner, washed and fed and silken-clothed organism had brought her to drinking tea and rum all day and staring drunkenly into the fire and opening her eyes uncomprehendingly to everything but the visions she saw in the parlor flame?

He heard Bevo in the hall introducing himself as Carter Thomas to Ephraim, who had evidently spoken to Bevo first since Ashby did not hear Ephraim give his own name.

"You're welcome here," Ephe said. "I'm sorry you come at a time . . ."

Ashby felt a nagging rage at the unctuous voice, so well-mannered, at a time when manners might be excusably forgotten. It seemed that even Semantha protested Ephe's courteous delay, for at the sound of his voice, she suddenly groaned and twisted on the bed. Or perhaps it was not the delay at all, but no more than the sound of his voice. Ashby made a soothing sound in his throat. "Now . . . now. . . ."

He looked up almost angrily at Ephe in the door. Ephe's eyes would not meet his. "I got Dr. Halman," Ephe said. "He's coming." He moved slowly to the bedside and looked down at her, avoiding Ashby's eyes, still.

"Why did she do it?" Ashby said.

"I don't know," Ephe said. He put his broad hand up to his mouth, rubbing reflectively, as if to cover the lie with an attitude of puzzlement. His knuckles were nicotine brown.

"What did she want to chop those roses for?" Ashby said. Semantha's breath came stronger now, a sibilant sound in the room. On the white spread there was an apple-sized ring of red.

"She never liked 'em," Ephe said. "She never liked wild things like that. She liked clipped hedges. . . You can see . . ." He still did not look at Ashby, who, bent over to hold the stick firmly, kept trying to find Ephe's eyes.

"I always wondered what they were doing there," Ashby said.

Ephe did not speak, but only stood there, corpulent and stolid, his blue eyes icy as they stared not at anything in space but at some vision of his own in time. The silence was heavy with old secret. Ashby had a memory of the white rose in June, hot and fragrant-scented in the night, opening to the moonrays and to the nightbees burrowing into the rich store of yellow pollen, and then of the petals falling, the de-flowering done, and the rose-apples swelling with seed on the stem. Then Semantha moved.

When Ashby looked, her eyes were opened. She tried to lift her head. Through pale lips she said a soundless something, full of an urgent hatred, at Ephe. Her mouth twisted to whatever it was she thought she had said, and her dark beautiful eyes flamed briefly as her lips moved. Then she dropped back on the pillow, her loosened purple-black hair spread carelessly about her head.

She shuddered. One bony hand, which had been lifted, dropped onto the spread. Ashby watched it curl a moment, and then relax. The sibilant breathing stopped. Before his eyes, all the tenseness and pain went out of her body, and she seemed to sink deeper into the mattress. The sharp line of her chin was blue-white. One hand, fallen over the edge of the bed, made a final twitch. From one of its thin fingers, her now too-large wedding band of gold slipped and fell soundlessly on the blue carpet.

Ephe reached and picked it up and turned it over in his hand and rolled it between his fingers. "It wasn't my fault," Ephe said, as if she could hear him, as if Ashby were not even there. "You blamed me, but . . ." Then his eyes touched Ashby. "She blamed me," he said. "But I tell you it was already done, time we married. It had been done a hundred years before. . . ." He shook his head and closed his mouth firmly. "Let go of it," he said, roughly, gesturing toward the tourniquet. "You don't have to hold it now." Then he touched Ashby's shoulder. "I'm sorry. Ashby, you won't go now, of course. You'll stay here, until . . ." He seemed terrified of being alone with whatever memory his eyes had looked on.

"I'll stay, of course," Ashby said. "But you've got to take care of Temp."

"Yes," Ephe said, absently. "Until after the funeral. Until then." He turned away. "I better wake Granny from her morning nap. I reckon I better tell her." He seemed reluctant to move toward the telling.

Then the door was blocked by Laurel and in the shafted sunlight her eyes were wide and fire-flecked.

"Somebody'd better come," she said, to Ashby. "Tilda is in her little house, and I only got the ax away from her in time. And she's in there yelling, and . . ."

When her voice stopped, he could hear the howling, a far keen of animal pain.

# Chapter XI

When he stepped into her cabin and closed the door behind him, it was still dark, the shades drawn against the sunlight drenching the pasture. In the darkness he could smell the mothballs from the cedar chest and the sweet urinal odor of an unemptied chamberpot and the white soap fragrance of some clothes soaking in a flowered crockery washbasin set on a marble-topped chest close to the door. He heard her slow desperate wailing in one blackened corner, before he could make her out clearly. Then when the shade on the back window flapped to let a brief patch of light in, he saw her. She had torn her clothes from her and now, naked, she crouched in the corner of the dim room. Her hair was disarrayed as if she had torn at it, and she swayed a little, moving from side to side the trunk of her now-thin, fine-skinned body, her long mobile hands cupped over the wasted unfirm paps.

The sound she made seemed near to rending her; it was filled with a sharper agony than any keen he had ever heard, a primitive and passionate suffering naked as her body.

He stood irresolute in the middle of the room, at the foot of the mahogany bed canopied in some faded splitting tapestry. He first thought to leave quickly, and then knew he could not leave her like that. He spoke. "Tilda . . ."

But the body continued to sway undulantly, she still rested on the spraddled toes of her strangely-light, almost creamy feet, and the sound of her mourning went on.

"Tilda!" he said, louder. The whole upper part of her body revolved, the thin muscles writhing under the close-grained skin.

"Tilda!" He caught his foot in her torn dress and kicked it away from him. The silence was sudden, and in it her steamy breathing began to grow until it seemed as loud as the wail.

She saw him now. Her eyes were like a caught animal's. She shrank back into the corner, her arms clasped over her bony knees, so that her tan wrinkled breasts swayed pendently in the arc her arms made.

He reached and pulled the crocheted bedspread from the bed and tossed it to her. She settled down on her buttocks, her sweat-gleaming flanks stretched straight before her. She pulled the crocheted spread about her. Through the holes in the spread her skin glistened yellowly. Suddenly he saw the tears start, slow globules down the shining copper of her cheeks.

"Peace," she whispered, in a tear-husky voice. "Peace." She reached a hand into the shadow of the cedar chest and held forth to him a dusty bottle of rum. She tried to offer it to him with words, but she was tear-choked beyond speech.

"Get up," he said. "Get up, Tilda."

"Drink," she said, the bottle held toward him, the dust specks flying about it in the shaft of sunlight from the flapping shade. "Drink," she said again, in her wet muffled voice. "Please, sir. You don't, I got to. You drink . . ."

"I don't want to drink, Tilda."

She held the bottle silently toward him, her eyes lifted up, luminous and urgent. Behind the spread, caught to her throat with her other hand, her whole body strained, pleading with him to take the bottle from her.

"I'll take it," he said. "But I won't drink it."

She jerked the bottle back with a smothered sound. Her whole body shivered now, with weeping. Slowly, she fumbled with the bottle, dropping the protective spread to open it. He stepped toward her, as if to take it. She put up a hand in fear.

"No. No sir." Her voice broke.

"All right," he said. He sat down on a stool a few feet away from her. "Drink it. Do you good."

She caught the spread to her again. Then, weeping because she had to drink, she lifted the bottle to her lips. He had his eyes averted, looking at the crucifix hung over her bed, remembering Granny saying, *Tilda's turned Catholic,* whispering the word Catholic as she always did, the way it was spoken in Protestant North Carolina and Virginia, the way her father had spoken it. *Tilda's turned Catholic and goes to confession and has one of those graven images over her bed. I saw that papist priest in Ephe's back yard with my own eyes. Why do you suppose Tilda did it? I never saw a Negro that wanted to confess. She's the only Negro Catholic there.* Maybe, he thought, that is why—she is the only one, and being neither white nor black, had rather be so. And maybe confession is just what she needs. Maybe there is no one else she can talk to except the priest.

He heard the liquid sound in her throat, and then he heard the bottle placed carefully on the floor.

"I got to do it," she whispered. He returned his eyes to her. She was pressed even farther back into the corner, and the hand holding the dress worked nervously at the cloth, kneading it. "If it's here and nobody won't drink it, I got to do it. I don't want to, but I got to." The other hand touched the bottle. She wept for herself.

"It's all right," he said. "Go on and drink it."

"I don't want to," she said, her voice small. "I don't want to but I got to." She rocked the bottle with her free hand. "Peace," she said. "Peace." The way she said it, it sounded like a prayer. Then she lifted her head up to him. "You don' need to tell me. I know it already. I knew a long time ago it would be this way. I knew she would go this way. The Lawd had writ it on her face."

He dropped his eyes on the floor, sapped by a nameless grief that had nothing to do with Semantha. He felt like Uncle Vance, that last summer before he had died, before they had put him in the lavendar-lighted burying ground under the marble obelisk chiseled with *Requiescat in Pace,* sitting there in the shadow of the columns copied from Corinth's, looking out on the pines they had brought by ox-cart from California, his mahogany stick trembling in his old man's hand, shaking the white mane on his head and muttering: "It's so bloody painful. God, boy, so bloody painful. And strange. Good God, boy, it's so hurtin' strange."

"Now he gonna kill me," Tilda said. "Now he . . ." Her voice rose.

"Hush," Ashby said. "Hush." He did not question who *he* was. He knew, without knowing why, without understanding any of it.

"She was all I had," Tilda said. "She was all. I'm nothing. Not black and not white, and she was all I had. Her and Father Conner. But she was the one, she was a savior to me, and now . . ." She spoke with a painful slowness, now without tears, but in a voice unsure and tentative, as if her throat might fail her any moment.

There was nothing he could say to her; he just looked at her and nodded. He thought to let her talk herself free of it, and in the second the thought formed itself in his mind, could hear Uncle Vance saying, *Free of it? Free of it? Nobody's ever free of anything that's happened to them. At eighty, I squint because of a raw stump I fell against in the river pasture at four; it took a chunk of meat out of my face and the scar still there draws my right eye.*

"I used to practice talkin' like her," Tilda said, in a low voice. "'Fore I paid any mind to what color I was, because even if I lived out here with old Crazy Mary, Miss Semantha used to bring me in and set me at the dinner table with her and Mr. Ephe. (I never knew why she did that, either, till later, or why when she did it, she never ate, but jest sat there with a little smile on her face and her arms folded, looking cold and prideful across at Mr. Ephe. And me sittin' there the color of floor wax and not the color of tallow, the way they was. And

Mr. Ephe never lookin' at me, until she would say, 'Give Tilda some cornbread, Ephraim.' Or, 'Reach and wipe Tilda's mouth for her, Ephraim.' Then, soon as she said my name, he'd give me one look, like he hadn't seen me before, and he'd turn to her and snarl and then rise up and pick me up and put me in the kitchen with Crazy Mary. 'And stay there, you goddam . . .' he'd say. And once I peeked after he had done it, and he stood there under the chandelier in the dining room, not only his face but all of him twisted with a terrible hatin' of her, and she sat never lookin' at him, just sat, smilin' down into her plate and making out to eat. And he turned and left her, madness all over him. And she sat there, not pretending to eat any more, but shakin' all over, and I didn't know whether with laughin' or with cryin'.) It was Crazy Mary told me I wasn't white, but I still tried to talk like her, praying God to change me. I can talk like her now. I can do it yet." She lifted the spread, from where it was caught at the pulse of her throat, to her eyes and wiped them.

"Used to sit there," she said. "Here late, she used to sit there and look at me. Talk in that pretty way of hers. She had a thing she always said. I can say it for you . . ." She looked at him, waiting for him to say yes. He didn't say anything. He would let her talk if she wanted to.

Then she was lost in remembrance. Slowly on her face he saw a change come; there was something there that looked like Semantha. The strained, haunted vitality of Semantha was there, the jerky nervousness. Tilda had become Semantha, and even the free hand she moved, moved with the intensity of Semantha's gestures.

When she spoke, her voice was Semantha's, too, the same vibrant tenseness. " 'We are the ones they outraged,' " she said, and he knew the words were not hers. He could hear Semantha saying them, with that certain glory in the rhetoric of tragedy with which a Southerner assuages the tragedy's wounds. *Let us talk of our ills, let us talk of our deaths and defeats, and give us time enough for oratory, and though we'll not forget, we'll heal the rawness of our remembering with words*—had Uncle Vance said that, or had he quoted it from someone else? Ashby didn't know, but he remembered. " 'We are the ones they outraged,' " Tilda said again, for Semantha. " 'They with their imaginings about the lust of the black they'd enslaved and now feared. Feared because they'd enslaved him and feared because they were pampered and weak and they could see his strength. And so they named him Lust, and said it would be dangerous to unslave him. That was their first lie, and then they made another one, to make the first one stronger.' " Tilda drank from the bottle, her hands cupped about it, her lips pulling at it with that same desperate hungriness with which Semantha had that morning drunk from her cup. " 'They put their women on a pedestal to show how different white was from black. They made the lie that their women had no bodies. And they worked so hard at it, they made us not women at all, but sort of wineless casks, empty and dry. And then their own lie caught them, and they did the very thing they had accused the blacks of wanting to do—they took the women of the other race. They took black women when they had ruined their own. They outraged their own women in one way, and then outraged the black women in another. And we are what they made with their lies. Me no woman at all, and you, Tilda . . .' " Tilda leaned forward as she said her name, leaned as Semantha might have when she first said the words. " 'You, Tilda? What are you? A soul in limbo.' "

When she stopped speaking, he came to himself with a shock. She had made Semantha live in that room, not precisely the Semantha he had seen that morning, but the Semantha who would sit and talk for hours in words he had not always tried to understand, because she could hypnotize him with that endless flow of rhythmic language and because a man looking at Semantha was often too fascinated to listen closely to what she said.

For a second Tilda was still. And then her body sagged, and

she was herself again. She wiped her eyes again with the spread. Slowly she shook her head.

"She almost never talked to me like I was colored. When we were alone, I mean, and she was drinking her tea. But he . . ." She put her pink tongue to her lips and wet them. "He never wanted me here. And she—at first, she kept me to make him look on me. She told me once she hated the sight of me, but she didn't hate me more than she loved to plague him with having to look on me. Then after a while, she didn't hate me at all. I reckon she loved me, the way I loved her. She was white and I was . . . nothin', but the Lawd had writ misery for us both." She lifted the bottle again to her lips.

"You better get dressed now," he said. "There'll be things to do in the house."

"Yessir," she said, from habit. Then she seemed to remember something, for he could see her lips part and her eyes glaze a little with remembering. "But first," she said. "I got to chop down those roses. I got to chop 'em down for her."

"I reckon Wesley will show up in a while, and if you want them chopped down, I'll get him to do it," Ashby said. "You get dressed now."

"Wesley can't do it," she said. "Even if Mr. Ephe would let him. Now she's gone, it's a thing for me to do. And when I do it, I reckon he gonna kill me, because he never would let nobody touch 'em. He kept these roses here to plague her, the way she kept me here to plague him. But I got to chop 'em down. It's a thing I got to do."

"Why would Uncle Ephe care?" he said. "I don't reckon he'll care. I reckon he would let you chop down roses if you want to."

She lifted her eyes to him. She looked at him a long time without saying anything.

"Why do you think he didn't like to look on me at that table? Aside from me bein' the color I am?"

"I don't know," Ashby said, not wanting to name to her the reasons he had imagined.

"Why?" she said.

"Well . . ." he said. "Maybe because they had no children. Maybe Miss Semantha was taunting him with that, showing you off to him. . . ." He knew as he said it that he had not said the truth, and that he was somehow afraid of hearing what the truth was.

She sighed. "You don't know. I talked a heap, but I haven't said anything yet. I told you he would kill me, and he will, maybe not straight out, but the way he killed her."

He stood up. "He never killed her," he said. "Quit saying that." He turned as if to go. "You'd better come on now, hadn't you?"

But she did not move. Even without looking, he knew she still crouched in the corner, her body showing yellowly through the flower-shaped holes of the crocheted bedspread.

He took a step. "Mr. Ashby. Please, sir."

"What, Tilda?" He turned.

She said, "You know this place here . . ." She indicated the cottage with her long fluid hand. "It's not like anywhere else. You know that, Mr. Ashby."

"You mean the roses and ivy and the wild look it's got?" he said. He was impatient now.

"It's got that look because Miss Semantha didn't like it. Miss Semantha always made him shamefaced, and then bein' shamefaced made him mad, and he just most of the time stayed mad at her without doin' anything except be a person who made him shamefaced."

"I've got to go, Tilda," he said. "You ought not to talk like that."

"I know it," she said. "I ain' . . . I haven't got any business saying it. Exceptin' I made him shamefaced, too, and now she's gone. And so what I got to do is chop down those roses and then leave. And I wanted to ask you to take me home with you when you go."

"I'm not going home," he said. "Temp's in trouble, and I

got to take him off somewhere." The shade flapped. In the brief sunlight her eyes were damp, regarding him.

"You could take me, too," she whispered. "I'm obliged to cut down them roses, and when I do . . ."

He went over closer to her and lowered his head. "All right," he said. "I didn't want to hear it, but go on and tell me. Why have you got to cut down those roses? Why did Miss Semantha have to cut them down? Why did Ephe insist on keeping them?"

"Because when he brought her here a bride," Tilda said, slowly, "because when he brought her here a bride, he had a black woman in this place. And the black woman planted those white roses. And he would never let 'em be touched because Miss Semantha hated the sight of them. Because this is the house where we were both outraged, like she said."

He nodded. "Both," he said, his voice dull.

"Yessir. The black woman died a-birthing me. She was my mother."

He nodded. "Yessir," she said. "What I aim to say is he made me. He made me and now he'll destroy me. And if he does, he'll be doing a better thing than he did when he made me. . . ." Through the echo of the words, which he could have said himself, so well had he known they were coming, he heard the thick sounds of her now-muted grief and saw her gold-tan body shiver under the crocheted flowers.

# Chapter XII

She had said what he knew she was going to say, and yet he stared at her a long time, feeling the strangeness of it. He could hear the ticking of the watch on his wrist above the low shuddering sound of her breathing.

Watching her, he felt that same hurtful misery he had known on that summer's day when he and Dale Tarnin, dead now of typhoid but that day six years old and alive, and Uncle Vance, dead also now but that day full of the live and pungent memory of an old man who has forgotten little and come to understand almost everything, had come, the three of them, on the convict stockade built in the oak grove beside the grist mill and the creosote-odored community cattle dip. They had come on the place suddenly, not knowing it was there, for the convicts came only once a year to ditch and drag and gravel the county roads, and they had had no way of knowing that they had arrived. So it was pleasant, at first, to turn the bend in the Old Sand Road and see the long-rail stockade surrounding what ordinarily was a picnic ground and to watch moving about inside it the overseers with black Stetson hats and ragged mustaches and the convicts in striped suits once black and white but now aged and dirtied to a gray and yellow. They had stopped to look across the ditch from the sunny road into the oak-shaded enclosure. Then they had seen, suddenly, the excitement in the men, and had watched while an overseer with a red mustache tied a great half-naked Negro buck to a post in the center of the compound, before which the other convicts were lined—their faces, black (for this camp was entirely colored) and frozen as they watched. The overseer had run the thongs of the long leather snake-whip through his hand, and then lashed out. Ashby had never seen any pain more graphic than that first helpless writhe of the agonized Negro. And suddenly Ashby had cried out, protesting, with what words he did not even remember. But he remembered that Uncle Vance had put his lean tobacco-smelling hand over his mouth and said, "Shush, boy," and then Dale, whose own lips were quivering, had said, "I won't cry. It doesn't hurt me."

"Come on," Uncle Vance had said and he had led them off down the road, away from the stockade, past the gristmill with its meal-dusty odor, along the hot sand ruts past the cattle-dip and run, across Old Sand Creek where the resin from the pine-board bridge stuck like hot glue to their bare feet. Then, across the creek, he had made them sit on the sand under an oak tree and he had seated himself gingerly on a rock, for he was all of seventy-five even then, and careful of his bones. He had put both his thin hands around the cane, about halfway down its length, and pushed it two or three times into the white sand before he said anything.

Ashby could remember now that certain old-man smell of him, that odor of old scrubbed flesh and nicotine and careless urination. When he had spoken he had been very grave.

"Listen to me," he had said. "What you saw up there hurt you. Both of you. Didn't it?"

"Yes," he had said. Dale had hesitated a second. Then he had said, "Yes. But I didn't aim to say it did. I aimed to be a soldier."

"Listen to me," Uncle Vance had said, "On the day that a thing like that doesn't hurt you, you take heed of yourself. On the day that another man's hurt is not yours, too, you'll know you're uncivilized. You hear me, boy?" He always spoke to them in the singular, as if they were one.

They had nodded, not quite understanding. And they had not understood at all what he had said after that. He had seemed to be talking to himself, anyway, or else addressing someone not there. Ashby could see him now, the yellowed white hair curling over the black collar of his cutaway, the boiled white shirt bunching over his old thin chest, the waistcoat soiled a little with his misdirected spittle.

"Do you think, sir," he had said, his old bleary eyes fixed not on them but on some dark mythical opponent of his own, "Do you think we are not all hurt by it? That all our faults and almost none of our virtues exist because of it—this dark web *Negro* that hangs like a pall over all of us? And aren't we arrogant, because they're there to serve us? And useless, often, too. And aren't we cruel, too often, because we're afraid of what we've enslaved? And God knows, sir, the question you're always asking—*would you have your daughter marry one*—is not just ignorance or facetiousness or emotionalism. It's one of the tentacles of the web, always there. It is, finally, you know, perhaps largely a problem of sex. And not just because we quail before the potency of the primitive and pagan, but also—and mainly—because any man is always in secret craving to experience the dark and unknown. Only the real drunkard can hate booze. And does that tell you anything about us and the Negro? Listen to me, sir. I am a man and I hurt when the Negro is hurt. But I hurt also to see what the dark web *Negro* has done to the white man, and if that is not the Negro's fault—as it is not—it is still no less tragic. Not even God can expect white and black to live side by side without each being burdened by the web of the other's strangeness. For the web is made of the odor of black and the odor of white, the alien smell of one race to another. And made of the alien form and color. Made, sir, of the fear of an alien thing, and a fear not cooled in a land of sun and hot rains. And, as I said, made out of lust, the constant secret craving for the dark and unknown. And out of hatred, and out of the love of a dollar, and perhaps out of the need to be master in a place where the skies and the soil dwarf a man and sap his potency. The web is made out of all these and more that are nameless, and if you can free us of it, sir . . . Then you are God, by God."

Though they were used to his long silences in which he seemed to talk to himself and then to his suddenly bursting into a rhetorical peroration in which he summed up what he had sat thinking about for some time, and though they usually sat unmoved through it all—the silence and then the peroration—that morning, when he had finished speaking, they had both felt a sudden fear. With the perspicacity of six years, they had felt in his voice his own deep and aged misery, sharp in him as the pain the cold brought in the shinbone shattered by a Minié ball at Chickamauga.

In the quiet when he had stopped speaking, Dale had said, almost whimpering, "I got to go home." And Ashby, so full of hurtful misery from all he had seen and heard and not understood, had nervously slipped into the huckleberry bushes to relieve himself. It was while he was standing watching the fizz of his urine on the sand that he had heard Uncle Vance rising and saying between his old-man grunts, "Just don't hurt when you can avoid it, boy. And if ever you can save a body from hurt, do it. You hear me, boy?"

Ashby had come from the bushes fumbling with his fly buttons.

"Yessir," he had said, and Dale (now dead) had said yessir too.

Now in Tilda's room he remembered that day. Perhaps he could remember all of what Uncle Vance had said only because Uncle Vance had never said a speech he liked only once. His favorite ideas he said over and over.

And now, remembering, Ashby imagined for a second that the filaments of the web were tightening upon him. Looking on her, he seemed to feel the pall of the web encasing him. He had a foolish urge to shout it away, knowing it would not leave, would not in any way be downed or denied. But he told himself, sardonically, that Uncle Vance was a romantic, a dramatizer, who after all had frankly admitted that his one real ambition had been to recite the iambic pentameters of Shakespeare before the footlights.

So he said, "You're making a big to-do about nothing. But never mind. I won't let him touch you. If you want to go home . . ."

She stood slowly and for a moment straightly, the spread held loosely now just at the rut between her breasts. Then her body seemed to sag and all the hope to drain out of her. "It won't do no good. Nothing anybody can do. I can't be unborned." She watched him with liquid eyes, shaking her head. "I can't be unborned."

"Hush," he said. "You hush." He straightened. "I'll tend to it," he said. He spoke flippantly, because he did not trust himself to say, "I'm sick of it. I'm sick of all of them and the way they do. Of the sheriff and of Ephe and . . ." He did not want to be dramatic like Uncle Vance, or Granny. He did not want any heroics. I am just plain Ashby Pelham, he thought, and I don't aim to do an imitation of St. George and the dragon. If it was St. George . . .

She did not seem to notice the flippancy. She shook her head. "God's done forgot how it is here," she said. "I don't know how you aim to tend to it." There was no blame in her voice, only a dead hopeless sound.

"You never mind. I will," he said, ashamed for the moment, seeing the hurt in her. He turned abruptly then and left her, shutting the door softly behind him, blinking at the warm bright sunlight in the yard.

He stood there indecisively for a second, looking absentmindedly at the raw stumps of the roses Semantha had chopped. He thought: They don't even die like other folks. And it's not only that they see visions and search for causes, but they can make a rosebush or a jimson weed into a symbol of darkness and evil. She even thought she could root out and destroy the trouble that had come on her by merely chopping down some rose bushes. They ought to all be on the stage. They even die dramatically.

When he looked up, Bevo was standing there a few feet away at the corner of the cabin. Bevo lifted his finger. "Ashby . . ." he whispered.

"What?" Ashby whispered, in a mock stage whisper. "What? Ghosts?" He walked toward him.

"Joshing again," Bevo said. "You 'member talking 'bout that sword? Well, I reckon you got it now."

"Good," Ashby said. "St. George." He put a hand inside his shirt, Napoleon-wise. Then, remembering that he had told Bevo nothing of his talk with Ephe, he sobered and looked puzzled. "What are you talking about?"

"Come here."

He followed Bevo around the cabin, past the stacked cords of stove wood, through the picket gate to the pasture and into the white-flowered copse of plum bushes.

"What is it now?" he said. "A maiden on the railroad tracks?" Then he saw Temp, half-crouched in the plums. He didn't have a hat on and he kept touching his head as if it were uncomfortable. He looked beseechingly over his glasses at Ashby.

"What's the matter?"

"I got to go on," Temp said, with that peculiar thickness of lips which betrayed his fear.

"The sheriff called a minute ago," Bevo said. "We were standing in the hall not knowing quite what to do, when your Uncle Ephe answered the phone. It was jest after the doctor came and called the undertaker." Bevo paused. With a big finger and thumb, he plucked at a plum bush, broke off a flowered twig. "I couldn't hear a heap because I was on the landing and . . ." He looked a little shamefaced at Ashby. "Talking to Laurel . . ." he said.

Ashby grinned carelessly at him, as if it did not matter about Laurel anymore than it mattered about anything else. "Well?"

"I heared him," Temp said. "I heared him. Maybe he never knew who it was. At first, I mean. Sheriff must 'a' asked for you, and Mr. Ephe said, 'Why, yes, he's here.' And asked if he wanted to talk to you. Then Sheriff must 'a' told him who he was. 'Cause Mr. Ephe sort of sputtered, and said he wasn't sure you was here. Said you had been here early this morning. And the sheriff said something else and Mr. Ephe said something about old folks having bad memories. Then he said he didn't know nothin' about who was with you. Then he told him 'bout Miss Semantha, and said he couldn't be bothered. That's when I left. 'Cause I know Sheriff Littlepage, and won't nothin', not Miss Semantha dead nor nothin', keep him from coming now. So I got to go."

Ashby regarded him soberly now, thinking that after this morning it might be foolish to trust Ephe too far, in spite of his promise after Semantha died, in spite of the fact that he had presumably been reared like Father, to think that a man's given word was inviolable. But you never know, he thought. You can't know. Even when what they do is too damn fantastic for a sane man to believe, he had better look twice before he refuses to believe. Because no sane man would have believed that Semantha would die chopping down rosebushes on a Negro cabin.

"All right," he said. "I reckon so. I guess we got to get you away from here right now."

"You jest let me go on," Temp said. "You done done enough. And all you gonna do is git yourself in trouble with the law. Because now there ain't no stopping that sheriff, and it will be better if you go on home after they bury her, and . . ."

"Hell," Ashby said, "I might as well be in trouble here as at home, and I reckon I was born in it anyhow." He smiled against Temp's fear, and touched Temp's shoulder, still gristle-hard and lean, old as he was. Bevo shifted uncomfortably.

"You better do something," he said. "I got a feelin' . . ."

"So has everybody else," Ashby said. He looked out over the pasture, rolling away from them in a series of low green hillocks, bounded by the flowering plum and haw. Far down below the springhouse he could see the distant haze on the swamplands they had skirted earlier.

He turned to Bevo. "You go on back in the house. If Uncle Ephe wants to know where I am, tell him you don't know. I'm gonna take Temp to a safe place, and then I'm gonna come back and make out like I'm surprised to find him gone."

"You going in the car?"

Ashby shook his head. "No," he said. "Gonna walk."

"Walk?" Bevo said. "Walk to a safe place?"

Ashby pointed to the far swamp. "That swamp goes down to the big river. And between yonder and the river, there are places no man ever set his foot. Even good bloodhounds would have a time finding anybody in those bayous."

Temp looked dubiously toward the swamp. "I never was one for no swamp," he said. "They sorta picks at yo' skin with ghost-fingers, swamps do."

"You won't have to stay long," Ashby said. "Just till I get Turkey steered away . . ."

"Well, yassir," Temp said. "I got to go somewhere and if you say that the place . . ."

Bevo said, "Then, when the funeral's over, we can slip him out to a safer place."

"Hell, time the funeral is over, Turkey will be chasing somebody else. Anyhow, by then Father will have straightened it all out." He touched Bevo's arm. "You go on. Hold Uncle Ephe off and look innocent at Turkey if he shows up. We're goin' on now."

"Wait." Bevo said. "If that sheriff comes, he's gonna call me Bevo Banes, and there Laurel thinks my name is Carter Thomas, because you went and made up that name for me, and I had to tell it to Mr. Ephe, too. And since I'm a competitor of Mr. Ephe's, it's gonna look funny . . ." His heavy face was set in an expression of stolid puzzlement.

"Well, keep out of Turkey's sight then. But get where you can listen to what he says when he comes." He turned as if to go.

"But . . ."

"What?"

"Well," Bevo said, "I jest wanted to ask you . . . do gentlemen eavesdrop like that?"

Ashby grinned, briefly, and then shrugged. "Gentlemen don't, I reckon," he said. "But I reckon, too, that for Temp's sake we might forget manners. Turkey's no gentleman. And the thing is that in a fight you usually have to swing on your opponent's level. Turkey's level is pretty low."

Bevo nodded. "All right." Then he smiled. "A man sho can be a fool about a little thing, can't he. At a time like this . . ."

Then, as Ashby pushed his way through the plum copse, with Temp following, Bevo raised his voice. "So you think it will be a fight?"

Ashby did not answer. He thought: I don't know. I'm sort of like a new inmate in a madhouse, who hasn't yet learned the peccadillos of the other patients. They might do anything.

Then he broke into a trot, running easily across the damp rich turf toward the distant swamp.

# Chapter XIII

Three hours later, when he emerged from the swamp, he could not yet admit the apprehension he felt. It was still a comedy he was playing and taking Temp to the swamp was no more than a serio-comic gesture which he was sure he would laugh at later. The unease in him he laid to his physical discomfort. In the warmth of the sun, he itched, because once inside the wooded border of the swamp, he had taken off his suit and his shoes and cached them away in the limb of a sycamore and had gone the rest of the way barefooted and in his underwear, so that on his return to the house there would be no telltale dampness and mud on his clothes. He had joked about even that precaution.

Since he had had to swim bayous and wade hyacinth-choked marshes, he had had to discard the underwear when he returned again to the sycamore and now the worsted suit scratched at him, and the sweat, seemingly generated in reaction to the icy water he had crossed, rolled naggingly down his buttocks and thighs. He supposed that Temp in the swamp was more physically comfortable than he was: Ashby had left him undoing the belt with which he had tied up his outer garments and hung them around his neck, so that, once at the lean-to Ashby had found for him to hide in, he could be dry and warm. Ashby had shot a squirrel and left Temp matches to make a fire. For the moment, Temp was safe.

Yet Ashby hurried, blaming the sense of urgency he now felt on the heat, the sweat, the itching, or else blaming it on the swamp, the sense of awe the swamp always imparted, even when a man was hurrying through it, jumping the puddled water and pushing through the tortuous undergrowth, the branches whipping his face and the sudden birds whirring up underfoot.

Yet when, swinging open the wrought-iron gate to the drive, he saw Bevo sitting on the stone steps before the cottage, he felt and admitted the apprehension, briefly. Bevo sat there unmoving, his tousled head lowered, in his whole figure a look of gloom and fatigue. Ashby did not have to ask if something was wrong. He knew it then, perhaps because the pose of Bevo's body was reminiscent of the way Uncle Vance had used to sit on the steps at Pelham and contemplate some new twist of circumstance and say, *Fate, boy, is like a tripwire in the dark. It'll tumble you into the mud, roll you into the gutter and then like as not you'll rise clutching a handful of silver dollars you've found under the palm you put out to break your fall; or else you'll rise muddy. You never know. Fate, boy.* To hear Uncle Vance say "Fate, boy" had always made goose-pimples on his back and a thin line of cold on the inside of his thighs. So when that first quick knowledge of something gone wrong was past, he told himself that it was no more than the attitude of Bevo's body, so like Uncle Vance's, that had touched him with a swift fear. I will be seeing ghosts next, he thought, and went swaggeringly toward Bevo.

He went and squatted on the ground at Bevo's feet and said, "Well?" grinning as he said it.

Then Bevo told him. The sheriff was there. Bevo had been in the upstairs hall when he came, talking occasionally to Laurel who was going in and out of Granny's room, comforting Granny about Semantha and helping Granny to dress. Then Bevo had heard the sheriff, had heard Ephe meet him at the door, and then had heard Ephe call upstairs for 'Mr. Thomas.' He had not answered.

"That sheriff knew my right name," he said. "And I couldn't go, but I couldn't tell Laurel why."

"What did you tell her?" Ashby said.

"I told her about Temp." Bevo said. "Why?"

"Nothing," Ashby said, thinking that he was being unreasonable to worry that she might perhaps tell her father where Temp was and that her father might tell Ephe, for even if Ephe knew now, he had given his word that Temp could stay without harm until the funeral was over. *I* haven't got any reason not to trust Ephe, Ashby thought. But I do. I don't like it, but at this minute I don't trust . . . I trust hardly anybody. And I haven't any reason for that, either. Unless that swamp did hoodoo me, the way Temp predicted.

"She already knew about some argument you and Mr. Ephe had," Bevo said. "Your Granny had told her."

"Go on," Ashby said. "About Turkey."

"Yes. So then . . ." Ashby listened to the low voice, droning the tale out. Ephe had denied knowing anything at first and had even blustered a bit and threatened to become angry with Turkey at the hint that he might shelter a runaway Negro. Then Turkey had mollified him by suggesting that Ashby might be fooling him by hiding the Negro somewhere on the place and not letting Ephe know about it. Turkey had revealed then, too, that the evening papers were carrying the story of Ashby's flight with Temp. It was then that Ephe had got really angry and called Turkey a fool. "Now we are bound to have trouble with the niggers," Ephe had said. But Turkey had pointed out that trouble with the blacks did not necessarily mean trouble for him and Ephe. In fact, Turkey said he had seen to it that the newspaper boys pointed out in their stories that even though Ephe was Ashby's cousin, Ephe had been a "lifelong battler for white supremacy" and would likely continue to be. "All you got to do is come out with a strong state-ment in the mawnin'," Turkey had said, "and a candidate running ag'inst you won't git ten votes in the whole dadgummed state."

"Running against Ephe?" Ashby said. "For what?"

"They never said," Bevo said.

"Well, I reckon I ought to have known that, too," Ashby said. "I reckon I ought to have figured that it was bound to be election year. That's what put Ephe in such a state this morning. What made him . . ." He grunted. "Go on."

"Well," Bevo said, Ephe had said, "If it just hadn't been Ashby. I don't see why it had to be my own flesh and blood." Then the sheriff had said that if Ephe made a special point of his sorrow at the treachery of his own blood kin, when he was making speeches, he would have the women weeping. Then Ephe had accused Turkey of cooking the whole affair up just to get votes. But the sheriff had acted hurt and had said, "Now, Mr. Ephe, you know I didn't. To tell you the truth, I jest got plumb outdone with Ashby and that nigger and them fool hounds, I got red-eyed mad at 'em all, and started out after 'em without thinking about a thing except catchin' them so that folks would stop laughin' at me. I was sick o' bein' humiliated. But when I got over here, I begun to think, especially when them newspaper boys started on me, and it come to me it was a fine chance . . ." "Chance for what?" Ephe had said. "What do you aim to get out of it all? Besides your name in the paper?" And the sheriff had acted indignant then. "Why, Mr. Ephe, I jest aimed to do you a favor. I knowed you'd do me one, did I ask you, and . . ." Ephe had said yes he would.

"Yes," Ashby said. He spat, disgustedly, onto the clay by the doorstep. "A favor. Like helping the sheriff get elected to Congress." He watched Bevo's finger touch a rosethorn.

"But that's not the worst of it," Bevo said.

"I didn't reckon it was," Ashby said. "I knew damn well that was just a summer breeze to what was coming." He grinned at Bevo but Bevo was staring gloomily off into space.

"You know somebody named 'Slim'?" Bevo said, bringing his eyes back to Ashby's face.

Ashby lifted his head quickly. "That's Laurel's step father. His first name's Slim. His last . . . I can't remember. Laurel told me, but . . ."

"Laurel's step father?" Bevo said, and looked in pained astonishment a second at Ashby and then dropped his eyes to the ground. "That's why she kissed him, then. I heard her kissing him when he came, downstairs. . . ."

"Is he here, too?" Ashby said, and without waiting for Bevo's nod, "Hell, they're having full regimental review."

The sheriff, Bevo said, had told Slim and Ephe about Ashby's being in jail with Bevo Banes.

"They never connected Bevo Banes with Carter Thomas," Bevo said, "Not yet. But that's why I got to get out of here. Before they do."

"Why?" Ashby said.

"Because Slim has told Mr. Ephe that if they can just connect Bevo Banes with all this Temp trouble they can run me out of business in this state. And that the papers this evening are gonna be hintin' that it was me that put you up to it, because I'm what they call a 'nigger lover.' "

"That bastard," Ashby said. "I knew he was a bastard all

along. . . ." He scratched at the wool pressed against his thigh.

"It does look like we are being pushed mighty fast from bad to worse," Bevo said.

"What do you think they aim to do?" Ashby said.

Bevo looked at him for a second without speaking. "I think," he said, "that they aim to let a lynching happen."

"Oh, hell," Ashby said, standing. "You know Uncle Ephe wouldn't . . ."

"I don't know nothin'," Bevo said, "except what I heard. And I know Mr. Ephe took strong to the idea that maybe they could get me accused alongside of you. But then he warned the sheriff against any violence . . ."

"I knew he would," Ashby said.

Bevo lifted his head. "And the sheriff said, 'I'm a sheriff of the law and couldn't be party to nothin' unlawful.' With a wink in his voice, though, when he said it. And Mr. Ephe said, 'Sometimes a man is forced to shut his eyes to a thing like a lynching. That is, if he aims to keep on getting elected.' And Turkey said, 'Sometimes, he is.' And then Mr. Ephe said the best thing to do would be to get you to turn Temp over to him without any fuss and bother. Because he said, 'If Ashby's done what you say he has—and I'm not saying he has—then I think I can talk him out of his foolishness. But I want to warn you I'm not going to be a party to any mob violence, and I want to tell you I hope you'll have the decency not to start any trouble until at least the last sad rites are over.' "

"He said that?" Ashby said. "He hinted that Temp might be around, and if they just waited till Semantha was buried . . ." He found himself gripping his hands, and then flexing the fingers, angrily.

"Oh, he said he wouldn't stand any lynching. But the sheriff didn't miss what Mr. Ephe was driving at. In fact he asked him. Asked him why did he think that if the boys got out of hand about this nigger trouble, it would disturb the funeral? Did Mr. Ephe think they'd find the nigger on his place? And Mr.

Ephe said he didn't know, but for the sheriff to keep in touch with him and he'd let him know what he found out."

"I believe Uncle Ephe has gone crazy," Ashby said. "We are all a little crazy, but I'm inclined to believe he has overstepped even our elastic limits this time."

"This isn't any time to be joshing," Bevo said, hearing the sardonicism in Ashby's voice. "I think Mr. Ephe really believes he can persuade you to give Temp up. I don't think he wants any lynching. But I think he's in a position where what he wants and doesn't want might not matter. About how the Temp business is handled, I mean. Because he stands to gain in his business and his politics any way it's handled. . . ."

"Except that people just don't lynch nowadays," Ashby said, "And you know it."

"Nowadays they usually just kill," Bevo said. "A fellow mad at a nigger shoots him and nothing's done. But the nigger's just as dead either way."

"Yes," Ashby said.

"But I wouldn't be too sure that a red-eyed mad politician couldn't manage a lynching if he wanted to."

"Maybe so," Ashby said, "but I don't think Ephe . . ."

"Maybe not," Bevo said. "Especially if I'm gone and he doesn't stand to gain from my being here. If my being here was a help to you, I'd stay. But if that sheriff sees me . . ."

Ashby heard their voices as the hall door into the greenhouse was opened. He reached out a quick hand to Bevo. "Get in the cabin," he said. He stood, straightening himself in front of the door, trying to hide it with his body while Bevo slipped through. Then he turned.

There, coming across the yard were Ephe and Laurel, and Laurel was walking close beside a tall thin man in a light tan suit. Out of small green eyes set close together in his head, the thin man eyed Ashby. Ashby waited.

# Chapter XIV

In the seconds which it took the three to reach him, Ashby watched them curiously. He noticed that Ephe had a certain blatancy about his stride, the walk of a man who has a guilt about his destination but moves brashly with a pretense at not caring. Laurel, on the other hand, held back a little, and she would not let her eyes look directly on Ashby, but with her whole figure seemed to be trying to pretend she was not there at all. But the thin man walked straight and sure, with something like sadistic delight in his pace, and as he came closer he cocked one eye at Ashby and on his weasel face there came an expression of cruel humor. He pushed his light tan hat back on his head so that the sun struck his face for a moment, and in that little time Ashby could see the naked sarcasm in his eyes.

Then they were very close to him. Ashby kept his eyes purposefully away from Laurel, because he knew that if he looked on her he could be caught unaware by whatever blow the thin man aimed at him. But he was as conscious of her as he would have been had she put her hand in his, and before any word was spoken he had an unreasonable feeling that she had done just that. The sunlight glinted on the gold streak in her hair.

Ephe spoke. "Ah . . . Ashby . . . We were looking for you." He put his heavy hand on the thin man's shoulder. "This is

Slim Lorrimer, Ashby." Ephe laughed. "He's sort of my factotum, you know. Miss Laurel's father."

He could not help letting his eyes touch briefly on Laurel. She did not avoid his gaze, but her usually mobile face was now mask-like and unalive, and her eyes looked stricken.

Then he put out his hand and Slim seized it and wrung it disinterestedly.

"Pleased," Slim said. He talked as if with closed nose, his voice high and nasal, so that the one word sounded like a jeer. His lips curled over it mockingly. "Pleased," he said again, dropping Ashby's hand.

Ashby said nothing. He stood with a waiting smile in the sudden burdensome silence. Ephe struggled with his throat; with one fat finger he pulled at his collar.

"Uh . . . uh . . ." he said, hocking.

With a delicate little finger, Slim explored a crevice between two teeth, contemptuously waiting for Ephe to talk. Ephe glared at him. He took the finger from his mouth, wiped the tip of it dry against his coat and, the while, stood grinning at Ephe, eyebrows raised. He was, Ashby thought, like an intelligent Turkey Littlepage. They were both dangerous. But Turkey had been colored by field sun: he was blundering, loud as the purple wattle on his neck, dangerous only because he fed on his own sudden, uncalculated angers. Slim, however, had the rodent cunning of the city about him. His flesh was pallid, a protective coloring to leave him anonymous while in the dark alleys and back rooms he plotted with rat-cunning and stealthy hatred. He did not lower his eyebrows until Ephe managed to speak.

"Uh . . . Ashby . . . where's Temp?" He did not look at Ashby. He pretended to be concerned about something to the westward, toward the river.

Ashby felt the hotness mount up his neck, the slow burning spread through his cheeks. He gritted his teeth against quick, unthought words.

Then he said, slowly. "I thought you had given me your

word about that." He fixed his eyes on Ephe. He could hear his own angry breathing.

"I'm not going back on my word," Ephe said. "Why'd you think I was?" He spoke blatantly now, as he had walked. Then he chuckled, unconvincingly. "You got the Pelham temper, son. I never meant . . ."

Deliberately Ashby pulled a switch from the rosebush beside him. Then he reached in his pocket and took out his knife and began to cut little slivers from the switch.

Watching the knife, noting, the way a man will note the unimportant and irrelevant under stress, the small patch of nicotine brown on his tanned middlefinger, he said, "You told me I could keep Temp here till after the funeral. That implied to me that I could keep him safely here. I'd have left three hours ago if I'd thought you meant to blurt to everybody." He looked slit-eyed at Slim. Slim's face was twisted while he worked again, with elaborate unconcern, with the little finger. "You ought to know that it was dangerous to tell that Temp was here." He shrugged. Out of the corner of his eye he could see Laurel, watching him. He wondered if he imagined that she gave him the briefest of nods. Somewhere beyond the anger in him, there was a heartsickness at seeing her beside the thin man, even suspecting that she did not want to be there.

"Why, son," Ephe said, heartily, "you ought to know I wouldn't tell anybody that would harm Temp. Why, Slim, here, why he's like family, been with me longer than I remember, and . . ." Ephe rubbed one hand over his jowls.

"Why'd you want to know where Temp is?" Ashby said. "You aim to protect him more than I'm already doing?"

Slim spoke. "Why," he said, "the Governor and me figgered we could git you safe out of it. When we seen that that sheriff was so hell bent on troubling you, we figgered . . ." His voice had the whining quality of a cat cry.

Ashby dropped the last piece of rose switch and closed his knife with a click. "I started out on this thing to get Temp to a safe place. Not me."

"Now, Ashby," Ephe said. "Don't be unreasonable, Ashby. You're in real trouble, now, whether you know it or not."

"That's fine," he said. "I feel right good knowing that. I'm beginning to think that a man that lives in this neck of the woods and isn't in trouble is either blind or yellow." He set his eyes first on Slim and then on Ephe.

"Well," Slim said, the mocking whine still there, "I reckon that tells us off, Governor." He grinned.

"Does?" Ashby said. "Well."

"What I'm trying to tell you, Ashby, is that this thing's got out o' my hands," Ephe said. With thumb and forefinger, he plucked at his jowls.

"I can understand that," Ashby said. "I thought I was setting out on a sorta picnic myself. A man can get mighty tangled up in circumstances before he knows it, can't he?"

Ephe swiped his lips with one hand. "No matter how much I might want to protect you and Temp . . ."

Ashby chuckled at that and Ephe, flustered, hesitated. Then he said, eyes narrowed, "Ashby, you make me so blamed mad I wonder why I'm fooling with you anyhow. You never used to be this way, but look like you got the devil in you over this thing, and if you don't listen to me now, you're gonna find yourself in jail—if you're lucky—or worse. I'm telling you, Ashby."

Ashby heard the quiet little gasp that Laurel made, but he did not look at her.

"If you want me to go on," he said, "if you'd rather I didn't stay, why don't you tell me? I thought maybe you needed me. I thought I'd stay until she was buried, because I thought for a minute or two up there in that room this morning that her dying mattered to you."

Ephe was shaking his head vigorously, evidently seeing in his mind Ashby escaping and making him and the sheriff look foolish to the voters.

"I wouldn't think of you going," he said. "Why, son, of course I need you. Now don't you get it in your head to go.

Why, what would your father say, when he comes and finds you not here?" Ephe was obviously wrought up over the possibility, and Ashby realized that it was not only the fact that it would make him look foolish to the voters that worried him, but also that Ashby's departure would be a violation of family ritual for which Ephe would be blamed. Funerals and weddings and anniversaries were sacred to the family, and Ephe knew it.

"I reckon Father would understand," Ashby said. "He knows what job I've got to do. And he wanted me to do it."

"Jason always was a dreamer," Ephe said.

"Dreamer or not," Ashby said, "This whole thing might have been settled by now, if he'd just been able to talk to Turkey before Turkey started out after me. But now I reckon everything and everybody have conspired to lead Turkey beyond any reason."

Ephe sighed, a heavy old man's sigh that sounded as if it came from the bowels. "No matter. I can't even pretend to protect you and Temp, Ashby, if you're gonna hide things from me. I mean, you got to tell me where he is. Suppose that sheriff should come back?"

"Come back?" Ashby said, feigning ignorance. "He been here?"

Then Ephe told him about the sheriff's visit, leaving out what it pleased him to leave out. "I of course never told him Temptation was here," he said. "I made out I didn't know anything."

"Course," Ashby said, calmly. He cocked his head and with one finger scratched in the hair at his temples. "And course you didn't even hint that the sheriff's little 'party' might have to be held on your place, once the funeral was over."

"Why," Ephe said, his mouth unclosing. "Why, what 'party' you talking about, Ashby?"

" 'Party?' " Slim said.

Ashby let his eyes go up and down the two of them, slowly. "I don't see any use of us talking any more," he said. "I reckon either one of you would get lockjaw on the truth." He half-turned from them.

"All right," Ephe said. "You gonna forget your respect for your elders, I'm gonna forget what I promised you. I'm gonna tell you like I told you this morning that I can't be involved in a thing like this Temp business. And no matter how much you make out that I'm just being mean and selfish about it, I tell you it's a bigger problem than me and you and Slim or anybody else, and you don't have any idea what you're doing protecting Temp. But I've warned you and if you don't choose to heed me . . ." Ephe turned. "Come on, Slim." He looked at Laurel. His voice changed. "We've got to go down to the undertaking parlor to pick out the casket. You'll take care of the folks that come? I don't know where Wesley is, and . . ." She nodded. Then he looked at Ashby. "I reckon you aim to get Temp out of here. I'm sorry you drove me to it . . ."

Ashby thought he could see Ephe's mind calculating how he would warn the sheriff that Ashby was leaving. He smiled. "Well," he said, "I'd be glad to get him out of here. But you see . . ." His smile broadened. "You see I don't know where Temptation is right now, myself. He's gone."

Ephe clamped his jaw to and stood a second without speaking, his breath coming in angry puffs. "You slipped him off somewhere," he said, finally. You . . ."

"Why, Uncle Ephe," Ashby said. "What you so het up about? You just told me to take him off. And now that I tell you he's gone, you fly off the handle. It couldn't be that you never really aimed to let me get away with him, could it?" He leaned forward, head cocked quizzically.

Ephe breathed with a rough, gravelly sound in his throat. Slim looked at Ashby with his little rodent eyes. Then, before Ephe could say anything, Slim said, "Like I told you, Governor." He glanced around the yard. Then he looked back at Ashby. "I reckon," he drawled, "I reckon that Thomas fellow is gone, too. Eh?"

Ashby wondered briefly if they had seen Bevo go through the

door, and, if they had, if they had known who it was. He chanced that they had not. "Why, I don't know. I hunted around a while for Temp, and so I haven't seen Carter lately."

Ephe opened his mouth, but Slim spoke again. "Carter. That his name? Carter Thomas." He made his eyes smaller. "Don't know as I ever heard of anybody by that name. No lawyer I know of. Where's he from?"

"He's from over home," Ashby said. He kept his voice level, usual, even a little bored.

"Must be new there," Slim said.

"You know home?"

"I been around there from time to time. I know most everywhere in Mississippi. This Carter Thomas must be sorta new over there." He rocked on his heels and with a gesture like a sneer he raked his tan hat farther back on his head. "Sorta new," he said again, meaningfully. "I'll be pleasured to meet him." Then he pretended to be impatient to leave. "Well, Governor," he said, "might as well get on, I guess." He looked with feigned casualness at Ashby. "I heard about you and Bevo Banes gittin' in jail night 'fore last. Didn't know you was friends."

Ashby met his eyes. "I never met him till that night."

"Seen him around since?" Slim said. Then, without waiting for Ashby to answer, he winked and turned. Ephe stared a second and then followed him to the stable-garage.

Ashby stood there in the sunbright yard listening to the sound of the motor starting, watching them back out and start up the road. He stood there conscious of Laurel beside him, waiting, and, when at last he turned, he wondered what he would say to her and she to him.

# Chapter XV

He did not, however, face her immediately. He thought that he had probably sounded smug and self-righteous to her in the talking with Ephe and Slim. He felt a little embarrassed at the seriousness he had shown. He wanted to say to her, "Sorry you caught me with my heroics showing." She was probably laughing at him. She was probably thinking that Ephe and Slim were sensible and that, beside them, he had acted like a yearling, engaged in a high school oratorical contest. He was embarrassed before her and then unreasonably angry that she should be there at all, and then within a split second, certain in his mind that she had come there to see him embarrassed by Slim, that her whole purpose in being there was to support Slim and Ephe. After all she had said nothing to indicate to him that she was on his side. For all he knew Slim might have brought her along on purpose. "Villains," he thought, as angry now at himself as he was at her, "Villains always use a seductive wench to lure their opponents off the straight and narrow. They do it that way in melodrama and God knows this is melodrama. And if it isn't, any Pelham can soon make it into one. Just any old Pelham you find lying around."

He was aware of his self-consciousness as he turned abruptly, awkwardly toward the cabin. He knocked on the door.

Bevo's head came out, his thick hair wisping over his forehead, as if he had been rumpling it.

"You hear?" Ashby said.

Bevo nodded.

"I reckon you were right," Ashby said. "You got to get away." He was whispering.

Bevo opened the door wider and stood in full view. He had taken off his coat and now stood in rumpled shirtsleeves there in the eave-shadowed doorway.

"No," he said. "I been thinking. When I thought it would help, me leaving, I didn't mind. But now they gonna use me as an excuse to do their worst anyhow, whether they know I'm here or not. So I reckon I'll stay and help you see that Temp is safe."

"You don't have any business . . ." Ashby said. He lowered his voice again. "If you do, they'll ruin you. Your mills . . ."

Bevo said, stubbornly, "It's a thing I got to do."

Ashby nodded. "All right. You stay here. We better wait till dark, and then I'll take you to where Temp is."

Bevo assented with a grunt, but his eyes were beyond Ashby, on Laurel. His eyes looked sadly, lingeringly on her, and then they closed briefly and looked away. He leaned to Ashby's ear. He whispered. "That Slim . . . I know now who he is. He's the fellow that might' nigh killed Papa once. Threw a brick at him. Papa was leading a strike and this Slim used to be a strikebreaker in the old days. Used to have a pistol with sixteen notches on it. For niggers he had killed." Then, before Ashby could say anything, he closed the door, as if he could not say anything else, as if he could no longer look on Laurel and say what he had to say. Ashby stared a second at the closed door, at the fingernail scratch marring one polished wood panel. Then he turned.

She stood in the same spot. When he looked at her, he swallowed, and found the swallowing hard. Again he felt awkward, and angry at her that he felt so, since it seemed to him that if she would only say something to indicate what she thought, then he would know what to say and do in turn. Perhaps he knew too that what he wanted of her was approval, and that on her slightly puzzled waiting face there was nothing, no expression in which he could take comfort. He did not think that she had suddenly, almost violently, been thrust into a situation where her loyalties were confused if not divided. He only knew that in her attitude at that moment he could read anything, and that, embarrassed at his own seriousness in the scene with Ephe, he chose to read mockery and doubt.

His voice was rough when he spoke. He said, "I reckon you will want to tell him that, too," though he did not even know that she had heard the words that had passed between him and Bevo.

"Slim?" she said. "I haven't told him anything." She came closer to him, shaking her head. "You know I haven't told him anything, because I never knew anything to tell. And I wouldn't have . . ." She shook her head at him with that strange almost childish excess which marked all her gestures.

He did not know then why he had said what he had. "There's nothing to tell anyhow," he said, shrugging. "Just a re-do of *Uncle Tom's Cabin* with minor changes in cast and plot."

"Are you sure?" she said, but he had already turned away, abruptly, angered now at the guilt of having been both unjust and rude to her. For a second he thought to turn back and say to her, "I'm a fool. Everything is getting mixed up and beyond me. When a man's spent thirty-four years grinning at his world, he can't change it from a comic spectacle to a tragic drama overnight. And he feels a fool when he tries—or when he's forced to." Yet, even thinking the words in his mind, he knew he could not say them. For one thing he knew he had probably never really laughed at anything, because he had never let himself cry at anything, not since that day when he was a kid and Num had said, "They named you wrong. You ain't . . ."

He went rapidly toward the house. He slammed the kitchen door behind him. He stood inside the too-warm room, breathing heavily. Tilda awaited him in the middle of the room, in her hand a steaming cup.

"You want something to eat?"

"No," he said.

"I thought maybe you wouldn't," she said. "Even if it is after one o'clock. But you can drink this." She held the cup toward him.

He shook his head. "No. Later, Tilda."

"You had no breakfast and no lunch," she said. "You drink it, now."

He took the cup and, holding it in two hands, gulped down the scalding bouillon. "Hot," he said, sticking out his tongue. He drained the cup. "Take some to Mr. B . . . Mr. Thomas, out in your cottage. And don't tell anybody he's there."

"Nawsir," she said. He handed her the cup.

"When the funeral's done, I'm gonna go," she said.

He had already turned away. He went through the butler's pantry, and through the dining room and into the darkened parlor. He stood quietly with his eyes closed for a second, as he had used to do when a child and confused by an adult world. He leaned against the door-jamb with his eyes closed and tried to make a pattern out of what was happening and tried to discern whether the pattern was leading toward a climax that might really test his mettle or whether it was really no more than the comedies he had lived through before. He tried to think the pattern through, so that he could keep out of his mind the picture of Laurel's stricken face. He could hear the sound of his own breathing in the still room.

Then he heard his name said. "Ashby . . ." When he opened his eyes, Granny was there, had been there all the time, sitting in a deep chair in a far corner of the shadowed parlor, her hair startlingly white against the deep red of the drawn draperies behind her. "Ashby . . ." she said. He noticed how white and luminous her old hand was, held up to him in the darkened room. He heard the echo of the name in his head, and knew all at once that she was not naming him, but that other one. Yet he moved toward her, saying nothing, moved silently on unreal feet in a place he had never seen before. This was a time he had made up in his mind, a moment in which the years fell away. He could have said the words she would say and the words he would say before ever they were said.

She put one white hand on the stool at her feet and he sat there. When she said "Ashby" again, there was only one by that name in his mind. There had never been but one; he and she were suddenly of one age.

"Windmill tilting again," she said. Her cool fingers were under his chin, scratching tenderly at his unshaven flesh, pulling his face up.

"Yes," he whispered.

"Tilt hard, Ashby," she said. "Tilt hard."

"Yes," he said. "I will." Her cool dry fingers stroked his face.

"Father said to me," she said, "Father said, 'He's mad. Fighting against slavery.' And I said, 'What is it you're outdone about? His fighting or what he's fighting against?' And he said both. And I said I would not want a man without fight in him, nor one without a thing to fight for or against. And that all I would ask is what is the thing he is fighting about? And Father said, 'I reckon if the day comes when the North attacks us over slavery, he will stand with them.' And I said, 'No.' Oh, I told him . . ." She chuckled and cradled his face in hers. Her voice was young and full in the room, but he did not wonder on that at all. He did not wonder on anything. "I said what you had told me, that when you were born in Virginia, they put a spoon in your mouth with 'Freedom' writ on it. And Father snorted and said it should have had 'Rhetoric' on it, you talked so much. Yankee talk, too, he said. And I said, '*All men are created free and equal.* I reckon you call that Yankee talk. Maybe I made a mistake thinking Jefferson was a Southerner.' And Father couldn't answer. He didn't have any answer, so he said it was a thing a woman couldn't understand, and unseemly for me to talk of it. And I said it was his history books I had read, and none of them had said anything about Mr. Jefferson being a Yankee. And left him sputtering . . ." She let her laughter go out into the room. She shook her head, tears glistening in her eyes. "You should have seen him," she whispered. "You should have seen him."

"I wish I had," he said, his eyes on her face. The years had fallen somewhere. His name was Ashby Pelham. The first and only Ashby Pelham.

"He was like that that day in the garden," she said. She touched her hair. "I can still feel the river-wind in my face and the ribbon sitting jauntily there, yellow it was . . . You remember?"

He nodded, remembering, could feel the wind at his back as he faced her, could feel the cold butt of the pistol in his hand, could feel himself pushing up his cuffs, and smiling at her where she stood against the ivied brick wall beside the miniature Parthenon summer house, could see the young gold of her hair and the yellow ribbon sitting jauntily. He could feel the blood speed warmly in him with the moment's daring.

"I can hear the shot," she said, "and smell the sulphur in my hair. And can feel the ribbon, loosened in my hand, and two holes in it, where the bullet had gone through the doubled part. And you remember Father? Choking there before us . . . ?"

Again he nodded. He could hear the words they had said before the older man had fallen there on the brick path at their feet, one twitching hand outstretched.

"He wanted me to be safe," she said, softly. "And I tried to tell him that all the safety I could ever depend on was in you. In your daresomeness. But it was that that frightened him, daresomeness. Afraid of fighting by them. Grown rich and idle, the land conquered, flush time everywhere in 1854. And they, all of them, depending on money and land to wall themselves in. Like William . . ."

"Yes," he said, "Like William." William he remembered, too. She had married William because her Father had made her believe he was dying, and begged her from his sick-bed to marry the man he had picked for her. But there had been only words to make the marriage, because the fire on the *Eliza Battle* had tended to that. He lived through those hours, too, the hours in which he stood on the side deck while inside, in the saloon, she danced with false gaiety with her new husband to the tunes of two Negro orchestras. And he stood outside watching, having come along on the voyage, the maiden trip of the elegant new *Eliza Battle,* because he had planned to come with her on their honeymoon, and was not a one to let circumstance face him down. So there he stood on the deck in the bitter wind watching now for the bonfires that meant another landing and now brooding over the lights patterning the muddy flooded nightwaters of the Tombigbee and now peering inside the saloon to see her in William's thick arms, dancing. But that was all of marriage there was for William, dancing, because the fire came along then, and . . .

"William tried to save himself," she said. "The man Father had married me to so I would be protected—because he was quiet and steady and untroublesome. But in the fire, he wasn't any of those things. He was only afraid and weak, as I'd known he would be. He tried to save himself, first, and he died. And you . . . Not you. You it was that thought about the cotton bales. I would never have thought of it, but you did. And gambled with your own life, when—the way you could swim—you could have saved yourself easily. But even there, you fought against the river and the fire, and didn't think about yourself . . ."

"You stayed," he whispered.

"Of course I stayed. While you told the Negroes how to save the women, putting them on the cotton bales and propelling them to where the tree tops showed against the flood. And then you tried to save William. Nobody can ever say you didn't try to save him. Although it would have meant . . ." She raised her head. "It was a strange miracle, that . . ." She fluttered her white hands.

He said nothing, snared and held by his remembering. Then finally she spoke again. "I have never been sorry," she said. "One battle fought, always you look for another one. The night the Negro was being lynched in Trent's pasture—I waited at the bedroom window upstairs watching the wet road in the flashes of lightning. I can remember rubbing my fingers over and over the naked figurines on that brass urn on the marble-topped table by the window. The mark of my fingernail is still there, on one of the brass maidens: I scratched it when in a sudden lightning clap I saw you coming on your horse, the Negro with his arms around your middle, and you crouched to the horse and the rain streaming down your face." She touched her handkerchief to her mouth.

"I have never been sorry," she said, again. "I was always glad you looked for a worthy battle. Glad . . . glad you helped to shape the place you lived in, to shape it better. And that you fought for something beyond yourself. And in '60 was both sad and glad that when you had to fight in a war that would never have been had your neighbors been like you, that you yet defended your neighbors, even though their cause . . . Well, I know what you said. That you weren't fighting for slavery but against war as a means of settling the thing. I wonder how many fought, feeling as you did?"

She put a hand out and stroked his head. "And now another fight. What this time? A Negro? Yes. Well, you will save him." She seized his arm. "Ah, you will beat them all. You hear me? You will. Because a man with a just cause is unbeatable. And you have always had a just cause, Ashby. Ashby, Ashby . . ." Her voice quavered, broke.

He felt her stand and without looking heard her move from him, heard the faint rustle of her black silk skirts. He turned and with glazed eyes watched her as she glided through the velvet portieres and out of sight. But in that instant before she disappeared, she whispered something to him, her old white head turned briefly in his direction.

"Bless you," she said, and then was gone. When he looked down into his hand, he found that she had left in it her handkerchief, a square of silky linen, lace-edged, had left it with him as she must often have left one with that other Ashby as amulet, his lady's colors. He had a ridiculous urge to put his head down into the dry lilac fragrance of the handkerchief.

# Chapter XVI

When he looked up, Laurel was standing in the middle of the room, watching him. He felt a fool. Laurel was very still and quiet and it seemed to him that she had been crying. But he could not think about that. He could feel the burn of his cheeks.

"You haven't got a padded cell on you, have you?" he said.

"I've been listening," she said, not smiling, her voice toneless, as if she expected him to speak harshly and accusingly to her. "I thought I ought to tell you."

"I'll go quietly," he said, still joking against the feeling of being a fool.

"I was coming to explain to you about . . . about . . ." Her hands went out helplessly, in one of her beautiful fluid gestures. "And then I heard you and her, and I stopped." She took a step toward him. "You talked to her like . . . Why did you talk to her like that?"

"Crazy," he said, standing now, the handkerchief wadded in his hand. "We're all crazy. See visions."

"But . . . she thought you were her husband. Is it Temp

that's worried her into . . ." She touched her tongue to her lips. "Or Miss Semantha?"

"It didn't take anything special," he said. "It was just a plain ordinary Pelham parlor game." He was lying and he was aware of it. Once, perhaps twice, when he was a child, she had played such games with him, had led him off into a world of myth more real than anything he had known since. But since he had been grown, there had always been his laughter there between them, his doubting. "Sometimes we play leapfrog," he said, wishing he could stop talking. "Or puss in the corner."

"Oh, Lord," she said. "Why are you such a fool?"

He grinned at her, liking the anger in her, glad that she could get angry at him.

"I've been telling you," he said. "It's inherited. The genes and chromosomes."

"No," she said. "I think you're ashamed. And afraid."

"Of what?"

"Of being what she wants you to be. What you want to be. What you really are." Now her breathlessness was returning and the eager movements of her head. He turned his head away, from the pulse beneath the three tiny freckles, like gold flecks in smooth polished stone.

"Am I?"

"Yes, and now you can't joke against it any longer. All the joking against what you really believe and are—it's caught up with you now."

He felt a strange pleasurable excitement in him for a second. Then he shook his head, still not looking at her, but looking away into the gloom of the heavily furnished room, even now faintly redolent of the rum Semantha had been drinking there only a few hours before.

"Got a sword?" he said, lightly, and then, posed with hand outstretched as if it held a weapon gripped. He laughed at her. "You've caught the germ. They will have you seeing visions sooner or later."

"All right. Yes," she said, and half-turned from him and

made a weak laugh. He could see her lower lip held tightly by her teeth. "Well . . ." she said quietly, and then started from the room.

"Laurel! Wait . . ."

Then, when she stopped and turned, he did not know why he had stopped her, or why he could say he had stopped her. Lamely he said, "Why . . . What did you come to tell me?"

She did not say anything for a moment. Then, speaking softly and swiftly, so that her words ran together, she said, "I came to tell you I would do anything to help you. I wanted you to know that being Slim Lorrimer's step daughter . . ." She lifted her head to look into his eyes. "You must have known from what I've told you already that Slim was never like a father to me. And never could have been. If you don't believe me—if you want to test me—ask me anything. Ask me what they said in this room this morning, and I will tell it to you. I'll tell you that without knowing what you're doing beyond saving Temp from that sheriff, you've somehow managed to give them a sort of dramatic situation that they intend to use to accomplish everything they want. They think this will elect Mr. Ephe to the Senate. . . ."

"The Senate?" he said. "So that's what he's running for?"

She nodded. "Yes, he is now. Now he thinks he can be elected for sure, by talking about white supremacy. And Slim thinks he can ruin Bevo Banes. He hates Bevo Banes because he hated his father before him. And Mr. Ephe would be glad to ruin Bevo Banes, too. Mr. Ephe and his partner, Tinney, a Yankee fellow who's building a mill over in your home town, they think that Bevo Banes is the cause of all their labor trouble. And Slim thinks that Carter Thomas is Bevo Banes."

He moved his head to indicate he had heard, but he did not say anything. He should have known that the Senate was the next logical step for Ephe to take.

"And now do you see why I say that you can't joke much longer?" Because it is going to take more than a laugh . . ."

He said, "I reckon," trying to make a sensible pattern out

of what she had said and wondering why she had chosen to say it—even while he could not think of anything except how close she was to him and how quiet the room was where he could hear her breathing. He found himself leaning forward and then his arms went around her. He kissed her, one hand cradling her head, her hair crisp yet soft to his touch. Under the scrape of his unshaven face her skin was smooth.

Her lips were as they had promised to be, warm and firm. The tip of her nose was cool against his cheekbone. He pressed his hands into the small of her back until it seemed that he could feel the flesh beneath the wool of the dress, the quality of her skin. He could feel the rise and fall of her breast against his chest. Flame mounted in him; his muscles tensed. He had no awareness of the house, or other human beings. He took his lips away a moment, and, with a little sob, she buried her face in his shoulder, her nose touching the sensitive spot along the ridge of his shoulder bone. He shivered with the feel of it, and caught her to him again. He could see the wetness on her cheeks, could taste the salt on her lips.

Then she pulled herself free and stood, still close to him, but with her head down. He put a finger under her chin. She looked at him with wet gleaming eyes. She waited, her eyes moving over him. His hand moved.

She whispered, her voice near to hoarseness. "You think I'm like Louise. You think . . ."

"I don't think anything of the kind," he said, softly. He caught her shoulder, roughly. "Don't say that."

"Then say it," she said. "Say it."

"Say . . .?" Then he smiled at her. "I love you," he said, and leaned to kiss her again. But she turned her lips away.

"You say it too easy," she said. "You say it like . . ."

He shook her then. "Listen," he said. "I never said it but once before in my life." He thought of Carol and how he would never say it to her again and how when he had said it, it had not meant anything at all, really—had not even meant as much as when, drunk, a man mumbled it to a waitress in a hamburger joint, because in the latter case "I love you" at least meant he would like to sleep with her. "It's a hard thing to say when you mean it. It sort of embarrasses me to say it, and so I say it easy that way, to keep from showing . . ." He shook his head at her. "I mean it," he said, fiercely. "Do you hear me?"

She turned her eyes back to him. "Yes," she said.

"I love you," he said. He kissed her cheeks, little quick kisses designed to hide his awkwardness, and then kissed her neck where the three gold flecks were.

She trembled and caught him to her and held his face in her hands. "I love you," she said. "I've loved you for forty-eight hours now." She smiled slowly at him. "I don't see how it could be. I never believed that in so little time, you could feel like this. . . ."

"But we do," he said. "We do."

"Yes. We do." She ran a finger over his eyebrow. "Have you really loved me all the time? Since the first?"

"Yes," he said. "Since I first saw you."

"Every minute since then? Every single minute?"

"Every single minute," he said. "Except when I was dodging the sheriff or doing all the thousand and one things . . ."

Again she turned her head away, just as he bent to kiss her. He felt the sudden rigidity of her body. Then all at once she relaxed and gazed up at him, laughing, a look of sudden sunlight on her face in the dim room. "I'm being female," she said. "Even the best of us . . . But I wanted you to think about me the way I do about you. Every minute." She touched his face again with her finger. "It's hard to be a woman and make sense. You want a man you're proud of, and yet . . . yet you can't help resenting the time he spends doing the very things that make you proud of him. . . ."

"Are you . . . ?" he asked, his voice husky, unable to finish the question. He was embarrassed again. He wanted her approval as he had always wanted Granny's, yet was unable now to believe, in spite of what Laurel had said, and in spite of his play-acting with Granny, that at this moment he faced a situation that might test him as a man. He was afraid to believe it much as he wanted to, and he was asking only for reassurance—that the job was there to be done and that she did not doubt he could do it. It was a stupid need for a grown man to have, he thought, even as he said again, stumblingly, "Are you . . . ?"

"Yes," she said. "Yes. When I think what you're standing up against . . ." She clutched him. "But I'm afraid," she said, burrowing her head into his chest, so that her voice came muffled to him. "I'm afraid for you. Because I know . . ." He felt the shudder go through her. "I know Slim. And that sheriff. And even though I'm grateful to him, I know Mr. Ephe too. And I wonder if you know what you're doing."

She lifted her head and looked at him and he tried to fight down the coldness that came on him.

"You've made it all so simple—even unimportant," she said.

Because I didn't dare do anything else, he thought. Because I didn't want to look a fool.

"But it isn't simple," she said.

All right, he said to himself. If it is going to be bad, then that's all right. I would rather it be bad than a joke. For me, I mean. For Temp, I'd rather it never had been at all.

"It seems silly and unbelievable to you," she said, "Their making such a fuss over what is only simple justice. But it's not a question of Temp and a crazy sheriff. It's like I told you, you're threatening an order of things they've built, and the very threat will help them strengthen their order. Not that they don't really, honestly, fear you . . ."

Do they? he wondered. Do they? Then at least they don't laugh. If they are afraid . . .

Her hands, holding onto him, gripped his arms tightly. "They're afraid," she whispered. "Only madmen could do what they intend to do to you and Temp, if you don't give up, give him up to them. But that's what they are—mad." She shook her head. "Don't you see? I love you for what you're doing, but I know how you'll call down on your head all the fear and hate in this country. They've wronged millions of Temps and they know it. But for you to tell them so by what you're doing . . . Well, in their nightmares, they see all the other Temps taking new heart against them, because of you. Oh, Ashby, don't let them. . . . They'll try to destroy you. They will. Ashby . . ."

He did not say anything. He could not reason against the coldness he felt. It seemed to him that in one breath she had told him that a difficult and great job needed doing, and in the next breath she had shown a fear that he could not do it. He drew back from her. He could not have said what he had wanted her to say, but she had not said it.

"Ashby! What's the matter?" she said, her voice still low. Ashby . . . ?" She reached a hand out to touch him again.

What had she meant, he wondered. If he had not stepped back from her would she have said in a minute that he had better give up the job altogether? And was her love for him the reason, the only reason?

He was angry at himself for doubting her, and angry at her for making the doubt. "I reckon," he said, "that Slim must have rehearsed you a long time for this."

"Ashby, don't joke now," she said, and then, mouth half-open, realized that it had not been a joke. He could see the realization on her face, and with it, the quick tears starting in her eyes.

He turned from her. "You ought to have known by now that I'm nothing but a clown," he said, and left the room.

# Chapter XVII

He went blindly, without sense of direction, away from her eyes and found himself in the upstairs bedroom where he usually slept in Ephe's house. Automatically, he bathed, shaved and dressed, taking his clothes from the suitcase which someone—Tilda, or perhaps Temp before the journey to the swamp—had brought in for him. He repacked the suitcase neatly. It was time to go. He knew that he was not thinking clearly, but what thinking he had done had convinced him that there was no reason important enough for him to stay there and that there might conceivably be many reasons why he should leave.

He went out into the hall with a carton of cigarettes in his hand. Downstairs he could hear the slow buzz of voices; already, from the sound, the house was filled. He went down the stairs, his feet quick on the carpet. Two women he vaguely recognized stood guarding the front door. In the light of the Minerva torches, their faces were yellow above the black of their dresses. One of them nodded to him, a short half-gesture of her face, as if she were not quite certain whether he was a member of the family or one of the undertaker's assistants. He nodded back, turned beside the Minerva to his left and went down the long hall away from the humming in the parlor. He stood aside for the man from the funeral parlor bearing Semanha back into her house in a gray casket. He thought that the family would be outraged at his departing before the funeral, but that in view of the things that might happen if he stayed, he would probably be showing more respect to Semantha if he left. He watched the men lift the casket onto the frame and roll it on rubber wheels toward the parlor. Behind the casket a young man with slick black hair and a professionally-sad mien bore a huge frame to which were attached what he would undoubtedly have called "the floral tributes." Ashby, flat against the wall, felt the wreaths brush his face as the young man staggered past; the inevitable cloying odor of tuberose flooded his nostrils. Ashby moved to the kitchen door, opened it and entered.

"I reckon we're going to have to raid Miss Semantha's pantry," he said. His voice sounded strained and unreal to him, perhaps because he was acting from a dimly realized instinct and not from any clear-cut logic or any understandable emotion. He was not angry or belligerent or excited or frightened. And he was only casually purposeful.

Tilda was bending over a box on the floor, half hidden by the jut of the cabinet. She lifted her head. He noted that the hair was again smoothly arranged.

"I'm doing it," she said, quietly.

She moved the upper half of her body to look at him, and he saw first that her eyes were strangely alive and quick and then noticed that even the miserliness with which she had held her body had gone out of it, that she moved freely and gracefully, like a person who has just regained the space to move comfortably in, like a person who has escaped from long years in a narrow cell.

"I mean," he said, "I mean . . . more than for just Temp."

"Yessir," she said. "I know. Soon as I saw those gun totin' men out yonder, I knew." She had dropped her head while she talked. She went on packing cans into the box and her voice came muffled to him, so that he thought he must have misunderstood.

"Gun totin' men?" he said.

She straightened and looked at him. "You didn't see 'em?" she said, her tan finger pointing toward the driveway. "Out yonder." He went to the door and looked but saw nothing. He moved a foot and gazed toward the side road. There, walking with an attempt at military precision, was one of Turkey's deputies. He had no gun over his shoulder, but he went back and forth across the driveway just outside the gate. Every now and then he self consciously touched the pistol in the holster on his hip, and when his hand touched it, his eyes went reflectively toward the house. He stopped once, spat, pushed his black Stetson back on his head so that the late sun fired his already wind-reddened face, winked one eye at somebody Ashby could not see, and continued his slow pacing. For a second he was lost behind the great black hearse parked beside Ashby's car. Then he reappeared and the pacing continued.

Ashby turned. "Are they all around?" he said.

Tilda nodded, grunting a little as she lifted a sack of flour into the wooden box which he could now see was closely packed with long-staying processed foods. "On every side," she said. She stood straight again. "I thought you must have seen them. I knew if you saw them, you'd know it was time to go."

He did not say anything for a moment. In spite of what Laurel had said, in spite of Ephe's attitude, he had not counted on this. If somebody had told him an hour ago that the house would be guarded by Turkey's deputies, he would have laughed. He could hear himself saying, "And those hounds, too, I reckon?" But now he did not know what to say. He had been so hell bent on not seeing visions that even so solid an object as the deputy outside did not at once become a tangible threat to him. When his mind finally comprehended what his eyes had seen, he shrugged.

"And you aiming for us to get all that food past them?" he said to Tilda.

"Yessir," she said. "I said to myself you would find a way. And if you didn't, the Lawd would find it for you. Her dying . . ." She looked toward the front of the house ". . . was a sign for me to leave, and now all I got to do is wait till you figure out how we can leave."

"Yes," he said. "That's all. And where we will go if we are able to get past them at the gate and past whatever road blocks they've got set up. It's as simple as that." He was smiling sardonically at her.

She paid no attention to his attitude. "Why I never thought there was but one place we could go," she said.

"You mean the swamp?" he said.

She nodded.

"Yes," he said. He wet his lips. "Yes. But getting that food there . . . I will have to slip past them and slip Mr. B. . . . Mr. Thomas past them." He rubbed his hand against his jaw and then pulled reflectively at his lower lip. "But now *you* could get by them."

"Yessir," she said. "They got no reason to stop me."

"You might," he said. Hesitatingly, he pulled again at his lip. "You might even get my car past them, so you could take all that food. If you could drive, that is."

"I can drive," she said. "When Wesley's off drunk, like today, I've had to drive Miss Semantha." She stood there in a swathe of sunlight. He was all at once impatient of the sunlight, wanting the day to end, wanting darkness. He tossed the carton of cigarettes into the box.

"All right," he said. "You think you can get that food in the car?" She nodded.

"Before the moon comes up," she said. "I'll think of a way." She frowned. "I could take those men their supper out yonder, and while they're eating it . . ."

"All right," he said. "And when you've loaded it up, you tell them Mr. Ephe is sending you somewhere. You reckon you can lie so they'll believe you?"

She regarded him gravely for a moment. Then she held out her bare arm and put one finger on it. "When you're this color," she said, "you lie like you breathe, because if you don't you wouldn't breathe long. You lie to live."

She turned her face away from him, and the thought came to him that she was remembering the scene in her cottage that morning, and feeling a sudden shame at so revealing herself. She pretended to be staring intently at the box at her feet.

He spoke brusquely. "Well, park the car off the road in the swamp. Somewhere in that part they call the Fox Run, in the bushes next to Cold Creek, where they can't see it from the highway."

"Do you know that the roads are blocked?" she said. "Do you know we got to go in the swamp?"

"No," he said, "I don't know anything for sure. But I don't think there's much chance they haven't blocked the roads."

"I know they're blocked," she said. "You must have, too. Without thinking, you must have known it. Else why did you say for me to raid the pantry without knowing I had already done it?"

He glanced at her and glanced away. "I don't know," he said.

"You knew they'd trapped us," she said.

"Not you," he said. "Temp and me . . ."

"And me. I been trapped here always."

He did not say anything for a moment.

"I don't reckon it matters," she said. "I just wanted to know if you felt it, too. I knew you did, though. When you said that about the pantry, I knew you knew that we'd have to go to the swamp and would need somethin' to eat."

"Well," he said, impatiently. "Anyhow, you park the car like I said. If the roads aren't blocked I'll get Temp and bring him there. If they are. . . I'll come and get you. You stay in the car, or near it in the bushes. Temp is in a hard place to find and you'd get lost."

She leaned against the cabinet. "If I was lost of my own doing, it would be all right. It would be like being found. It's being lost because of somebody else's doing that's . . ." She spread her tan hands, and then lifted her head and smiled at him. "I'll do anything you say. Anything." Then she stooped to her box and began to move the food around, busily.

He went to the back door and put his hand on the knob.

"You lookin' for Mr. Thomas?" she said.

"I was going out there," he said, not turning.

"He's not there," she said.

He turned. "Not there?"

"No, sir," she said. "He came through here a while ago and went in there?" She made a question out of the statement, as if she thought he had known Bevo was in the house. Her finger pointed toward the front of the house.

"Lord," he said, turning quickly. "If Slim Lorrimer should see him . . ." He hurried across the kitchen and pushed open the door of the butler's pantry. He collided squarely with Bevo's broad back. Bevo flinched and ducked aside from the place where he had been peering through the diamond-shaped glass in the door to the dining room. He backed into the corner, against the pantry cabinets. Then he saw it was Ashby. "Hell," Ashby said, recovering his balance, "you didn't have to knock me winding." He grinned. "Thank God you're hiding. I was afraid you'd shown yourself off to Slim. . . ."

"No," Bevo said, straightening. "I jest wanted to come in and see how they acted. I been peeping and eavesdropping." He looked so dead serious that Ashby laughed. "I wanted to see how they acted," he said again.

"How who acted?" Ashby said.

"Gentlemen," Bevo said. "And ladies, too, for that matter."

"Are there any in there?" Ashby said, jerking his head toward the door.

In the near-darkness of the pantry, Bevo nodded. "They must be ladies and gentlemen. They act funny enough to me."

"Do?" Ashby said. "Let me see." He put his face to the pane and looked out on the soft lighted rooms. To his left, against the outside wall of the dining room, before the stained-glass window Semantha's casket rested, behind it the frame of flower-wreaths, the pale flowers touched yellowly with the last sunlight through the window. Laurel, in a black dress, sat not far away, in a straight chair near the wide door into the parlor. He moved his eyes quickly away from her.

Suddenly, Bevo's head was against his, crowding to see through the narrow pane. "Tell me who they are," Bevo said. "Tell me about them."

"All right," he said, because he did not want to go in and face them then.

He pointed out first his cousin, Young Sandy Pelham, who came from the family branch which Granny called the "Mule Pelhams," and who was called "Young Sandy" even at sixty, to distinguish him from his father, Old Sandy, named Alexander. It was Old Sandy who, after Appomattox, when the slaves marched off and left him with a thousand acres of land to be planted, did the first plowing he ever did in his life, but never changed his customary demeanor: he plodded behind his one decrepit old mule, still wearing his morning coat, his brocaded waistcoat, and his tall silk hat.

"Why?" Bevo said, his nose pressed against the window pane.

"Because he always had dressed that way and he wasn't going to change even if he had lost seventy-five slaves. If he had to plow, he'd plow. But by God, he'd still dress as he'd always dressed."

"It sounds sort of crazy to me," Bevo said. "He must 'a' got them good clothes awful muddy."

"Reckon he did," Ashby said.

"Well . . ." Bevo said, reflectively. Ashby took his face far enough away from the pane to look at him. "Well, now, he was a gentleman, though."

"Yes," Ashby said. "I guess so. I guess he was one if you define a gentleman as one who adheres to a course of conduct for which there is no longer any reason. And against which there are plenty of practical considerations. Like now . . . you can see 'em wearing full dress and doing some new dance step that can properly be done only in acrobatic tights. But your gentleman wears tails, the same clothes he wore to dance 'The Blue Danube' in."

"You wear 'em though," Bevo said. "I bet you wear 'em yourself."

Ashby grinned at him. "Yes. I wear 'em." He put his face back to the pane, thinking: Good God, yes, I wear them. But don't ask me to make any sense out of it.

"Who's that yellow-headed girl over yonder in the corner?" Bevo said. "The one with her hand in the hand of that good-looking brown fellow?"

"That's Cousin Lissa Tillman and her husband, Junius." He watched her while he told Bevo about her. She was pregnant, and as some women are, beautiful in pregnancy. "It must be strange for her to sit here and think that Semantha is dead of the same fable she suffered so much from," he said.

"What fable?"

"The fable they teach ladies here: that their body ends at their neck and begins again at their ankles."

Bevo said, "Oh," and listened while Ashby told about her. Her father, old Major Tillman, was known as the wildest man in South Mississippi, and had made the mistake of marrying a woman who was thin and cold and believed the fable. After a while, they no longer lived together though they were under the same roof. One night, drunk, kept from his poker game and cockfights by a flood on the river, he had looked up to see his wife coming down the stairs and all the frustration and crazy love he had welled up in him. He caught her at the foot of the stairs and dragged her, with her feet bumping, upstairs and into her bedroom, and there outraged her. But in the end, she was victorious. Lissa was born as the result of that night, and his wife, her mother, died in childbirth. The major, in morbid repentance, attempted to rear Lissa to be an exact copy of her mother, though she was clearly not made of that same cold flesh. Even after the major's death and Lissa's marriage to Junius, however, she had not been able to escape the major's repentance. Dying, he had left her in the care of the strange perverted preacher who had helped him rear her. When she married Junius she sent Father Benjamin, the preacher, away, but two years later, at the moment when she was blossoming into the woman she was meant to be, the preacher returned to begin his work on her again, to tell her that she was childless because she had married "in the lust of the flesh" and the Lord had punished her for it. He almost destroyed her then, and her marriage with it. She came to look on him as a thing immortal, and not until another man—who loved her and saw that Junius was paralyzed by his own love for her—ran Father Benjamin away and burned down the church the major had built for him, did she see him for the person he was. Now she stood there in the room next to the bier and any man looking at her could see she was happy.

When Ashby finished, Bevo turned to him, frowning. "I knew a fellow had the same trouble with his wife," he said. "Festus Blue's wife wouldn't sleep with him a-tall after she got religion. But Festus jest beat hell out of her a couple of times and everything was all right after that."

Ashby laughed, softly. "You think Junius ought to have beat Lissa?"

"He's a gentleman," Bevo said. "I don't reckon he could beat her." He still frowned. "But it's still funny to me. Somehow, I didn't think that gentlemen and ladies would have the same kind of trouble that old Festus Blue had."

"Hell," Ashby said, "I tried to tell you before, but you wouldn't listen. Flesh and blood is flesh and blood. I don't reckon a spirochete knows the difference between a gentleman and a roughneck."

"But there is a difference."

"Not in what they do," Ashby said. "Only in how they do it."

"Yes. All right. How they do it. They do whatever they do mannersome-like."

"Yes," Ashby said. "And long as they've got manners about it, they can get by with anything." Only, he thought, there are some things they would not want to get by with. They would not kill or steal or lie—that is, all of them except Ephe. Outside of Ephe, their sins are decent sins, little adulteries, little delusions, little arrogances. They sin from the heart and not the head; and it is usually they who suffer and not anybody who is innocent or helpless. Because they are really decent people, even if sometimes they are a little fire-struck and mad.

He pointed through the pane to a little woman with white hair and black eyes. "You see Cousin Vettie Tillman yonder?" She sat very straight on a ladderback chair next to the fireplace and on a stool beside her sat her husband, Jubal, a pipe in his loose, humorous mouth, his satyr ears pink and youthful next the peppered gray of his hair. Ashby told about them. He told about how Vettie (christened Olivette) had fallen in love with Jubal, who was her distant cousin, and how, since both of them were chock-full of pride and touchy as a sensitive plant, they had quarreled often. After one of the quarrels, Vettie had gone to a party, and, pridefully, without thinking, had wagered her prize mare that she would never marry Jubal but would instead marry a man "as you'd pick out a piece of furniture" and then come to love him afterward. She was not the kind who could back down. Stubbornly, she married not Jubal but his brother, and scarcely spoke to Jubal during the five years the marriage lasted. Then her husband died and she, clinging even more tenaciously to the notion that she had learned to love him, buried him outside her dining room window and erected a bust of him over the grave and pushed the dining room table up to the window so that his face was opposite her in death as it had been in life. There and in that manner she lived with her one small son and one servant, while her money and her property gradually slipped away and her house began to crumble around her. Then Jubal came one day to see her, and she swore that she'd never leave that house while it stood about her. She spent her time looking out at the bust, which she had had made from a death mask, but which nevertheless had to be changed in several details before she would admit it was a good likeness of her late husband. Jubal knew nothing of the change and did not pay much attention to the bust. But he did know that only something startling would move her out of that house—which was not even, in fact, her own, since a dishonest factor who staked her crops had long ago got a mortgage on the place and was at that moment ready to foreclose. So Jubal set the house on fire.

"On fire?" Bevo said. "Like that fellow and the church . . .?"

Ashby nodded. "I'm kin to a long line of pyromaniacs. Evelina says it's because we're most of us born under fire-signs. You know, the stars." He felt the sudden strangeness of that. It was true: they seemed fire-born.

It was in the light of the fire, he said, when Vettie stood in the dining room window refusing to come out to Jubal in the garden, that all at once she looked at the bust and then at Jubal. Then she saw what she might have known, except for her pride: that the changes she had had made in the bust had made it into a bust not of her husband but of Jubal, that Jubal's face was the face of the bust. Even Vettie had to believe her eyes, then. She reached a hand out and Jubal lifted her over the sill.

"They have a genius," Ashby said, "for being like nobody else."

"I reckon," Bevo said.

"Look at Aunt Adele yonder," Ashby said.

"She's smoking. The one smoking, with her cigarette in that holder." He peered anxiously through the pane at the woman of whom he could see only the claw of her hand with its blood-red fingertips holding the ivory holder, the bony shoulders under the sheer of her black dress, the fantastic hair dyed a purplish-red.

"Now move over here," Ashby said, "and look at Aunt Parthenia." Bevo stood in front of him. "The old woman there. Lissa's aunt."

"I see," Bevo said. "She's sort of thin-lipped."

"She's not really," Ashby said. "She's a sort of gay old girl. But still full of religion and decorum. And got too much religion and decorum in her to approve of Adele. That's why she looks that way—I can hear her saying, 'A woman's got as much right to smoke as a man. But I say she should choose the places she smokes. She ought not to smoke on the street or anywhere in public and certainly not at a wake.' " He laughed softly as Aunt Parthenia waved a white age-freckled hand before her and sniffed perceptibly at the drifting blue smoke of Adele's cigarette. Between her long, puffed, setter's eyes, her great nose twitched. She toyed with an aged, crooked mahogany cane, leaning a little on it. "She hit a young preacher over the head with that cane once. Decorous as she makes out to be, she couldn't stand his arguing that Genesis shouldn't be taken literally. She believes that the seven days were seven days by a dollar alarm clock and not any millions of years, and she believes that the whale swallowed Jonah, and she'll scourge any agent of the devil who suggests the Bible might be allegorical."

"I wouldn't think a lady . . ." Bevo said.

"Of course you wouldn't," Ashby said. "I knew you had cooked up in you some fantastic notions of ladies and gentlemen." He jerked his head. "Look . . . Look at Adele. She's likely talking French to Aunt Parthenia now, just to shock her with bad words which Aunt Parthenia will know damn well from having read every blasted paper-back novel the French ever published, but won't admit she understands a thing Adele is saying. And Adele is busy defying them, the way she joined the Catholic Church to defy them—after she was through with her four divorces, which she like as not got just to defy them, too. The way she went abroad to live . . ."

"Four divorces?"

"I think it's four," Ashby said. "Though Aunt Adele always counts it as three because two of them were from the same man." He shrugged. "So there they are. And there's not any one thing true of all of them except that they're old. Whatever their age, they're old, old as hell. Because they haven't lived just their own lives—they've lived the lives of every damn person whose seed helped make 'em in the last two hundred years. No wonder we're all a little haunted. Our minds are like old houses, tenanted by the ghosts of our grandfathers' deeds. We've never forgotten anything and we've known everything but peace. Nobody in this family ever had peace. I reckon we'd sicken and die on it."

He stood in the deep darkness of the pantry, the darkness unbroken except for the flickering of the candles Laurel had now lighted at each end of Semantha's bier.

"So . . ." Bevo said, softly, his face heavy, with a strange sadness touching the corners of the mouth, the luminous liquid hound-eyes unwaveringly sorrowful. "So . . ."

"Yes," Ashby said. "So."

"I was a fool to think . . . I mean, that being a gentleman meant . . . I don't know." He shook his head, and turned.

"That a gentleman wasn't human. That it?"

"I reckon. But they do act human in a different way."

"Maybe," Ashby said, "Maybe it takes them longer to act human."

Bevo put a hand out toward the kitchen door. "And I thought to learn . . ."

"You don't need to learn anything," Ashby said.

"No. Maybe not," Bevo said. He touched Ashby's shoulder. "I'm goin' back out yonder now."

"Don't let anybody see you." Ashby watched him push the door open into the lighted kitchen and slip through it into the odorous vapors of baking ham and vegetables boiling with fat-back. The door swung shut behind him, blowing the food smells into Ashby's face. He was suddenly terribly hungry, but he turned and pushed open the door into the dining room.

He stood there just over the threshold, a few feet from Semantha's casket, and hesitated a second, facing them. When, at the sound of the closing door, they looked up and turned their faces toward him and cut off the low hum of their conversation, he knew that they all knew about his having taken Temp away. He supposed they had read it in the papers. For a moment they looked at him as they might have looked at a housecat which jumped on Semantha's bier. He could not say they were horrified, but certainly their faces were frozen, in that moment, with fascination, and they could neither speak nor move. Irritably, he thought: Good God, why are you staring? You ought to be used to the unpredictable in your own blood by now. God knows none of you has ever been able to foretell what another will do next. Of course I know you're outdone—that my particular unpredictability should have got on the front pages, but this is the age of publicity and I don't reckon I could hope for the anonymity Colonel Ashby Pelham enjoyed after his exploit in Trent's pasture.

He moved his eyes from them to Laurel and then quickly away from the hurt he saw in her face. The clock ticked and no one moved. Then at last Aunt Adele, who had turned her head to see him, raised one crooked finger and beckoned him to her, as she had no doubt beckoned many young men in her time. He walked past Laurel and Young Sandy to where she sat, and took the hand on which the finger had been crooked, and leaned and kissed it in the continental manner she insisted on. The hand was parched and white.

"My dear Ashby," she said, looking at him with the awful archness of the aged. "We hardly expected to see you still here. I thought you would have been across the river by now. . . ."

"On chunks of ice?" he said, raising an eyebrow at her.

She gave a low laugh, restrained just enough for the occasion. "I played Little Eva once in an amateur theatrical in Paris. You've never seen a Simon Legree until you see the French version. A sort of cross between that sewer-rat of an inspector in *Les Miserables* and Fyodor Karamazov." She frowned, a particularly strong frown because she was so adequately equipped with the wrinkles with which to make it. "Yes," she said, shaking her head with sudden emphasis, "Yes, more like old Papa Karamazov, I should say. The French version hinted at some sort of sex interest between Legree and Little Eva." She smiled, widely. "Lord, the French. . . But then . . ." She waved her bone-thin hands. "But then all this could never be happening in France. The French are so tolerant."

He looked into her eyes, darkened by the ring of eye shadow and the thick mascara on her short eyelashes.

"I've heard tell we used to be, too," he said, casually. "Before we were defeated."

"Yes," she said. She made a grimace with her rouged cheek. "But then, what can you expect. The whole place . . ." She swept both hands out. "The whole place is run by new-rich poor whites."

"Oh, now . . ." he protested, making conversation, so that he would not have to turn to the others and face the questions they might ask and which he would not know how to answer. "Like Uncle Ephe?"

Her face hardened, her eyes fired with a youthfulness he had not seen before. "A new kind of Simon Legree," she said, "with a Southern accent." Her hand patted nervously on the chair arm. "And Yankee masters." She looked over her shoulder at the casket. Her eyes softened. "I know why she was chopping those roses. Do you ever feel that maybe this terrible black thing will destroy us all?"

He did not answer her for a moment, because he could not speak lightly and laugh at a moment when she was concerned with Semantha's death, and also because her words recalled Uncle Vance to him, Uncle Vance and the phrase he had used: the dark web. Then he knew that he did not know how to answer her anyway, so he only shrugged.

"You mean it's up to us," she said. "You mean we can destroy ourselves because of it. And that . . ." She considered for a second, frowning again. "And that we make it what it is."

"I don't know," he said. "I reckon so."

"But you must . . ." she said, protesting.

"Look, Aunt Adele," he said. "I got into this whole thing out of something like instinct. I'd do it over again tomorrow if the necessity came. But I don't aim to do any Pelham preaching about it if I can help it."

"But how dull of you, Ashby," she said, smiling. "But then what do I expect? The grand manner is gone. And it's a pity, too. My God, Ashby, but I hunger sometimes for words that will move me." She shook her head. "But inarticulateness is a virtue now. And we're ashamed of our dreams as well as our decencies. Too bad."

"Yes," he said, aware of the others waiting for him to speak to them.

She leaned toward him. "Where is he? Temptation?"

"I don't know," he said, looking straight at her.

"Liar," she said. She rose and put her arm around him. "You must remember your manners, Ashby," she said, for the room to hear. "Come speak to the others." She led him to Aunt Parthenia.

"I was wondering when you would see me, son," Aunt Parthenia said, lifting her hand from the cane and giving it to him.

"I'm sorry, ma'am," he said. "Aunt Adele and I . . ." Adele had already returned to her chair.

"Adele," Aunt Parthenia said, "has a fascination for men I've never understood. Too skinny and sometimes quite raucous." The mauve-colored mole with three sprays of hair in it twitched beside her mouth. "But her Venus is strongly placed in the heavens."

"Evelina been talking astrology to you, Aunt Parthenia?" he said.

"Astrology," she said, "is a logical adjunct of predestination. If we are predestined, it seems reasonable to me that God might mark our destiny in the stars."

He smiled. Geology and Genesis she refused to reconcile; but astrology . . .

A hand touched his shoulder. "Howdy, Ashby." It was Junius, and behind him Lissa. Out of the corner of his eye he saw Young Sandy move toward him. Vettie and Jubal had risen. He greeted them all, conscious of the constraint in the room, a constraint stronger than even death could account for.

He stood talking to them for what seemed a long while, all the time watching Laurel out of the corner of his eyes. People came and went, stopped to speak to the family, filled the far corners of the house with the bee-buzz of strained conversation. Laurel sat beside the casket, standing now and then when callers came to look at the body. She was so paradoxically alive, standing there, her face flushed now and her hair curling damply around her forehead and her quick mobile hands saying words unvoiced, she was so alive she made death an outrage, and the women, looking at her and then at Semantha, would be seized with sudden uncalculated tears and would hasten away to weep quietly not for Semantha but for the fleetingness of time.

He saw this more than once as time passed. He avoided looking at Laurel, as he avoided the questions on mouths and in eyes. He sensed the low undercurrent of excitement in the house, and his ears sometimes caught the whispered phrases: "In all the papers . . . whatever is he doing here? . . . The radio said Mr. Ephe has demanded he tell where the nigger is . . . The Governor said . . . are they going to arrest him? . . . not yet, the nigger might try to contact him and give himself away . . . not till after the funeral is over anyhow . . . oh, whatever made Ashby do it anyhow?"

He had a great nervousness in him, an impatience to be gone, but he waited, for what he did not know. Though when six o'clock came and it was well dark, he looked up and saw his Father's face in the door and it seemed to him then he had waited until he should come. Behind Father he saw the face of Evelina. He pushed past the people around him and went toward the hall. Then he saw that the hall itself was filled with people, and that behind Father and Evelina, Ephe was there and with him his partner, Tinney, and Slim Lorrimer and the sheriff. All their eyes were fixed on him as he went through the suddenly silent crowd.

# Chapter XVIII

Ashby could sense in their eyes that they expected him to be grim or resolute or even angry: that, in a word, they looked to him for an emotional reaction on a scale they could understand, and they would not comprehend him if he should tell them that he was acting out of no conscious and clear-cut motivation, but only out of necessity, the push and jostle of circumstance, which now had decided that he must take Temp and depart Ephe's that night. He could not tell them that he was not yet dead-sure that circumstance, or Ephe, might not change. They stood waiting for him with that unconscious drama in their expressions he had known so long.

Father was ostentatiously usual in his manner. In the jaundiced light of the Minerva torches, his lean face was ashen, but everything else about him was the same as ever. His eyes retained that strange unseeingness in which he seemed to be looking inward always. He put out his hand and held Ashby's only a second longer than usual and said simply, "Son . . ." Ashby wished desperately for a ready joke, though even if it had been there on his tongue, he could not have said it because of the death in that house.

Evelina was worse to face than Father; she had tears in her eyes. She held him tightly for a moment and he was inarticulate with embarrassment. He could smell the faint odor of dried rose geraniums that was always about her. "I've been so worried," she whispered. "Oh, Ashby." He kissed her forehead and, self-consciously, patted her back. The deadly silence of the rooms remained unbroken. He could feel the eyes waiting behind him, curiously, and could see the fixed hard eyes of Ephraim on him.

Then, when Ashby was wondering what he would say to Ephe and what Ephe would say to him, was wondering if he should not leave as quickly and quietly as possible, Father said, "Take me to Granny," and put his hand on his elbow.

"Yes," Evelina said, and took his other arm.

"I guess she must be in the back parlor," he said, and took a step.

But before he moved farther, Ephe checked him with a pudgy black-furred hand. "Ashby, I'd like to see you. You know Tinney, I think. We'd like to talk to you—in my office."

Again he was angry because he was embarrassed. They were all demanding that he behave in a new pattern to which he felt unequal, and so he felt self-conscious and then enraged. He spoke coldly. "If you think there's anything to say." He shrugged. "In a minute."

The sheriff and Tinney stepped aside. Ashby and Father and Evelina went down the hall and into the back parlor next to the greenhouse. Granny sat alone in the dark. All he could make out of her was the white crown of her hair touched flittingly by a light that seeped through the hinge-crack of the door. Evelina went ahead and leaned and kissed her.

"Granny . . ."

Granny did not speak. Father leaned then, and touched his lips to her cheek.

"Don't you want a light in here?"

"I like the dark. I find I see better the things I want to see. Bring your chairs near me." She sat by the empty fireplace. Ashby pulled a chair close for Evelina and then he and Father sat beside each other on the small sofa facing Granny. The room was heavy with the overpowering scent of Granny's sachet. He sniffed.

"I can't bear tuberose," Granny said. "Have I managed to kill it?"

"Yes," Ashby said, wanting to joke again, to laugh against the waiting strain he felt in them. I never should have come here in the first place, he thought. Only I never thought it would be so complicated. But even so, I should have left them out of it, as much as I could. Because they have got a big enough burden of remembrance without bearing this, too.

Yet he did not know what he could do about relieving them. Certainly there was nothing anybody could do to relieve them of the past. They had chosen not to forget it, the crack of the Minié ball into the bone, the odor of the burning dead in the inferno of the Wilderness, the red hole in the throat at Shiloh. There was nothing he could do about their remembering, but if violence was coming, he could at least move it out of their sight and hearing. That had a plenty of bloodstains on their furniture, and an ample sufficiency of *Requiescat in Pace* chiseled on marble.

He heard Granny talking. "I'm glad you've come, Jason. I want to go home with you. Now that Semantha is gone, I'm not coming back here. I've only come these years because I thought some Pelham owed her something for the misery another Pelham had caused her."

And Father said, "We'll take you home."

They sounded weary, he thought. The youthful timbre that had been in Granny's voice this morning when she had mistaken him for the other Ashby was now gone. She seemed to have forgotten he was here in the room with her. For a moment, he wondered why he had thought to leave at all, why he did not go into that other room and repeat that he did not know where Temp was, and, since Temp was in a place where they could hardly find him, leave it at that. Then he could go home with them, back to Pelham. But he did not suggest this.

He had a feeling that, even tired as she was, Granny would scorn him for thinking it.

He moved impatiently in his chair. "I guess I ought to go see what Ephe and Tinney want."

Then, when she spoke, he was glad he had not said what he thought. "Tinney?" she said, suddenly galvanized, her voice ringing the name. "Is that man still living? Oh, how I hate that name . . ." There was no surrender in her, he thought.

He heard Father say, "This is his son."

"I don't know him," she said, disdainfully. "But I knew his father when he and Ephraim were partners. In the lumber business. They cut it all." She made a gesture of pain and bitterness with her white hands in the darkness. "All. Not just the big trees. The little ones, too, and those they didn't cut, they destroyed with their carelessness. When they got through, they had stripped the ground of everything green and growing, and often as not stood by and let it be burned over to make sure. And all the good top soil washed into the rivers—no roots to hold it. And many a year passed before the thin pitiful little crops of new saplings managed to grow in the gullies they left—and then they were no-good, loblolly pine." He watched the gesturing hands. There was a core of hard resolve in her that was tireless and without age. He wondered that he had thought her old and tired.

"Ah," she said, "I've seen what their kind does to the land. To fill their pockets today, they'll empty it for all time. And the money—driblets of it went to Ephe and piddling sums to the sawmill hands and the landowners—but precious little, really. Most of it went somewhere else, where it all goes, the fruit of our land, the oil, the coal, the iron, the timber, all the riches the good Lord blessed us with. And the Ephraims among us help them. It's bad enough to be conquered and to have the conquerors steal all your wealth. But when your own people team with them, and in the name of your own tradition, help destroy the land you . . ." The slow brooding voice, half-regretful, half-angry, ceased suddenly. Evelina sat still and silent, but Father stirred uneasily.

"Mother . . ."

She paid him no mind. She spoke angrily. "Why does nobody see it? Ephe will run for the Senate, and I can hear him now, invoking tradition, talking about 'states' rights' and 'white supremacy.' And the only rights he wants are the rights of unlimited theft, and the only supremacy the supremacy of him and Tinney and their robber gang. But everybody will believe him, and give him the rebel yell. . . ." She leaned back in her chair and put a hand briefly to her brow. "The pass we have come to is enough to make our dead weep in their graves. . . ." Ashby could hear her breathing in the dark, a quick soughing sound; then she sighed. "I sit too much and think. And have so few people I can talk to, because I remember what nobody remembers. I'm glad you and Evelina are here. I want to go home." She was looking at Father.

"We'll take you home. Tomorrow."

"Yes," Evelina said. "We've missed you so."

Ashby rose. "I'll go talk to Ephe."

Granny said, "You're in trouble, aren't you?"

He looked down at her, at the hands now quiet in the lap. He knew then that she had not been talking idly, as the aged do. He knew she had been talking to him, and that what she had really been saying was, "You cannot laugh at this, Ashby. Or shrug your shoulders. From the moment those hounds bayed behind you that night, you had no chance but to stand and face what would not be laughed at or shrugged off."

Yet now he said, "I don't know for sure. I'm going in to see if they aim to call my cards."

She only looked at him, silently, without speaking, and he felt that he had hurt her. He turned away.

Father rose. "All right," he said.

Evelina said, "Ashby . . ." She raised one plump hand. "Be careful, son."

"Yes," he said, not hearing. He turned and he and Father left the room together.

In the gloom of the jaundiced-lighted hall, Father put a hand on his arm.

"Ashby, you don't seem to know . . ." he said. "I mean, this whole thing has assumed the most astonishing proportions. The whole state . . . Why, not since that terrible lynching at Parchman, can I recall . . ."

"Yes," he said, again, automatically.

"I never thought . . ." Father said. "I mean, it was so simple a thing, a Negro falsely accused by a quick-tempered sheriff, angry at the inefficiency of his bloodhounds. It's strange to think that a little thing like that could cause all this fuss—strange to think how it all fitted together, to make an issue so much bigger than you and Temp."

"Well," he said, "Uncle Vance warned me that things happened like that. Uncle Vance and his tripwire. . . ." He grinned as if he still did not take Uncle too seriously.

Father said, "I won't ask where Temp is. I'd rather not know. I won't ask what you're going to do if you find no reason in Ephe. Or how. But I want you to know . . . to know that I'm proud you haven't backed down, or . . ."

"Yes," he muttered. They did not look at each other. He felt a terrible inarticulate tenderness for his father, but they were so unused to the feeling of spiritual closeness, so afraid of naked emotion, that he knew there was nothing for him to say unless he embarrassed them both. They moved without speaking up the hall, past the lighted Minervas, to the library door. Ephe was not in sight, and when Father looked in the library was empty and dark. But when Ashby went to the door of the parlor, Ephe was standing in one corner, talking gravely to Junius and Young Sandy and a tall spectacled man Ashby did not know. When Ephe saw Ashby he excused himself and came toward him. Tinney appeared behind him, and then the sheriff and suddenly Slim Lorrimer, as if they had been watching from burrows and emerged all at once upon seeing Ashby. The silence fell again upon the crowd, strained and intent. Ashby turned from the door, and Ephe brushed past him, and went into the dark room and switched on the light. Ashby and Father followed him in. Behind them came the other three men, Tinney coughing explosively.

Ashby heard the door shut behind him. He noted that the door to the room where Evelina and Granny sat was ajar, but if Ephe noticed it at all he did not bother to close it. Red-faced, his thick white hair rumpled, Ephe took his place behind the desk. Slim leaned against the wall behind him, leaned in an arc with only his buttocks touching the wall, and his long gooselike upper parts bowed forward to avoid Ephe's law degree and the portrait of Robert E. Lee. Out of one corner of his mouth, a toothpick rolled. The sheriff took a straight chair a few feet from where Ashby stood, and when Ashby looked at him, he saw the gloat on his face, the way he seemed to swagger even when perfectly still in the chair, the way the purple wattle on his neck moved.

"Well," the sheriff said, nasally, "well. You give me a chase, Ashby."

Ashby narrowed his eyes. "Good practice," he said, "for whatever running you aim to do. You figure on going to Congress as a reward for saving the state from Temptation Pelham?"

"Might," the sheriff said, dead serious. He showed his yellow teeth in a grin. "Yessir. Might at that."

Ashby turned away. Harold Tinney had taken a place at Ephe's side, half sitting on the right-hand window sill. He was a thickly built man, and, as he crossed his arms on his chest and leaned casually there on the sill, he had that earth-rooted poise of a man who has never been uncertain about anything, and who has never plagued either himself or the world about him with unnecessary questions. He gave the impression of being colorless, so all of a piece was he, his brown-gray hair, his brown eyes, his brown suit: there was nothing, no feature about him, to intrude spectacularly on the consciousness of the beholder, and only after gazing at him steadily for a moment did Ashby realize that what he disliked about him was an essentially humorless self-righteousness epitomized in the very poise with which he stood there. On one heavy finger he wore a university class ring of gold, in his lapel there rested a civic club insignia, and on the gold chain across his vest there hung a fraternity alumnus key. It needed only a glance to ascertain that Tinney had never doubted that his class and his university, his club and his fraternity were the best of their kind in the best of all possible worlds. Ashby turned his eyes away.

Father sat close to him, in the chair behind the desk. He looked quiet and dignified, his eyes mild, and, in his posture, there was just enough easy slouch to hide whatever concern he felt. He had about him that judicial air of the scholar who has seen too many axioms disproved, too many pat formulae exploded, until he can no longer take a position about anything, because in his mind he knows that right and wrong are only too mutable. If now he stood by Ashby, he did so out of sentiment, out of a residue of emotion he still retained—the strength and violence of the issue were beyond him. So that he sat there, with his lean, firm, tolerant face in strange contrast to Ephe's thick, slightly apoplectic visage, the difference in them the more marked because they had the same white thick hair and dark blue eyes.

Ephe cleared his throat. He had one hand hooked in the top of his trousers and his fingers drummed on his round belly.

Ephe spoke. "Ashby, I've asked you in here to reason one last time with you."

Ashby smiled. "You brought along mighty near a whole ball team with you, too."

Ephe's fingers played scales on his abdomen. "I don't know if you know the things that have happened since you came into this room this morning. But if you do, I should think you'd look on this a bit more seriously."

Ashby met his cold eyes steadily. "It's not so easy to believe a nightmare in the daytime. But now that it's dark . . ."

"Let me tell you briefly what has happened," Ephe said, crisply. "When I told you this morning that I didn't approve what you were doing, I never thought the whole incident would enlarge as it has. And I want to tell you I'm not responsible for what has happened. I didn't plan for Temp to get in trouble and for you to help him escape jail, though from your attitude a person would think I'd sat here thinking up the whole business from first to last."

"No," Ashby said, interrupting, "I never thought you were any Machiavelli. I just realize that between me and fate, we played right into your hands."

Ephe went on talking. ". . . and what has happened since is not all my doing, either. Though, as you can imagine, I don't disapprove of the stand certain people are taking."

"I can imagine," Ashby said. He could see a muscle twitching in Ephe's jaw; he wondered if the man were afraid.

"Naturally," Ephe said, "when Turkey had to come half across the state after you, questions were asked. It got into the papers."

"Of course nobody involved was looking for a little publicity," Ashby said. He let his eyes fall a minute on Turkey. Turkey squirmed, pushing at his lips with his tongue.

When Ashby looked back at Ephe, he saw the quick and momentary hardness in his eyes. "I hardly see how Littlepage could have done anything but what he did do."

"No," Ashby said. "I reckon you're right. The crazy hate Turkey has for a black man is more your fault than his."

"What do you mean?" Ephe said.

"You know what I mean," Ashby said. "You wouldn't rest very easy at night if the poor white and the poor black ever stopped hating each other."

"Are you calling me white trash?" the sheriff said, half rising from his chair, his flaccid lips baring the stained teeth.

Ashby turned his head to him. "And not blaming you for it," he said. "You make me mad as hell, Turkey, but I know you can't help being the crazy, touchy fool you are. . . ."

Turkey was out of his chair then and now stood close to Ashby, the wattle on his neck moving furiously, the rank sweat-odor of his black dusty suit sharp in Ashby's nostrils. "Don't you call me no fool, Ashby Pelham!"

". . . a poor fool," Ashby said calmly. "And the thing is, he knows it, and so is busying trying to convince everybody he's not a fool. That's how he started all this mess. Those bloodhounds had made a fool out of him, and he had to prove he could best them. Just like he's always having to prove he can best some poor Negro. . . ."

"At least I ain't no nigger lover," Turkey said, shaking his head in Ashby's face.

"No," Ashby said. "If you're proud of that, you can thank Ephe for it. He's the one profits from your hate." Then he turned from the sheriff back to Ephe and went on from where Turkey had interrupted. "So here was a chance to prove he could best those hounds and best a poor Negro, too. And for something that didn't matter a hoot in hell, he got those hounds out and paraded 'em through town and told everybody he was after a dangerous criminal. He couldn't resist making himself into a hero for the voters, and so he had to blow Temp up into a super badman. That was the beginning. He'd committed himself before his precious voters, and when Temp got away, he lost his mind completely. . . ."

"We know all that," Ephe said, impatiently.

"Do you?" Ashby said. "Anyhow, I'm going to tell it. Because it's damn near unbelievable, and maybe I can get it straight in my own mind by telling it." He cleared his throat. "So he followed me outside his county. He told the newspapers what he was doing, again making Temp out a man who was dangerous to the life and limb of everybody in Miss'ippi."

"Look here now, Ashby . . ."

Ashby went on, ignoring Turkey. "He's spent twenty-four hours now blustering and bragging and making himself a public hero. But I wouldn't worry about that if it weren't for the fact that Turkey's crazy doings happen to fit into the plans of some folks not so crazy. And those folks have got ways of using the Turkeys in this world for their own ends." He moved his eyes from Ephe to Tinney and then to Slim and back to Ephe. Tinney scratched at his head and pretended to be engrossed in some distant spectacle, on his face a quiet little smile. Slim's eyes narrowed jeeringly. Ephe took a long breath.

The sheriff was shaking Ashby's arm like an impatient feist dog. "You better hush that kind o' talkin' about me," he said. "You fool much more with me, Ashby Pelham, and I'm gonna fergit my promise to your Uncle Ephe and put you behind bars."

Ashby glanced casually down at him. "Why don't you do it now? I'm ready."

"Get away, Turkey," Ephe said, impatiently.

"Yeah," Slim said. "Shut up, Littlepage. You want to mess everything up?" He moved lankily toward the sheriff.

Ashby realized all at once that they still hoped he would turn Temp in: only that could explain their sudden turning on Turkey.

Turkey sat and dropped his eyes before Ephe's glowering glance. He muttered to himself something indistinguishable.

Ephe turned to Ashby with feigned patience on his face. "Ashby," he said, as if talking to a child, so that Ashby felt resentment cold and hard in him and stood with set face under the glaring light and never moved his eyes from Ephe's face, "Ashby, I'm not going into the justice or lack of justice in Littlepage's charges against Temp. I've been trying to make you see that isn't what's at stake here."

Ashby said nothing. He could sense the mild protesting movement of his Father, but Father remained silent.

"I've always regarded you as a son," Ephe said, slowly. "I've always thought you were a stable young fellow. Even when you were sowing your oats. I never thought to see you in a position like this. . . ." He stopped to breathe again.

"Anybody would be stable to you as long as you could push him around," Ashby said. "Or as long as he didn't make any objection to your pushing somebody else around. And the thing is, I've been too busy sowing oats, as you say, to notice any pushing around. Or if I did notice it, I whistled it off. And as long as I did, you approved of me. Well, I don't know that I'd feel happy about your approval now."

Ephe's eyes went up and down him, appraisingly. "When you've destroyed yourself, it won't be a question of approving or disapproving."

"If you're measuring me for a casket," Ashby said, "I'm five feet ten and a half."

"You josh as usual," Ephe said. "But you may not be far from the truth, if you persist in . . ." He flung out his heavy, black-furred hands. "Because the thing is out of my hands now. Whatever justice may be on your side, no one will ever know. There's no voice in this state with courage enough, even if it believed in you, to raise itself for you."

"I never expected it," Ashby said. "I never raised my voice before for anybody or anything, so I never expected anybody to raise it for Temp, or me. But it's a hell of a thing to brag about —that nobody will speak for justice. If they won't speak for that, I don't know what they will speak for."

Ephe went on as if Ashby had not interrupted. "And no voice can be expected to raise itself for you. Because what the people of this state see is that a Negro has committed a crime . . ."

"Good God," Ashby said, the anger exploding in him. "How can you stand there and say 'crime' when he only attempted to discipline his own daughter?"

"That's what your Father claims," Turkey said, his humiliation forgotten now. "But ain't nobody proved she was his daughter. She got a birth certificate?"

Ashby turned his face slowly toward Turkey. "I don't reckon she has," he said, raising his eyebrows. "I don't reckon she has, since her skin's not white, and we don't pay a heap of attention to dark-skinned babies. For all we know, maybe she wasn't even born." He smiled at the discomfort on Turkey's face.

"Nevertheless," Ephe said, imperturbably, "nevertheless, all the people of this state know is that a Negro has committed a crime. There are reasonable grounds to think he may be guilty of other, unsolved crimes."

"Yes," Ashby said, nodding. "Just as reasonable as supposing you or I committed them."

Ephe paid him no mind. His voice went on, droning. "He has been aided in his escape from the law by a white man. And cooperating with that white man is another white man—don't deny it, Ashby—another white man who is known all over this state as a nigger lover, who has worked niggers and white together in his mills, no doubt letting black blood mix indiscriminately with white . . ."

Ashby laughed at him, then. Their eyes met and Ephe knew that Ashby had learned about Tilda. Ephe's face grew redder. He clenched one fist, so that, for a second, Ashby thought he was going to lunge across the desk and hit him. Ephe's eyes had a strange yellowish cast. He seemed to quiver with the sudden rage of a fearful man. Ashby realized anew the terrible fear that was behind him, a fear perhaps as strong as his opportunism.

Even through the folds of fat on Ephe's neck, the cords stood out like white ropes on the red flesh. He held his teeth together for a long moment. Then he spoke thickly.

"Listen to me," he said. He leaned over the desk and rested both his hands on it: only then did the hands stop trembling. "Every man with eyes can see the danger of what you're doing. You're tearing up a tradition like a scrap of paper. You're displaying contempt for an order of things which, if it ever breaks, will break the white race with it. I don't give a holy damn about Temp, one way or another. Temp, personally, is unimportant. So, personally, is a crawfish in a levee. But in floodtime, one crawfish hole can burst a levee and bring the waters down on you. And that's what Temp's case may likely be—a hole in the levee the white race has built up against the black. I don't give a holy damn about Temp. I give a damn only about my own people, and about what will happen to them if ever the black race thinks it can defy the laws we make for it, whether those laws are just or unjust, and whether they're enforced justly or unjustly. And you . . . you're digging at the levee, and with it threatening our lives. What do you think the niggers around us are feeling tonight?"

Ashby put a hand in his pocket and waited a moment, while Ephe breathed stormily. Then he said, "I reckon they're less dangerous to you and to every other white man than they've been in a long time. I think if I were black, I'd be feeling good tonight, to know that a few white people somewhere were willing to do anything to get justice done them."

"Don't be a fool," Ephe said. "You know they're only resenting you. You know as well as I do they resent a white man's helping them."

"Some," Ashby said. "Some of them do. But Temp's kind doesn't. And if I were black and like Temp, I'd feel a little hope in me tonight where I hadn't had any hope before." Then he took a step toward Ephe. "After all, would you be as afraid of them as you are if you hadn't wronged them?"

Ephe lifted one hand and slammed it on the desk. He gritted his teeth and through them muttered something Ashby could not hear plainly. Then Tinney, who had remained leaning against the windowsill back of Ephe's desk, came and stood beside Ephe. He smiled his professional, neatly calculated smile at Ashby.

"Now, look here, fellow," he said, his slightly nasal voice attuned to that sound of bored jolliment with which a levelheaded businessman approaches the offer of a bargain he is attempting to make seem unimportant to him. "I'm not a fire-eating Southerner. So it seems to me you and I ought to be able to talk this thing out. I'm from Chicago. Even had a grandfather fought in the Union Army from Illinois—though I usually don't mention that around old Ephe here." He chuckled, smoothly, and patted Ephe's shoulder. Ephe watched Ashby grimly. "So," Tinney continued, "I don't think you can accuse me of having any prejudice about this question. I'm just a plain corn-fed fellow from Illinois. But I want to tell you that up there in Chicago we know there's a limit to how far you can let Negroes go. The real white men know that, and they've never yet hesitated to attend to any darkies that threatened to get out of line. Of course now, we've got a foreign element—Polacks and wops and sheenies—and some of them give Negroes big ideas, but just the same, we real white men, we draw our lines up there, and we keep them drawn, I tell you."

Ashby made a mock bow to him. "Let me congratulate you. So now you've come down to help us draw our lines." He did not turn his head to look at Father, but he heard the brief smothered laughter.

Tinney smiled, with self-assured patronizing. "Now, fellow, you don't get my goat that easy. We grow tough in Illinois, and I like to see toughness in a fellow. All I'm trying to say to you is that a fellow has got to be careful not to let his sentiments lead him astray. It's sentiments that have pretty near ruined the business setup in this country. Now you take your uncle and me. We've got a pile invested in cotton mills in this state. Now you know as well as I do that with the way those radical politicians in Washington are doing, an honest business man is having a devil of a time making a dollar."

Ashby raised an eyebrow at him. Tinney gestured with one hand, the gold class-ring flashing. "Oh, I know you think that a fellow who owns cotton mills is bound to be cleaning up. But when I think of how the Governor and I have put thousands of dollars into those mills, so we could hire people that were out of work and raise the living standards down here . . ." He ignored Ashby's eyebrow. "When I think of how we've worked and what a little return we've got out of it, I tell you, it's enough to make a man lose his faith. An honest businessman is having a tough time, I tell you, with all this folderol about labor—got to do this that and the other for labor, until a man never knows from one day to another where he stands. You can't blame me for wanting to see the Governor here in Washington in the Senate, where he can look out for the interests of sound businessmen. Why, I came down South here in the first place because you didn't have all this labor trouble everywhere. No sir. And why? Because pure Anglo-Saxon white workers weren't going to organize themselves into labor unions with Negroes. I came because of that. And people down here appreciated me coming. They're glad to have new capital. Need it. They gave me tax-free land to build on, and then the taxpayers voted bonds and built my mills for me."

"We're right hospitable," Ashby said. "We not only leave the door open to thieves—we give 'em a present for coming." The anger in him seemed beyond containing. He looked for a moment into the bland face of the man, who still smiled tolerantly at him. Then he half-turned, as if to leave the room.

"Ashby!" Ephe said. When Ashby turned, his hand was lifted.

"I don't guess you need tell me any more," Ashby said. He had trouble keeping his voice even and low. He could feel his fingernails biting into the palms of his hands. "You've made it pretty clear. You've made it clear that you're scared, that you're having a perfect nightmare about the Negroes you've outraged. And you've made it clear that your main interest is in your pocketbook and in your power. And that you're using Temp's misfortune for your own ends, like you've been using the Negro and the poor white for your own profit ever since that War you talk so much about. I guess you'll be elected Senator now, all right. And I guess you and Tinney won't have to worry about any strong labor unions, either, long as you keep white and black hating each other. And then, too, you'll be destroying your biggest competitor. You'll be able to ruin Bevo Banes with your kept press yapping your lies all over the state. Oh, I ran into quite a combine, didn't I? Ran smack into a Negro-hating sheriff, a power-hungry politician, and an opportunistic Yankee industrialist—the princes of the new South. Of course it worries you a little that it had to be me—your own cousin. But I'll be a minor sacrifice compared to what you'd lose if you lost your empire. Well, go on. Try to find Temp if you can. And, if you can't, put me in jail, and make your speeches. You may win this time. I don't know how far your plans go, but you may even manage to kill Temp—to make him into the symbol of your mastery, a sign to everybody that this is your world to run as you please. But what I wonder is, how do you think you can win in the long run? And what will winning profit you when you still have nightmares?"

He turned then and looked at his father. "I know," he said, glancing at Ephe. "I know you're going to tell me that you never made the system, and that you've got to keep the Negro where he is so the system can run at a profit. But Father and I do all right, we run our place and make a living, and, no matter what you and Tinney might say, we pay good wages like we always have."

Ephe straightened. A strange smile twitched feverishly in one corner of his mouth. Then his face became cold. He leaned toward Ashby.

"You fool," he said. "You fool." Ashby felt a surprised unease in him; he looked quizzically at Ephe.

"Where," Ephe said, "do you sell your cotton every year?"

"Why," Ashby said, "to you." His palms were damp.

"And did you ever notice," Ephe said, sarcastically, "that you get more than the market price?"

"Why, yes," Ashby said, "I have. And you told me why. You said it was a special long-staple. You had me plant that kind."

"That was all a scheme," Ephe said, his voice now low and charged with triumph. "All a scheme to save you and your Father, to save your damn Pelham pride." Ashby felt the cold unease sweep through him. "That fact is that blasted plantation would have been under the hammer years ago, running it like you do, like it was nigger-heaven, paying those crazy high wages, building tenant houses with screens in 'em, hiring doctors to birth babies that could get birthed under the nearest bush if the nigger wench having 'em worked anywhere but in Pelham

Heaven! But I let you run on in your crazy way on account of Granny, on account of what I owed her . . ."

Ashby felt a sickness in him, an acidulous humiliation sharper than any he had ever known. His face burned and smarted as if someone had rubbed it with peach-fuzz. He pressed one fist into the palm of his hand and faced their smug faces, arrayed before him, Slim slouched by the desk grinning slantily from his crooked mouth, Tinney on Ephe's other hand rocking confidently on his heels with that bland smile on his face, the sheriff chortling behind his hand. He turned his eyes away from them and brought himself to look at his father, who was standing there, his face ashen, a little yellow, as it had been in the light of the hall. Ashby looked him in the eye.

"I can't say I didn't know it, son," he said, making his words precisely through his fine-cut lips, which trembled slightly. "I can only say I didn't let myself know it. I kept trying to pretend that we could do the way we'd always done, that we could all of us, black and white, prosper out of the soil, even when I could see our neighbors going down . . ." He shook his head. "But I knew. I knew, I guess." Then he averted his head, trembling a little, as if ashamed at being called back into the real world from that place where he lived in company with his ideas.

Ashby put his tongue to his dry lips. But he would not let his eyes waver from theirs, now.

Then he spoke. "Even if it is so, it can't matter in what I have to do."

Ephe regarded him, now comfortably unbelieving. "You would lose Pelham Place for a nigger?"

"I would lose that land before I would lose my right to the name."

"Your grandfather was a good businessman," Ephe said.

"A little wrong on the slavery issue, but a good businessman," Ashby said, satirically.

"A good businessman," Ephe said, ignoring his remark. "And is it his name you're talking about? I reckon they named you wrong."

Ashby felt his fists double.

"I reckon they named you wrong," Ephe said. "*He* ran that place and made money."

Ashby felt the rage tense his whole body. He had never wanted to do anything as he wanted to smash Ephe's face at that moment. But before he could move or say anything, Granny came through the half-open door to the back parlor. She stood just inside the room in her black dress, her old thin face exceedingly white and fine-lined, her faded blue eyes blinking a little with the light. She stood almost unnaturally straight, facing them all, her eyes fixed on the spot where she knew Ephe was.

When she spoke, her voice had that youthful throb in it he had heard earlier.

"Yes," she said, "my Ashby was a man to make the earth produce well. And he stored up riches. But not with injustice. Because those were the days when we were not a conquered people. It was only later that the carpetbaggers came—" and she turned her eyes to what must have been to her only the blurred outline of Tinney—"to steal our wealth, and that there arose from our own people, scalawags—" and she looked back at Ephe—"to help them. That was before defeat had forced us to mortgage ourselves to thieves." Her eyes went from one to the other. "In those days, we sold our cotton for its worth, our labor was worthy of its hire. Now we sell it for what the scalawags and carpetbaggers pay us for it." Then she turned and took one step toward Ashby. "Lose it," she said, the word strong but tremulous in her throat. "Lose it. I love that land like my heart's own, but it is not worth betraying one letter of your name. I would rather see you buried under those cedars at Pelham than see you turn into an Ephraim and join with a Tinney to ruin the land you live in."

When she stopped there was a deadly silence in the room. Their eyes could not meet her face as she looked from one to the other of them. She looked without triumph of malice or condescension. She looked on them with a strength stronger than she was. Somewhere beyond his hurt and his anger, Ashby felt a great pride in her well up in him, and at the same time a wonder that she could not only know she was right but know *why* she was right. Swept with emotion too confused for him to think clearly, he wished that he had in himself that hard core of certainty which she owned.

He turned at her bidding and walked from the room beside her. At the foot of the hall stairs, she stopped him. Across the hall, people stared from the lighted parlor. But he paid them no mind, nor did she, nor Father when he came and took Granny's arm to lead her upstairs. She went up one step and put out her aged white hand and curled it around the slim leg of one bronze Minerva. Her voice quavered with an emotion now beyond her strength. "We named you right. Ah, how right we named you."

Father looked down at him. "Yes," he said. He put out his hand to Ashby. "I won't ask what you're going to do. Or how. But I will pray, Ashby. And wait." Then he turned abruptly.

Granny leaned and kissed him. She caught him to her and patted his back, murmuring. When she released him, he turned blindly away from them and went down the dim hall.

All at once, then, Laurel was there, as if she had waited for him. "I heard," she said. "I heard, and wanted to tell you I was proud." There was a tremor in her throat: like a bird-throat split on a note too sweet to hold.

He saw the face of Slim Lorrimer, and he saw Ephe striding the fields of Pelham, and through these visions her face loomed unclear. Clumsily, he pushed open the back door.

# Chapter XIX

Ashby put his hand out into the darkness, into the shadow of the cottage eaves. He found the knob and slowly turned it. It made a slight grating sound. The door creaked as he pushed. His breath came with the short pants of one winded. He gave a brief furtive glance back of him, into the silver swaths of moonlight patterning the yard. Then, seeing nothing, he slipped quickly through the door and shut it softly behind him. He let out a lungful of air in a long shudder. He closed his eyes and opened them on blackness, unrelieved except for the slim finger of moonlight through the window toward the pasture.

"Bevo." He whispered the name.

There was no answer, only silence and darkness, and the by now familiar odor of Tilda's cabin, the smell of stale soapsuds and cedar and mothballs.

"Bevo," he said again, his voice still restrained yet urgent now, thrusting against the silence. Outside he thought he heard a motor starting.

There was a sound like linen sliding on the bed and then a sleepful mutter. He put out his hands and moved like a blind man toward the sound. He waved his hands uncertainly before him, trying to find the bed, until all at once his left hand struck one of the bedposts, hard.

"Damn." He put a hand down on the mattress and pushed it gently. "Bevo?"

Bevo's voice answered with startling loudness. "Ashby? That you?"

Now Ashby could make out his form, could see the dark outline of him as he sat up, and smell the faint sweetish odor of his sleep-sweat. "Hush," he said. "Hush." He sat gingerly on the side of the bed, facing Bevo's sitting form.

"What's the matter? You sound like . . ."

"Hush," Ashby said. "For God's sake, you want one of the sheriff's deputies snooping in here?"

"Oh," Bevo said, whispering. "I'd near-'bout forgot. They back?"

"Yes, they're back. So that a man would have to look twice to tell whether this is a funeral or a hanging."

"Is Laurel in there, too?" Bevo said. Ashby knew that his eyes were fixed on him, though in the dark he could not see where they were focused.

"Yes," he said, shortly. "Why shouldn't she be there?" In his mind, he could hear her voice, that tremulous huskiness peculiar to her, that vibrant enthusiasm she put into any word she spoke. He felt suddenly unsure, not of her, now, but of himself. Remembering her in the hall, the candid gold-flecked eyes, the sculptured curve of her throat sweeping down to where her dress parted, the half-open lips revealing the minute gap between the two white teeth, he did not know for a moment how he had turned away from her so brutally. For, quite apart from the beauty he had invested her with in his memory, he realized that in her voice and in her poise there had been nothing but the open honesty he had from the first felt in her. Uncle Vance would have laughed at him, he thought. *The one quality every female has,* Uncle Vance used to say, *is guile.* But not Laurel, Ashby thought.

Yet, even trusting her as he did, he would have turned again from her, had she entered the cottage at that moment. He would have turned from her as he wished somehow to turn from everybody and everything. Now he knew what Uncle Vance had meant on those days when he had remembered too much too well and would suddenly tell him, Ashby, to begone: *I am sick at soul, boy. And the only physician that can cure me is loneliness.*

In his mind, Ashby saw again Ephe's face at the moment when Ephe had smiled strangely and said "Where do you sell your cotton every year?" The question drummed in his ears, not as a sound he had heard only a few minutes before, but as one he had heard in some far unremembered past and yet only now heard it consciously. It seemed to him that, like his father, he had known that he had lived at the sufferance of Ephe and had been unable to admit it. It seemed to him he must have known it on that day—yesterday?—when he had said to Bevo that he felt a stranger in a strange land. For that he undoubtedly was. The life he had lived at Pelham had no existence in fact. It had been no more than a stage play, a puppet show, with Ephe backstage directing the scenes; he had been an actor in the spectacle, barely conscious that it was a spectacle. Now he knew. Now he knew that the theater was Ephe's. The land belonged to Ephe and those like him. Ephe had allowed him and Granny and Father to pretend it was theirs, but they had known it was not.

He was all at once aware that Bevo had spoken. "What?" he said.

"She's a mighty live person," Bevo said. "I thought, looking at her this evening, she's mighty near too live to be in a house where death is."

Ashby stood impatiently. "Well, she can go away, for all I care." Unwittingly, he had raised his voice to his normal tone. He checked himself, then shrugged, since it did not seem to matter much whether the sheriff heard him or not.

Bevo did not say anything for several minutes. But Ashby heard, before he did speak, the sudden quickening of his breath, and then a heavy sigh, like that of a child in sleep. "You never told me," Bevo said, slowly.

"Told you what?" Ashby said, turning on him almost angrily.

"Told me you . . . told me you loved her."

"Loved her?" Ashby said. "Did I sound like a man who loved a woman when I said it didn't matter to me if she went away?"

"That's all you did sound like," Bevo said. "I reckon if she didn't mean anything to you, you'd never be so wrought up about it."

Ashby turned his back on him. "It's not that I'm wrought up about."

"It's that," Bevo said, "and maybe something else. But it's that."

Ashby said nothing.

"What is the something else?" Bevo said.

Ashby turned and told him, slowly, as if he had memorized the scene, what had been said in Ephe's office. Bevo listened without comment. When Ashby had finished, he still sat silent. "So you see," Ashby said, "it doesn't matter. None of it matters. I don't belong here and there's nothing here that belongs to me. So I'm thinking about chucking it. I came out here to tell you you'd better slip away tonight."

Bevo regarded him quietly. Then he spoke in a level, monotonous voice. "When Tilda brought me something to eat, she said all the roads were blocked, and so she was goin' to take your car past the guards out yonder and park it in the Fox Run in the swamp with food in it, so in case you and Temp didn't get across the river tonight you'd have something to eat until you found a boat. . . ."

"That was before," Ashby said. "I planned that before. Now . . ."

"Have you told her?"

"No," Ashby said. "I came straight here."

"Nor Laurel either?"

Ashby moved impatiently. "You've got to get out of here. I told you what they said. Unless I'm wrong, you're going to find all hell breaking loose at your mill. I tell you they know who you are and are using what I'm doing to try to ruin you."

"If the white men and the black men in my mills turn on

each other," Bevo said, "I'd as soon fight what made 'em do it here as there."

Ashby put a hand on the hard waxed post of Tilda's bed. He curled his fingers around the hard post. "Listen," he said. "There was something I should have told you there this afternoon, when you were in the pantry looking through the glass at those men you took to be gentlemen. There was something I thought then, and now I know it's true, because I don't just think it, I can feel it in my bones. And it's this: that the Young Sandys and the Old Sandys, the Jubals and their ilk are gone. The South —hell, the whole world—sees them dying off every day. Now there are not enough left to count. Oh, I'm not fool enough to think that we haven't always had money grubbers and swindlers, but in their day we used to be ashamed of them, and now it looks like we're proud of 'em. The highest compliment some folks can pay a man nowadays is to say he's a slick bastard— which is a roundabout way of saying he's a thief. Why, even I can remember when a thief had to pretend at least to honor and to truth. But now—all he's got to do is proclaim his theft and he's canonized."

When he paused, Bevo sat silently waiting for him to continue.

"Well . . ." Ashby shrugged. "The South doesn't belong to me. Or you. Or to the disappearing Young Sandys and Jubals. It belongs to Ephe and Tinney and Turkey Littlepage and Slim Lorrimer. Well, they can have it." He held his lower lip fast between his teeth.

"When a fellow takes off his dark glasses, there's always a kind of hurting in looking," Bevo said slowly.

"All right," Ashby said. "Yes. I've had dark glasses on a long time." He grunted. "Dark rose-colored glasses, I reckon. But it's not just what I'm looking at for the first time that's got me riled. It's that I'm so . . ." He turned again, not showing his face to Bevo. "So damnably alone."

"Your Granny . . . your father . . ."

"Relics. Like Jubal and . . ."

"And me?"

"An anachronism."

"I don't know what that means," Bevo said. When Ashby looked at him, he stood beside the bed, his white shirt open at the collar, his dark eyes gleaming faintly in the room where the moonlight had gradually encroached.

"It doesn't matter," Ashby said, tiredly. He could feel the tiredness like a drug in his muscles and joints.

"What do you aim to do?" Bevo said.

"I don't know," he said, thinking: Now I am back to that, to the not-knowing, but not quite back to the not-caring, which is what makes the lack of decision painful. "I don't know."

"You aim to leave Temp in the swamp?"

"They'll have a helluva time finding him there."

"He won't have a very good time of it, though, even if they don't find him."

Ashby rubbed his hand up and down the waxed bedpost; his dry palm made a skid-squeak sound on the wood. He said nothing.

"Alone?" Bevo said. "I don't reckon a man doing right is ever alone."

"Maybe not," Ashby said. "You and I, for instance. We've got a goodly company with us—of ghosts. What the living do doesn't make much sense to either of us. The only sense we've known in the world is in the doings of men long dead. And we can't even be sure that they're anything more than tales told to put kids to sleep."

"I saw Papa," Bevo said.

"All right," Ashby said. "You're luckier than I am. Everything I've known and heard has had the foundations knocked out from under it. I thought Pelham was real, anyhow. But not even that . . ." His hand on the bedpost had grown moist. He rubbed it dry on his coat.

"Ghosts are pretty strong sometime," Bevo said. "There are some ghosts that a man can't say no to."

Ashby said nothing. In the swath of moonlight from the window dust particles roiled about.

"She could tell you that."

"She?"

"Laurel."

"What has Laurel got to do with it?"

"Nothing, maybe." Bevo was sitting on the edge of the bed, now, with his feet on the floor. "Nothing except that you can look at her and know that what she loves she understands, and that she'd understand you enough to know that there's no giving up for you, that your ghosts are a heap stronger than the misery you feel now."

"Bevo, I . . ." He made a helpless, futile gesture with his hand.

"Never mind," Bevo said. "I know. I've known it all along, I reckon, since she came down the stairs that night at Miss Miranda's. I can remember how she looked at you, how she turned when we were going in the parlor to see you over her shoulder. And through that pantry door today, when you weren't looking at her . . . I saw how she never moved her eyes from you. I saw her laughing with you on the road this morning, before Miss Semantha . . ." He let out his breath in a slow sound, like the sound of skidding leaves. "I know. Have known."

"Hell," Ashby said. "You don't know any more than I do. How do you know what she wants? Anymore than you and I can be sure we want her? We neither of us saw her till day before yesterday. It's been such a wild crazy forty-eight hours a man's not responsible for anything he might feel or do."

"Who are you trying to talk out of the notion he's in love with her? Me or you?" Bevo said.

"She's Slim Lorrimer's stepdaughter," Ashby said. "How do I know I could trust her? Even if I did love . . ."

Bevo rose and came toward him, his tread soft but heavy on the bare wooden floor. "Trust her?" he said, and his voice seemed loud in the room. Ashby could feel the sudden terrible anger in the man. "You know you can trust her. You're not really worrying about that. It's yourself you don't trust. You don't trust yourself to tell her you're giving up. Like you're trying to excuse your giving up by talking about how wrong everybody else is. As if you won't be as wrong as they are, if you quit now." Ashby felt the blood flush hotly across his face. Bevo breathed heavily in the quiet. "I'm sorry," he said.

"That's all right," Ashby said, thinking: Maybe he's right. Maybe if I just knew how she really felt . . . or maybe I do know. And yet if I could only have a sign from her, a sign other than words. For no matter what Bevo says, she may feel that I am being a little foolish about all of this Temp business, and the words she has said she may have said in pity, without ever understanding any more than Ephe understands.

He turned toward the window looking out over the pasture. He had stood there for what seemed a long time in silence before the knocking came, muffled but urgent on the wooden door. They stood tensely a moment. Then Laurel's voice came speaking his muted name. They breathed easily.

"It's Laurel," Bevo whispered. He was standing close behind Ashby. "You can't shake her off as easy as you can a ghost. Or deny her."

"Ashby, Ashby." She sounded winded.

"If you can say to her . . ." Bevo said. "But you can't. Can you?"

"I don't know," he said. "Let her in."

Bevo turned and went wordlessly toward the door and opened it. She slid into the room, framed a split second in moonlight until the door closed behind her.

"I can't see anything," she said, letting out her breath. But Ashby could see her, the luminous white of her skin above the black dress, the faint spark of her eyes. He could see her so clearly he could mark the rise and fall of her breast. "Ashby?" she said, looking without direction into the dark space of the room, the area unlighted by the invading moonlight.

"I'm here," he said.

From somewhere, Bevo drew a chair to her: it scraped loudly across the floor, so that Ashby said, "Hush. Those deputies . . ." said it involuntarily, without thinking.

Laurel laughed, quietly. "You needn't worry. I've been getting them drunk one by one. Sort of a Mississippi Molly Pitcher, if you could have seen me. Tilda and I mixed up a whole big crock of lemon and whiskey, and I took it around from one to the other. That's the excuse I used to get the car out—told the guard on the back gate, I wanted to take a drink down to the boys on watch along the swamp road. And I did. Took 'em drinks all down the line, and when I came to the last one, at the swamp edge, I told him I was going to the turning around place, and he gave me advice, free—told me I better not go more than half a mile down the road because the first of the road blocks was there and there was a strange guard there that might not know me. And so I went to where Tilda had told me and parked the car and walked back up the highway and told the guards I'd had a flat and would have to send for a garage man. They even wanted to go back with me to help, but I told them they'd better stay on duty."

Bevo muttered. "Now tell her. Now."

Ashby was close to her. She had not sat down, but stood, one hand on the chair back.

"You did that?" he said.

"It was so much easier for me than for Tilda. I introduced myself as Slim Lorrimer's daughter and they never suspected anything. . . Of course I had to keep out of the sheriff's sight, because he'd remember Miss Miranda's and . . ." She laughed and leaned close to Ashby and he felt the quick chill at the back of his neck and along the underside of his arms.

The door beside Laurel suddenly shut, without Ashby's having known it had opened. When he looked, Bevo was gone.

He stepped toward her. He seemed to hear in his mind the echo of Bevo's taunt, "Now tell her. Now," and he knew that he would say nothing to her of the bitter misery he had felt, the misery not yet forgotten, but lighter, easier to bear now.

He would pretend that he had never wavered, for he now saw that there was never a chance for him to do so: she would not have allowed it.

He stepped toward her. There was still that astonishing tightness in his throat. He knew he was going to touch her and it seemed there was no breath in him.

They held each other tightly for a moment, wordless, until she said, "Ashby!" from a breaking throat. They clung together, he holding her as if he yearned to sink into a darkness of feeling that would blot out thought. He closed his eyes.

Then all at once from the yard the voices came, shouting a sober fear into him, and then a hard, resolute anger. He heard his name said. He broke from her. He lifted aside the shade at the window and peered out. There in the back yard were half a dozen men, including the sheriff and his deputies, Slim and Ephe. Ephe stood on the back steps in the glare of the flashlights. "Where's Ashby's car? You've let him get away." The deputies answered all at once, telling about Laurel. Then Ephe said, "She's not here. Where is she? You damn fools . . ." The sheriff stood in the middle of the confused men, his face empurpled. "Search around. Look for him, you blamed idiots. . . ."

Ashby found his hand gripping Laurel's arm. "I'm going out the back window. Bevo must be out there. Bevo Banes."

"Oh. Mr. Thomas. He is . . ."

Ashby nodded and turned. She caught his arm. "You stay here a minute. Let me go out and distract them. That way I can head them off until you and . . . Bevo can get away."

He heard the sheriff's strident voice yelling at the men. He fumbled at the window, maddening himself with his own ineptitude. Finally, it gave, jerking upward with a shrieking sound. He lifted a foot and kicked the screen out. Then he turned to her.

"All right," he whispered. "Now." They stood for one taut, agonized second looking at each other. He gave her arm a quick grip. Then she went across the room to the door, opened it and went through it. There was sudden silence in the yard. He waited to hear no more. He went through the window, striking his head against the frame and dropped onto the ground outside. As he regained his balance, his outstretched hand touched somebody. He looked up. It was Bevo.

"Come on," he said, his voice harsh. "Let's get going."

"She wants to go too," Bevo said.

"She?" Then he saw Tilda, standing there in the white flowered plums, her skin rich almost to brownness in the moonlight. He was angered that he should have to waste time now explaining to her that she could not go. He pushed aside a plum branch and went to her. "Listen, Tilda, we've got to go now, and if you go you might endanger Temp. The more of us there are, the more danger . . ."

She said nothing. Her lips trembled and she put one hand up to the hollow between her breasts.

"You understand? I'll come back for you sometime. I mean it. I will. I'll do anything I can to help you against them. Anything." He seemed to spit out the words. "Later," he said. Still she said nothing. He patted her arm. "That's a girl." Then he looked over his shoulder at Bevo.

"Let's get the hell out of here," he said, and began to push his way through the plum bushes, showering the blossoms underfoot. He heard Bevo plowing his way behind him. They headed west, away from the back road, and then, at the fence line, turned north, since he planned to make a wide arc northwestward through the swamp to that place near the road where Laurel had left the car. They ran crouched through the startling and now dangerous moonlight toward the waiting swamp.

# Chapter XX

Then, for the second time that day, he was again in the swamp.

"Now, by God . . ." he said, and then said it again, "Now, by God . . ." and kept repeating it to himself, like a talisman, not even completing the meaning in his mind, not even saying to himself, "Now, by God, I have dallied long enough with reason and hope and uncertainty, have talked and waited as long as a man can talk and wait, and now I am sick of words and hesitation." Perhaps he did not say that because, acting now, he was ashamed of his inaction, as he had been ashamed that time in prep school when the tennis coach had yelled at him, "Great God, Pelham, don't you give a damn whether you win or not?" and then had muttered reflectively, "I'm damned if I don't believe you'd die about as careless-like as you play tennis."

He had not known how to tell the coach that it was only because winning was so important to him that he could not even try to win, for fear he would fail, and failure after effort would be immeasurably more humiliating than failure from carelessness. Perhaps now he knew that he had played the game with Ephe and Turkey careless-like: to stop off at Miranda's (good God, why Miranda's? When I'd been there the night before, and was not a randy adolescent needing a female ride come nightfall, and ought to have been old enough so that anger at Father need not have called forth the reaction of a sulky spoiled kid *I'll show 'em*); to get himself in jail (when at that moment Temp should have been more important to me than Laurel, whom I did not really know and might have guessed could have taken care of herself with more ease than Temp could protect himself); to take the broadest highroad out of town (because I would not even let it enter my head that Turkey had done anything but forget Temp; because I would not let myself think that Father had given me a large commission in asking me to save Temp); to dally on the road like a tourist (and talking about myself, and perhaps trying to talk myself into thinking that this was no ordinary outing in the countryside, yet unable to, stopping like anyone else to get a drink of whiskey so that for a while I would not have to face the fact made obvious by my stopping, that I gave not one holy hoot in hell); to come to Ephe's (thinking that I could unload Temp there and have that the end of it, when I must have known that even had Ephe been another man, Temp would not be safe anywhere in the state boundaries, since I knew by then that Turkey was maddened beyond reason); and then to wait there (even knowing as I did know that Ephe was not to be trusted, and even after he was surrounded by men I trusted even less than him). He had been afraid through it all, and now he could not say what he had feared, whether he had only carelessly underestimated the stakes in the game because he feared losing it, or whether he had not dared hope that the stakes were high enough, so high that for once he would play with everything he had and would play to win. Yet, whatever the reason, the fact was that he had played careless-like up to now: "Like a damned Boy Scout," he muttered. "But now, by God . . ."

"What?" Bevo said, behind him, fighting off from his naked flesh the whipping swamp-branches, since they had undressed except for their shoes once they were safely inside the swamp borders. ("It's a question," Ashby had said, "of putting up with mosquitoes and thorns now in order to be dry later when we have got across river.") So they had stripped then and made their clothes into bundles secured by their belts around their necks and resting like pilgrim's packs on their backs. But Bevo had said, "Mosquitoes this time of year?" "I don't believe they ever die here," Ashby had said, and had found himself glad to say it, as if the prospect of one added discomfort could be marked up by the hand of God on His Ledger in partial payment for the comfort in which he had dallied while Temp was in danger. "What?" Bevo said. His water-filled shoes sounded a *whish-scrunch* as he walked.

"Like a damned Boy Scout," Ashby said.

"What? What like a Boy Scout?"

"Nothing," Ashby said. He waded into the slow creek. The night was warming, with clouds blowing over the moon and darkening their path when the heavy overlace of moss and leaves and vines did not shut out light anyway. Yet even in the warming night, the water still held its winter iciness: Ashby could feel the shrinking in his loins when the searing-cold water lapped at them. But he went on grimly and faster than necessary, now that they were safely within the swamp borders, following the long arc he had planned to follow in order to reach the spot near the road where Laurel had put the car.

Carefully, a little awkwardly, Ashby held his pistol above the waters. They came at length to a bayou noisy with striking fish and the wet slap of an occasional muskrat. The foamy skum on the dead waters of the sloughs now clung stickily to their bodies.

"Feels like turpentine and tar," Bevo said.

"You ought not to have come," Ashby said.

"I ain't complaining," Bevo said.

"It's none of your business," Ashby said.

"I know what my business is," Bevo said.

Ashby grunted. Now they traversed a stretch of relatively dry land, filled with the great hulks of insubstantial trees and the soft-waving tendrils of moss, the whole space lighted with so phosphorescent a glow that the scene for a moment was as unreal and as undeadly as some dream-picture of a swamp. Then Ashby put out a warning hand and they picked their way along a fernbank on the edge of a gumbo of quicksand.

"Lord," Bevo said, "I wondered when we passed this place this morning why nobody had ever cut this fine timber. I don't blame 'em, now I see it. It'd be easier to go timber prospecting in hell."

Ashby grunted. "A tough virgin to make, this old swamp. If she weren't, Ephe and Tinney would have raped her long ago, the way they've raped all the other land around her. But she's stood 'em off. And will stand 'em off again—for us."

"Well," Bevo said, "if she gets much worse, she'll be standing us off, too. She ain't a easy lady to lay with."

"Thank God," Ashby said, and no more, as if he knew Bevo would understand. He stretched out his hand to push aside a limb.

"Yes," Bevo said, "thank God." And Ashby, turning, saw him standing there framed in the arc of an oak-limb, his great white body erect and unmoving, the streaks of muddy water on it like the faint plumed swirls in a smoky marble, his whole being still as a carved thing except for the half-clenched hands which while not moving yet seemed to move in a gesture Ashby had noticed before and yet only now recognized, thinking: What he needs is to do something with his hands; I never thought it before but what has always been awkward about him is his hands; and he thought to be a gentleman . . .

"You damn fool," he said. "Why don't you go home and push a loom or whatever it is you do in a blasted cotton mill?"

As if he knew by some instant divination of his own what had passed through Ashby's mind, Bevo lifted the half-clenched hands and stared at them, flattened them out and inspected the heavy, still-calloused ridge at the base of the thumb, the blunt strong fingers, turned the hands over and looked at the thick blue veins and the black crisp furring on the back and between the knuckles of the fingers.

"Yes," he said, slowly. "Yes. I will." He looked at Ashby with his liquid luminous eyes. "Even when I thought it was Laurel, I don't reckon it was in the way any man would want a woman. It was to have something to hold, to touch, to . . ."

"You're sure that was all . . . with Laurel?" Ashby said, merely using the question, the words in order to speak of what had to be spoken of between them sooner or later.

Bevo nodded. "All," he said, simply, and went back to looking at his hands and said, again, "Yes. I will. When we are through here."

"Hell," Ashby said, turning suddenly, "at this rate that'll be next year." He pushed through the matted vines ahead. Their shoes made a slopping, pneumatic sound as they moved.

"Careful," he said. "Mud. Slick as greased okra." He led the way cautiously across the sink, where the dry top layer of earth flaked off, leaving exposed a substance like heavy crude oil. The moonlight touched them briefly there, and then they were again in a sector of thick underbrush, fighting the trailing vines which caught and scratched their flesh, the limbs which whipped their faces, silent now, moving quietly toward the place where the car was parked.

When they reached Cold Creek, it was very dark. Ashby led the way through the shallow water, wading slowly so that the thin trickling of the water was lost in the louder gurgle of the stream. On the bank, shivering a little, his body prickling from the icy water, he leaned to his shoes.

"Why?" Bevo whispered.

"Might be deputies on the road," he said. "Might hear the water sloshin' in 'em." He struggled with the wet knot, while behind him Bevo leaned and removed his shoes without untying them.

"Leave 'em here," Ashby said, the whisper hoarse in his throat. "We come back this way." He picked up the pistol from where he had placed it.

Crouching, he pushed his way through the huckleberry bushes, his feet moving softly on the deep muck of the creek bank, the thick limbs parting to his hands with a rustling as quiet as the sound of a faint breeze threading the leaves. The going was slow. Behind him, Bevo suppressed a cough with a gurgling sound. When the moon appeared capriciously, Ashby cursed, and yet never uttered more than half the damnation he intended, for in the sudden light in the clearing the car loomed up, closer than he had looked for it, and there beside the car, three men.

He bit off the curse with his teeth and flung out a hand behind him and caught warningly the hard nakedness of Bevo's knee, so that Bevo halted with an almost inaudible grunt. Behind the thick screen of bushes, he regarded the men.

They had found the box of food and they had quite evidently eaten some of it: they crouched now among the debris of the meal, the tin cans, opened jaggedly with pocket knives, glinting in the moonlight, waxed scraps of bread-wrapping littering the ground around them, as if in their hungry—and perhaps guilty—haste they had grabbed and torn at the food like animals, and doubtless had even fought among themselves over it, though they might have known they could not have eaten it all then, and though they now sat with food still uneaten and yet were satiate. They rested there on their hams, and on their faces—on the faces of the two facing Ashby—there was that absolutely blank and unmoving expression of repletion, so that he wondered how long they had been sitting there after the satisfaction of that sharp outrageous hunger. On close inspection they would not have been identical, and yet, from where Ashby watched, there was an astonishing sameness about them—their bodies lank, stooped, the skin of their faces, hands and necks, thin, freckled and permanently reddened by the sun, the uncut hair wisping beneath their dusty black hats, the faces hollow-cheeked and weakly-chinned and marked by a mouth of thin pale lips held loosely and almost idiotically open. Even silent and unmoving, there was reflected from the pale blue eyes that sullenness which was the apathetic portrait of the fear and impotence and outrage with which they were always marked. They did not have to speak for Ashby to know that they were not of that country, but of the country of the eroded hills. And he knew also, before ever a word was said, why they were there, and was only surprised that they were there so soon. Like they knew about it before it even happened, he thought; like they had a nose like a dog, and do not even need to be told about it in words, but can catch the scent of their quarry on any stray wind that passes, and get up and start the right direction and inevitably come on the cotton field or warehouse or railroad car or swamp where the game they are hunting has chosen to hide this time.

So he remained, watching them in a kind of mute and helpless rage, knowing even then that their patience was longer than his, and that momentarily he and Bevo must turn and slip away; but he wanted to hear what they said, once digestion uncrowded their diaphragms. Finally, the taller of the two men facing him licked his lips.

"We had luck," he said.

The other two did not reply; the short man, whose face Ashby could see, only blinked his pale-lashed eyelids. Then, at length, the man with his back to them, moved a little nervously.

"I reckon we best git on," he said. "The city feller that owns this here car . . ." He turned his head jerkily toward the automobile.

"Who you figger owns it?" the short man said.

"Some city feller," the nervous man said.

"And what's it doin' here?" the tall man said, a little contemptuously.

"Why," the nervous man said, "why, he's likely come out here a-picnicking in the woods . . ."

"A-picnickin'," the short man said, making a grunt at once derisive and lecherous. "Hell, he's *a-dicking* of some gal in the skirt of the woods, and not thinkin' about no somethin't'eat."

"I reckon he will be soon, though," the nervous man said.

The tall man looked from one to the other, meanwhile running his tongue around the inside of his mouth. When he was satisfied with the job his tongue had done, he spoke.

"I don't reckon the feller owns this car is aimin' on doin' no picnickin' nor no *dickin'* either tonight. I reckon he's either in jail or 'bout to be in jail, unless he has done got loose from the big house up yonder, an' if he has done that, I reckon he's hid hisself out somewhere along with that black man, since he is enough of a nigger lovin' bastard to do a thing like that." The tall man said the words slowly and with relish and when he was through he breathed audibly and the faintest trace of outrage flared on the face that up to that moment had been only sullen.

The two other men regarded him silently for a moment. Then the short man said, "You know a heap," still with his voice edged with derision.

"Yes," the tall man said. "I do. I know that them fellers up yonder at the big house is still talkin' and arguin' an' figgerin' on doin' somethin' legal. Legal. An' while they are talkin' 'bout a legal way to do what they know has got to be done no matter how it's done, that nigger has done slipped loose ag'in an' hid hisself in a swamp that nobody but a crazy man would go into even if it was a cache for ten thousand gallons of the smoothest moonshine ever made." The tall man never once raised his voice, so that his words did not give off the sound of anger but rather the deadly and implacable monotony of a slow-burning hatred.

"Well," the nervous man said, tentatively, as if he were trying to apologize to the tall man for the way things had gone.

"Well," the tall man said. "Well. Do you aim to go in this here swamp to look for him?"

"Who?" the nervous man said. "The nigger or the white man that . . ."

"Either or both," the tall man said. "Would you go in this here swamp after 'em?"

"I reckon . . ."

"I reckon not," the tall man said. "Nor me either. Nor any man with sense enough to step out of the way of a cottonmouth."

"That nigger went in there," the short man said, looking at the tall man.

"Nobody never said he had sense, either," the tall man said. "And anyhow, I reckon I would go, too, if I was him. Whatever happens to him in there couldn't be no worse than what will happen did he stay out and git caught. But I ain't in the nigger's shoes, and much as I would like to see him caught, I ain't aimin' to git me no tow-line an' go in yonder after him. There are tales told about this here swamp to make a man's hair frizzle on his head."

"Well," the short man said. "Then I reckon we've done wasted our time comin' here. If the nigger is in the swamp, an' ain' nobody goin' in after him, then I reckon . . ."

"No," the tall man said, not looking at anybody. "No, there's a way. There's a way." He tried to smile. "A way that will make even them who are talking about a legal way have to help us. A way that that sheriff can even help us with without havin' to wink, the way a sheriff has to do sometime, since he is supposed to be a officer of the law and so not to let no lynching happen. And even the Governor . . ." The tall man hesitated.

"Pelham?"

"Even him," the tall man said. "Even him."

"I don't know why you say 'even,' " the nervous man said. "Nobody can say that Governor Pelham is any nigger lover. Or was you thinkin' that since it was his nephew that . . ."

"Cousin," the tall man said. "His cousin. But I warn't thinkin' about that. I was thinkin' that even lovin' a dollar the way he does, the thing has done gone too far for him to hold back even if it means he might lose a dollar." In the bushes, Ashby breathed softly.

"Hold back from what?" the short man said.

The tall man turned his head toward the short man. The rage and the fear and the impotence were all there now, clearly marked on his face, so that it seemed he was not looking at the short man at all, but rather at himself, as if he could see reflected in the short man's face the rage and fear and impotence that was on his own. His hand touched an unopened can at his feet. He picked the can up and flung it away, cursing, but not taking his eyes off the short man. "Nigger food," he said. "Food stored here fer that nigger, when there's white folks . . ." In the thin corded neck, the swallowing was convulsive. "And a white man doin' it. A white man feedin' a nigger, when there's white folks hungry and . . ." He reached without looking and found another can and threw it from him. "All right," he said, and the urgency was gone from his voice and in its place that implacable hatred, like a steady, slow-winded fire. "The year the big flood came I sat in that tree, me and my woman, and the water under us ten feet deep and boilin' and churnin' an' all night long I had to beat off the snakes, all the snakes in Miss'ippi a-writhin' at our very feet, an' me cursin' the day I'd come to them damn flatlands where it look like a man never gits his feet dry an' where them folks in their fine houses speak like human to a nigger but don't even see you a-tall if you're white but don't own no blackland nor no sixteen-cylinder sin-house on wheels. An' me cursin' and beatin' them snakes off till daylight come and then hearin' that boat and hollerin' until it come out o' that red fog that was ever'where, even the air you breathed the color o' that water, an' the boat come toward us an' a white man—one o' them sixteen-cylinder white men I could see, even if he did have on coveralls, since you could see that coveralls was not what he wore all the time but more likely a white suit that wouldn't last five minutes in a cotton patch an' was made in the first place only for the kind of sixteen-cylinder sin that such fellers spend their time doin'—" The tall man licked at his flaccid lips. "An' him standin' there, a white man, an' me hollerin' from that tree full of snakes where I had spent a whole night above that water that didn't have no end to it—him standin' there a-wavin' a hand that had been manicured by some peroxide blonde in the Peabody Hotel in Memphis, standin' there a-wavin' that white hand at me while his motor roared, an' then him hollerin' at the very minute I was knockin' off a cottonmouth that come writhin' t'ward me, hittin' the snake with one hand and a-beckonin' to him with the other, an' then him hollerin' 'I'll be back in a little.' 'In a little,' he said. An' I watched the churn his motor made, and the boat a-fadin' away into that fog that was the color of flood water. That boat a-fadin' away, leavin' me an' my woman in that tree with those snakes up above that water that didn't have no end to it an' was even then eatin' at the very roots of the tree we was hangin' to. . . That boat a-fadin' away, full of . . ." He looked at the other two. "Full of *niggers*. Room in it for ten niggers. But not for me nor my woman. A white man, an' his boat full of bastard niggers, an' me that had fought snakes and river-flood a whole night long, an' was *white* to boot, had to wait there till he in his own good time got them niggers to high ground an' then come back fer me—a white man."

In the quiet, Ashby noted the tall man did not make any particular sound, did not breathe heavily or in any way indicate that a sudden anger had come on him; rather he sat quietly in that even flow of his hate, which did not even seem to affect him physically, as if he had lived so long with it and so constantly that his very blood and nerves now accepted it without changing his metabolism by so much as a breath.

"Well," the nervous man said. "So you're here."

The tall man looked at him. "I'm here. An' ain' leavin' until I see done what I came to help do. An' will do my best to see that what others has come don't leave either." He rose. "I'm goin' up to the big house. I got a thing to tell to Slim." He made that grin that was like a grimace. "Slim is one not to worry about a thing bein' legal. We was boys together, me an' Slim. An' now I got a thing to tell him."

The short man rose. "All right," he said. "I don't know what it is, but I ain' come half across Miss'ippi fer nothin'. I lef' my plowin' to come to this here party, an' I aim to see it done right. So I reckon I'll go 'long with you and have a word with Turkey Littlepage. He was the one told me there might be doings over here an' I aim to remind him of it."

"I don' reckon Turkey needs no remindin'," the tall man said.

"But you can come if you want to." The two of them looked down at the nervous man. "You aim to stay by this food? We all might be gittin' hungry, come mornin'. And I'm derned if that there eatin' don' set a mite better than ordinary, I reckon because ever' mouthful I take I can think I'm takin' it from the mouth o' that nigger-lover an' that limb o' Satan he's hidin'."

"All right," the nervous man said. "If you're sho he ain' comin' to git it . . ."

"I ain' sho o' nothin'," the tall man said. "I reckon he aimed to git it sooner or later. But you in hog-callin' distance o' them deputies on the road, an' if he comes, you jes' got to holler a little for us to git his damn sixteen-cylinder carcass in our hands."

"All right," the nervous man said. The tall man and the short man looked down at him and on their faces there was a faint and enjoyable condescension. Then without speaking they turned and made their way toward the road.

Even after the two were gone, Ashby could see in his mind their faces, and could see them endlessly multiplied, until they became not faces at all, but one gigantic caricature of a face, an exaggerated representation of all fear, all impotence, all rage. It was a face he had seen all his life, and yet had not seen at all, so that now he remained for a moment unmoving, thinking: My God they'll do it. You are always hearing about it, you talk about it, there has been a time when you have even seen them on the squares holding up to the sunlight the jars of formaldehyde in which there swim two joints of a black finger, yet somehow you don't believe it. Perhaps because nowadays they usually don't kill in mobs, and when they do it is so seldom and so far away that you read about it the way you read about the death of a person you do not know, shaking your head and folding the paper and wiping the breakfast napkin across your lips. But all you have to do is look into the face to know that they will do it, are always ready to do it: that it is possible for it to happen anywhere, anytime, given a man who has had to wait his time in a tree above a flood that has no end . . .

In the instant he thought this, he felt a new coldness in him, not of anger so much as surprise, the reaction of a man who, knowing he has a river to swim, dives in, and then discovers that the water he thought was warm is icy instead: he is not enraged, only shocked that the element of cold has been added to the elements of distance and wetness. For one moment, Ashby contemplated the store of uneaten food, resting in the box near the lone nervous man who had not yet moved, who remained crouched and immobile, as if he did not dare even turn his head for fear he might see what he did not want to see, as a child by covering its eyes thinks to negate all evil. It was not any particular anger at the tall man, nor any particular desire to deprive the three of them of food that made Ashby want to retrieve the half-full box; it was only that he had planned to get the food on his way to Temp and he had a childish desire not to change his plans, as if failure here would presage failure later. Yet he forced himself to turn and motion to Bevo, squatting close at his side, to follow, and they made their way at a gait so slow as to seem interminable through the bushes, feeling safe—in their nakedness in which they seemed doubly exposed—only when the live oaks at length shut out the moonlight and they were once more in the dark phosphorescent glow of the deep woods. They were at the place where they had left their shoes.

"What you think they aim to do?" Bevo whispered, sitting on a log and crossing his legs, a shoe in one hand.

"I don't know," Ashby said, lying, because he thought he knew. "But we've got to get out of here tonight. Not in the morning or tomorrow night. This night." He reached for his waterlogged shoes, laid the pistol down, and seated himself beside Bevo.

"We could 'a' taken that food," Bevo said.

"Yes," he said. "But if we ever need that food—because we are encircled in this swamp—then we'll need other things more than food. I don't reckon we'll even be worrying about something to eat then."

"What will we worry about?" Bevo said.

Ashby worked his foot into the wet leather. "I don't know what," he said, lying again, knowing that he could have said what they would worry about in one word, and yet not quite believing his own deduction, thinking, I don't believe even they would try that. In a swamp seventy-odd miles square . . .

"They're not comin' in after us, though."

"No," Ashby said. "Nobody's coming in after us. There aren't three men in the state of Mississippi who'd go in that swamp."

"And we're two of 'em," Bevo said. "And Temp . . ."

"Yes," Ashby said, leaning to his shoelaces. "Well, one more maybe. If he's alive. He used to live in here. Bootlegger. I used to come down at Thanksgiving, when I was in college, and stay with him and hunt. He knows this place like he knows the back of his hand, and he taught it to me. Not just the fringes—plenty of people hunt and fish on the fringes—but the heart of it. Nobody will be coming into the heart of it. Nobody." He stood up, the pistol in his hand, and all at once discovered that the hand was trembling slightly, and realized that he had probably been trembling a long time, from the moment it had come to him, not what they might do to Temp (he had at least thought of that before), but how they might get Temp in order to do it. "I don't reckon they will have to come in the heart of it," he said, his voice sounding harsh to him.

"You think that crazy beanpole back yonder has an idea . . .?"

"I don't know," Ashby said. "If he hasn't, somebody else will. All I know is we got to get out of here before they have got their receiving line formed."

When the creek water touched him now, he did not notice, just as on that long hectic walk that followed he noticed only those landmarks he had trained his eyes to note, and noticed those only in some remote corner of his consciousness, not ever naming them to himself, not saying, "Turn from the Fox

Run at the oak uprooted by lightning and go through the tangle of smilax and moss until you come to Red Pond (with water the color of port) and skirt Red Pond and follow the branch through the palmetto flat and at the end of the flat find the opening in what will look like a solid wall of bamboo and plunge into the marsh and sight, across it, the charred stump where the bay trees begin and make your way through the thick-clumped bays and then into the Hell-Hole itself, the deep heart, where not even God could find room for even a seedling, where no path lasts longer than a week, even when hacked out with axes, and where a man has to steer by nothing but intuition, since every tree and every length of moss and every smilax vine looks alike, until you come to Deep Creek where the footbridge (a felled log) crosses to the clearing where Temp is." He did not name these places to himself as they came to them, though he went from one to the other as unerringly as he might have walked a straight broad road, and with as little concern. For now he was concentrating only on that end-place, the lean-to under the oak where Temp was. He walked in a feverish haste through the now-cooling swamp where the swampsteam rose from the black water and curled whitely and made the moon light milky, so that at times they seemed to be curtained in milky light, yet he paid no mind to this either, no more mind to it than he paid to the caterwauling of the occasional wildcat, or the sudden freezing of a deer on the bank of a slough, or the breaking of a quick quietness by the swift up-flapping of a white crane, its wings fanning their faces as they trudged through the wiry whistling marshgrass. No more mind, indeed, than he paid his own body, scratched, torn, mosquito-bitten, that body which at times he had to use like a swimmer who breasts not deep waters but vegetation, who can move only with a constant flailing motion of his arms against the entanglement of vine and limb and moss which impedes his way. Once he heard Bevo mention, in the peevish voice of a man who has more important things to be worried with, the dropping of a snake from a limb overhead, and he glanced about in time to see the cottonmouth writhe into the brush. And once it seemed to him that he heard a sound behind them which was somehow foreign and intrusive to that medley of swamp-noise to which he was by now so accustomed that he scarcely heard it at all: he stopped and turned and strained his eyes through the trees and tangled vines, through the pale luminosity of the swampsteam, and then, seeing and hearing nothing, shrugged and went on in the rhythmic plodding urgency which marked that whole long walk from the place where the three men had sat around the car. It was only shortly afterward that they sloshed through the stretch of gumbo mud and pushed aside the bamboos and stood on the brink of the felled-log footbridge which spanned the final creek.

"A footbridge," Bevo said. "I never thought to see another one."

Ashby said nothing. He stood still a second, breathing heavily, relievedly, as if he had not quite dared to take a full breath until now, until he had seen the footbridge spanning the silver line of the creek. He wiped his hand across his face with one gesture, and with a second scratched at a bite on his thigh.

"This is it," he said. "Now to get Temp and get on to the river . . ."

"And what?" Bevo said. "Swim it? I swear, I don't believe I could swim across a tin washtub right now."

"We'll get across. Somehow. By God, if we've come this far, we'll get across that damn river." He stepped onto the log, walking carefully, against the slick mud coating his shoes, conscious suddenly of a cramping in the hand in which he had held the pistol gripped and had forgotten that he held it there until now, until the sudden pain. He turned, once he had touched the solid sand of the other bank, and, holding the pistol loosely in the hand that was uncramped, working the fingers of the tingling other hand, watched Bevo come with the slow sure tread of an animal, the muscles in his powerful legs knotting ropily, his great mud-streaked body looking in the moonlight like some huge white-skinned animal from which the fur had been shed in patches. Where the fur remained, on the legs and arms, across the chest and around the genitals, it was thick and wet, like the coat of a seal. Ashby turned as Bevo jumped onto the bank and squinted into the darkness, taking a step forward and suddenly feeling his skin creep not from cold but from the strange oppressive silence of the spot. In the quiet steamy dark he could hear nothing.

"Temp . . ." he said, tentatively, his voice strange and unnatural, already at that moment without any assurance in it, his eyes toward the spot under the oak where the lean-to was built. "Temp must be sleeping," he said, but he knew all at once that he did not believe it—knowing as he did that Temp was too frightened of the swamp to sleep so soundly as not to hear them. He knew this, although he had not once thought of the possibility of Temp's not being there when they arrived, although he had only a moment before spoken confidently of proceeding on to the river. He knew it instantly, before even he found himself running through the trees, stumbling, with eyes blinded by the brilliant silver of the creek, the moss slapping his face. He dropped on his knees before the lean-to and felt with his hands beneath it. He touched only the thick bed of moss. Nothing breathed there. He closed his eyes and remained on his knees, a little stupefied, not quite willing yet to admit that his hands rested on nothing but the faintly electric, furry moss. Then in one quick blind gesture he jumped to his feet.

"Temp!" he bellowed, and then, "Temp. Temp. Temp," as if merely yelling the name could controvert Temp's absence. His words rang hollowly through the swamp space. "My God . . ."

Bevo stood beside him. "He's just likely gone off somewhere."

"Temp!" Ashby called again. Then, to Bevo, "He's too scared to go off by himself. Somebody would have had to take him off. You reckon somebody followed us this morning?" He turned another direction. "Temp-ta-tion!" He began to search the clearing, moving haphazardly, without plan, finding a certain satisfaction in the mere movement. He cursed the overarch of trees and vines which shut out the light. "Temp-ta-tion!"

Nothing sounded except a mocking bird. Ashby wiped his forearm across his brow and stood, slumping with tiredness, looking down at the empty lean-to, as if he could will Temp back there. Then he sat down on the ground, the sand gritty to his buttocks and genitals, the trailing moss tickling his face, and he noticing nothing, staring bitterly into space. He did not even move to take the clothes from around his neck.

"He likely just went off a piece."

"He promised me he'd stay. If he was anywhere close, he could have heard me. If he went farther he'd be breaking his promise, and Temp wouldn't do that, wouldn't break a promise anyhow, and wouldn't break that one because he was too scared of this swamp. No, somebody took him off. And even if it was somebody friendly to him, if we don't get him out of here tonight . . ."

Bevo had no answer. He sat down beside Ashby. They sat in the dismal place for what seemed a long time, not speaking because the only words they could say would be more futile than silence, not moving because there was now no reason and no urgency to move.

Then, all at once, there was a sound close by, a sound that Ashby heard, picked out, and yet did not react to until it was repeated; even then it took him a moment to recognize it: footsteps.

He rose slowly, unbelievingly, hearing without mistake now the soft thud of feet on earth. He looked back through the trees whence he had come.

"Maybe it's him."

"No," Ashby said, narrowing his eyes. "No. It's a woman."

He did not even think that he was naked. He went toward her where she stood a few feet from the bridge, her flesh, still touched by the moonlight, glowing yellowly, and the startling black of her hair reflecting a light like a halo about her head.

# Chapter XXI

He stopped a few feet from her. It was Tilda. Her dress clung wetly to her, and in the faint light—the half-shadow where she now stood, unmoving, like a carved figure—he could see the swollen scratches on her face.

"I had to come," she said, not raising her voice, speaking in a whispered monotone. "I knew you wanted me to stay, but I followed you. That was me you heard behind you that time you stopped and turned and looked." He was aware of the charged quality of the words, a quality more exaggerated than minimized by the monotone in which she spoke, and he wondered if it were the racking trek through the swamp which had unnerved her or only the possibility that he would send her back (as if, he thought, he could send her back, since she could not have found her way and would no doubt have ended up, as many others had ended up in that swamp, smothering in quicksand or drowning in Red Pond whose placid port-colored waters were subject to sudden, inexplicably violent eruptions.)

"It's all right," he said. She said nothing, then, and it was her quietness, more than the unseeing stare which she directed at him that made him suddenly conscious of his own nakedness, and, even while he fumbled at the belt which bound his bundled clothes around his neck, grimly amused at the instinctive modesty which made him turn from her and stumble awkwardly into his pants without even taking time to dry his damp body.

As if it mattered a good goddam now, he thought. He let the rest of his clothes remain on the ground where he had dropped them, and turned back to her.

"All right," he said. "You can stay."

She lifted her head to him. "How come you look like that?"

"Temp's gone," he said.

He saw the slight shiver of her body. "Lord," she said. "Lord," and he knew she was thinking about Temp, about the things that might have happened to him. Then she spoke quickly, "But this an easy place to get lost in. He likely just lost."

"He was too scared to wander,"

"He likely come home in the morning," she said.

"Home?"

"I mean here," she said, and he looked intently into her face, but said nothing, not feeling like saying anything.

"Ashby . . .?" Bevo's voice came muffled to him, from the lean-to.

"Uh?"

"Y'all go over yonder by the footbridge so I can get dressed. No matter what you said about me in that jail, I'm not the nudist around here, and I haven't got any room in this lean-to to put my pants on . . ."

"All right," he said, unamused, and he turned and without speaking to Tilda, went tiredly toward the creek, and, unthinkingly, began to tear down moss and pile it on the bare sand under an oak. He knew that Tilda was standing close by, as if waiting for an order, or at least for an assurance, a casual word that would indicate he was aware of her presence. But he continued silently to arrange the moss carefully on the ground and did not even look up until he felt her shadow fall across him and heard the strangle, the half-sob in her throat. Then he raised his head, quickly.

"Do you think they . . . they got him?" she said.

"Who?" he said, wishing she would be quiet.

"Them men . . . All them men that have come from all over

and are out yonder sitting around their campfires now, waiting to get him?" She spoke very slowly, against some obstruction in her throat.

"Da—" he said, and then, seeing her face, did not say the whole word, but stood impatiently and went and kicked at the footbridge and stared intently at the silver-shining creek. "I don't know," he said, without turning. "I didn't know it was going to come to this," he said, more to himself than to her, excusing himself to himself. "How could I have known? You don't take it seriously when you hear about it. It's just words, a thing that has happened and may again, somewhere a far piece from where you are. And even when I heard that the sheriff had hinted . . . Well, dammit, I didn't think . . ." He bit his lip. That's it, he thought. Didn't think, period. That's what I didn't do.

Behind him, he heard her say, still in that strangled voice. "It's a terrible thing to feel like you got to kill," and he did not know whether she was talking about the men out there or about herself or perhaps about both the men and herself. But he did not ask her. He turned impatiently back to the bed of moss and began to smooth it, not because it needed smoothing but because he wanted something to do with his hands.

"I'll make me one," she said.

He turned and looked at her. "You sleep in the lean-to. You can't sleep in those wet clothes. Take 'em off and hang 'em up to dry and I'll give you the coat to my suit—it won't cover you all the way, but it'll help, if you sleep scrooched up a little."

She did not question his plans, but he noticed that she hesitated a second before she spoke. "I'll make one for Mr. Thomas then."

"His name's Mr. Banes. But I'll make his. You sit down and rest yourself. You've come a long way . . ."

"So have you," she said.

"It was my own fault," he said. "I took the long way and

I reckon the wrong way, and it won't be me that will pay for it being wrong."

She did not say anything, because Bevo appeared then.

"What are we gonna do?" he said.

"There's nothing to do but stay here till morning, when we can look for some signs of Temp. If he doesn't show up then . . ." He shrugged, and turned impatiently and went a few feet away and tore again at the thick hanging moss, dropping it haphazardly on the ground around him. In the tree above him there was the sudden raucous night-chatter of a squirrel. He lifted his head. "Yah, yah, yourself," he muttered.

Bevo was beside him then. "What?" he said.

"Nothing," Ashby said.

"You do a heap of talking about nothing," Bevo said.

Ashby looked down at the moss around his feet. "There's your bed," he said. "Just smooth it up a little . . ."

"All right," Bevo said. He squatted and then sat on the moss and then looked up at Ashby, blinking, and then silently sank back onto the unevenly piled moss, and slept, leadenly. Ashby watched him a moment and then turned and went back to where Tilda waited. He stooped and picked up his coat from the sand where he had dropped it and handed it to her. She stood looking at him, a strange soft gleam in her eyes.

"Sleep in the lean-to," he said.

"In the lean-to," she said, tonelessly, not having yet touched the proffered coat.

"Yes."

"And cover myself with your coat," she said, a tinge of wonder in her voice.

"Yes," he said, impatiently.

She took the coat from his hand and held it clasped against her.

"It doesn't matter to you?" she whispered.

"Why should it matter?" he said.

She arched her neck and drew her breath in, shudderingly. "It matters to me that it doesn't matter to you," she said, still in that same strained voice. "You can't know what . . . what it means to me . . ." She put her free hand to her mouth and then she shook her head against sudden weeping and fled from him, running through the curtain of moss toward the lean-to.

He watched her for a moment, surprised, and half-embarrassed. Then he lay down on the moss, feeling only then the ache and tiredness of his muscles and the sting of his slashed and bitten skin. He thought of Temp and clenched his teeth, but sleepfulness caught him up, and he blinked only once at the moon before he slept.

He woke to the sting of a mosquito on his cheek and to the knowledge that he had overslept, since the morning was already past the crimson of sunrise. The sun-yellowed sky above him was the sky of almost nine o'clock. He reached for his watch. It was twenty minutes to nine. He looked at the watch for a long time, half-stupefied still with exhaustion; when his head had cleared and he could gaze at the sunlit sky without closing his eyes against it, he still sat, indecisively, helpless for a moment against the cold unease which swept him with the remembrance that Temp was lost. He's not coming back, he thought. He's had plenty of daylight in which to find his way here, and with his sense of direction he would have been here by now if he just wandered off and got caught by the dark somewhere. So that means either that somebody is holding him against his will or else the quicksand has got him or a wildcat has smelled his fear or . . . Because even in this swamp, I believe Temp could find his way back unless . . .

He did not know what to do, but he could not sit any longer, so he rose and began to inspect the ground around the creek. He found no trace of Temp, and it was only after perhaps thirty minutes of close inspection that he came on the heelprint, across the footbridge from his bed. It was a heelprint made by a heavy boot or shoe, unlike the shoes Bevo and he wore. He squatted for some time looking at the print in the damp sand. But when he tried to find other prints, he noticed nothing, or at least nothing that could have been made by a human foot either shod or naked.

He stood then, again indecisive, beside the creek. Bevo and Tilda were apparently still asleep, protected from the sun by the thick umbrageous oaks. He supposed that he should wake them, tell them that Temp had not re-appeared, and that after they made one more effort, the three of them together, to find some trace of him, they would give it up. And then do what? he thought. Go where? Not back to Ephe's, and not back to Pelham. Then where? He did not know.

He did not wake Bevo and Tilda. Instead, because his muscles were cramped and sore, and his skin smarting, he crossed the footbridge and standing by his bed of moss, he stripped off his clothes and then stepped into the sun and stood a moment thrashing his arms about and bending his hard, lean winter-white body. Then he walked on bare feet to the footbridge, thinking: No doubt Tilda will wake up and catch me buck naked again. He sat down on the sand-grainy log and lowered his feet into the icy water. He thought about the times Temp had taken him swimming in the river when he was little and Granny had forbidden it. "No bathing in the river," she had said. But then it had got hot and he had thought about the cool river and the sandbar at the foot of the limestone bluff where he went to hunt for petrified shark's teeth which Uncle Vance said had been deposited there when the ocean covered all that part of the world. Then he would go and find Temp, because then, no matter how much he wanted to swim in the river, he was a little afraid to go by himself, after Granny had pictured the horrors of drowning. And every time, at first, Temp would refuse. "Miss Granny say no. No bathing." "I'm not gonna bathe," he would say. "I'm not gonna take any soap with me. I'm just gonna swim." Temp would speculate a while, then. "Now it do look like you got to have soap if you gonna bathe." Ashby would nod eagerly and Temp would speculate some more. "And if you ain't got soap, you ain't bathing," Temp would say. "Course not," Ashby would say, knowing he had won but not showing he knew, because then Temp might change his mind. "And it is hot," Temp would say. "Hotter'n the hinges of hell," Ashby would say, sometimes. "Ain't no use cussin' about it," Temp would say, "but it look to me like there ain't no reason us can't go git ourselves cool in the river." By that time Ashby would be jumping impatiently at his side. "Per-vided . . ." Temp would say, "pervided you don't say nothin' to nobody about it. There is folks that don't make no difference between swimmin' and bathin'." "I won't say a thing," Ashby would say. And then they would make their way through the pasture and down the cliff to the sandbar and undress. Temp would stand a moment stretching his powerful black body, hairless and smooth and rounded as a sculptured thing. Then he would hold Ashby's hand and they would wade into the water. "Jest don't git yo'self drownded," he would say. "Because if you do, I will have to tell yo' Granny you went in the river and there's no telling what she'd do to us."

Now, with his feet in the cold water, he could remember Temp's saying, "It ain't no use to slip easy into cold water. Like a heap of other things I could tell you about, it's better to dive in head first and feel all the coldness at once, than to feel it inch by inch." So Ashby did it the way Temp had said to do it, all at once, only not diving for fear of waking Tilda and Bevo. He slipped off the log and straight down into the water ducking under and jackknifing his body against the sudden cold. He came up gasping, his skin seeming to shrink on him, ducked his head again, and then, coming to the surface, struck out up the deep creek, swimming with long near-silent strokes against the slow current. The black water was so clear he could see the sandy bottom and occasionally note a dawling trout or a darting bream in the depths. When he had swum perhaps thirty yards up along the bamboo-hedged bank, he turned on his back and let the current carry him down to the footbridge. He closed his eyes, letting himself drift. He thought: When I get out of here, I'm going to be hungrier than a man in the middle of a swamp without a fishhook ought to be; I reckon I will have to try to shoot us a squirrel with my pistol.

He opened his eyes only when he felt his big toe touch the log. He straightened in the water and reached with his hands for the bridge. He pulled himself half-up, and then, the muscles of his arms bulging with the pulling, he lifted his eyes to a near shadow.

Temp swayed there on the bridge above him, one lens of his spectacles broken, a welling red wound across his left forehead and a terrible sickness heavy on his whole body.

# Chapter XXII

Temp swayed there a moment. Through swollen lips he muttered, "Mr. Ashby. That you, Mr. Ashby?"

Then he fell, crumpling, one hand raised helplessly above him, and his body splashed into the water. Ashby caught him, grasping the collar of his open shirt. One hand on the footbridge, he managed to slip the other arm under Temp and get a hold on him around the chest. Then by means of the bridge, he pulled himself toward the bank. When his feet touched the shallow water near where his bed of the night before lay, he stood and put his arms under Temp and lifted him onto the bridge, since the bamboo cut him off from climbing directly onto the bank. He drew himself up out of the water, put his hands under Temp's armpits and dragged him from the bridge to his bed of moss.

Gently, he laid Temp on the moss, imprinted still with the shape of his own body. He knelt and felt inside Temp's wet shirt and found the beat of his heart. The dark eyelids, however, were still closed and the breathing came in irregular shudders. Ashby reached hurriedly for the pants he had thrown down, stood and drew them on, not troubling to dry himself. His skin tingled warmly, yet there was a chill misery in him for Temp, an ache in his own forehead in the place where the gash was on Temp's temple, so that he thought, grimly: A hell of a doctor I'd make; I'd hurt every place a patient hurt. He stared helplessly for a second. Then he turned to call Tilda, but found her already there, standing close to him, staring with sleep-swollen eyes at Temp. He did not know how long she had been there and he did not trouble to find out. He did note that she wore her still-damp dress.

"Will water help him?" he said, and then, angrily, "There was whiskey in the car, but those bastards were sitting there," and then he said, "I'm sorry," but she acted as if she had not heard.

"I got some brandy," she said. "I brought it with me."

"Oh," he said. "Yes," as if he should have known it, expected it.

She went hurriedly toward the lean-to.

He dropped to his knees beside Temp. With hands still a faint blue from the cold water, he chafed Temp's thick veined wrists. The lips, puffed and purplish, muttered something and the eyes opened but closed again almost immediately. Ashby leaned, trying to hear what Temp's lips were trying to say. He made out only one word, *cold*, or perhaps *coal*.

Tilda was beside him. "Give me those shorts of mine by my bed." He raised Temp and unbuttoned the wet shirt and pulled it from him. Then he took the shorts which Tilda handed him and rubbed Temp's muscular brown chest, rubbed it dry and then kept on rubbing it, thinking to bring warmth back to the flesh. Breathing heavily, Tilda squatted beside him.

"Is he . . . is he gonna die?" she whispered.

"No," he said, turning on her angrily, the wet limp cloth dangling in his hands as if for a moment he contemplated striking her with it. "No!" he said, again, his voice harsh as it might have been had she predicted his death instead of Temp's. She did not say anything. She dropped her eyes and held out to him the bottle of brandy. He took the bottle, which she had already opened, and poured a measure of the liquid on the shorts. With them he wiped the gash on Temp's forehead. Temp's legs writhed, briefly; he moaned.

He handed the undershorts to Tilda and then, still on his knees, leaned over Temp and put one hand under his head and lifted it. He put the neck of the bottle to Temp's parted lips and let the brandy trickle between the clenched teeth. Temp swallowed. His eyes opened, but they stared sightlessly upward. Ashby put the bottle again to his lips and now Temp swallowed without urging. Ashby thrust the bottle back upon Tilda.

Temp rubbed his tongue across his lips. He blinked at the narrow sweep of sunlight which lay across his face. Then suddenly he began to whimper, a terrible plaintive sound.

"It's all right," Ashby said. He put his hands on Temp's hard-muscled shoulder, gripping him. "It's all right."

"Not like no man," Temp whispered. "Not like no man. Like a dog."

"What?" Ashby said. Temp's eyes, turned to him, were glazed and vacant. He spoke, Ashby realized, in delirium.

"Sho he save you," Temp said, thickly. "Sho. Like he'd save one of his huntin' dogs. And treat you that-a way. Feed you and talk good to you and git the doctor for you, long as you does what he ask you to do. For the world the way he treats a good dog . . ." The words trailed off. Ashby did not look at Tilda but he reached for the undershorts. In his hands, he rolled the wet shorts. Then he heard Tilda cry, and lifted his head, quickly.

"Hush," she said, one tan hand catching Temp violently by the shoulder. "Hush yourself. Quit talking about Mr. Ashby that way. You hear me? You hush, you, Temp. He's not like that. He's not. He gave me the best bed here last night, like I was a real woman, and not a high-yellow one, you hear me, he gave me . . ."

Ashby grasped her wrist and jerked her hand loose from Temp. She sobbed.

"Hush," he said, quietly. "Leave him alone. He doesn't know what he's saying."

He did not look at her. She had cried out against the truth, for, though it was not untrue that he would have done what he was doing for a dog, it was true that he and Temp were master and servant and not merely man and man. He thought of what Uncle Vance might say to that. "Good God," Uncle Vance would likely have said, "Good God, do you require that a man bathe with another man in order to prove that he's just toward him? Or eat from a common plate, in order to substantiate equality before the law? And what other equality is possible in the nature of things? You and I, for instance? Equal? My God, I've got a game leg from a Minié ball at Chickamauga and could walk at my best no more than a couple of miles, while you . . . And no female would say we're equal. I couldn't sport with the most wanton, flesh-rife female in Mississippi, but you . . . could you not swive her now? Hah! No, son, if the Lord requires that we equalize ourselves, he'll have to stop the earth in its orbit and do a remodeling job."

"Like a dog . . ." Temp muttered painfully.

"And it's not true that you're saving him because he's served you, either," Uncle Vance might well have said. "You would do the same for any man. So what is this business of master and servant, anyhow? I dare say you'd save me if I got in hot water. And you'd treat me just as you've treated Temp, except that perhaps you'd say 'sir' to me. You'd act inferior to me, because of my hoary head. And would that be wrong? Hell, son, it would only be manners. Just as Temp's saying 'sir' to you is only manners. Oh, I'll admit that, given an equal chance you might have been the servant and Temp the master. But wouldn't the relationship have been exactly the same, and only the participants reversed? You may bemoan, if you must, the inequality of opportunity which has made you what you are and Temp what he is. The unequal chance, yes; the inequality before the law, yes: those are wrong. But do not spell me any sentimental lessons about complete equality of man and man. Man will never be equal to man until each man on earth is whole and self-sufficient. For, as it is, we must divide the labor of living among ourselves, according to our individual capacities. And the man capable of the most valuable labor will always stand above the man capable of less valuable labor."

Through Temp's stifled moans, Ashby could hear in his mind everything Uncle Vance would have said. "The guilt you feel at the gap between you and Temp is stupid and sentimental. What in the devil are you doing in this swamp, boy, but fighting to see that you and he are equal before the law? Good God, what else can you do to prove you look on him as a man?" And yet . . . Ashby thought. And yet. He closed his eyes against Temp's contorted face.

"Let Num . . ." Temp cried, suddenly, twisting his body. "Let Num sit in balcony at church." His blue lips moved slower, then stopped. He rolled his head and cried out. The cords in his neck were swollen and taut. Ashby wiped his face. He quieted. "Let Num in balcony. Sho. Balcony. Even in church, a special place. Num don't sit 'side Mr. Jason or Mr. Ashby, do he? Naw. Sit in balcony . . ." Temp's tongue flicked across his lips. Ashby thought, Now what, Uncle Vance. Have you an answer for that one? Surely, if you're going to grant him the right to equality before the law, you might grant him the right to equality before God?

"Sho, Mr. Jason made 'em let him sit in balcony. Sho. Won't let Num be hurt. But won't let his dog be hurt, either."

Tilda stood up. "I'm not gonna listen to him," she said. "He's doing bad nigger-talk. I've heard it before, and I . . ." Then she turned and ran. Ashby followed her with his eyes until she disappeared in the moss-laden trees. She was not angry at Temp, but at the truth of what he said. He felt a sickness in him.

Temp lay quiet a second, then he reared up, suddenly, and said, "It's a lie. It's a lie, Coal Black. A lie, lie, lie." Then he fell again. "Like a man," he mumbled. "Mr. Ashby doing like a man. He my best friend. Treat me . . ." He turned on his side. "It a lie. Lie, Coal Black. Don't hit me, Coal . . ." Ashby leaned, listening: the word was coal, not cold. And Temp said Coal Black, as if it were a name, the name of an antagonist, with whom he was arguing. "Lie!" Temp cried.

"There," he said, knowing that someone else had said those other bitter words to Temp. "There. Course it's a lie."

"Lie!" Temp said.

"Of course," he said, wanting to bite his tongue as he said it. "Of course, Temp. It's a lie. Go to sleep."

"Yessir." Temp spoke without seeing, and yet the word was now quiet, resigned, as if he had been waiting, Ashby thought grimly, for a command from a white throat, an order which, when he obeyed it by sinking into that untroubled slumber, confirmed the very fact which he had been so agitately denying. *I'm a man, I'm treated like a man* he had cried to whoever had tormented him, and yet he did not rest until he was commanded as a child—or perhaps a dog—might be commanded. Perhaps he was frightened of freedom, too old now for rebellion. Ashby did not know. He was as confused as Temp. He sat gazing down at the dark now peaceful face, thinking of Uncle Vance, thinking, *The web is made out of all of these and more that are nameless, and if you can free us of it, sir . . . Then you are God, by God.*

He rose, and would have gone to call Bevo, except that there facing him across the bridge stood a man with a ten-gallon black hat on his head and a shotgun slung carelessly under his arm.

# Chapter XXIII

Ashby stood stock-still for a second, his eyes fixed on the man. The man rubbed a casual, reflective hand over his jaw and looked back at Ashby out of narrowed eyes. Thinking desperately, Ashby stepped forward, imperceptibly he hoped, and let himself fall suddenly on the moss of his bed. With quick fingers he felt the pistol there. He closed his hand around the barrel, drew the pistol out of the moss and behind his back, his eyes never leaving the man, who now sauntered toward him across the bridge. Ashby flipped the pistol, caught it by the butt and leveled it at the man. He did not say anything, but merely held the pistol on the man, feeling foolishly inadequate sitting there glowering at the stranger, thinking: What in the hell does a man say in a moment like this, "Halt" or "Put 'em up" or "Reach for the sky" or whatever the devil they say in the moving pictures.

When he did manage to speak, he felt a fool. "Stop!" he said, managing to find his feet again. The man paid him no mind, but came forward with that same careless, aimless gait of his, unperturbed and even a little scornful. Then, all at once, the man laughed. He had a great, belly-born laugh that seemed to vibrate his whole body. For a moment Ashby, feeling foolish, was angry. His finger on the trigger tightened slightly, but then the man suddenly put down his gun when he had stepped off the bridge and stood there with the stock on the ground, laughing at Ashby without any hostility in his laughter. Ashby continued to hold the pistol level on the man, but now examined him curiously.

He was a strapping fellow, of undetermined age, dressed in well-washed and faded overalls and a shirt from which half the sleeves had been torn, so that his heavy-muscled arms, tanned and marked by the blue line of taut arteries, displayed their ropy strength. His face was tanned, too, and heavy not only with flesh but with an expression of open sensual humor, an expression particularly apparent around his large mouth, now spread to his laughter. This laughter that he made was so without threat, so evidently intended not for mockery of Ashby but for Ashby's sharing, that in spite of himself Ashby found himself grinning. There was a certain familiarity about the fellow, yet Ashby could not name him. What was it Temp said? "I knows your favor but I can't call you?"

When the man saw that Ashby was grinning at him, he stopped laughing long enough to say, "I'm damned. I'm damned if it ain't College Boy."

Then Ashby knew him. "Lafe!" he said, and flung the pistol down and put out his hand. "Lafe, I figured the revenuers had buried you deep by now." He squeezed the huge calloused palm.

"How you, College Boy?" Lafe said, still chortling. "If you didn't look a sight, a-sittin' there in that damned moss fumbling fer that gun. Why, had I a notion to, I could 'a' picked you off six times before you could 'a' turned that pistol right side up, and then I reckoned there'd 'a' been women all over that state of Miss'ippi weepin' in their beds at night."

"You did sort of catch me with my pants down," Ashby said.

"And it not the first time, either," Lafe said. "What kind o' gal you got now, College Boy?"

He only grinned at Lafe and said nothing, but the thought skimmed across his mind—My God, things have happened so fast to me I haven't even had time to brood about Laurel.

Then he said, "You wouldn't have caught me that way, but I was taking care of Temp there, and . . ." He looked around at the sleeping Negro.

Lafe glanced down at Temp. "What ails him? Why, when he left my place this morning, he wasn't exactly blue-jay happy, but he wasn't . . ." He leaned and put one finger just above the wound on Temp's forehead. "Hell," he said. "He must 'a' met up with some trouble . . ."

"You mean you had Temp with you?" Ashby said. But before Lafe could answer, Bevo had appeared at Ashby's side, his hair mussed, his eyes sleep-sanded, his suit rumpled. "Well, you finally dragged your carcass up."

"I slept gentleman's hours last night," Bevo said, grinning and then breaking the grin to yawn noisily.

"Lafe," Ashby said, "This is Bevo Banes. Friend of mine."

"I've heard of you," Lafe said, shaking hands with Bevo. "Read your name in print this mornin', but never thunk that that Ashby Pelham they was writin' about was ole College Boy."

"College Boy?" Bevo said, looking at Lafe. "You call him that?"

"Never knowed him by no other name," Lafe said. "Oh, I reckon I might 'a' knowed, if you'd pushed me right hard, that he was named Pelham, 'cause I've seed him here in this swamp too many times with other Pelhams." He pushed his black hat back on his head, so that a wisp of reddish hair fell across his forehead. He chortled. "Last time I seen College Boy, him and his girl was buck naked, a-runnin' from the Ku Klux Klan." With one finger, he scratched at the dimple made by his grin. "He called her Honeybreeches, I 'member."

"Honeybreeches?" Bevo said. Ashby said, "Shucks," remembering.

"That's what he called her, and it don't take no long imagination to guess why. Anyhow, him and her was swimmin' one moonlight night up yonder in Cold Creek. Swimmin' in their altogether, naked as jaybirds, and it a time when the

Ku Klux was a-runnin' all over creation tryin' to stamp out sin, which was the Klan's name for a good time. In them days, the Klan would chase a fella if they caught him parked with a girl, and I heared about one place where the Kluxers drove so many of the whores out o' town the men-folks jest had to sleep with their own wives for want of somethin' better And another time not twenty miles from here they caught a bunch of young folks swimming naked, male and female together, in the river, and the Kluxers wrapped up the gals in sheets and took 'em home to their folks that way and tole their folks what they'd been doin'. So you would 'a' thought College Boy would 'a' been sorta sharp-eyed, but a randy man ain't got eyes for but one thing, so the Klan caught him." Ashby watched Bevo. Bevo was chuckling, and the chuckle was without shyness, as if with his entry into the swamp he had actually shed the restraint and timidity with which he had been clothed from the moment Ashby had met him that night in front of Miranda's house.

"The Klan caught him," Lafe said, "but it couldn't hold him. He knowed this swamp better'n those Kluxers did, even if they'd had the guts to run after him and his gal, which they didn't. But o' course, College Boy and Honeybreeches had had to get out of that creek and get gone sort of hasty-like, and didn't have no time to fool around for clothes. So they come to my place. I reckon College Boy's feet jest naturally led him there, he'd been there so much a-buyin' moonshine from me. I always said it was a pure shame I couldn't get my rightful cut of all that stuff College Boy got with the help of my good moonshine. Why, he averaged three virgins to the gallon . . ." Lafe closed his eyes and rocked on his heels.

"Hell," Ashby said, "I bet you tell that to all your customers. That watered-down stuff of yours . . ."

They chortled together, but Ashby was thinking: How long ago? How long and how far? The clack of poker chips, the self-conscious oaths, the ostentatious puffing of the Havana fillers in the room back of the Greek's looking out on the square; the smoke-smudged face of a blond girl sleeping on his shoulder and breathing a sweetish whiskey-breath into his face on the swaying football special in the car heated by a little Franklin stove and littered on the return trip with orange peels and empty bottles and students sprawled debauchedly on the gritty velveteen seats; the brass braying of Blue Jesus and His Twelve Disciples and she, when his arms went around her, saying "Sounds like Basin Street to me," and he saying, daringly, "Not the way Basin Street sounds to me," and she pretending not to understand and then giggling and saying, "Oh, you men . . . have all the fun," and pushing herself closer to him, murmuring through her rouge-pouted lips, "If you waltz as well as you foxtrot, I don't believe I can stand it," and he saying, "Baby, why stand it? Tonight we live. I got a snort in the car," and she saying, "You . . . you're awful," but looking over her shoulder and then saying, "Well . . . if you're *sure* we can get past the chaperones," and he, peacock-proud, thinking, Forrest never got there first with any more, fustest with the mostest, boy! Good God, how long and how far. Tonight we live. Hell. Thinking back on it was like coming on a picture of himself taken years ago, and turning to someone and saying, "This me? Why, that's not me?" And the someone would say, "Why, of course it's you. As you were then."

Yet the feeling passed, the swift vision fled, and he came to himself still laughing at the pure comic flow of Lafe's language, but laughing with a part of himself which seemed to act automatically, so that at the very moment he was laughing he was conscious only of his worry about Temp and the now-hardened anger that made him chafe at standing there still and listening to Lafe.

"Anyhow, here him and his gal come through the glade and when she seen me a-settin' on the steps, that Honeybreeches, she hid her pretty little self 'hind a bush, and College Boy run up to me out of breath and a-cussin' the Klan." Lafe spat. There was no use, Ashby knew, in trying to hurry him. "Now my ole woman, dead now but live then, she was drunk. And nigh asleep. And woke to see that pair come glidin' toward us through that misty moonlight. And she started a-hollerin' like in Holiness meetin', a-shoutin' out loud, 'Lawd Jesus, He's done done it. He's done tuk me back to Eden . . .' and she got up out o' her rocker and she waved to College Boy and his gal and she said, 'Adam 'n' Eve. I see you, Lawd Jesus, I do. Adam 'n' Eve.' That was when College Boy's gal hid herself behind the bush and my ole woman fell down in a fit. Even after I give that pair some clothes and sent 'em off to their car . . ." He cocked his eyes at Ashby. ". . . the ole woman laid there, and when she got up, swore to me the Lawd had showed her Eden. I never could git her to believe it was College Boy and his gal. Said I was jest bein' mule-headed, wantin' to spile her vision. 'I've seed Adam,' she said, 'With my own eyes, I've seed him. An' he was a right pretty man, too. Now I never thought so much of Eve, though. Too skinny.' "

They stood there, the three of them, laughing lustily at Lafe's tale, Ashby as loud as the other two, though it still seemed to him that Lafe was telling a tale about somebody he once knew rather well but had not seen for a long time now. Yet actually, he thought, I saw that College Boy fellow less than a week ago. I saw College Boy my last time on Sunday.

Lafe's laughter stopped and he searched Ashby with his mild blue eyes, looked him over appraisingly in unembarrassed silence.

Then he said, "I never would think it. I never would think to see you now, that you could be the same fellow always showin' up with some college gal, lookin' fer a quart. You got a man look about you, College Boy."

"Well," Ashby said, joshingly, "It's time enough, I reckon."

"Yeah," Lafe said, "time enough." He eased himself down on the bridge-end, laid his gun on the ground and took out a plug of tobacco from his pocket. "Chaw?" he said.

Bevo squatted beside him. "Reckon I will," he said.

"So you a chewer," Ashby said, seating himself on the sand near Bevo. "What other secret vices you got?"

Bevo flushed, taking the sliver of tobacco Lafe pared for him. "I ain't no layer of virgins," he said, joking Ashby as Ashby had not known him to do before. "Not," he added, "that I wouldn't like to try." His eyes looked past Ashby and lighted on Temp for the first time. "Is that Temp?" he said, half-standing. "That's Temp. What's he doin' here?"

"He got here a while back," Ashby said. His eyes were on Lafe. "Lafe was fixing to tell me when you came up."

Lafe, chewing busily, scraped at a fingernail with his knife. "I come in here last night," he said, "a-pullin' up some whiskey that I had fixed on a trot-line in the creek. An' I heard a low moanin', a kind o' yowlin' sound that I took to be a far hound at first, and then realized it was close to me, and not no animal I'd ever heard befo'. So I crossed this here bridge and scouted around and finally turned my flashlight on that lean-to back in yonder." Lafe pointed to the moss-hidden lean-to where Tilda was. "And there was that poor devil asleep, but a-twistin' and a-turnin' in a nightmare, a-yowlin' like a scared female cat, a-callin' fer 'Mr. Ashby.' When I woke him up he was scared. I never saw a man so scared, and I never saw a man hide it so quick. He scrambled out of that lean-to and stood there lookin' at me through those glasses of his and derned if I didn't feel a little buffaloed. I knew he was scared, but he stood up there before me straight as a turkey-cock, and I thought to myself, 'Black or white, that fella's a man.'" Lafe raised one eyebrow in Ashby's direction. "Maybe he'd let you see him scared, knowin' you all your life. But I got to admire a man waked up in the middle of a nightmare by a rough looking bastard like me in the middle of a swamp he's hiding out in and bein' manly like that fella was. Oh, I knowed he was scared. He wouldn't talk. Anyhow, when I asked him did he want to come to my place to sleep the night—thinkin' he was lost, maybe, and in daylight might find who he was lookin' fer—he never said anything. Jest nodded his head and come after me. I found out afterwards he thought I was the law. Thought I was the law, and knowed what that meant for him, and yet he come with me without a whimper. I don't know that I could have done the same. Or anyhow, not with the guts he showed." Lafe let his eyes wander to Temp and back.

"You sho gave me a scare," Ashby said. "When I got in here last night and found him gone . . ."

"What you reckon happened to him?" Lafe said. "He never did tell me what he was doin' here, jest said he had to find somebody, and when I sent him off this morning, after he found I wasn't the law, he was all right. Nothin' wrong with him, then, and now look . . ." He gestured with the knife to the wound on Temp's forehead.

"He kept hollerin' somethin' about Coal Black," Ashby said, gazing questioningly at Lafe.

Lafe pared a new plug of tobacco and feigned unconcern. Then he lifted his head and said, "Coal Black" and some intonation in his voice belied the casualness of his glance.

Ashby nodded. Lafe put the plug back in his pocket and chewed silently for a second. Then he looked back at Ashby. "I oughta knowed."

"What?" Bevo said, thrusting his head forward, chewing with a faint liquid sound of enjoyment.

"I didn't know that sonofabitch was still in this swamp," Lafe said. "I tole him last time I saw him he better get his ass out of here. He's sorta shrink-tailed about me, though, and I reckon he's been hidin'." Then, seeing the questioning still on their faces, he said, "Y'all done heared about Coal Black. The one that was a nigger preacher an' said he had the call from God to lead a nigger rebellion ag'inst the white folks?"

Ashby shook his head.

"Why," Lafe said, "you must 'a' forgot it, but the papers had a heap to say about him at the time. What started him out on all that foolishness, I don' know. Folks tell different stories. Some say he was a brother to that nigger trusty at

Parchman that they lynched a while back after he'd kidnapped the keeper's daughter. Some say he got het up because his woman was layin' for a white man. I don' know. All I know is he got him a bunch of niggers together up in Washington County and tried to shoot up the county seat one night. They say he'd been a-preachin' to all the niggers up there how the land belonged to the niggers 'cause the Lawd had made niggers stronger than white folks, and how niggers had to take the kingdom the Lawd laid out for 'em. What he really railed against though was niggers that got white blood in 'em, an' nigger sluts that lay for white men, an' niggers that do what he called 'bow down to white men 'stead o' God.' The niggers testified afterward that they wasn't aimin' to shoot no white men that night but was after what they called 'impure niggers.' Said that in court, but some of 'em admitted they aimed to go after the white folks after they'd killed all the high-yallers in Washington County, which would take some time and some doing seein' as how they ain' a white man in Washington County that ain' got himself a couple of half-black yard-chillun." When Lafe paused to grin, Ashby heard the slight sound behind him, and, turning his head quickly, thought that he caught a fleeting glimpse of Tilda lurking behind the moss oaks nearest them. But then, seeing no more, he turned back to Lafe.

"They oughta knowed the fella was crazy," Lafe said. "I've seed crazy white folks that thought that bein' white was all the guarantee of heaven they'd ever need. An' here this Coal Black was spoutin' the same kind o' foolishness, only sayin' that bein' black made a fella automatic the child o' God." Lafe spat. "Well, enough niggers believed him to stage his shootin'-mess. And the ones that did got in bad trouble, but he got loose. The law was so humiliated at him gittin' loose, they made up a tale about him drownin' tryin' to escape. It come out in the papers, an' I seed it myself. I seed it after I'd already come on him in the swamp one day, a-preachin' his craziness to nothin' but the mist. That was when I told him to git away from here. Evidently, he ain't got." Lafe was grim.

Ashby nodded. "It all makes sense now. When Temp got here, he was out of his head. He must have had a fight with Coal Black, because Coal Black told him I was tryin' to save him like I'd save a hound dog that was valuable to me."

Lafe spat. "I never heared of a fellow standin' up ag'inst the law an' his own blood an' all the prayin' jackasses an' snarlin' po'-buckras in a community jest to save a hound dog. I don' reckon you'd do that for anything less than a human bein'. An, tell the truth, it don' make much sense to me what you doin', but if you doin' it, College Boy, it must be right. Fact, 'fore I knowed it was you doin' it, when I seen them fellas comin' on my house from all directions this mornin', I figgered that if ever I found the man that was bringin' out all them pious ass-holes, I'd give him a hand."

"What?" Ashby said. "What's that? They came to your house?"

Lafe nodded. "How'd you think I knowed what was goin' on? Yo' nigger never tole me. Ole Littlepage an' Sheriff Twigge o' this county an' ole Governor Ephe—he's your cousin, I notice by the paper they give me—they all come. An' Sheriff Twigge tole me if I'd turn y'all over to them, I wouldn' have to pay no protection to him for a whole year. He had a notion that if I didn' already know where y'all was at, I'd be the one man that could find you." Lafe spat again. "Well," he said, looking down at his overalls, "to see me, I don't reckon you'd think I was a moneyed man. But I pay that bastard Twigge nigh onto five hundred a year so he won't arrest me on the prohibition law he's always speakin' out so strong fer in church. An' be derned if I don't have to furnish him his own private drinkin'-whiskey, to boot, because he says I make the best whiskey o' any bootlegger in this state. Anyhow, here I had a chance to make myself four or five hundred a year, an' all I had to do was tell the place where I'd found yo' nigger last night. But then I looked over that bunch o' fellas. An' I thought to myself, if ever I saw a bunch o' bastards hog-tied together, this is them. I had sold ever' one of 'em whiskey an' paid most of 'em for lettin' me sell it without gittin' arrested, while I had to listen to 'em makin' speeches fer the dry law an' watch 'em votin' ag'inst legal likker. Course it's their law that makes me my profit, but a bastard is a son of a bitch and I know him when I see him, even if I do turn a dollar or two out of his way of doin'." Lafe grinned and shifted his tobacco and shook his head. "They give me a gut-ache, jest lookin' at 'em, there this mornin'. An' I thought to myself, from what I know about that bunch, anybody that's ag'inst 'em must be a pretty honest fella. An' I never told 'em a thing, not only 'cause of that, but 'cause they plumb riled me with all their threatenin'."

"But they know we're in the swamp?" Ashby said.

"Why, hell," Lafe said, grinning "you might as well 'a' blazed a trail. With that car and all them groceries . . . How did you figger . . . ?"

"I never figured," Ashby said. "I never figured a-tall. I was just minding my own business. . . ."

Lafe nodded. "You was lightin' your corn-cob and never noticed that drum o' gasoline next you. And now there's hell to pay." He looked off over Ashby's head, meditatively. "Well, I don't understand none of it. Not why you should try to keep the nigger from the law nor why they should all be so yearnful to scorch your hide for doin' it. It's away beyond me, the whole shenanigans, but I come a-lookin' fer you to tell you I'd be pleased to help you. I ain't even been able to find out what they aim to do, but we can tend to that . . ." His eyes narrowed laughingly at Ashby, and Ashby looked back at him, puzzled, not understanding the expression. "All I know for sho is they got you surrounded."

"On land," Ashby said.

"Well, yes," Lafe said. "At least I don't guess all them hill rednecks and Delta peckerwoods and courthouse-square politicians are dustying up the roads leadin' here for no Ladies' Aid picnic. But now they're a-churnin' up some water, too."

"Water?" Ashby said, and for answer Lafe pointed river-ward and touched a hand to his ear. Ashby heard the faint buzz, which he had not heard before at all, and which he now listened to with that sudden cold foreboding with which a man will note the sound of trouble, the ambulance siren, or the wail of a police car in the dark streets of early morning. He felt himself sicken a moment and then grow angrier, with an anger not hot and impetuous, but frigid and reasoning. "All right," he said. "They're patrolling the river, too. But it will be dark, come night, and it will take some patrolling to keep us from slipping over . . ."

"Swimming?" Bevo said.

"Or in Lafe's boat," Ashby said. He looked to Lafe for confirmation.

Lafe chewed quietly a moment. Then he said, "Ain't a man one of 'em got guts to come in here. Oh, no, that ain't gonna be their way. But what their way is gonna be, I don' rightly know. And look like to me you ought to find out, College Boy, before you go to thinkin' you can slip past 'em easy-like."

"The devil," Ashby said. "I'd be glad to find out. Only I don't aim to walk out yonder and ask 'em."

Lafe's mouth was spread wide, the laugh-lines crinkling around his eyes. "Well, now," he said, "I don't reckon it will take any goin' out. Seein' as how she knows and come to tell you . . ."

"She?" Ashby said. "Who . . . ?" He was on his feet looking across the creek, knowing beyond reason the name Lafe did not say, seeing nothing there, however, but the immobile greenness of the morning-drenched swamp.

"I can do anything," Lafe said, "except out-talk a woman. Especially a woman that threatens to holler if I don't lead her where she aims to go. And especially when her hollering might bring—might 'a' brung—them damn bastards back to my place jest as I was burying in Cold Creek the best copper still in Miss'ippi. So I brung her along. Not that I ever had a chance to do anything else, since after they had got riled at me, I figgered I needed to know what they was aimin' to do myself, and if she knowed, I had to keep her with me to find out. Only she won't tell me. She won't tell nobody but you, she says, and . . ."

Ashby interrupted the wry sing-song of Lafe's words. "Where is she?" he said.

"Who?" Bevo said. "Who are y'all talkin' 'bout?"

"Laurel," Ashby said. "Where is she?"

"The last I seen of her," Lafe said, deliberately, "she was a-standing wet an' a little mud-dirtied down at the sandbend a-waitin' fer me to git gone so she could bathe her pretty self befo' she let you see her. I didn't aim to make it so hard fer her, but I had to make sure they wasn't follerin' us, and I reckon the tracks we made through this swamp is still sizzlin'. She is sho a woman to keep up, though, and I never had to help her much a-tall. But she did git herself scratched up some, and . . ."

Ashby, by then, was out of sound of the voice, pushing through the bamboo, thrashing his way through the undergrowth with a noise no louder than the beat and pump in his chest.

# Chapter XXIV

When he came upon her, she still sat upon the triangle of white sand, legs stretched bare before her and bare feet soaking in the clear eddying water. A faint dew clung still to the rose-tan skin of her neck and face, and the brown dress she wore was muddied and torn. He could see a scratch on one cheek and briar marks on the golden legs. Her hair, wet somewhere in that hectic flight into the swamp or else newly-washed in the creek, dripped a little yet. She looked, to him, damp and weary and lovely.

She had not yet seen him, and before he moved forward from the pendant moss where he had halted, she all at once began to kick her feet in the water, churning it with a kind of childish delight, so that she did not hear him as he moved shoeless across the sand. The sun here was warm now when it touched his chest and shoulders, for he had not yet had time to put on his shirt and coat. He hesitated a second before he knelt beside her, feeling the warmth and blinking in the diamond light.

His shadow touched her before he spoke and she started and turned her head and made a smothered gasp.

"You fool," he said, half-laughing and half-serious. His hand tightened hardly on her arm. "You're a plumb fool of a woman."

"I know it," she said, her voice cracking with huskiness. For a moment they neither moved. He was aware of her breathing, of the slow life-movement of her flesh. She smelled of the subtle musk of swamp water. A bead of bright blood oozed from the scratch on her cheek. He put a finger to it. He heard a choking in his own throat when he kissed her lips; they tasted of creek water.

When he spoke again, he tried to make his voice harsh. "You didn't have any business coming in here. You might have been snake-bit. Or drowned. Or . . ."

She put a hand on his shoulder, and he saw her laughing at him with her eyes. "Even in a swamp," she said. "Even half-naked and with hair all tousled up and . . ." She mocked him.

"What?" he said.

"A Southern gentleman," she said, and the laughter was sounding in her throat. "Oh, Ashby, you're the fool. I had to come to tell you what they're going to do."

"You could have told Lafe," he said.

"I didn't know I could trust Lafe," she said.

"You trusted him with your life, coming here," he said. "If he had wanted to be rid of you . . ."

"I never thought of that," she said. "I reckon I didn't do much thinking at all, not after I heard what they were planning. I just followed them to Lafe's and hid until they were gone, and then made him bring me . . ."

He took the hand she had not moved from his shoulder. He held it between his two hands, warming it. Even in the sun her flesh was cool to the touch.

"How did you follow them?" he said.

"I made Mr. Ephe take me down to the road they turned off to go into Lafe's place. I told him I wanted a walk, and that I'd walk back to the house from there. And then I didn't, of course—didn't walk back. Instead I slipped down along the road and watched them talking to Lafe and then waited for them to be good gone . . ." She laughed softly, pleased with her trickery.

"And then surprised Lafe burying his still in the creek," he said. "It's a wonder you haven't got your lungs full of buckshot right now."

"I guess so," she said, unconvinced. "He was sinking it out of the way of snoopers and I guess I looked like a pretty bad snooper. But he must have thought I could be trusted because he agreed just pretty as he could to bring me where he thought you were."

Ashby grinned at her. "You're a liar, too," he said. "You're practically shameless. Lafe said you threatened to holler. . . ."

She laughed aloud then, and put her head down on his shoulder, so that the damp hair touched silkily against his flesh. "Shameless," she whispered. "I am. You know, Ashby, I am." She lifted her face then. "Now I am." She spoke the fact with that curious intensity of hers, as if she had only then discovered it, yet she said, "I thought about it on the long way here. I thought that if I hadn't met you on the stairs of Miss Miranda's house . . ." Her eyes widened a little, her mouth was parted, wondering. "I never would have come in the swamp," she said. "Aunt Martha would be outdone. And with any other man, met anywhere else, I'd have thought how outdone she'd be. But with you . . . Ashby, it wouldn't ever be with us like it was with Miss Semantha and Mr. Ephe. It won't ever be that way, will it?"

He was holding her hand. "No," he said, and he was thinking that it would not be as it had been with him and Carol, either; nor, for that matter, as it had been with him and Honey-breeches. I have never known, he thought, a woman as a woman before Laurel; I have known only 'ladies' or pushovers. He chuckled. "Is that what you came to tell me? That you aimed to give up being a lady?"

"Don't laugh," she said. "It's only that I don't intend being the Miss Semantha kind of lady. And it wasn't easy to decide that. Any more than it would have been easy for you to love me if we'd met across a bridge table."

"I'd have loved you instantly," he said, "if we had met at a parchesi board."

"No," she said; and shook her head vigorously. "You'd have been very proper and gentlemanly and remembered all the stuff about 'protect the ladies from the niggers and Yankees.' . . . And then taken yourself off to Miss Miranda's to kiss that . . . that Louise . . ." She half-pouted but her eyes smiled.

"Oh-ho," he said. "You know her name."

She smiled with glinting eyes and moved closer to him on the sand. He put his arm around her. "I was there when she saw you drive up that night. I think I began to be a little suspicious of that house right then. What she said about you . . ." The laughing bubbled in her throat. "She didn't know I heard . . ."

"What?"

"I won't tell you."

"Tell me," he said. He grasped her wrist, tightly.

"No," she said. "I can't. I really can't." He saw the blush

spread fanlike across her cheeks. Joshingly he pushed her back on the sand, with mock threats, and she lay there, twisting in half-hearted effort to free her wrist, and laughing uncontrollably. "No. Really . . ." The protests came in gasps on the exhaled breaths. "Ashby, I can't . . . I can't . . ."

They scuffled in the sand like children. "Are you going to tell me?" he said, making as if to choke her.

Still gasping, she said, "Louise . . . called . . . you 'Skinny.' Said . . . 'What do y'know, yon's Skinny ag'in.' And the other girl said something I didn't catch and Louise said, 'Honey, he's skinny, all right, but I want to tell you . . ." She put her hand to her mouth to smother the memory and the laughing of it, but the laughing came again in spite of her. "I can't. I can't," she whispered, exhausted.

He loosened his hold and stretched out on the warm sand beside her. "You don't need to," he said. "I can imagine the rest. Louise says that about all her boys. 'He's fat, but I want to tell you . . .' Or 'He's skinny,' or 'He's bowlegged . . .' "

But the moment for comedy had passed, and they lay silently side by side, savoring the closeness of each other, the odor of creek-washed flesh, the slow movements of half-held breaths, the roving caresses of the eye. Then, all at once, he turned his body toward her, a half-cry caught in his tense throat, his flesh racked with wanting. In taut violence they clung together.

When the earth shook to a far rumbling, he did not at first think it was anything but the rock of his body to the still-demanding blood. It was only when, with a stifled sigh, Laurel pushed him away, that he heard the faint noise as a thing outside his own frame. Already the flush was gone from her cheeks as she sat there and clenched her hands.

"What?" he said. "What is it?"

"Just because they know how to strike a match . . ." she said, with a kind of quiet bitterness he had not seen in her before.

"A match?" he said, knowing the question was rhetorical,

having known from the moment the tall man had left the car last night that a match would be their way.

She turned her head to him. "They're going to burn it," she said. "The swamp. It was what I came to tell you."

"Yes," he said.

"They wouldn't dare come in here," she said. "But to burn you out . . ."

"Yes," he said.

He rose and put a hand down to her.

"My shoes," she said, and reached for them where they lay on the sand.

"Yes," he said, "We are all of us gonna need our shoes. In a hurry." He looked at her as she slipped the shoes on her slender white feet. He wanted to touch her once more, briefly, but not with any urgency. His blood raced now not in desire at all, but in a kind of exultant anger. Yet he wanted her to share the anger as she had shared the desire. He stood immobile, waiting for a sign. Then she looked up at him and put out a hand. He helped her to her feet.

She looked around the spot, the sand walled in with trees. Her hands were clenched again. She smiled at him when a mocking bird sounded derisively from an oak nearby. But her hands did not unclench at all until he seized one of them and drew her after him along the way toward the lean-to.

## Chapter XXV

On that hurried walk back to the lean-to, she told him all she had learned, speaking quickly, but her voice for once showing no emotion, except when she said, "I did think Mr. Ephe would hold them off until they had buried Miss Semantha. I did think he would have that much decency. . . ."

Ashby, beyond surprise now, for the moment nerveless even to the whole diabolical scheme she had revealed, spoke then for the only time on the walk. "The funeral's over now. It's noon or later."

"Oh," she said, "Yes. Only still . . . for him to raise a hand and give the order . . ."

"Is the easiest way for him to forget Semantha quickly," Ashby said. "And to forget how he felt when he knew he'd killed her."

She did not say anything, for by that time they were at the footbridge, and she loosed her hand from his and, without asking any aid, balanced herself and went gracefully across. He followed, and when he stepped down from the log, Lafe and Bevo and Tilda were standing huddled together. They nodded wordlessly to Laurel and then looked at him. He looked to where Temp still slept, peacefully, and then he spoke.

"They are making themselves a fire," he said.

"A fire?" Bevo said, and left his mouth open, as if he did not even believe the word in his own mouth.

Lafe squirted a stream of tobacco juice on the sand at his feet. "I ain't surprised. I had thunk of it when I buried that still. I thunk to myself, 'If I was a yellow-bellied coward too scared to come in this swamp but wantin' to git somebody out of it, how would I do it?' And I thunk of firing it. Only I hoped they wasn't smart as I was."

Tilda did not say anything. She stood there impassive, waiting, but Bevo looked at Ashby and then at Laurel and rubbed his hands on his pants and said, "Burn the swamp? Burn all this water? You crazy?"

Lafe pushed the butt of his gun into the sand with a sudden angry gesture. "You'd be surprised what a few drums of gasoline will do, especially now, before all the spring sap has riz up. You git some gasoline on slow creeks, you git the sedgebrush started up, you dry out the muck until the very ground burns like coal. . . . Hell, you'd be surprised. . . ." He chewed, viciously. "After all," he said, "all this swamp north of Cold Creek is mine. And even if it warn't . . . My ole woman, who was a right godly soul, she use' to say the good Lawd made this a wild and dangerous place a-purpose. So it would be a refuge, she said, fer them of His critters that need a place to hide in. Fer bears an' squirrels an' bootleggers an' niggers drove crazy by more wildness and dangerousness than ary man ever found in quicksand or rattlesnakes. It's the Lawd's land, she use' to say, fer them of his critters as are fearful of mankind. Well, I don't know about that, but if it's so, He ain' gonna take no more kindly than me to them de-stroyin' it. And I ain' takin' kindly to it a-tall. No more'n a squirrel would, bein' burned out o' his nest."

In the quiet, when his words had stopped, they did not say anything for a second; if the swamp was even then burning on its distant edges, as Ashby assumed, no sound of it reached their ears. He knew they were all listening, as he was, and then he realized, startled, that they were all looking at him. He felt Laurel's hand reach again and hold his own.

"Well," Bevo said, "what do you say?"

"Laurel brought a piece of news for you, too," Ashby said.

"I already know it," Bevo said. "Lafe saw it in the paper Mr. Ephe had with him this morning."

"You mean about the riots?" Ashby said. "The Negroes and whites in your mill?"

Bevo nodded, a leaden grief on his face.

"They told them . . . told your workers you were protecting a Negro rapist."

"I know," Bevo said.

"Well," Ashby said, "you've got to get out of here and over there. You've got to stop it. I told you last night they'd use what I was doing to ruin you."

"I knew they would," Bevo said. "And I knew they could, too. But I chose to stay then and I aim to stay with you now." In the green-yellow light filtering through the oaks, his face was set, stubborn.

"Well . . ." Ashby said, and shrugged. "You'll have to get out the river way anyhow, same as we will. So we can talk about that on the way."

No one, not even Bevo, said anything to that. Their faces stared at him, waiting. Lafe chewed silently, contemplatively. Tilda had not moved. Bevo had hooked his thumbs in his pants pockets. Laurel's hand rested loosely in Ashby's. He could hear Temp's sleep-breathing in the quiet waiting. Then it struck him that they awaited his judgment, his plan, and he found his tongue frozen. He had, all along, been aware of a responsibility toward Temp, but the sense of that responsibility was a thing of habit, like manners in a drawing room, and had chance not contrived to make it now sharp and even dangerous, he might never have been any more aware of it than he was of his manners. But suddenly to be responsible for the lives or at least the immediate physical safety of Bevo and Laurel and Lafe and Tilda was a tongue-freezing burden. Granny had frequently and regretfully spoken of his irresponsibility, as if it were a stage of human life, like adolescence, which he might outgrow. It occurred to him that if he had not outgrown it by now, if the last two days had left him unmarked, he might never have a chance to outgrow it. Time had trapped him, and he fought only briefly against the urge to malinger. Then he found his tongue, thawed.

"All right," he said, feeling a little foolish, like a kid who has yelled to be captain of a wooden-gun army and all at once finds himself elected. "All right. I've got only one plan. If any of you've got a better one, talk loud and quick. If not, I reckon we'll have to do this . . ." He looked at Bevo and Lafe, wondering if they would think his idea hopeless, and tell him, in front of Laurel, how idiotic it was. "They're patrolling the river. They've got . . ." He questioned Lafe. "How many boats?"

"At least three, I hear," Lafe said.

"Well, say three. That means that wherever we choose to get out of the swamp and head downriver, there'll be at least one boat down there between us and a getaway. The only way Temp and I can get loose is to divert all the boats to some spot upriver and to keep 'em diverted long enough for us to get a good start downstream. That means that the rest of you—everybody except Temp and me—are going to have to make the diversion." He felt Laurel's hand tighten on his, and he wanted to turn to her and tell her that he did not want to leave her any more than she wanted to be left, but that she could not go with him. He did not, however, even have to look at her.

He heard her say, "Yes. That's what we will have to do," but he heard also the sharp intake of breath before she spoke. He looked at her, then, and smiled.

"Well . . ." he said and cleared his throat, quickly. "Temp and I have got to get away fast, so if it's all right with you, Lafe, we'll use your motor boat."

"Course," Lafe said. "She's a-settin' yonder in the mouth o' Cold Creek, primed to go."

"And the rest of you . . . Well, you'll just have to paddle out in Lafe's skiff. You'll have to manage so they think Temp is there, or that you'll show 'em where he is. Delay as much as you can. I know it's a long chance that they'll call up all the patrol boats to that point. They'll be looking for black skin, and . . ."

"I'll be there," Tilda said, whispering. "I'll be there and I can dirty my face and . . ."

" 'Cept'n there's a hitch," Lafe said. "The bottom of that dern skiff is plumb rotted out. I got me some planks down there to fix it, but I ain't got around to it yet. . . ."

"I can fix it," Bevo said. He looked down at his huge, black-furred hands. "That's what I can do. I can put a new bottom in it."

Ashby frowned. "We haven't got time for that," he said. "It will be nearly sundown when we get to the river, and the fire will be close on us by then. No, all we can do . . . You all will just have to get on one of those hammock islands and lure the boats into there."

"I don't calculate it'll be too hard," Lafe said, drawling through a grinning mouth. "If Miss Laurel jest stands herself on a hammock in the light o' that fire, them boats is likely plumb to fergit they're nigger huntin'."

They laughed, all except Tilda, who stood there lost in that place where she frequently traveled far from the flesh that mortified her. Then even their laughter, spontaneously and gratefully as it had sprung, subsided. As with one ear, one nose, they searched a second for the sound and smell of fire. They heard and smelled nothing except the pulsing swamp.

"Well," Ashby said. "I reckon we had best be heading for the river."

# Chapter XXVI

The swamp steamed broodingly as they toiled toward Lafe's anchorage. Lafe himself had long since ranged far ahead of them, and the last they had heard of him was the bark of his gun as he dropped a quail or a squirrel. Hunger had enfeebled them all. They would meet Lafe later in the palmettos near the riverbank. Then, perhaps, they could steal time in which to eat, though they knew they could not count on a fire observing a convenient timetable.

Ashby, leading the way, could feel the sweat roll itchingly beneath his clothes, burn with acid sharpness the mosquito bites and lacerations on his skin, and stop its downroll only when it dropped from his knees onto the rough wool of his pants where they were molded wetly to his calves from the shallow marsh they had waded. He carried Temp in his arms and when he looked down at him, he could see Temp's tongue lick at a crack in his lips the salty sweat had found, the tongue licking while the brain which commanded it still slept. Temp had protested the being borne only when Ashby had first lifted him from the mossbed.

"I can walk, Mr. Ashby."

"You need rest, Temp. I'll carry you a while."

"I can walk, please sir"—as if he were embarrassed or unaccountably guilty of some mannerlessness.

"You can walk later on. Now you need carrying."

"You been carrying me a long time."

Ashby imagined that he spoke in delirium. "And will carry you till you're stronger."

"I'll be able to walk good as anybody," Temp said, "in a little while."

"That's what I say," Ashby said. But Temp did not hear, for he had already drifted back into that forgetfulness, which was not like sickness so much as it was like the willful sleep of a child who has been reassured of the unreality of a nightmare.

Only Bevo found a strength beyond famishment and fatigue. Laurel, who plodded behind Ashby, and Tilda, who brought up the rear, scarcely spoke at all. But Bevo kept leaving his place between the two women and falling into step beside Ashby and talking.

"I'll help you carry him," he said, when they had gone only a short distance. "But you ought to have let him walk, like he wanted to." With a big hand, he pushed a branch out of Ashby's face, held it until the women had passed and then caught up again with Ashby.

"He ought to have a hand in his own saving," Bevo said, with an urgency Ashby had never heard in him before. "Don't, he'll turn on you one day, and plumb despise you."

"The heat's got you," Ashby said, winded, thinking only to reach the bank, to escape the flames and the patrols, and be gone far down the quiet and placid river.

"I been thinking . . ." Bevo said.

"You better stop," Ashby said. "If you think Temp would hate me for . . ." He snorted.

"Did you ever hate your father?" Bevo said.

"Hate . . . ?" Ashby said, and then said no more, thinking that there had never been any reason for him to hate his father; he had had reason to hate only that first Ashby Pelham, who lived in Granny's mind, but who was dead and beyond hate: all his life he had fought the shadow of that Ashby, and now the shadow had won, and he was not sorry.

"I been thinking about the men in my mill," Bevo said. "Them fellows . . ."

"Biting the hand that feeds 'em," Ashby said. "Ungrateful bastards . . ."

"No," Bevo said. "Why . . . why should they be fed? Why can't they feed themselves?"

"What?" Ashby said, unthinking, his arms and shoulders aching with the burden of Temp. The ground they walked across was clumped with wiry swampgrass; they stumbled as they moved.

"They're men," Bevo said. "And I never got 'em. And even if I had done the begettin' of 'em . . . A man outgrows a father. A man comes to hate the fellow that feeds him. Because as long as he's fed and not feeding himself, he's not a man, and has no say about what will happen to him, but has got to wait on the fellow that feeds him to say, or else not be fed."

"I'm too worn out to make any sense out of all that," Ashby said.

Behind him, he heard Laurel's voice, soft, gentle. "Go on, Bevo."

"I got to go on," Bevo said, without turning to her. "And Ashby's got to listen. Tired or no tired." He put a hand on Ashby's shoulder, stopped him, and held out his arms. "Give Temp to me. Since you figger he's got to be carried . . ."

Without speaking, Ashby let the relaxed body settle in the cradle of Bevo's big arms. He rolled his shoulders a second, against the tightness and ache that was in them. He glanced back and put a hand out toward Laurel and smiled at her; the hand did not quite touch her, and he was all at once too tired to make more than the brief gesture. Her eyes were bright as the eyes of the fevered. She smiled back at him, but they said nothing. He turned and the four of them trudged on, across the open space toward a line of cypress rearing above black waters.

"All right," Ashby said. "You were saying about your workers . . . But all I can see you did for them is give 'em jobs. . . ."

"No," Bevo said. "I played father. I gave my kids more than any other kids in the block had. That put 'em in my debt. That was what put 'em in jail, and me with the keys. I was a fool. No wonder Mr. Ephe's man could go in there and stir up white against black, and against me that had put 'em to working side by side." He brooded a moment, and grimaced at the unaccustomed effort of logic. "They're men. They're men and will have what they have because they're men and not because I'm pleased to dole it out to 'em. And they choose this way to tell me. I don't reckon they even know in their own minds what they're telling me. No more than they know what it was made 'em hate what they thought they'd forgot how to hate. Killing without knowing why they're killing. Only I know it's because they're sick of being children, and carried . . ." He looked down at Temp in his arms. "Just like one day you might find Temp sick of it, of bein' a child and being protected and fed by you and maybe even striking back at you. . . ."

"Temp? You're crazy." He made his voice hard and certain, but there was an unease in him, an unease he had felt once before today.

"All right," Bevo said. "I've likely said it wrong. I ain't much hand to string words together. Or maybe I am crazy. But you know I ain't. You know I'm saying the truth and you know that's why Temp took so much to heart the things Tilda told me that Coal Black told him. And no man could blame Temp for it, since any man in his place . . ."

"Blame him for what?" Ashby said.

Bevo turned his great dark head toward him. "For someday gittin' a hate in him. Not a hate at you, but a hate at a time and a place where he never had no justice in his own right, but only because you got it for him. And so hittin' out at you because a man can't land a solid blow on a time and a place. Not hatin' you so much as hatin' bein' saved, as hatin' not saving himself. Like them fellows in my mill ain't really strikin' at me . . ." His words trailed off into silence, as if he now were ashamed of having said so much, and a little uncertain of his own rightness.

"Yes," Ashby said, reluctantly. "I see."

"Well," Bevo said. "Well. Then I hope the seeing takes the itch out of your pants. Because it ain't over when you got him safe."

"Well, I can worry about that later. If I get him safe—not to mention us gettin' our own carcasses out of here before we get singed—I don't reckon I'll give a damn. . . ." He stopped short then, catching up with Bevo, said, "What do you aim to do?"

"What?"

"About the mill? About . . ."

"Why, the only thing I can do. Give it to 'em."

"Give it to 'em?"

"Why sho," Bevo said. "Give it to 'em. Each an equal share. White and black alike. If they want me to be president, they can elect me. Then I'll be their man as much as they'll be my men and no more." He chuckled. "I reckon that will scare Mr. Ephe and Tinney more than anything I ever did. That ought to put the fear of God in 'em. Because they're in more danger than we are, anyhow. They've never even been father to anybody. And an out and out slaver, like them, is more likely to git his throat cut than you an' me, who're nothing but chillun playin' at bein' papa." Bevo lifted one black bush of an eyebrow. "Mr. Ephe and Tinney were licked a long time ago, and don't know it yet. And you an' me—we were . . ."

Laurel's gasp cut off all other words Bevo might have said. When Ashby turned in quick alarm, she was saying, "Tilda . . . Tilda . . ."

Abruptly, Bevo stood Temp on his feet, and Temp opened his eyes and remained upright.

When they looked behind them, along the way they had come. Tilda was not there.

# Chapter XXVII

It was Bevo who went back to look for Tilda. For Ashby, who, with Laurel and Temp, trudged on to the palmetto flats and there ate the squirrels Lafe had downed, it was a bad time, the darkest hour of all, even though fading daylight still shimmered hotly high above the overarch of oaks. Filling his stomach with the roasted gamey meat had been little comfort; he had sweated the salt out of him, and if he had known of a handy saltlick he would have lain on his stomach and lapped his tongue on it like an animal.

But, more than the discomfort of his body, a dourness of mind overcame him. Uneased by Tilda's disappearance and Bevo's near-hopeless search, by the concern which had led Lafe again away, upriver, to measure the southward run of the fire, he brooded at the waiting, so that not even Laurel's presence could lighten the misery he felt.

When, on the trudge from the cypress marsh, Temp had finally insisted on taking to his own feet, Ashby had been shocked at the change in him. He had walked with head lowered, shamefaced, and once he had said, "I causin' you misery an' I ain' worth it."

"Don't be a fool, Temp," Ashby had said, but he had looked at Laurel, and he knew they had both thought of what Bevo had said. There was, he had seen then, a rankling sore in Temp at his own helplessness.

"I don't understand it," Temp had said. "I don' understand none of it. Not that Coal Black . . ." His body shrank at the name. "Nor that Mr. Sheriff Littlepage. It look to me like I ain't right in my mind when I try to think about 'em. I . . ." He bit at his dark lips. "I ain' harmed nobody. I ain' done a soul on dis yearth no harm. But I got to run like a yeller dog an' hide. . . . From a bad nigger downwind and a bad white man upwind . . ." He had stopped a moment for breath; under the tattered shirt the muscled black chest rose convulsively; he gulped at the air. "It's a new time and I don' like it."

There was nothing Ashby could say. He and Laurel had not looked at each other then—or for a time after.

Now, squatting by the fire over which they had roasted the squirrels, he stared moodily into the flames. There was still no sign of that larger fire they awaited, unless the faint gray draperies that occasionally coiled overhead were smoke from it, and unless the unnatural heat in that place was reflected from it. It could not yet, however, be heard.

Temp slumped against an oak tree, his feet and the lower half of his body hidden in palmetto fronds. Laurel sat, tailor-fashion, on the sand near him. Once she reached out silently and held his hand.

"Granny sent you a message."

He turned his face to her. "Granny?"

She nodded and he saw the three gold freckles move as she swallowed.

"Early this morning, she told me. She didn't know I was coming—she couldn't have. I wasn't sure myself, then. But she said, 'When you see Ashby, tell him I will wait for him. At Pelham.' "

His jaw hardened. "I don't aim to trespass on Ephe's land." It was near to dark by then; it was almost blackness, with only a faint luminosity, that he gazed into when his eyes searched far. He was by now taut with waiting, counting in his mind the separate fates that might overtake Tilda and Bevo and Lafe. When Laurel spoke, he had been playing a childish game in his head. He had been saying, over and over, "I will count to a hundred. If one of them is not back by then, it will be a sign for us to go on. No, I will count two hundred and then . . ." He counted perhaps a thousand, and did not move, but waited on. "Not on Ephe's land," he said, his voice harsh.

"Ashby . . ." He felt her hand tighten on his arm. But whatever she had intended to say, he stopped. He turned and seized her and kissed her and they held each other tightly against time and danger and loss, not speaking even when the miserable kiss was ended, but instead making those sounds on lips and in throats which, with lovers, pass for speech.

Then the low cry welled from the darkness near them. He dropped his arms from about her and stood suddenly alert, peering into the black jungle depths from which the sound had issued. Laurel stood, too, quietly, seemingly without fear or question. Yet, sensing her fearlessness, he was afraid for her, and he grasped her shoulder and pushed her behind him and then walked a step or two toward the dark curtain of looped and matted vines. He was only vaguely aware of the apathy in which Temp still slumped, so that not even a dark cry could arouse him.

At first he saw nothing save the blackness and the night mists coiling like insubstantial parasitic tendrils above the limbs of the oak and cypress. Then one of the milky tendrils moved, was stirred. Tilda stood there, alone, outside the pale light of the fire, nearly obscured in the tangled growth.

"Tilda."

She came toward him and stopped a few feet away in the half light, mist-filled, so that she looked like a figure in a dream, unearthly. She put her hand down into her bosom, groped in the shallow furrow between her breasts and drew out a dark object and handed it to him. He felt the steel of the pistol, warm from her flesh—his pistol which he had been without all this time and had not even missed.

"Where's Mr. Bevo?" Ashby said, knowing he should not

have let Bevo go, knowing at once that Bevo was lost somewhere in the swamp.

Tilda did not even answer him. "I couldn't do it," she said, as if she had not even heard. Her eyes were distended, as the eyes of the dead sometimes are. "I couldn't kill him."

"Who?" Laurel said. "Who, Tilda?"

She did not look at Laurel, but kept her wide luminous eyes rigidly on Ashby's face.

"Coal Black," she whispered. "I went to find him. I took your pistol while you wasn't noticin' and I slipped off to hunt for him. And I found him, but I couldn't do it." She held out her hands and across the pale tan of her wrists, he could see the broad welts, red and chafed, where rough hands had gripped her. Then he saw that one of her cheeks was suffused with blood and slightly swollen in a half moon under her eye, as if she had been slapped hard several time.

"Coal Black?" Laurel said. "Is he the one . . . ?" She looked to where Temp sagged against the tree.

"You ought to have something on your face," he said to Tilda. I got some brandy still in my coat . . ."

"No," she said. "No sir. Let me tell you." Her head shook in protest and when Laurel would have taken her hand to lead her to the fire, she shrank back, huddling her body. "I got to tell you how it was. I couldn't kill him." She thrust her still-huddled body forward from the hips. "You don't know how it is not to care enough about living to be able to kill."

Ashby gazed at her, curiously.

"I got a despair in me," Tilda said. "I got a despair in me so big I couldn't fight for or against anything. I couldn't kill Mr. Ephe or Coal Black, even to help you and Temp. But if them killing me would help, I'd let them kill me. I got a wish to die in me. Maybe I got a deadness already in me, the way Mr. Ephe is got destruction in him, the way you got liveness in you."

Ashby dropped his eyes to the pistol in his hand. Even in the tight, water-shrunk dress, faded and streaked with mud, she seemed naked, even more embarrassingly naked than that day in her cottage.

"You could have killed him," Tilda said, her voice lower now. "You could have killed him, because you got the will to live. And Mr. Ephe could have killed him because he's got the will to destruction. But I haven't got any use in me."

When she was quiet, he raised his eyes to her. "Why didn't he kill you?"

He knew she had heard him, and yet when she spoke it seemed to him that she had planned what she would say before even he asked the question, and that she was saying only what she had intended to say, unhurriedly, in that monotone to which her voice had now come.

"Stood there," she said. "I stood there with the pistol aimed at him and then couldn't pull the trigger. And he knew I couldn't pull it, and he came toward me, not even putting up his big black hands to brush the moss out of his way. He walks like something not human, on the balls of his feet, so quiet it scares you. He's big, all twisted black muscles and shining. Big, like a black cloud. And when he was coming toward me, I felt smothered. I could smell nigger, and it was like being drowned in a cloud of nigger." She shuddered, almost imperceptibly. "It wasn't me I was scared for. If I'd been scared for me, I could have pulled the trigger. For myself, it seemed like I thought, Well, I'm half-blackened now. Now I'll be blackened all the way and that'll be the end. Like in killing me, the blackness of him would rub off on me, and I would be all black, and not a half-thing. But I was scared for you. For you and Miss Laurel—and for Temp. For all the good folks like you that might be drowned in that black cloud, all because of what the bad folks like Mr. Ephe have done. I could smell that black hate the way I could smell the white hate in Sheriff Littlepage when he come to the kitchen yesterday." She buried her face in her hands, huddling her body again. "I couldn't kill him though," she said, parting her hands just enough, at the point where they touched her lips, to make the sound audible.

Ashby opened his mouth to speak, but before he could say anything, before Laurel could touch Tilda with a hand impulsively protecting, Tilda was talking again.

"It couldn't have been long that he was coming toward me, but I thought all that and more. And I tried to call up a hate of my own. I tried to hate him like sometimes I've hated Mr. Ephe. But I couldn't. All I managed to do was slip the gun into my dress and hope he wouldn't get it and leave you without any pistol against him." She looked directly at Ashby then. "He knocked me down and almost broke my arms. But he didn't kill me, because he wanted to send me back to you. He knocked me down and sat on me, holding my wrists, and talking like some crazy animal . . ."

"Did he . . . ?" Ashby said.

"No sir," she said. "I'm half-white. He might have done that to a white woman, in hate for what white men have done to black women. But to me . . . No sir. I'm the no-color he only wants to kill. He told me. He called me 'filth.' 'Filth.' But he didn't kill me because he wanted to send me back to you to tell you to get out. He said he was making a heaven here for black folks and he won't have you destroying it." She moved a step toward him. "He didn't take the gun though, and he hasn't got anything except his hands to kill with, and if we watch there won't be any danger from him. I'll watch. I'll watch and . . ."

He reached and took her hand, to cut with the gesture the rising hysteria. "You didn't see Mr. Bevo?"

"No," she said. "I never saw anybody but Coal Black."

"You go and rest yourself," he said. He was conscious that her hand was warmer than his own; her story had chilled him. He could feel the quick frosty fingers of apprehension on his spine. On the river the patrol boats made their distant drumming and somewhere in the darkness Coal Black lurked and somewhere there, too, Bevo struggled to find them again, and the fire ate steadily toward them. Yet it was not the danger as such that he feared, but the waiting, the inaction, since they could not move, unless fire-driven, until Bevo found them.

"Bevo's bound to find us," he said. "Bound to." He was reassuring himself. "I told him exactly how to find the palmettos. And after all, if the fire is as close as I think it is . . ." By now even his nose could detect a subtle acrid smell in the air, but there was yet no sound of burning. "He would be hemmed in. If it is coming downriver and upriver and from the road toward us, then it's leaving only a smaller and smaller space for him to be lost in. But we have got to wait until . . ." He did not finish. He did not say, "until the flames drive us out."

Tilda gripped his hand tightly. "We can't leave Mr. Bevo. Not if he came looking for me, and . . . We can't . . ." He reassured her with a shake of his head. "Yessir," she said, simply, yet it seemed to him she said something else, something like "It will be all right." Then she moved away and squatted beside the fire, holding her gold-tan hands toward the thin flames.

He stood unspeaking, holding in his hands the pistol she had handed him. When his eyes met Laurel's, he saw that her face was drained white. He saw the swallowing in her throat.

"It's always there," she said. "There never is any time we're free of it."

"You're tired," he said. "I'll build up the fire and . . ."

"To keep it way? Drive it back?" she said. "As if there's not always a darkness for it to hide in. . . ." He could see her amber eyes darting into the swamp shadows around them. He had never heard her speak so, with such violent fear.

"You're unstrung," he said.

She turned her face back to him. "No," she said, slowly. "Only it just came over me all of a sudden. Thinking of Miss Semantha. Thinking that I thought to outrun it, deny it, by coming into the swamp . . ."

"And did," he said. "Did."

"Did in one way," she said. "I wasn't a half-woman when I did it." She caught his arms. "But if it takes you away from me,

I will be mad as Miss Semantha." She was whispering. He could smell the fragrance of her still-damp hair.

"You're not Semantha," he said. "Semantha never followed Ephe into a swamp. 'It'—as you call it—'it' had already ruined her. She never had Ephe and so she never really lost him. It was herself she'd lost. And you haven't . . ."

"But it can take you another way," she said. "If that Coal Black . . ." Again her eyes went past his shoulder into the darkness. Her hands loosened and then dropped from his arms.

He said, "I'll . . ." and, not even bothering to finish the sentence, stooped and with his free hand picked up a piece of wood to throw on the fire. He hesitated a second, noting that Tilda had moved away and now lay unstirring on the sand, near Temp, at the very edge of the flickering light.

Laurel caught his wrist before he could toss the wood. "Don't," she said. "He won't come into the light."

"He?"

"Coal Black. He won't come."

"But Bevo . . . It's Bevo I'm keeping the fire for. I don't care whether Coal Black comes or not . . ."

"Oh . . ." she said. "Oh. Of course. Bevo. I . . ." she looked ashamed and confused a second and he grinned at her. "It's just that I . . . I've watched you clenching your fists all day now, and I knew you were sick of fighting shadows. . . ."

"So you wanted me to shoot Coal Black," he said, slowly. "To land one solid punch, anyhow? Is that it?"

"I wanted you to do whatever you'd have done if I hadn't come in here. Do you think I don't know that you let Bevo go look for Tilda because you felt you couldn't leave me? And because of that, we're bogged down here, and will only just get out ahead of being roasted?" She shook her head at him. "I just wanted to be sure you were not building up that fire for me, when what you really wanted to do was wait in the dark and have it out with Coal Black here and now. Because, after all, he is a danger."

"Yes," Ashby said. "He's a danger. But there's nothing I can do about him, unless he chooses to expose himself. I've got to leave the fire as a signal to Bevo."

He could see that she was shivering, and he did not understand it because the heat had grown with the dark, and the usual night-cold of the swamp had been dissipated by the hot flames which must now flank them on three sides. Silently he took off his coat and helped her on with it.

Then he led her back to their own small fire, where they sat down and began again that waiting which was now almost unbearably painful. Ashby put a stick of wood on the fire that had burned down to only one fast fading ember in the piled gray ashes. He laid the pistol near his right knee. He reached in the pocket of his shirt and took out the crumpled package of cigarettes and offered it to her. She lifted her face to his, and he could see the color coming back into her cheeks, so that her skin was once more flushed with that shading that was like nothing so much as it was like the tan and pink of a rose which Granny grew at Pelham but the name of which he had forgot.

"It's strange," she said. "You don't know whether or not I smoke, do you?"

"No," he said. "I don't know anything about how you do in civilization." He smiled. "After all, I've only seen you in a bawdy house and at a wake and in a swamp. And you might say those were all uncivilized circumstances."

"And a good thing, too," she said, bantering as he had done. She shook her head at the cigarettes. "I don't. I tried to like cigarettes, but I never could. I wish I had learned to like 'em, because I would like to smoke when you smoke, but I would only look a fool, coughing and sputtering."

He put a cigarette in his mouth, found a match and leaned to the fire, the ember, and thrust the match into the faint glow until it flamed. As he leaned, he smelled the damp perfume of her hair. For a moment while he was lighting his cigarette, he kept his eyes on her, caught for a moment by the candor of her face, with its smooth skin and golden freckles. The match burned his fingers and he dropped it quickly. In his throat, the smoke was sweet, too sweet.

"You burned yourself," Laurel said.

"Yes."

"You've got to watch. Whoever comes may be Bevo or Lafe, but then again it might be Coal Black. You've got to be on the lookout for Coal Black. If you're going to keep on looking at me, I'm going to move."

"I'm looking for Coal Black," he said—and for Bevo and for Lafe, too, he thought. Though Lafe may be waiting at his anchorage, where the boat is, we have still got to wait until there is no hope at all of Bevo's coming here. Then we will have to make fast tracks toward Cold Creek.

She did not say anything. The lone stick flickered feebly. The swamp sounds seemed louder around them. Yet he could hear his own breathing and the pump of his blood, sitting there in that tense immobility, wanting to touch her, unreasonably, as if the need for her were heightened by dangers closing in upon them. "Laurel?" He whispered the name from a constricted throat.

"Yes."

But he knew it was no good, saying anything or moving. Now he did not even know what he had planned to say or whether he had planned to say nothing and merely to slide toward her and touch her and let the flesh speak what the lips could not. So he said, "Nothing. I was just thinking. There isn't any freedom from it. Like you said."

"There will be for us. We're already half-free." She was whispering. "We're at least not like Mr. Ephe—or Miss Semantha. Her dead and him . . ."

Ashby felt his teeth grit, involuntarily.

". . . pacing his library, like a prisoner in a cell," Laurel said. "And crying out, 'Good God, what does she expect me to do?' That was when he sent for me this morning. 'How would she like it if niggers were running Pelham Place, if niggers owned it?' he said. 'Which is how it would have been if I had sat and done nothing, if I sat and did nothing now.' "

Ashby was quiet, swept again with the bitter thought that it had taken an Ephe to save Pelham, that without Ephe the Corinthian columns and the marble mantels might now be rearing nakedly in a chaos of tumbled brick on land the wild grape had reclaimed. He turned his eyes away from her, from her form dim in the phosphorescent glow.

"It took me a while to realize it was Granny he was talking about," Laurel said. " 'She's only civil to me, nothing else,' he said. He said he could stand your father moving gloomily around the house, with eyes that accused him. 'But her . . .' he said, 'I can't stand that terrible cold politeness.' I only sat and listened—that's all he wanted me to do. 'I came up in a time when it was black or white,' he said. 'One or the other. But she would never recognize it. Never admit that if I hadn't done what I did, this would have been a black man's land. All she saw—all she sees now—is that I sold out to them that had conquered us.' He turned angrily to me then. 'As if I could do anything else. I had to do as those before my time had learned to do—either be content with some crumbs from the conqueror's table, or see the crumbs go to the blacks. If there hadn't been any white men the North could have depended on to develop . . .' Then he stopped and said Granny's word was 'exploit.' 'But if there hadn't been any white men for the job, there would have been plenty of black. And we might have gone down under them.' " Laurel paused.

In the silence, Ashby strained his ears. He thought he had detected the scud of a leaf somewhere in the near blackness; yet now he heard nothing, and he made no sign to her to stop talking. When she had remembered how the talk had gone after that, she went on.

"A little later, he began to laugh, a low choking sound, terrible to hear. 'And the funny thing was,' he said, 'I did it all for her. The whole time it was for her. To make her proud of me, more proud than she was of that husband.' And he told me how when he was little he had thought that your Grandfather and God must look exactly alike. And he said that what he was doing now, about Temp, was only so he could be senator, and that he had wanted that for her, too." She frowned. "I'm trying to remember how he said it. I think he said, 'But it's no good. It'll be no better than the first time I was elected to Congress.' He told how he came home late to find her still up. He thought she had waited up to hear how the election came out, but he found out later she was up because Temp was sick with pneumonia. But he was pleased she was up and he told her proudly that he'd won. I can hear him describing it: 'She stood there and looked at me and then she said only two words. *Elected?* she said, and I said yes. *How?* she said and turned and left the room like a cold storm.' You see, somebody had told her that Ephe had paid poll taxes and distributed free whiskey to get votes. 'It was what the opposition had done and I had to do it or not get elected,' he said. 'But she never could see I had to do it. That if I didn't do it, everything we had would slip away from us. But there is no use talking to her. Whenever I get elected or make more money, there is always the *How?* in her eyes and the question she asked me once, *Ephraim, when will you learn it is not what a man gets but what a man is that matters?* And then he shook his head and said, 'But what under God's name she would have me be, I don't know.' "

"He must have been drunk," Ashby said. His eyes moved constantly, accustomed now to the darkness beyond the fireglow, watching for the tremor of a vine or the stirring of the mist that might mark the passage of a body.

"No," Laurel said. "Not drunk. Caught in his own net. Wanting nothing but the affection of Granny, the approval, and yet knowing no way to get it except a way which outrages her. I believe that he really wanted to be senator only to please her. Just as he has imagined that black skin is a menace to her and has seen himself saving her from it. Or maybe he has forgot all that now and just wants to get elected. I don't know.

I don't think he knows. All I know is that he's defeated. That he has defeated himself."

"Or she has defeated him," Ashby said, still intent on the dark spaces. "Granny. And not intentionally. But she's defeated him, because the voice she speaks with is bigger than she is, and I reckon unbeatable. And don't ask me what voice it is. A legend, maybe, a tradition. Or even a conscience. I don't know, but it's stronger in you than any mere mother love. And you either listen to it, or you get beat. I know." In a moment, he would replenish the near-dead fire.

"But would it have beat him, Mr. Ephe, anywhere?" Laurel said. "If the hate hadn't been here, the black and white . . ."

He put a quick hand out and touched her into silence. It seemed to him that there was a new sound in the swamp, a sound like a far wind, and yet the trees and vines were dead still. Then, quite close, he heard what only an ear now trained to the swampsound and acutely attuned to any noise foreign to that sound could have heard. But he heard it and knew what it was. He knew it for the ball of a bare foot pressed on mucky soil. Had the man been walking on sand, Ashby might never have heard him, but in the underbrush where he lurked he had stepped on a thick layer of wet leaves, twigs and acorns underlaid with a marl firm enough for the twigs and acorns to crack softly when the spongy mass of which they were a part was stepped on. It was not the kind of step Bevo made.

He reached slowly for the gun. He could feel the sudden sweat on his buttocks, and he held himself rigidly against the desire to turn immediately, knowing that if he moved too soon the foot would flee. He waited. He could hear the quick breathing of Laurel. The thought came to him that he was likely going to kill a man, but the thought came fleetingly and went easily, since he had been forced to choose violence a long time before—or at least had been chosen by violence.

His hand on the pistol sweated. He remained rock still, rooted, wondering that he could have the sensation of frost on his spine at the same time that he felt the trickle of perspiration down his thighs and in the palm of his hand. He held firm against the powerful impulse to rise and wheel and dash toward the place where the foot had paused. Then another foot stepped, and a leaf skidded, with a soughing so low he could hardly hear it. It seemed to him that he could smell the man, an odor of rancorous armpits, of sweat-stained and urinous cotton; but perhaps Tilda had put that in his mind. He waited for another step. He sensed a hesitation in the man. For a long time no other sound came. Against the panic he felt at the idea the man might make a soundless step toward him, he put the thought that he might have imagined it all, the sound and the odors. The step was long coming. He scarcely trusted himself to breath, and he was tense against a sound by Laurel or the awakening of Tilda. Then he heard the step.

He rose and wheeled, the pistol cocked before him. He looked into shadows not as dark as he imagined they would be, strangely light, and yet saw only the black gleam of the man's eyes.

"Come here," he said, his voice unready and hoarse from his tense throat. Then, on an off-chance, he said, "Bevo? Is that you . . ."

He could make out now the gigantic hulk of the man, unmoving there before him, draped round with virginia creeper and smilax.

"I've got a pistol," he said, feeling foolish at the waiting patience and unexcitement of the Negro.

"It save you now. Not always." The voice was deep throated and edged with a fanaticism cold as snow-crusted steel. The eyes turned suddenly away.

"Come here," he said. But the body lunged away. He shot, twice. Over the echoing explosion of the second shot, a high unearthly howl sounded in his ears; when the echo had drummed into silence, he heard the man lunging through the undergrowth, howling still, like some mindless monster maddened by an injury he had not only not expected but could not comprehend now that he felt its hurt in his flesh. Then even though the man was still in range by the sound of him, Ashby found that his finger would not move again on the trigger. He stood there with his finger frozen and all the rest of his body seeming to melt, as if his blood and juices had congealed in those few seconds since the first foot-sound and only now were running free again in his body. The tension drained out of him, as he listened to the howling gradually smothered by distance.

He was relieved at what happened then, not only because it meant the waiting was over, but also because it meant he did not have to reveal to them the childish and almost cowardly relief he felt that Coal Black could still howl and run. He did not know how he could hide the relief from them or how he could tell them that even though he would shoot Coal Black again if he had to, he would not shoot him with any feeling save a sickness at having to pull the trigger. He did not know that they, any of them, would understand.

Not even Temp would understand, for now Temp, awakened from that benumbed apathy in which he had fallen, was standing before him, shaking, saying, "I could have done that. At least you could have let me do that. It was my place to do it." He reached imploringly for the pistol, and Ashby looked at him, and was heartsick. It was clear that Bevo had spoken the truth, and that a man could resent very much his own salvation, if he had no hand in it himself.

Yet this moment too passed, and was swallowed up in the sound, which had no doubt been growing around them for several minutes but which Ashby only now heard, when the howling and Temp's bitter words died on the air. It was a sound of concerted fear, still distant at that moment, but coming closer, like a song passed from voice to voice. The animals in the swamp were crying.

When he turned his head, he looked into Laurel's face. She stood beside him, her face again white. He did not say anything until he felt Tilda's hand on his arm, gripping it.

"Fire," she said. "Fire, Mr. Ashby. I can smell and see . . ."

He looked up and knew then why the shadows had been

lighter than he expected, why he had heard a far wind where no wind was, and why the animals cried. The sky above them was rosy with what could only be the reflection of flames too close for them to wait there any longer. His only hope was that Bevo had somehow found his way to a point of escape beyond reach of the flame—if there was any longer anything for Bevo to escape.

"We'll go on down to the anchorage now," he said, and was surprised that his voice had the quality of a butler announcing dinner.

# Chapter XXVIII

If, on the way to the anchorage, he had understood what it was Tilda planned to do, he might have tried to stop her; and, had he stopped her, then it would all have ended differently.

But the moment when the idea came to her passed too quickly, and he agreed to her plan without even realizing what it was she aimed to do. He could be pardoned for that, too. For the swamp had become in what seemed a slim second of time a place of such unbelievable chaos that a man's whole instinct was to flee it, no matter what lay in store for him beyond its flaming borders.

By the time he had seen the fireglow in the sky, the swamp was well toward its end. Fifteen minutes after he had first heard the crying animals, all the flesh and blood in these precincts seemed to be swarming through the undergrowth along their path. He had not understood, at first, how the fire could have come so close—within a mile at most—before he was aware of it. Yet, reasoning, he realized that the light from it had grown gradually in the sky, and the sound had been only a slow-growing rumble. And the fear of the animals had taken time to spread from the advancing rim of flames. Now both the fear and the fire were progressing geometrically, not by slow addition but by swift multiplication. No doubt the licking flames did not have to cross the space from tree to tree, for a tree fifty feet from the closest burning would be hot enough to burst into instant combustion. And an animal five hundred yards from the stampede could hear the sounds of fright and begin his own stampede toward the river.

"Like a nightmare," Laurel said, when they were hurrying through the thickets toward the anchorage. "A nightmare of the world's end."

It was at the very moment when a wildcat, yellow in the smoky light, sprang across their path, its throat opened to one long shuddering whine, apparently unaware of them as human beings. Before they could move another step, a great buck deer crashed by, following in the cat's path, as if in the face of the common enemy fire it, like all other breathing things there, was unaware of any animal enmity at all. Around them, the sounds of flight swelled, underbrush cracking to plunging bodies, hooves stampeding on the mucky earth, bird's wings whirring.

"A nightmare of the world's end," she said, and when she said it, she, who had all this time been strangely calm and had not yet flinched at either sight or sound, dug her fingers into his arm. He knew it was not the wildcat or the smoke she spoke of or flinched from. He knew she was saying *Now what? Because we can't leave this swamp together. I knew that without even you telling me. And I don't mind that because you have got to get Temp out safe. But after? What then? And where, since you do not intend to set foot again on Pelham?*

He did not move for a second after the deer had crashed through the curtaining smilax. Then he leaned to her and spoke.

"Or the beginning. Maybe it begins in fire. With Pelhams anyhow."

She looked up into his face. The hot air had dried her hair and her dress. She still wore, as a woman might wear a wedding ring, with a certain self-conscious pride, the coat Ashby had put on her. Its sleeves were too long for her arms, so that when she loosed her hand from his arm, the hand disappeared in the sleeve. In the eerie shifting light from overhead, he saw her acknowledge the separation.

"Yes," she said.

He did not have time to say any more. Behind them, Tilda began that chant which had no particular meaning to anyone, then, including Tilda herself. Only Temp was obdurately silent.

"What we gonna do? What we gonna do?" Tilda said, chanting. "What we gonna do? What . . .?"

"Hush," Ashby said. "You know what we're gonna do. You knew it would be this way. You didn't have to come." He saw her shrink from him, her eyes flaring with a faint wild glitter. "I'm sorry."

She quieted and looked at him gravely. "No sir. I didn't have to come." Her eyes were wet, but since his own were stinging from the smoke, he did not know whether she was crying or not. The smoke drifted in lazy clouds, flesh-colored, curling, around them. The air smelled of burning pine and cypress, astringent, medicinal. "I was only wishing there was a way for me to do something. Wishing there was a way that me dying could help."

"Don't be a fool. Your dying can't . . ."

"I know," she said. She wet her lips with her tongue, but made no other movement, holding her body rigid so in that light she looked like a figure hammered finely out of rich copper, while behind her on the vines the shadow of her body leaped and jerked in the gyrating light. Then he saw her mouth open and her palm reach halfway to the mouth and a look indecipherable to him contort her face. He wheeled.

Ephe was standing there, facing them. Laurel said, "Mr. Ephe . . ." in a voice faint and unreal. Ephe looked at Temp, behind her, and dropped his eyes.

Ashby did not have time then to see Ephe's face clearly, to see that it was haggard and white, and that, with his body hidden in shadow and smoke, the face stood out ghostlily, with no more threat in it than could be seen in a face on a severed head served up on a platter. Ashby pulled the pistol from his belt.

"Where are they?" he said.

"They?" Ephe said. "They, Ashby?"

"Where's Bevo?"

"Bevo?" Ephe said. "How should I know? I only saw Lafe at the anchorage."

"He's safe?" Ashby said. "By God, if you . . ."

"I'm alone, Ashby. If you don't believe that, you ought to. You ought to know I would be alone."

"Know?" Ashby said.

"Because no other man out there had the courage to come in here," Ephe said, bitterness on his tongue. "The common man," he said, laughing shortly. "What a text we have heard on the common man. Well, you ought to see your common man out yonder." He snorted. "It's your bloody common man wants to lynch Temp now. Turkey Littlepage wanted to wink at lynching and all the other Turkeys in Mississippi wanted to do it. So long as they didn't have to do it by themselves. I've seen enough of your common man to . . ." He checked himself.

"I don't know why you say 'my' common man," Ashby said.

Ephe regarded him silently, then shrugged. "No doubt another of my sins. I'll have to tell St. Peter I made the common man."

Ashby grunted. "Maybe not. Maybe that you just helped to keep him common. But I haven't got any time . . ." The smoke was choking him. Beside him, Laurel coughed, holding onto her throat with one hand. "We've got to get on . . ." He still held the pistol in his hand and made no move to put it up.

"Do you object to my walking along with you toward the anchorage?" Ephe said.

"I reckon . . ." Ashby said, but did not have a chance to say any more.

"No," Tilda said. "No." When Ashby turned, she was still in the place she had been, and her shadow still danced fantastically on the screen of moss and vine. Her mouth was twisted as she looked at Ephe and shrank back toward her own shadow. "No. He'll bring us bad luck. Send him away. I don't know why he's here, but I know that what he touches dies. Not just Miss Semantha and me, but even a swamp like this, even God's earth dies under his hand, and . . ."

Ashby looked back to Ephe. It was then that he noticed the haggardness, the whiteness of the face. Ephe did not look at Tilda. "Dies," he said, his eyes on Ashby. "Dies. Good God, dies, she said. And who would she like to walk with? Jason? Your father? Or your grandfather, that other Ashby?"

"We've got to go," Ashby said. Behind them, he could hear the crackling of the flames, the hiss of the sparks in water. "We've got no time . . ."

But Ephe stood squarely in the path, unmoving.

"I reckon the earth lives, for them," he said, bitterly. "When you know as well as I do where they would have ended up. A good thing that Ashby Pelham died when he did. And a good thing for your father that I came along. Because Jason . . ."

"Uncle Ephe, I . . ."

"I'm going to say it," Ephe said. "I'm going to say it if we all get roasted. And you're going to listen." The tiredness had gone from him. "Where would your father be, if I hadn't saved Pelham? I know where he'd be. Think, Ashby. Can't you see him? You ought to, because he's everywhere. He's the high-minded, pious fellow, tall and thin, wearing an old shiny suit, bowing with long-gone gallantry to the ladies . . ." Ephe gasped for breath but held up a hand against interruption.

". . . thumbing the pages of his leatherbound Shakespeare if he hasn't hocked it, sitting on the gallery of his paintless, columned house and watching the chickens root up the lawn and drinking moonshine whiskey in silver goblets and talking about 'Befo' the War.' Every bank in the South has stacked papers carrying his fine thin signature to first and second mortgages. Every man like myself sees him every month, walking into his office with that thin-lipped prideful air, sitting there and talking in his pleasant even voice and then asking with a shamefaced but rigid pride for a little money to tide him over until the cotton crop comes in. Or until his son who's gone North can send him a few more Yankee dollars. Or until some lightning from God strikes his land and spreads gold along the ground for him to pick up."

Ephe was breathing heavily. Ashby said, "Uncle Ephe, I don't give . . ." but got no farther.

"Well," Ephe said, loudly, "Isn't that so? Isn't that where your father would be, how he would be, if I hadn't known that a lot of blather about honor and idealism never paid a grocery bill? And yet . . ." He shrugged angrily. "Pelham has got paint on it and a fence around the chickens. And there's fertilizer in the ground. And nothing's been pawned. It's all there, better than Ashby Pelham left it. And yet I'm cursed for saving it. While Jason, who would have been too high-minded to save it, and you who've shown clearly enough . . ."

"That I want to save something else," Ashby said, his voice loud in his ears. "Get out of my way, Uncle Ephe. If you've come down here just to defend yourself, I haven't got time to listen." He took Laurel's arms and stepped forward. Ephe turned and walked ahead of them. Ashby heard Tilda following, and Temp.

"I didn't come to defend myself," Ephe said, over his shoulder. His words sounded small, remote above the wind-noise of the fire. Even the animals had passed beyond them now. "Nor to hear you tell me I have saved the substance and lost the spirit. That's what she told me this morning. Granny. But I didn't come here for that, either—to prove to her I had some of her 'spirit' left." He pushed his way through the moss ahead and waited until they caught up. He had stopped in the gloom of a thicket, where the fireglow was shut out. "I came here to make you a proposition." He had turned to face them again.

"No," Ashby said. He made as if to move forward.

"Listen," Ephe said. "I won't pretend. This thing is to the interest of both of us."

"No," Ashby said. He felt Laurel's hand tighten on his arm. Behind him, he heard Tilda make a smothering sound, strange and unidentifiable. He still had the pistol in his hand.

"I'll admit," Ephe said, "that what gave me the notion of coming was her. Granny. Because, without ever saying a word, she let me know your blood would be on my hands. Even though I never thought up any lynching, and I certainly never aimed to burn the best timber in Miss'ippi just to drive you and that nigger—" he looked scornfully in Temp's direction,—"out of this swamp. You ought to know I was forced into that and if I hadn't agreed to it . . ." Temp stood unbending, his lips tight.

"It won't help," Ashby said. "Granny won't ever call you senator anyhow. If that's what you want. Now, if you'll . . ."

"Wait, Ashby!" Ephe held up his hand again. In his heavy jowl Ashby saw a nerve twitch. "I don't give a . . . I don't care whether she calls me senator or not. Not now. Yesterday, talking to Miss Laurel, I did. But now . . . I'm too old. Too old to change, Ashby, and too old to care that she despises me as I am. If I defended myself a few minutes ago, it was from habit—because I've tried to defend myself from her for half a century now. But I am through with that. Now I want to be senator. In my own way and whether she approves or not. And that's why I came in here."

"I thought so," Ashby said. "But even if I wanted to listen to you, I don't reckon I can count on that fire waiting while we talk." Without seeing the fire or even its reflection there in the thicket, he could feel the heat.

"All right," Ephe said. "Go on, then. But I reckon you know there are three fast patrol boats on that river. And this fire is burning not only from the road to the river, but from the north border of the swamp down and from the south border up. It was set that way, so that if you didn't leave until it got started good, you would have to get out within a short length of river that three boats could cover easily. I don't reckon there's more than a mile of swamp-shore that'll be left unburning time you are ready to leave."

"Don't listen to him, Mr. Ashby. Don't . . ."

He shook Tilda's hand from his arm. "All the more reason for me not to waste any time talking," he said. Yet he did not move, hearing the sounds of their breathing, quickened it seemed in the dark. "If you didn't think I might get away, I don't guess you would be making a proposition."

Ephe hesitated a moment, his eyes narrowing, his dark-clothed body an indistinct blur beneath the silver of his hair and the white of his face, so that his head again stood out as something disembodied.

"All right," he said. "Yes. I do think you might get away. Yesterday I thought you were a fool. Now I don't think different, except that I think you're a grown fool. And a grown fool can sometimes pull off what a grown sensible man would not even try." He stuffed his hands into the pocket of his coat, almost as if he were cold, in spite of the heat in which Ashby could feel his own body perspiring. Beside him Laurel stood quietly, waiting, without any question, as if, having settled the doubts between him and her, she had no doubts left, and could stand in a flaming swamp or face an uncertain river without qualm. Her very passivity gave him a strength to wait patiently for Ephe to speak after that angry gesture of the pockets.

"Yes," Ephe said. "I think you might get away, and if you did, I would be a laughing-stock at best, and, at worst, I would be a traitor to them that would elect me. I never thought this thing would go this far, but now that it has, I aim to come out of it on top. And I don't intend for anybody to say I was a fool or that I willingly let you get loose with Temp because you were kin to me. So I came in here to make you this proposition: I will guarantee Temp a fair trial, if you will surrender him to the law and . . ."

Ashby snorted. The hot words tipped his tongue, but he held them there and turned deliberately to Temp. "It's your neck. You hear?"

"I hears, Mr. Ashby." Temp's voice was hardly more than a whisper, and once more he was draped in the apathy he had briefly flung aside.

"And what do you say?"

They all stood there watching him, as if he would now do what he had never done in all his life before, make a decision as a man, and not wait, as a child waits, for guidance.

But Temp said, "It's for you to say, Mr. Ashby . . ."

Ashby felt himself flush, guiltily, remembering that in that moment when Temp had tried to shape his own end by reaching for the pistol in order to deal with Coal Black, he, Ashby, had put the pistol back in his own pocket, as he would have hidden a toy from a child. He was heartsore at the crushed thing that was Temp's manhood, and he heard himself saying, "Dammit, it's not for me to say. It's your . . ."

Then he checked himself, for Temp only backed away a step, bewildered and confused. "I jest wants to go back to Pelham, please sir," Temp said. "Anyway us can git there."

"Of course," Ashby said. "Course, Temp." Pelham was the place where Temp had had an illusion of dignity, and he thought to regain the illusion when he regained the place; but Ashby knew that would never be. The illusions he and Temp had had were gone; it was no longer possible to play on a stage already afire. And if in this second Temp waited and he commanded, it was only because the roles were too familiar to be instantly abandoned. Sooner or later, they would have to take up buckets together.

And if they did not, he would not have saved Temp at all, but only the crushed and dispirited hull of a man who now faced him and waited for him to decide what should happen to him.

He turned to Ephe. "A fair trial? When even if you could get him through that mob out yonder, you couldn't find a jury in Miss'ippi that would take more than five minutes to send him to the pen? You must take me for a fool." He saw Temp's fingers touch his gold-rimmed eye-glasses; he saw the fingers tremble against the lens shattered somewhere in the violence of the day.

"I take you for a man that's young enough to want to go on living," Ephe said. "And one that must know that the chances against his getting out of here with Temp are one in a thousand. I don't think I'd have come—would have thought coming would do any good—if I hadn't known Miss Laurel had followed you in here. And when I knew that—though nobody else thought it possible for her to come through this place, and Slim thinks she has gone back to her aunt—" Ephe coughed against the smoke, now drifting more thickly around them, puffing through the walls of the thicket. "But knowing that I thought, now he will not be fool enough to risk his neck. Now he will want to save himself because there will be something to save himself for, even if he is not gentleman enough to realize that he owes it to her to save himself."

Ashby did not have a chance to answer. In passing, Laurel brushed his arm. She stepped forward, toward Ephe, and when she spoke her voice was low and strained.

"Do you think I'd want him if he saved himself?" she said. "Do you actually think a woman could love a man who'd compromise and betray himself in the name of her safety and happiness?" Her eyes were bright with anger. "I'd hate him. You told me yesterday that you'd never been loved by anybody. I know why now. I . . ." Then she caught at her strained throat, coughing. Ephe's face was lined, heavy, and he had turned his eyes away from her. "I'm sorry," she said, the tears running down her face. She turned to Ashby. "I'm sorry. I didn't mean to sound self-righteous. But it was just that I didn't want you to do anything because you 'owed' it to me." She seized Ashby's hand. "You don't owe me anything except to be you," she whispered.

He watched Ephe, whose body had grown suddenly heavy, old, like his face. Now even the thicket could not keep out the light of the fire, any more than it could muffle the sounds of the hissing sparks and the occasional crash of timber and the lick-lick of flames. In the thin light that crept through the thick growth, he saw Ephe straighten and make a smile with pale lips.

"I'm sorry," Laurel said, again. "Mr. Ephe . . ."

"Never mind," he said. "You may be right. I don't know. I'm not very clear in my mind about anything any more. I'm just a man that has got to win, no matter what. I could tell you that . . ." He checked himself. "Never mind," he said, and turned as if to go. Tilda continued to watch him, warily, as if her eyes did not believe the defeat he showed.

"Uncle Ephe!" Ashby raised a hand. Ephe turned his head. "I . . . I can't let you go."

"Can't?" Ephe said.

"No, sir. I'm sorry, but I can't take the chance. You've got to go out in the boat that surrenders. Your boat, since I reckon you came in a boat. We needed two boats, but never thought to get . . ."

"Surrenders?" Ephe said.

"Yessir. Laurel and Lafe and Bevo and Tilda are going out in your boat to attract the attention of the patrols, while Temp and I slip downriver in the other."

Ephe turned full toward him then. The smile he made was not now tentative.

"You think it will work?" he said.

Ashby shrugged. He could feel the hot breath of the fire, again the acid sweat on his lacerated body, the scratch of wool against his damp flesh.

"At least," Ephe said, a small triumph in his voice, "At least I had a plan that chance favored. Telling the sheriff I was coming in here to get you to give Temp up to him—so that he, of course, could pretend that the mob took Temp away from him. And then hiding you and Temp in the bottom of my motorboat and going out and telling the patrols you wouldn't give up. And then, once out of their sight, go on past my own landing to Mussel Bluff and slip Temp ashore and to a jail. But you . . ." He leaned toward Ashby. "I thought you would plan better than that. What makes you think the patrols will all be diverted toward one boat in which there is no nigger?"

It was a thing Ashby had thought about but had not faced, thinking that time and chance would somehow solve the problem. Now, the question put, he felt a swift unease, and, as a man will, an anger at Ephe for having said the word that brought the unease.

"Of course, if I wanted to, I could adopt your plan," he said. "I could put Temp and myself in your boat and force you at pistol point to take us through the patrol." His voice was cold.

"I reckon so," Ephe said. "Only I could not take you downriver. I was scheduled to take you upriver, and even those idiots in those boats out yonder would think something funny if I changed direction. And upriver, above the swamps, I don't know any place the gas I've got in that boat would take you that you'd be safe: a young white man and an old nigger. Not with all South Miss'ippi looking for you."

"Check," Ashby said. He pressed his lips together. "So I still aim to try what I aimed to try in the first place. Only now we will have a better chance. Because Lafe and Bevo and Laurel and Tilda will go out with you in your boat. And Lafe will have a gun handy in case you aim to say anything but that Temp and I have already gone, escaped."

"And he and your friend Banes will be in jail by sunup," Ephe said, clipping the words, angrily.

"You will look too big a fool by sunup to want anybody to give public testimony," Ashby said, grinning now, the unease not gone but no longer crawling along his backbone.

Ephe let out his breath. "Look a fool? I? When those patrols are looking for a nigger, and . . ."

"Tilda will be in the boat." When he said the name, Ashby looked in her direction. She was tense, her body held so that in the phosphorescence of that place she seemed to crouch as if ready to spring, against what he did not know until he saw that her eyes were fixed on Ephe, unmovingly. Ephe turned his head nervously.

Scorn was in his voice. "They're looking for a male nigger," he said. "It's well known that Tilda's in the swamp."

"But far enough away," Tilda said, "on one of them islands, standing in the undergrowth and with my face darkened with a little mud . . ."

"No," Ashby said. "You go out in the boat."

"I'm gonna stand on an island. Until I see all the patrol boats are there, and know you and Temp have had your chance . . ."

"They're looking for a male nigger," Ephe said. "And they can count. Can you do anything about that?" For the first time he looked full at her, more hatred in his eyes than a man can direct, Ashby thought, at anything except himself. It was as Ephe were hating not Tilda but himself.

When she answered him, her voice was almost inaudible. "Maybe I can do something about that, too." She turned her head away from him after a long moment during which Ashby sensed that somehow, somewhere the initiative had subtly passed not only from Ephe but from himself, and that Tilda had within her some power, or perhaps even some plan, unknown to all of them. But the sensation lasted only a minute. When she looked at him and said, "It's all right? I can do it?" he could not think of any reasonable objection. He started to say that it was dangerous, and yet he knew that the patrols would not likely use their guns, at least not on anything dark-skinned, since they did not aim at anything quick and clean as murder. So, as it was, he nodded.

"I got to go pick my island out." She said, and then with a certain primness, "if you will excuse me," she seemed to bow to

Ephe, mockingly, and there was a sudden sound in her throat, like swift hysteria, only it had a note of brief pleasure in it.

When she had disappeared in that way of hers, with wraith-like suddenness, Ashby saw that Ephe's hands were clenched and his face again that gray-white, even in the now rosy light. But Ephe said, "A male nigger. That's what they're looking for, and she . . ." He laughed, but there was no conviction in the laughter. Ashby wondered why, for even though he had won a victory of words over Ephe, he had changed nothing. He still had to face a danger in which, as Ephe had said, the odds were against him. The chance of eluding the patrols was slim; and time, he suddenly realized, was running out, the funnel of his escape being narrowed by the flames racing down from the north and up from the south along the river bank. He touched Laurel's arm and spoke, his words guttural.

"We got to go."

Ephe led the way. When they emerged from the thicket, Ashby got his first glimpse of the actual fire, seeing it through a long vista, the wild flames racing through the hanging moss and along the looped twining vines. Laurel gasped, a short throttled sound and they hesitated a second, fascinated as children by the fire-patterns, so used now to their stinging eyes and smoke-roughened throats that the actual flames were for a moment unreal, as undeadly and remote as a display of fire-works at a county fair.

Then he took her arm again and they followed Ephe, stumbling, hurrying toward the Cold Creek anchorage, where, Ashby trusted, Lafe would be. From time to time, he paused and looked around him, wondering about Bevo. The palmettoes fanned their legs, the long coiled smoke eddied like water to their passage. Ephe moved swiftly ahead, not turning to see if they followed, his back set, his shoulders rigid as if, not knowing where he was going or what would happen to him, he was yet bent on walking as a man with a purpose walks.

They padded through a marsh and onto the sand of the flat near the anchorage. Ashby, helping Laurel, was slowed, and when they stood on the dry sand, he stamped his feet, without any particular purpose, so that the mud in his shoes made a slurping sound. It was above this sound and the fire-noise that he heard Lafe's roar.

"Stay where you are, by God!" When Ashby looked up, Lafe had barred Ephe's passage. "You aim to slip out of here . . ." Then, blinking, Lafe saw Ashby and Laurel and Temp. "Hell, I thought he'd done a murder or something. That yallow woman told me y'all was on the way, but nobody can't blame me for expecting the worst. All this damn wildness goin' on. First that yallow woman starts a-runnin' up and down the bank talkin' 'bout pickin' her out a island. And then somebody slips up behind me out o' that devilish smoke and I'm ready to blow him to Kingdom Come, since he was appearin' from the other side o' Cold Creek, and then he hollers and its . . ." Lafe gulped.

"Bevo!" Ashby said. "Is Bevo with you?"

Lafe nodded. "He got hisself a mite lost and had to find Cold Creek 'fore he could even know where the river was. He's right bramble-tore, but outside o' that he's all right. Exceptin' he's mournin' over how he could have fixed that there skiff so we could 'a' used it."

Ashby turned to Lafe and explained to him in a few words the plan for them to go out in Ephe's boat. Glancing at Ephe, he said, "I guess you know, Lafe, that it's up to you that nobody talks out of turn."

Lafe looked at Ephe, too. Ephe stood stolidly facing them, his eyes unblinking, unwavering, his jaw thrust out.

"I got a mighty fluttery finger on a trigger," Lafe said, caressing the barrel of his gun. "You might say I'm almost careless-like, if somebody surprises me by opening his mouth when he ought to be hushed up."

"You needn't worry," Ephe said, smiling that smile of the wet pale lips. "I won't talk. Because I won't need to. Your plan is the only one you can possibly try. But even it won't work. So . . ." He glanced from face to face, smiling, his confidence returned, his nostrils seeming to dilate with the scent of a victory he was now convinced of.

"If it don't work," Lafe said, "I reckon we will have us a good crowd in hell." Then he turned to Ashby. "I reckon we best git on an' tell your friend down yonder that even if he could 'a' fixed that skiff, it wouldn' 'a' been no use, since the Lawd's seen fit to send us the boat of our enemy." He spoke with mock seriousness and then chortled, winking toward Ephe.

"What?" Bevo stood there, near them, one of his pants legs split from thigh to ankle and the white lining spilling out of the shoulder of his coat, his face swollen and bruised, and his hair even more tousled than usual.

"A whole congregation," Lafe said.

Ashby took Bevo's hand. "Dammit," he said. "You near-'bout had me worried."

Bevo grinned, briefly, and his dark eyes rested a second longer on Ephe than they did on the other faces before him. "I reckon I've been more trouble than I been worth. It looks like I can't do a thing right." He looked at Ashby for what seemed a long second then. "If we get out of this place whole, it will be 'cause the Lord has seen our hearts, not 'cause he's given us any minds."

"You did all right," Ashby said. "I wouldn't have wanted to do all this without you. I reckon if it hadn't been for you, I'd have laughed it all off a long time ago . . ."

Bevo nodded, embarrassed, and then spoke hurriedly. "We got to go. I got Lafe's motorboat tied to that little south island yonder . . ." He pointed. ". . . below the mouth of the creek. That all right?"

Even while Ashby was saying yes, Bevo was remembering his manners and for the first time greeting Laurel, saying with unfeigned casualness, "Howdy, ma'm." He held his hands easily and did not even seem aware of his torn and dripping clothes, wetted in the swim back from the island. It was as if the danger and exertion and isolation he had endured had now gained him a new understanding with himself. His glance passed over

Laurel and back to Ashby. "What?" he said, and Ashby told him yes, again. On the river a patrol boat passed, its light flashing, so they could see the flash to their right in the moss-decked trees.

"I almost hate to leave this place," Bevo said. "A man needs to wrestle sometime with the devil, and this swamp is his own work." Then he smiled, guilelessly, at Ephe. "Though I reckon there will be plenty for me to wrestle with if I git out of here."

Ephe did not say anything at all, but he looked briefly discomforted, and he turned his face away from Bevo's easy confidence.

There was a second's hesitancy in them all, like the short pause of a diver facing deep cold water. Ashby brought himself to look at Laurel in that second. Then, speaking quietly, above the spit and roar of fire, through lips parched by its reflected heat, he said, "I reckon this is it."

"Unless we aim to git singed," Lafe said.

Ashby looked up to where the sparks showered now, to where they every now and then whirred upward, high in the air, like coveys of electric birds, miniature and brilliant. He brought his gaze back to Laurel. Without moving his eyes, he said, "You and Bevo, Lafe, go bring the boat you're going out in to the mouth of the creek. And Ephe, too. Laurel and I'll meet you there."

"All right," Lafe said. "But mind you don't git in a place where that searchlight will pick you out. This ain't no time to git shot."

Ashby nodded. When they had gone, he turned to Temp. "Our boat's straight yonder," he said, pointing. "You got to swim over and get in it. Keep out of sight of the light—drop down if it starts flashing in there. And when you get to the boat crouch down in it, if you have to, to keep your head out of sight."

"Yassir." The voice was still humble, and yet it was without fear of anything now, and its very fearlessness was probably a measure of its despair.

"Wait for me there, Temp," Ashby said. He touched Temp's shoulder, affectionately.

"Yassir." The hand fumbled at the eyeglasses again and then Temp walked away, disappearing in the layered moss and flesh-colored smoke.

Laurel remained still, her head turned up to him, on her cheeks the faint smudges where tears had run through smoke-grime.

"I must look a sight," she said, without coquetry, only, he realized, in an attempt to say something natural and unstrained. But hearing it, he felt an anger grow in him, that she should not be able to say it lightly, an anger not at her but at those whose sounds were fire hissing in a swamp and patrol boats buzzing on a river.

"By God . . ." he said, inarticulately. "By God . . ." The smoke was blinding him now, but he did not want to move. He caught her to him. He held her fiercely but their lips only brushed and their bodies scarcely touched at all, except for his hands grasping her elbows. Then he seized her hand and wordless they turned and he led her toward the creek mouth. Under his breath he cursed the river and the swamp, the fire and the boats, Ephe and Turkey Littlepage and Tinney and Slim.

At the mouth of Cold Creek, protected from view from the river by the innumerable jungle-rank islands of a delta, the boat waited them. In the hazy light Ephe and Bevo and Lafe sat—Lafe with his gun already below the boat-side fixed on Ephe's back, so that with one motion he could bring it up for a clean shot between the shoulder blades or in the back of the head. He grinned at Ashby and Laurel on the bank. Ephe sat rigid. Bevo turned and looked at them and then faced away.

"Tilda went up yonder," he said, without turning. "To that biggest island. Jest disappeared in all that cypress. She said it was the best, 'cause on the river side it's got a beach and back of the beach a lot of undergrowth she can hide in so only her face will show. She swam clean up yonder with the sparks hissing when a breeze hit the fire coming from that end. And they gonna be hissing around us, don't you hurry . . ."

Ashby wet his lips, parched now from the heat, as all his skin was. For a moment, he felt panic mount in him, not as panic is described, cold, but hot, burning his already-parched skin. In that moment, nothing made sense. It seemed to him that not only could this not be happening to him, but that the plans he had made to escape what was happening were fantastic, beyond reason and certainly beyond hope. He licked his lips again, looking at Laurel, speechless, tense.

It was she who spoke. "You know where I am going, don't you?"

He did not understand. "Going? Back to Aunt Martha . . .?"

"No," she said. He followed her eyes. He had to turn his body to follow where she looked. He saw Ephe, lifting his chin confidently, already self-proud in his victory, as a patrol boat swerved so close to the screening islands that they could hear the shouts of the men and see the backwash lapping in the red waters around the cypress roots. Ashby looked at Ephe a long minute.

"I don't know where . . ."

"To Pelham. To wait for you."

"Pelham?" he said, seeing Ephe's proud face in his mind's eye now.

"And you will come back there," she said.

"No," he said. "Not on his land . . ."

"What a thief steals is not his," she said. "Maybe it is not yours, either, but you've got the chance to make it yours. Or can you think of a better place to fight."

He looked down at the ground, the sand at his feet. Then he lifted his face. "Yes," he said. "I've known it all along. That I'd go back. That I couldn't retreat always, and would have to fight somewhere, and that was my own battleground." He was dead serious inside himself, but in his voice there was a note of the old banter, the mark of that Ashby who had jeered at everything, even himself.

So that she said, "You're not laughing, are you?"

"Laughing?" he said. "Not the way I used to. I'm not shrugging, anyhow. Or closing my eyes. Or waiting any longer on fate."

She put out her hand, gravely. "Then I will wait there for you. With Granny. At Pelham."

He took the hand in his. "At Pelham."

He could see Ephe's eyes, and he knew Ephe had heard. He saw the eyes grow hard and cold and the faint supercilious smile touch Ephe's lips.

"You wait for me there," he said, unable to think of anything else to say, yet still not wanting to move, to leave.

She lifted her chin. "Yes."

"You . . ." he said, and reached out to touch her and then knew he had best not, and so said, lamely, ". . . wait."

Then, all in one movement, he lifted a hand to Bevo and Lafe, and glanced only once, quickly, at her as she stood there, still wearing his coat, her hands hidden in its too-long sleeves, so that she looked little and forlorn. But she smiled briefly at him before he turned from sight.

He plunged away, pushing through the moss, wading, sliding, tripping through the cypress marsh, keeping well-hidden from the river, moving south toward the boat and Temp. Behind him, he heard the sputter and cough and then the roar of Ephe's boat. He imagined Bevo's hands fondling the wheel, Lafe's sardonic finger caressing the gun trigger.

He waded out into the narrow channel and struck out, swimming, toward the southernmost end of the south island. He saw the boat tied up there, rising on the glinting red water, and Temp sitting stolidly in the double front seat. Ashby pulled himself out of the water and up onto a huge cypress root. Temp questioned him with a glance.

"Stay close to the boat," Ashby said. "I got to go up and watch." He shook the water out of his face.

He swung himself around the tree and pushed through the grove, creeping, always keeping between himself and the river a sufficient thickness of growth. When he glimpsed the river he could see the smoke dropping and rising and then dropping again, in long rolling billows out over the wide water.

By the time he had reached a vantage point, he saw that Ephe's boat was already out on the river. Just as he pushed aside the obstructing moss, Bevo cut the motor, and, with a paddle, tried to hold the boat against the current, although they had obviously gone out into the river a good piece farther north than the island where Tilda was, so that the drift would not push them too close to Ashby and Temp.

Out on the river, one patrol boat had already stopped and was circling around, suspiciously. Ashby could see a man standing up in it. He saw the man raise a pistol. The signal shot vibrated in the air. Almost immediately Ashby heard the northernmost patrol boat swinging around, well up the river.

"That's right," he said. "Come on. Come on down." He turned and narrowed his eyes, looking downriver. He heard Temp behind him. "You hear that one downriver?"

"Nawsir," Temp said.

"Hell," Ashby said. "Can't be out of range. With only a couple of miles to patrol." He could see only the backs of the four in Ephe's boat. He heard the man standing up in the first patrol boat say, "Where's the nigger?" Ashby cursed, even as Lafe raised a hand and waved it toward the long S-shaped island, now naked, now clothed with purplish smoke.

"There a blowin' sound from down yonder," Temp said, but when Ashby twisted his body to look downriver, all he could see were the antlers of a big buck moving toward the distant other shore.

"Watch and keep hidden," he said to Temp. "Do you see Tilda?"

From the north, the second patrol boat came in sight.

"Come on down," the man in the first patrol boat said.

"We better keep spread out," the second boat answered. "That ain't all of 'em there, is it?"

"Mr. Ephe's yonder. There's a nigger on the island."

"That high-yaller woman?"

Ashby held back the oath, crouched tensely now. Ephe had been right. They were not to be fooled by Tilda. Even in that smoke, she did not look like a black man, but only even more like what she was.

"I'm afraid we're gonna have to make a break for it. If we get shot . . ."

"What Tilda doing?" Temp said, his breath warm on Ashby's neck.

"Damn 'em," he said, not paying Temp any mind. "One chance. We had one chance and they have to be smart."

"What Tilda . . .?"

He looked. The island, well-lighted now in that roseate glow, thrust out into the river like a great sprawled S. He saw Tilda come out on the open sand and then retreat into the bushes. He saw her repeat the movement.

"What . . .?" he muttered and then thought, watching the taunting move of her body: maybe she thinks to get them there that way if no other. Knowing the plan's blown to hell and back, she still aims to try, and so is trying with what a woman will usually try with, sooner or later.

"You see anybody else there?" Temp said. "Look like to me . . . That smoke, though . . ."

"What?" Ashby said, glancing downriver again, seeing in a sudden flare of light the swimming buck now near the shadowy, insubstantial far bank.

The man in the first patrol boat was the thin man Ashby had seen that night in the swamp. He was still standing in the bow, bracing himself as the boat slowly circled. Now he called to Lafe, "Go git the nigger."

"No room," Lafe called Bevo, keeping the boat inland, away from the other two.

"Three damn waterbugs," Ashby said. The plan was lost. He could feel the lostness of it, like an ache. There was nothing he and Temp could do but try to outdodge or outrun the south boat. "I bet Lafe is cussing," he said. "Where in hell . . ."

"Yon it is," Temp said. "It coming."

He heard it now. Over the express train sound of the swamp fire, over the slow murmur of the river, he heard the motor. "It's got to get past us, though." The palms of his hands were wet. No boat had ever moved slower. Without thinking, he wiped his wet palms on his river-wet trousers.

He could not yet see the boat coming up. Then the thin man cupped his hands and facing downriver hollered, "Keep spread out. We ain't seen no nigger yet."

"The bastard," Ashby breathed. "The lousy . . ."

"Yassir," Temp said. "Sho is."

Ashby could see the south boat now, circling, criss-crossing, several hundred yards down through the gauzy smoke trailing over the fire-glinting waters. "Take some fancy dodging," he muttered. "Take a boat that can ballet dance to get past those bastards yonder . . ." When he looked back upriver, he saw Tilda. "Good God, what's she mean, showing herself so clear? She knows by now she's not fooling 'em. You reckon she really . . .?"

"It ain't doing, Mr. Ashby," Temp said. "Like Mr. Ephe said . . ."

"Then, dammit, we'll run for it. I reckon if a boat can do a ballet act, Lafe's can. If Tilda had only . . ." He didn't say any more. It seemed to him that all the blood in him drained downward; he felt strangely lightheaded, and at the same time, calm, as if he had never really counted on getting free. "All right, let's go. By damn let 'em shoot us. We'll give 'em a run, anyhow."

"Wait," Temp said. "Wait, Mr. Ashby. Great Gawd, Mr. Ashby, look yonder. Look at Tilda."

The fire by then had swept downward to the bank immediately across from the island Tilda stood on. It was as if she stood in spotlight. On the flat sand bank, she stood, facing downriver, so that even at that distance, through the long gray nets of smoke, Ashby could see enough of her face to note the taunting expression of the mouth and the defiant triumph of the flung-back head. And there, approaching her, on the stealthy balls of his black feet, was what Ashby knew could only be Coal Black. Through the rags on his body, his muscled back gleamed. He moved with his long dangling hands half-clenched toward the taunting copper woman.

"My God," Ashby whispered. "She told Ephe . . . No wonder she picked out her own island. She looked for him. And knowing what would happen, went . . . That's why she was showing herself. She didn't have to fool 'em our way. She had her own way, all planned, and I never realized . . ." He was muttering swiftly, almost incoherently, to himself.

He heard the shouts of the men in the boats. "Come on in, boys," the thin man called. "Yon's the bastard."

"Yes," Ashby whispered. "Yes, come on in. Come on. Come on." Tilda dodged and twisted, always eluding the black hand, in a movement not of hope but of delay. Ashby could see her laughing, almost as if she took pleasure in savoring the delay.

"He'll kill her," Ashby said. The south boat went past them. The river was clear, open to them now, but he could not move.

"We got to go," Temp said. "Mr. Ashby . . ."

But now the ropy black hands had fastened on her throat. Beyond the beat of his own blood in his ears, Ashby heard the raucous surprised shouting of the men in the boats. One boat had pulled alongside Ephe's boat, but Lafe waved them inland so quickly Ashby knew Ephe had had no chance to speak, or if he did, no one had heard. The north boat swerved upriver and came down as if to get in behind Coal Black and Tilda, who now circled slowly, like two wrestlers in a death grip.

Then all at once there came a succession of shots from the north boat.

"They shootin' our way," Temp said. "Them bullets . . ."

Through the breeze-coiled smoke, he could see the man in the prow firing the tommy gun.

The thin man's voice rose cryingly, *Don't kill 'im. He's killin' the woman.*

*Don't kill the bastard. Don't . . .* the thin man called from the center boat.

But the shots came again, an angry fusillade, just as Ashby thrust himself forward, unthinking, moved to cry out to her, even knowing she would never hear it, moved to say, *No, Tilda, No,* even certain that she would answer, *I told Mr. Ephe I would beat him and I will.*

He lunged forward with his mouth opened to shout to her just as the second fusillade spattered from the north boat. Later it seemed to him that he touched his shoulder before he ever felt anything. He had paid Temp's warning no mind. Then he felt the sudden burning, no more at first than a bee-sting, but when he drew his fingers down and looked at them, there was a smear of dark red blood on them. Temp was all at once in front of him, holding his arms out to protect him with his own body. He heard the cry in Temp's throat. "Great Gawd, Mr. Ashby."

"Come on," he said, his voice dulled with surprise. He turned and would have fallen but for Temp. Temp lifted him up and hurried through the island underbrush and, still holding him, stood knee-deep in the channel water and leaned and put him in the seat.

"Get in," Ashby said, hoarsely. "I'm all right. It was just . . ." He touched his shoulder. "Nothing much. Way up, high . . ." His lips felt stiff, as if frost bitten.

Temp lifted himself over the side of the boat and slipped, dripping, under the wheel. With his good arm, Ashby reached, grunting, and turned on the ignition.

"Ready?" he muttered.

Temp looked at him. "Us can't start no motor now. They hear it." He reached behind him for the paddle.

"Course," Ashby said. "Don't know what I'd do without you . . ." He felt the boat sway along the dark, smoke-roofed channel between the glowing swamp and the nestling islands. He slumped against the back of the seat and closed his eyes to pain and the terrible growing heat.

He opened them to sunlight and the sudden explosion of the motor.

"Where are we?" he said. Temp turned quickly to him.

"We good an' safe," Temp said, grinning. The boat shot forward. "Good an' safe."

"For now," Ashby said. "Safe for now, Temp. But we're going back and fight 'em. Later on."

"Yassir," Temp said. "Mr. Ashby . . ."

"What?" He felt his shoulder. It was stiff and aching and when he put his hand inside his shirt the flesh was feverish.

"I aim to thank you," Temp said.

Ashby turned to him. "Thank me? You thank me?"

"Yassir," Temp said.

"And what would I have done back yonder without you?" Ashby said.

Temp looked at him a second, blinking in the startingly bright sunlight reflecting on the spring-green banks sliding past them. The sun glinted, too, on the fine gold rims of Temp's spectacles, and he all at once looked through the broken lenses more proudly than he had ever looked through them when they were whole. He sat very straight and tall in the seat and his hands on the wheel were sure.

"I reckon we both needed each other," he said.

"Yes," Ashby said.

"And where we goin' now?"

Far ahead the great gulf swamps loomed and beyond them the wide open water. Ashby felt the sun warming his body.

"Is we goin' back to Pelham?" Temp said.

"We have got a long way around to go," Ashby said. "And if ever we get back there—it won't be ours. It hasn't really belonged to us for a long time."

"Ain't?" Temp said. "Ain't belonged to us?"

"No," Ashby said. "But if we get back there, maybe . . . maybe if we work together we can own it again."

"Yassir," Temp said. "We can do that."